Heaven Official's Blessing

TIAN GUAN CI FU

4

WRITTEN BY
Mo Xiang Tong Xiu

TRANSLATED BY
Suika & Pengie (EDITOR)

COVER & COLOR
ILLUSTRATIONS BY
**日出的小太陽
(tai3_3)**

INTERIOR ILLUSTRATIONS BY
ZeldaCW

Seven Seas

Seven Seas Entertainment

HEAVEN OFFICIAL'S BLESSING: TIAN GUAN CI FU VOL. 4

Published originally under the title of 《天官賜福》
(Heaven Official's Blessing)
Author ©墨香铜臭(Mo Xiang Tong Xiu)
English edition rights under license granted by 北京晋江原创网络科技有限公司
(Beijing Jinjiang Original Network Technology Co., Ltd.)
English edition copyright © 2022 Seven Seas Entertainment, LLC
Arranged through JS Agency Co., Ltd
All rights reserved

《天官賜福》 (Heaven Official's Blessing) Volume 4
All rights reserved
Cover & Color Illustrations by 日出的小太陽 (tai3_3)
Illustrations granted under license granted by 2021 Reve Books Co., Ltd (Pinsin Publishing)
US English translation copyright © 2022 Seven Seas Entertainment, LLC
US English edition arranged through JS Agency Co., Ltd

Interior Illustrations by ZeldaCW

Seven Seas press and purchase enquiries can be sent to Marketing Manager Lianne Sentar
at press@gomanga.com. Information regarding the distribution and purchase of digital
editions is available from Digital Manager CK Russell at digital@gomanga.com.

Follow Seven Seas Entertainment online at
sevenseasentertainment.com.

TRANSLATION: Suika
EDITOR: Pengie
INTERIOR DESIGN: Clay Gardner
INTERIOR LAYOUT: Karis Page
COPY EDITOR: Jade Gardner
IN-HOUSE EDITOR: Lexy Lee
BRAND MANAGER: Lissa Pattillo
PREPRESS TECHNICIAN: Melanie Ujimori
PRINT MANAGER: Rhiannon Rasmussen-Silverstein
EDITOR-IN-CHIEF: Julie Davis
ASSOCIATE PUBLISHER: Adam Arnold
PUBLISHER: Jason DeAngelis

ISBN: 978-1-63858-352-3
Printed in Canada
First Printing: September 2022
10 9 8 7 6 5 4 3 2 1

HEAVEN OFFICIAL'S BLESSING

CONTENTS

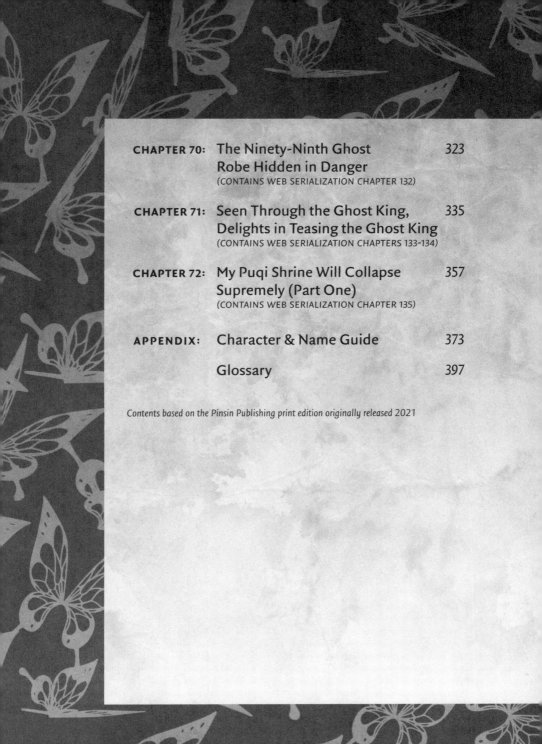

Contents based on the Pinsin Publishing print edition originally released 2021

52
Three Gods, One Ghost, Reverend Nowhere in Sight (Part Two)

"IT DARTED IN and tampered with the array when we left Puqi Shrine?" Shi Qingxuan wondered, then instantly dismissed his own theory. "No! It couldn't have."

"That isn't possible," Xie Lian agreed. "We had already opened the door, so even if it crept in to meddle afterward, we should've still arrived at our original destination. The array was already activated; changing it wouldn't have done anything at that point. It only had a split second to interfere."

Which meant it happened in the moment after Ming Yi had finished drawing the array—when Shi Qingxuan blew out the candles and Puqi Shrine fell into darkness. However, that contradicted Xie Lian's own theory.

"But there were only the four of us in the shrine," Shi Qingxuan said.

There had been three heavenly officials and one ghost king in tiny Puqi Shrine. Wouldn't they have noticed if there was anyone or any*thing* extra? And if someone among them had meddled in the darkness, who was the most likely culprit...?

Shi Qingxuan couldn't help but steal a glance at Hua Cheng. Although he stopped himself quite quickly, Hua Cheng didn't miss it. He smiled.

"What's with that look? Personally, I think Lord Earth Master is the more suspicious one here. Don't you agree?"

Ming Yi's eyes also swept over.

"Rather than worrying about who meddled after the fact, consider whether the array he drew was wrong from the start," Hua Cheng pointed out.

Ming Yi neither refuted nor acknowledged the accusation, but Shi Qingxuan couldn't let this line of questioning continue.

"Hua-chengzhu, you stop right there, all right? I know the two of you quarreled in the past, but Ming-xiong really isn't like that. I dragged him on this expedition at the last minute to help me, so he has no reason to meddle."

"One doesn't always need a reason to do something," Hua Cheng said. "Lord Wind Master, you're very suspicious too."

"Huh?!" Shi Qingxuan hadn't expected the tables to turn on him, and he pointed at himself. "Who? Me?!"

"Mm-hmm. It's common for a wolf to *cry* wolf to shift the blame," Hua Cheng said. "Why exactly are *you* here? If you and your esteemed brother are genuinely scared of the Reverend of Empty Words, why were those raggedy scrolls so sloppily cobbled together? It's not a stretch of the imagination to think that the two of you schemed to intentionally lead us here."

It was easy to tell from his expression that he was being cheeky and spouting nonsense. But he'd made such a good point that anyone was now worth considering as a suspect. Even Shi Qingxuan was almost persuaded.

"Am...am I that ridiculous?"

Hua Cheng chuckled. "The same logic applies to me. I'm not that ridiculous either."

He would strike back with whatever others used to strike him. But Xie Lian was still busy mulling over the evidence, so he waved dismissively.

"All right, everyone, *stop*. Nothing's clear yet, and we've already started doubting our own people."

Hua Cheng laughed out loud and stopped talking. However, his attitude was more than obvious: he was purely there for fun. He wouldn't help, but he wouldn't cause mischief either. There was no point in expecting anything from him, but there was also no need to guard against him.

After thinking for a moment, Xie Lian said, "Actually, there's another possibility. When Lord Earth Master was drawing the array inside the shrine, someone else might've already been drawing a stronger array on the other side of the door."

Shi Qingxuan had cast an isolation spell to seal Puqi Shrine and prevent Qi Rong from listening at the door and eavesdropping on their discussion. But that spell also made it hard for those on the inside to easily detect whether someone was tampering with things outside. When two similar spells collided, the more powerful one always won, and "power" wasn't solely based on the caster's abilities—it also depended on the materials used when spellcrafting. Ming Yi had used the aged cinnabar that Xie Lian picked up while collecting junk—stuff that had been discarded by his cultivation peers. If someone had used fresh blood to weave their own array, it would naturally be stronger.

Shi Qingxuan eagerly accepted that possibility. "Outside the shrine...could it have been the Green Ghost? Can he do *anything* in his current state?"

"I don't think so..." Xie Lian said.

"He won't even dream of moving for the next week. But it wasn't just him outside the shrine," Hua Cheng said evenly, an implication hanging from his words.

"In any case, let's not panic, and let's not hurt our trust in each other,"

Xie Lian said. After pacing for a few steps, he added, "But the monster's words were very strange. Why did it say that this place will become Lord Wind Master's 'nightmare' that he'll 'never wish to recall'? Are we going to encounter something here?"

Shi Qingxuan looked around and wrinkled his brows. "Wait. This place looks like...?"

Before he finished, Ming Yi's expression suddenly turned sharp. His hand struck out in a flash, and the move was aimed at the back of Shi Qingxuan's head.

"Lord Wind Master, look out behind you!" Xie Lian shouted.

Thwump! Ming Yi's hand-chop cracked a large rectangular object in twain. The object had tumbled down right as Shi Qingxuan passed under it. He leapt a few paces away, patting his heart.

"Whew! That was close!"

He looked down, and his pupils shrank. Xie Lian approached to take a look, and he tensed as well.

The object was an establishment plaque painted blue with golden characters that proudly spelled: *"Temple of Wind and Water."*

Shattering the establishment plaque of a heavenly official's temple was an enormous taboo. Ming Yi dropped his hand, his expression icy. Shi Qingxuan stood in numb shock for a moment, but he then spirited away the broken pieces of the plaque with a sweep of his sleeve.

"Keep this a secret, a *secret*! Nobody speak of this," he said in a low voice. "If my brother found out one of his plaques got smashed, he'd be totally furious!"

Xie Lian turned to look around the room, and his tone was one of disbelief. "This is...a Temple of Wind and Water?"

Indeed, the broken-down house they had been transported to was a Temple of Wind and Water.

The Water Master was the God of Wealth. No one hates money, so the temples that worshipped him always had donations in abundance. To see one of his temples desecrated was as unimaginable as seeing a bundle of cash discarded on the street, exposed to the elements and ignored by passersby. Shi Qingxuan rushed back into the main hall. The interior of the temple was desolate from neglect and heavy with cobwebs and dust. He rummaged around, then finally pulled two wretched-looking divine statues from beneath a pile of rubbish.

The divine statue of the Lady Wind Master was missing a leg and an arm, and the head of the divine statue of the Lord Water Master was broken off altogether. The damage didn't look like it was from decay but rather like someone had used something sharp to smash them, as if they were venting immeasurable hatred onto the statues. The divine statues were extremely realistic too—almost lifelike. It was exceedingly unsettling to see them lying on the floor of this eerie old temple in such a state of abuse, one still wearing a curved smile on its face.

Shi Qingxuan hugged a divine statue in each arm. "What kind of hatred provoked this?" he wondered aloud. "What grudge?"

Even though Xie Lian could sense a strong malicious intent from this scene, he replied gently to keep Shi Qingxuan calm. "Lord Wind Master, steady yourself. As long as there are those who worship, there will also be those who desecrate. It's a common thing in the mortal world; no need to pay it any mind. The creature must have set this up intentionally to fan fear in your heart and allow it to absorb your spiritual power."

Ming Yi, however, was more succinct in his response. "Are you okay or not? If you can't handle this, leave."

Shi Qingxuan brushed away some of the dust off the divine statues. He gritted his teeth, gripped his Wind Master fan, and leapt to his feet.

"I'm fine! Now I *have* to see what this creature's got up its sleeves!"

The four of them exited the rundown Temple of Wind and Water and walked around the little town. It was a very quiet, peaceful place. Not bustling, but modern and well kept. Nothing out of the ordinary. Rather, the most peculiar thing there was the four of them—their appearances, bearing, and dress were much too conspicuous to blend into a crowd of mortals. They ducked into a small alley for a costume change.

Xie Lian was already dressed quite plainly, so he didn't need to change. However, the other three changed their looks thoroughly from head to toe. On one side of the alley, Shi Qingxuan voiced his critique of Ming Yi's new getup. On the other side, Hua Cheng changed into a set of refreshing black robes. His long hair was tied up neatly and properly, which was a rare sight. Complemented by a white jade hair accessory, the new style changed his languid appearance into something more spirited. He looked like an extraordinarily handsome and intelligent young disciple of some renowned orthodox sect, as intensely eye-catching as always—an emperor simply couldn't look like a beggar, even if you forced him to dress like one. As he gazed at him, Xie Lian couldn't help but remember the saying: *"For men to impress, in black they must dress."* He reflected on the profound truth of this statement.

Once his mind came down from the clouds, he looked at the Lords Wind and Earth Master and remembered something.

"San Lang, there's something I've been meaning to ask you," Xie Lian whispered.

Hua Cheng fixed his sleeves. "What is it?"

Xie Lian clenched his hand into a fist, then pressed the fist to his lips. He cleared his throat lightly and tried to sound extremely casual. "...What's the verbal password to your private communication array?"

To directly send a message to someone's private spiritual array, one had to have their verbal password. For example, to reach Shi Qingxuan, one had to loudly recite in their mind the following doggerel:

"Lord Wind Master is divinely gifted,

"Lord Wind Master is funny and carefree,

"Lord Wind Master is kind and righteous,

"Lord Wind Master is aged sweet sixteen."

Of course, other heavenly officials didn't set up verbal passwords that were so embarrassing to say; most were much more normal.

The Upper Court heavenly officials didn't freely give away their verbal passwords; they only provided them to close friends or associates. As a Supreme Ghost King, Hua Cheng would naturally have the same standards. But although he and Xie Lian might not have known each other for long, their relationship was fairly good, and it was a little strange that they hadn't exchanged passwords yet. They'd always seen each other face-to-face every time there was something to address, so exchanging passwords hadn't ever seemed all that important.

Xie Lian had never asked for the verbal password of any heavenly official. He'd call out in the general spiritual communication array whenever he needed assistance; if he wanted to speak to anyone privately, he would just ask for them in there. Since this was the first time he was the one asking for someone's private communication, he didn't have much prior experience and was a bit worried he might be acting too forward. And now Hua Cheng's eyes were twinkling, but the man didn't respond, so Xie Lian felt a little awkward.

"Is it inconvenient? If it is, don't worry and don't mind me," he hurriedly added. "I was just asking, nothing serious. There's something I wanted to discuss privately later, which is why I made such a presumptuous request. I can also figure out a way to speak to you in secret..."

"It's not inconvenient," Hua Cheng interrupted him. "I'm very glad."

Xie Lian was taken aback. "Huh?"

Hua Cheng sighed. "I'm very glad that gege finally asked me. You never brought it up, so I thought it would be inconvenient for *you*—that you didn't want to exchange passwords with anyone. That's why I never asked either. But, gege, now that you've finally asked, how can you dismiss it as 'nothing serious'?"

Xie Lian let out a breath of relief and brightened up, grabbing Hua Cheng's hand. "So we were both concerned about the same thing! It was my fault just now; my 'nothing serious' was the unserious comment. I apologize to San Lang. So...your verbal password is...?"

Hua Cheng's eyes shimmered, and he leaned over. "This is my verbal password. Gege, listen closely, I'm only going to say it once."

Then he whispered a phrase.

Xie Lian's eyes widened once he heard. "What...? Is that really it? San Lang, you didn't make a mistake?"

Hua Cheng was perfectly composed. "Yup, that's it. If gege doesn't believe me, why not give it a try?"

As if Xie Lian dared. "Then...then doesn't that mean every time someone wants to talk to you, they have to mentally recite *that* phrase three times? W-wouldn't that be *extremely* embarrassing?"

Hua Cheng snickered. "I set it to that phrase *because* I don't want anyone to talk to me; it lets them know to back off. But if it's gege who wants to talk, I'm always free."

Xie Lian felt a little incredulous. *That's so mean...*

He hesitated. He wanted to initiate the private communication array, but he just couldn't bring himself to utter that password no matter how hard he tried. It was difficult, even in his head. Xie Lian pressed his hand to his face and twisted his head away, unable to make up his mind for the longest time.

Seeing him fretting, Hua Cheng finally had his fill of teasing.

"All right, fine. If gege dare not recite it, then I'll be the one to reach out to you. What's your verbal password?"

Xie Lian turned his head back. "Just recite *Dao De Jing* a thousand times."

"..."

Hua Cheng cocked an eyebrow. A moment later, Xie Lian heard his voice next to his ear:

"It's the phrase, 'Just recite *Dao De Jing* a thousand times,' right?"

The two stood facing each other, but their lips were closed and unspeaking. They were communicating with their eyes, whispering secrets to one another using a voice no others could hear. Xie Lian replied using the private communication array as well.

"That's right. I can't believe you weren't fooled."

Hua Cheng blinked and continued to reply to his messages. "Ha ha ha ha, I almost was. How *fun*."

Xie Lian's delight was apparent as he blinked back.

It must be known that this verbal password was something Xie Lian spent serious effort coming up with when he first ascended eight hundred years ago. He used it because he thought it was funny, but not many other heavenly officials appreciated the joke; even after he revealed the trick, they were more speechless than entertained. Mu Qing told him bluntly, *"Your Highness, your joke is bad. Forgive me if I can't laugh at it."* On the other hand, Feng Xin laughed to the point of rolling on the ground screaming himself hoarse—but he laughed at almost any joke no matter the quality, so sending him into hysterics didn't make Xie Lian feel the least bit accomplished.

However, if Hua Cheng laughed, maybe it really was somewhat amusing after all.

The original plan was to go to the best restaurant in the imperial capital to drink, but since they didn't make it to the imperial capital, it made no difference where they went. The group reserved a room at the biggest restaurant in town, and they lounged at the table, bored out of their minds.

When the waiter brought their drinks, Xie Lian inquired, "May I ask where we are?"

Although it was a strange, blunt question, it was still the most direct and effective way to gather information. The waiter was amazed.

"Did our honored guests not come because of our reputation? This is the town of Fu Gu."

"Reputation? What reputation?"

The waiter gave a thumbs-up. "Our town's Fire Social! It's really famous around these parts. At this time every year, a number of outsiders come to watch the spectacle."

Shi Qingxuan was curious. "What's a Fire Social?"[1]

"Celebratory festivities during folk holidays," Xie Lian explained. "There will be busking, local plays, and so on. They're worth seeing."

They were similar to the Shangyuan Heavenly Ceremonial Procession of Xianle back in the day. However, Heavenly Ceremonial Processions were sponsored by the monarch and hosted by the state. Fire Socials were the entertainment of commoners.

"But it's not a holiday today," Shi Qingxuan commented. "The closest thing is that tomorrow is Hanlu, the official end of autumn."

---

1   *Fire Socials [Shehuo / 社火] are Chinese folk festivals. They were originally intended to drive away evil spirits and pray for abundance in the harvest, but evolved into celebrations of acrobatic feats.*

"It doesn't have to be a holiday," Xie Lian explained. "Sometimes they're for commemorating a person or event. The common folks pick a special day to celebrate and have some fun."

Just then, there was a huge commotion on the main street that stretched out below the restaurant.

"Move aside, move!" someone was shouting. "Women and children, don't stand around! Back away, the troupes are coming!"

The four looked below, and what a sight they saw! Xie Lian's eyes widened. A long procession paraded down the main street, and everyone in the line was painted with thick layers of vivid makeup and dressed in all sorts of bizarre costumes. There were also weapons embedded in each of their heads.

Axes, butcher knives, iron tongs, scissors—implements both sharp and dull, all were deeply buried in their skulls, piercing their brains. Some even had their eyeballs squeezed from their bleeding sockets and dangling down their cheeks. Some had been stabbed all the way through their foreheads, and the weapon jutted out the backs of their heads in an exceedingly gory display. Every one of the paraders had tightly knitted brows and expressions scrunched in agony, and every face was covered in blood. And yet they continued to slowly march forward amidst the trumpeting music like a procession of phantoms.

53
Gods and Ghost Learn of the Bloody Fire Social

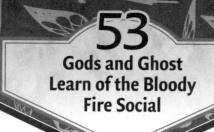

XIE LIAN SPRANG TO HIS FEET. Shi Qingxuan stomped a foot down on the table, rolling up his sleeves as if ready to charge right down there; however, Xie Lian hastily held him back.

"It's nothing, don't worry. Lord Wind Master, please calm down."

Shi Qingxuan was quite alarmed. "Is it 'nothing'? Their eyeballs got squeezed out!"

"It's nothing," Xie Lian reiterated. "What a rare opportunity—it's a Bloody Fire Social!"

Shi Qingxuan quickly removed his foot from the table. "Bloody Fire Social? What's that?"

The two sat back down, and Xie Lian explained.

"Different regions have different kinds of Fire Socials. A Bloody Fire Social is a special type, and extremely rare. I've only ever heard about them; I've never seen one in person. Since the performances are gruesome and unusual, and the makeup artistry is a trade secret, there are fewer and fewer of them every year."

Shi Qingxuan was astonished. "Makeup? It's all fake? I-I-It's…it's just too real. Here I thought it was the work of some sort of evil magic!"

What he said was no exaggeration, and Xie Lian sighed in awe as well.

"There are some extraordinarily talented people in the world."

Not only did the performers in the parade have weapons "deeply embedded" in their skulls, some also had exposed innards and missing limbs, and they crawled on the ground, crying and howling. A few were carrying a large wooden frame, and a woman was hanged by her neck from one of the beams. Two performers marched while dragging a woman by her legs; the woman's clothes had been torn to rags, and she left a long trail of blood as her face was scraped against the road. It was truly a realistic vision of hell. Even though it was a performance by humans, it was more horrifying than the ghosts of Ghost City—in comparison, Ghost City was practically an ordinary, bustling human market. Just how had all that makeup been done? Xie Lian knew of the tradition, but he'd also thought it was a procession of evil at first glance.

There were quite a few women and children who tried to squeeze to the front of the crowd to watch out of curiosity, but they screamed in fright and backed away when they actually caught a glimpse.

"Your Highness, didn't you say that the point of Fire Socials was to celebrate? Who celebrates like this?" Shi Qingxuan commented. "People are running scared, and those little girls are going to have nightmares. Do people really have fun watching performances like these?"

It really was hard to tell whether people enjoyed watching such performances. But in truth, slaughter and the sight of blood did get people excited. A rush of adrenaline would wash over them after the initial shock wore off, regardless of whether they felt true terror. It seemed there was another name for Bloody Fire Socials in the local dialect: "Stabbing Ecstasy." That meant that when a person was violently stabbed to death, the heart in that moment would be filled with ecstasy—at least, that was how Xie Lian understood the phrase.

The lust for slaughter ran deep in the hearts of humans.

Of course, Xie Lian didn't voice these thoughts on the subject and only watched the spectacle intently for a while. In that impressive parade, there was a pale-faced man dressed in black, tall but skinny as a twig. Knife in hand, he struck at the head of one of the lavishly dressed performers and plunged the weapon deep into their skull. Next, he took out a long spear and used it to skewer the other performer and hoist them up to hang in the air. It was cruel and gruesome, almost like there was a real murder happening right before them. The crowd screamed in horror, though some also cheered.

"I'm guessing they're acting out a story," Xie Lian said. "The black-clad man should be the protagonist and the people he's killing should be the antagonists, the villains. The story tells of the defeat of evil and the triumph of good."

Having said that, something clicked in Xie Lian's mind. "Lord Wind Master, watch closely."

"I *am* watching," Shi Qingxuan said.

"No, I'm telling you to watch for the story," Xie Lian explained. "Watch for the characters they're performing and the kind of story they're telling. There must be a reason why the Reverend of Empty Words brought you here and picked today of all days. Maybe it was so you'd watch this Bloody Fire Social."

The black-clad man's brow was deeply furrowed, and it looked like he was drowning in grave misery. As he single-handedly "butchered" hundreds of "villains," he was also stabbed all over his body by all sorts of weapons. At the end, he dragged along a number of mangled "corpses" with white bandages around their throats, and then he lowered his head and moved no more. Surprisingly, the ending was one where everyone perished together. As one troupe went past, another troupe followed and performed the tale again. The parade cycled endlessly like this.

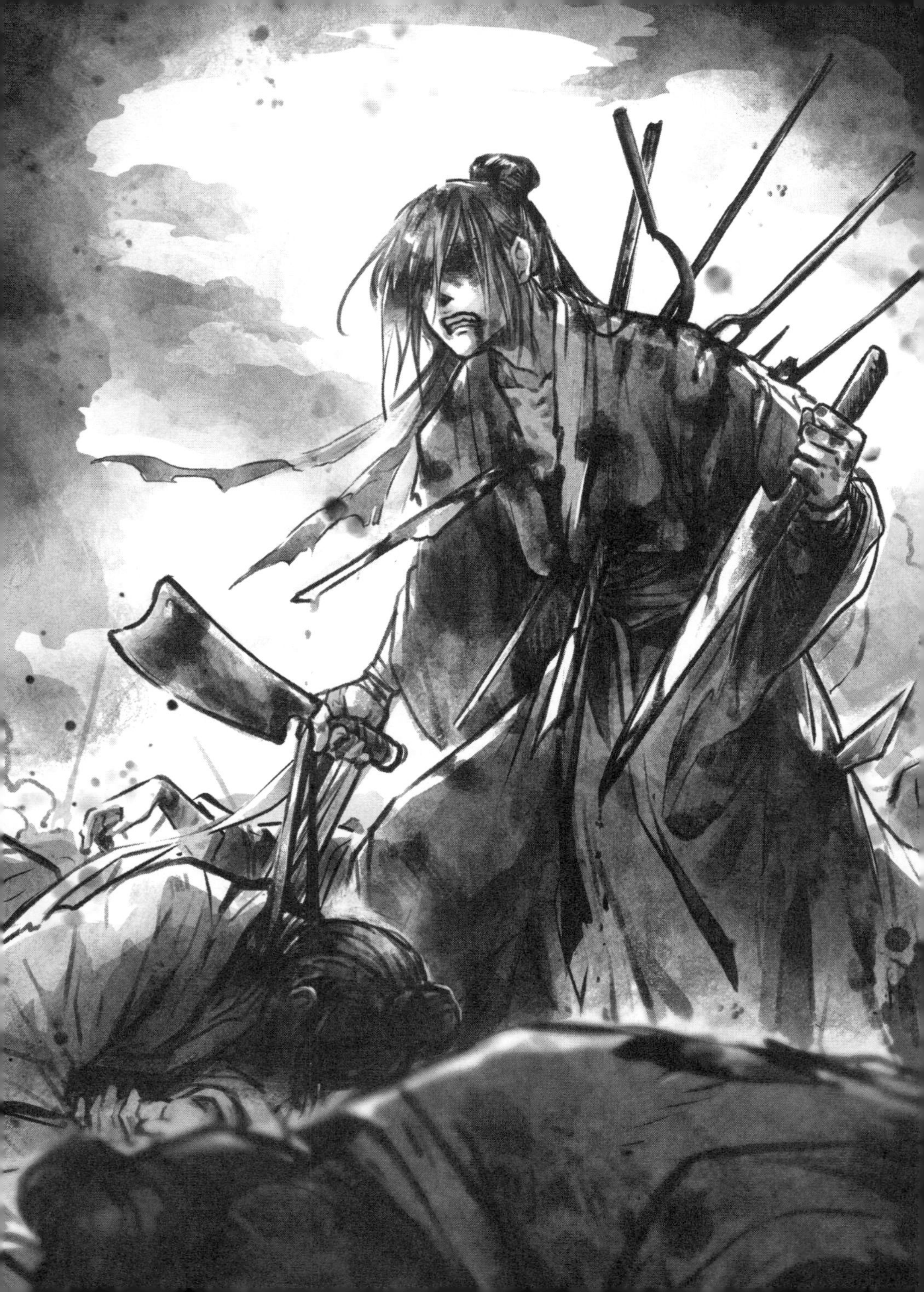

"Have you figured out what the story is about?" Xie Lian asked.

Shi Qingxuan knitted his brows. "No. I don't think I understand. He's doing nothing but killing people."

Next to Xie Lian, Hua Cheng said leisurely, "I imagine it's not a widely known story. Ask a local and see if it's about someone renowned from the area."

Coincidentally, the waiter came by again to bring their orders. "Honored guests, how's the show? Is it exciting?"

"It's good. Very exciting," Xie Lian responded. "May I ask who the main character of this Bloody Fire Social performance is?"

Sure enough, the waiter said, "Oh, outsiders usually don't know and always have to ask. Our town Fu Gu's Fire Social tells a tale that was once passed down through word of mouth alone, starring a character from local legend. Many centuries ago, there was a scholar with the surname He.

"Although this scholar He's family was very, very poor, he was a talented man. Since his youth, he was frighteningly intelligent and picked things up quickly and expertly. He was also widely known as a good son; there was really nothing bad to say about the guy in any respect. Unfortunately for him, he was also very unlucky. For him, nothing good ever lasted.

"When he studied and took the state exam, even though he got the highest marks of them all, he offended the officials because he didn't give a gift to the examiner. They hid his test scrolls and exchanged them for blank ones, so for years he couldn't land a rank.

"When he got engaged, it was to his childhood friend; she was beautiful like a flower, kind, and compassionate. But both his fiancée and his little sister were forcibly taken by a wealthy household to serve as the lowest kind of concubines. One wouldn't obey and was beaten to death, the other couldn't bear the shame and committed suicide.

Scholar He went to seek justice, but those criminals accused *him* of committing adultery. He was locked up in jail and almost died of starvation there.

"His old ma and pa, both over seventy years old, kowtowed an entire night to beg for him to be shown mercy. But it was no use, and he rotted in jail for two years. His mom had no one to take care of her and was long dead from illness when he finally got out. His dad had to labor for the family by himself and was hanging on by a thread. Scholar He was forced to abandon his scholarly pursuits and went into business instead, but he was too good at it and the other merchants ganged up to suppress him. All the money he made was fleeced away, and instead he drowned in debt."

"..."

"So what do y'all think?" The waiter sighed aloud. "How could anyone be so unlucky?"

Xie Lian cleared his throat quietly and agreed earnestly, "Yeah."

How *could* someone other than Xie Lian be that unlucky?!

After that brief lamentation, the waiter was radiant with cheer as he continued the tale.

"And then, one fateful night, the guy went crazy—just completely mad. On the eve of Hanlu, he grabbed a bunch of sharp tools and butchered everyone who had ever caused him harm! It was a bloody sight, I tell ya! Flesh and gore flying everywhere; he hacked 'em all to tiny bits! Since everyone he killed had been bullying the town's citizens for ages, everyone cheered for him. So that's why the town commemorates him with a Bloody Fire Social every year on the eve of Hanlu. Pray Lord Scholar He watches over us and slaughters the wicked."

Supposedly, evil had been defeated and good had triumphed, but it seemed like it still didn't end well. After the waiter left, Xie Lian noticed that Shi Qingxuan seemed contemplative.

"Lord Wind Master, do you have any thoughts?" Xie Lian asked.

Shi Qingxuan snapped out of it. "Some baffling thoughts, but... they're too confusing, so I can't exactly explain. What about you, Your Highness?"

"I was wondering if that Scholar He could've been the previous incarnation of the Reverend of Empty Words."

As they spoke, another troupe started performing the same story again. Shi Qingxuan looked over.

"Its previous incarnation?"

"That's right," Xie Lian said. "Spirits and monsters that resemble humans are usually born from extreme cases of human resentment or obsession. For example, I've heard of a monster in Dongying[2] that was formed from the resentment of women. It's called the Bridge Princess. Some say it was born from the grief of women who waited for husbands who never returned, and others say it was the madness of jealousy. If the Reverend of Empty Words was born of someone plagued by misfortune, one could say it was formed by that person's jealousy of another's good fortune or their hatred of their own unfortunate fate."

"Investigate the local history. The timeline needs to be verified," Ming Yi said.

"Right. We need to investigate," Xie Lian said.

To determine whether their theory was true, they had to investigate when the "Scholar He" character first appeared in these tales. If he first appeared after the earliest records of the Reverend of Empty Words, then their theory didn't hold.

Shi Qingxuan nodded. After a moment's thought, he continued, "There's one small thing..."

---

2   Dongying is the ancient Chinese term for the country of Japan.

Suddenly, a voice laughed heartily from the crowd below. "Just wait! Your closest family, your best friend—they'll all die a disgraceful death because of you!"

Shi Qingxuan's face immediately changed when he heard. He slapped the table and pushed off, leaping out the window of the restaurant and soaring through the air as light as a feather.

The voice had come from the parading crowd!

"Lord Wind Master! Come back!" Xie Lian yelled from the building's upper floor.

Shi Qingxuan landed in the crowd of bloodied living dead.

"Come the hell out!" he raged. "Come *out*!"

However, the performers all bore wooden expressions; they ignored him completely and continued to march as though sleepwalking. Shi Qingxuan was shoved around by the crowd as they flowed past him. He couldn't decide who among them was the most suspicious—he saw one that looked dubious, but just as he was about to strike with his Wind Master fan, he spotted another who looked even more suspect. If his aim was not true, there would be a life on his hands.

Hua Cheng hadn't touched his vegetables, and he pushed them around on his plate to form a smiley face. He never looked up once. "It's pointless. It's too easy for a thousand-year-old monster to hide its tracks."

It would be simple for something inhuman to infiltrate this peculiar parade, and Venerables of Empty Words already commonly took on human form. It would be child's play for the Reverend, who was the strongest of them all.

A moment later, Ming Yi jumped down too and pulled Shi Qingxuan out of the crowd. The group left the restaurant on the main street and walked toward the Temple of Wind and Water.

Shi Qingxuan gripped his Wind Master fan with a still-trembling hand, but the trembling now seemed like it was from anger rather than his initial fear. He dangled a small wine jug from the restaurant from his other hand; after walking for a while, he tossed back the jug and took a drink, and the seething redness in his eyes finally faded away.

"Ming-xiong, maybe you shouldn't be my best friend for the time being. Wait till I've killed that thing first!"

Ming Yi, however, replied without a trace of restraint: "Who's your best friend? *I've* never been."

"..." Shi Qingxuan took a moment to process, then his expression turned to outrage. "Ming-xiong, that's too much! Don't turn your back on people so quickly when things get tough!"

They were off once again, bickering away. Xie Lian shook his head and fished out two small items from his sleeve.

"Here, Lord Wind Master. I think you'd best use these after all."

Shi Qingxuan took them. "Earplugs?"

Xie Lian nodded. "The idea might be silly, and it doesn't address the root problem, but it'll work for the time being. The creature can't do anything to you if you can't hear it. I made a new group communication array; the verbal password is 'By heaven official's blessings, no paths are bound.' If we need to talk to you, let's do it in the array."

Sure enough, Shi Qingxuan could hear nothing after stuffing in the earplugs. One after the other, the four entered the array.

All of a sudden, Xie Lian heard Hua Cheng's voice calling softly next to his ear. "Gege, gege."

Xie Lian looked over and saw Hua Cheng pointedly blinking at him. His lips weren't moving, but his voice was still resounding in his ear.

Didn't you say you wanted to talk to me? You won't come to me, so I've no choice but to come to you."

Xie Lian grinned. "It's your fault for setting *that* as your password."

"Fine, fine. My bad," Hua Cheng acquiesced.

Shi Qingxuan adjusted the earplugs and saw the two of them staring at each other, smiling without saying a word.

"Your Highness, Crimson Rain Sought Flower, what are the two of you doing?" he asked in the communication array, puzzled. "Did you exchange verbal passwords? And now you're exchanging secrets?"

Xie Lian softly cleared his throat and deadpanned in the communication array, "Nothing of the sort."

Hua Cheng raised his brows slightly and passed him another message. "You liar."

Xie Lian stumbled in his step.

Looking straight ahead as he walked, and keeping an equally straight face, he replied, "San Lang, stop teasing me...I need your help with something."

The two of them walked side by side, not looking at each other.

"What is it?" Hua Cheng asked.

"Work with me to test whether a certain someone is the Reverend of Empty Words."

54
In the Temple of Wind and Water, Night Chatter to Discern Truth

HUA CHENG TURNED AROUND upon hearing this, and his gaze fell on Shi Qingxuan and Ming Yi, who were strangling each other behind them. He gestured at one of the two.

"Him?"

Xie Lian nodded.

"How do you want to test this?" Hua Cheng asked.

"Many years ago, I encountered two Venerables of Empty Words, and one even clung on to me for over half a year," Xie Lian replied. "During that period, I tried worming information out of them and discovered a unique quirk they have. They didn't realize they were doing it, so they can be easily identified with just a bit of effort."

Xie Lian then passed on the secret. Once Hua Cheng heard, he said, "That's easy. Let's do it like this..."

Just as the pair finished their discussion, they arrived at the broken-down Temple of Wind and Water. The autumn air was slightly chilly, and the skies were dim. Shi Qingxuan searched all over for the head of his brother's divine statue and secured it back in place. He righted the two statues and placed them properly on the altar anew. Meanwhile, Xie Lian started a small campfire using rotten logs he collected from around the temple, and the four sat around the fire.

Shi Qingxuan's ears remained plugged. He petulantly drank a few swigs from his wine jug, then he finally couldn't sit still anymore.

"We can't possibly sit around like this just waiting for that thing to show up. Is there anything we can do for entertainment?"

He brought it up first—just as Xie Lian wanted.

Ming Yi poked at the fire. "You can still think of entertainment at a time like this?"

"It's important!" Shi Qingxuan spat. "That thing wants me scared? Well, I ain't scared! This Wind Master will play as happily as he pleases, happier than ever before. It'll be like New Year's! I hope it dies from frustration."

In the communication array, Xie Lian suggested, "Why don't we roll some dice?"

Shi Qingxuan pulled a long face. "Dice? Betting on whose roll will be lower or higher again? Your Highness, you're not addicted, are you?"

"What? No..." Xie Lian denied.

"Never mind, there's nothing else around anyway. Dice it is. But there's four of us here, won't things get a little confusing?"

"It won't. Here," Xie Lian said.

He opened his palm and revealed two small, exquisite dice.

"The four of us can split into two teams," Xie Lian explained. "San Lang and I will be one team, My Lords can be the other. We'll compete to see who has better luck. With two dice, each team gets one turn, and each person rolls one die. Then we add up the rolls of that turn. If a team's roll is bigger, they win, and they can ask any question that the losing team must answer. Or they can have them do something instead."

"I have a question," Shi Qingxuan said.

"Go ahead," Xie Lian replied.

Shi Qingxuan jiggled his leg impatiently as he spoke. "Why are the two of you so naturally paired together? Did you take our feelings into consideration when you divided the teams?"

Xie Lian softly cleared his throat. "Um, well, if you want to switch up the teams, that's fine too. It makes no difference."

Shi Qingxuan stuffed his whisk into the back collar of his outer robe. "It's fine. I don't actually have any complaints about the team split, but Crimson Rain Sought Flower has such good luck—won't my team be at a disadvantage?"

Xie Lian cheerfully smiled at him. "That's not entirely true. San Lang might be extremely lucky, but my luck is extremely bad. With the two of us together, one good and one bad, don't we cancel each other out?"

That did make sense when Shi Qingxuan thought about it, so he smacked his thigh and exclaimed, "Good! Let's have at it!" Then he elbowed Ming Yi. "Ming-xiong, did you hear the rules? Don't drag me down, all right?"

Ming Yi gave him a look, and his callous voice came through the spiritual communication array. "Forgive me, but I won't be joining you."

Shi Qingxuan hastily backtracked. "I-I-It's okay if you drag me down! Never mind, never mind, come, come, *come*! Just play. It'll be too sad for me to be on a team all by myself!"

Thus, the four swore a simple oath to follow the rules and started playing. In the first round, Shi Qingxuan rolled a five, Ming Yi rolled a four, Hua Cheng rolled a six, and Xie Lian rolled a one.

Shi Qingxuan was overjoyed and dissolved into laughter. "Ha ha ha ha ha ha! Your Highness, your luck really is bad; *so* bad! Ha ha ha ha ha ha ha...."

Xie Lian rubbed his forehead and said gently, "Although what Lord Wind Master says is true, can you not say it with such glee?"

"*Ahem!* Fine. So our team won. This Wind Master will ask you two to do something," Shi Qingxuan said. "So. Your Highness and

Crimson Rain Sought Flower! I order you to...to strip off each other's clothing!"

Xie Lian was first speechless, then alarmed. "...Lord Wind Master?!"

Ming Yi turned around with obvious disgust, and his hand covered his face like he wanted to shield himself from having to witness this terrible joke. Shi Qingxuan, on the other hand, was hollering.

"Come, come, come! Don't be sore losers! An esteemed heavenly official and an esteemed ghost king, you won't back out now, right? Your audience is seated, so please start the show!"

"..."

Xie Lian looked at Hua Cheng, and Hua Cheng shrugged helplessly, mouthing the words, *"Gege, it's not my fault."*

Feeling helpless as well, Xie Lian could only ask, "How much do we strip?"

Shi Qingxuan was only playing around—he wasn't actually trying to embarrass them. He laughed and gleefully jiggled his legs.

"Just one layer is fine. Keep a few on for later! Hee hee hee hee hee."

He actually wanted to keep this going... Xie Lian hesitated and secretly whispered into their private array.

"San Lang..."

Hua Cheng's face showed no reaction, but his voice next to Xie Lian's ear comforted him, sounding earnest.

"Don't worry. Didn't we agree to let them win a few rounds? They'll lose eventually."

That was indeed something they had agreed upon. But Xie Lian hadn't expected Shi Qingxuan to play like *this*, and he felt like he was shooting himself in the foot. He reluctantly shuffled over to untie Hua Cheng's belt, and it took him a while to remove Hua Cheng's black outer robe and reveal the snow-white inner tunic. Hua Cheng also helped him out of his outer robe, looking as calm as he always did. His hands were slow and gentle, and he carefully avoided touching any part of Xie Lian's body. The two of them only removed their outer robes; it was nothing extraordinary and nothing unseemly, but Xie Lian still felt extremely weird.

After assuming a proper sitting position, he stammered, "A-again."

The second round, Shi Qingxuan rolled a three, Ming Yi a six, Hua Cheng rolled a six once again, and Xie Lian still rolled a one.

Shi Qingxuan pounded the ground, laughing uproariously. Xie Lian looked to Hua Cheng again and spoke through their private communication array.

"...San Lang!"

This was not what they had agreed on!

Hua Cheng apologized profusely. "Sorry, sorry, I forgot. Don't be mad, gege. It's my fault this time."

Shi Qingxuan cheered once more, rolling up his sleeves. "All right! This round, I order you to..."

"Stop!" Xie Lian hurriedly cut in. "Last round was a request. We did it and stripped. This round should be questions."

Shi Qingxuan laughed heartily. "Ask questions? That's fine too. Then here's my first question: Crimson Rain Sought Flower, to you, what's the worst suffering in the world?"

Hua Cheng's smile suddenly faded, and silence settled in the Temple of Wind and Water.

"Don't misunderstand," Shi Qingxuan added. "I don't mean anything by it—I'm honestly just curious. Is there really anything that can cause pain to someone who's made it to the position of a ghost king like you, Crimson Rain Sought Flower? Maybe there *isn't* anything...?"

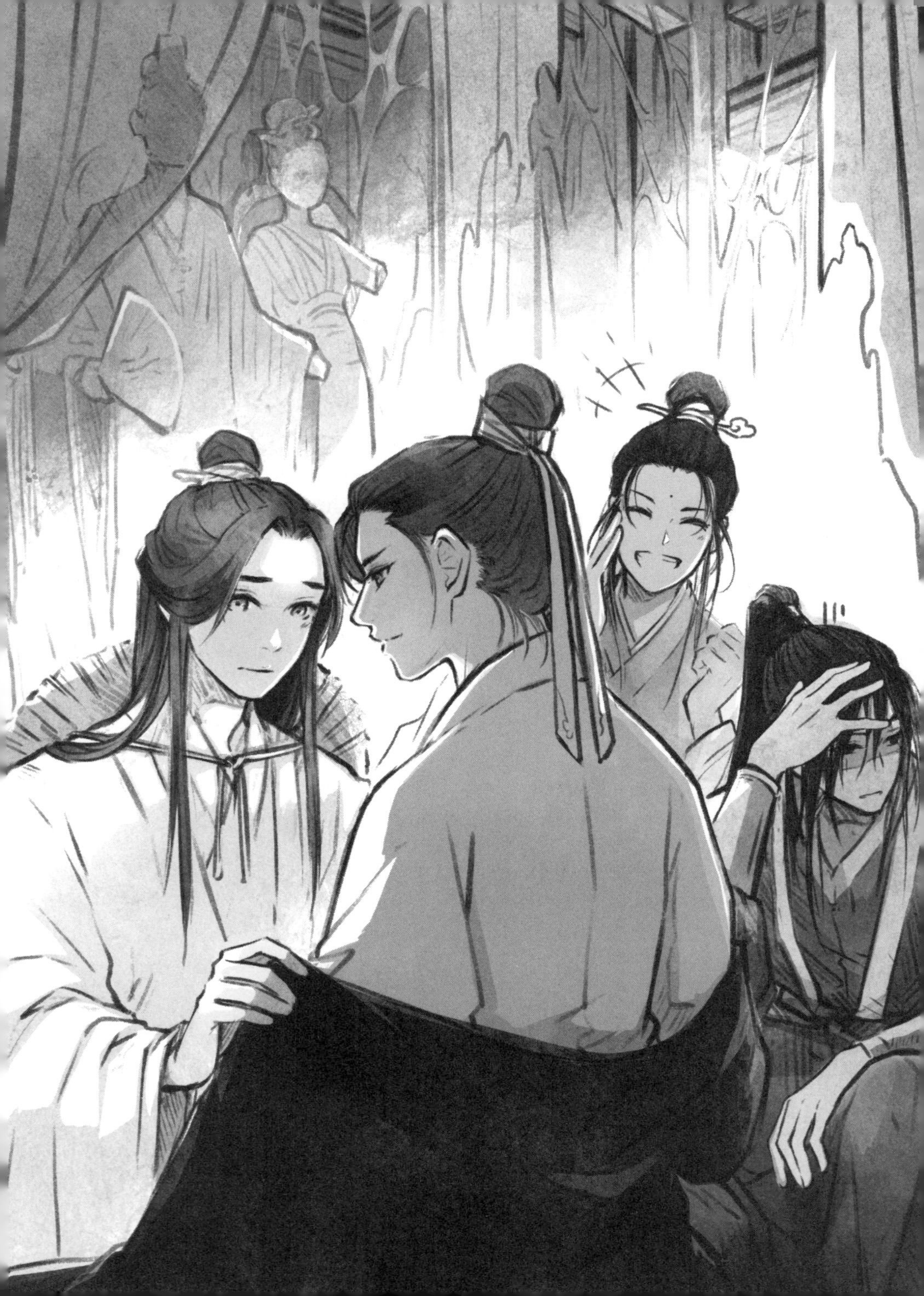

"What do *you* think?" Hua Cheng asked back.

Shi Qingxuan pondered for a moment before making his guess. "The City of Gu at Mount Tonglu?"

There were many who'd suggest that answer when they considered the question. However, Hua Cheng only smiled faintly.

"That's nothing to fear."

Shi Qingxuan was amazed. "That's not it? Then what is it?"

Hua Cheng's lips curled, but the curve soon disappeared.

"I'll tell you what it is," he said softly. "Watching your beloved be trampled and ridiculed with your own eyes and being unable to do a thing about it. You understand that you are nothing, that you can do nothing. That's the worst suffering in the world."

Xie Lian's breathing stopped as he listened with rapt attention. Not a single soul spoke in the rundown Temple of Wind and Water.

Shi Qingxuan couldn't think of anything to say for the longest time, until he finally managed to squeeze out, "...Oh."

Ming Yi's face remained sullen as he poked at the fire. "Continue."

Shi Qingxuan scratched his head and waved. "I'm done. Ming-xiong, you ask something."

Ming Yi glanced up and stared at Xie Lian. "Your Highness."

Xie Lian snapped out of it. "Hm?"

"What's the biggest regret of your life?" Ming Yi asked.

Ming Yi was usually quiet and spoke little, but when he finally opened his mouth, he unexpectedly asked a question of such weight. Xie Lian was floored.

Was it his disregard of advice and warnings, and his insistent and illegal descent to the Mortal Realm? Was it his hubris in thinking himself powerful enough to create rain for Yong'an? Was it his wishful thinking that he could save Xianle? Or was it his reluctance to kill certain people?

He knew it was none of that.

It took a moment for Xie Lian to answer.

"My second ascension."

The other three in the temple looked at him, unspeaking. Xie Lian seemed lost in his thoughts, and it was a while before he came back to himself.

"What is it? Everyone, I've answered the question."

"It's nothing. Let's continue," Hua Cheng said quietly.

The third round, Shi Qingxuan rolled a two, Ming Yi a two, Hua Cheng rolled a six, and Xie Lian a one.

Seeing this, Xie Lian let out a huge sigh of relief. By the heaven official's blessings, they'd finally won!

It was now the other team's turn to be punished, but Shi Qingxuan was eager and clearly afraid of nothing.

"Come at me! Hit me with your best shot!"

Xie Lian smiled. "Then I will. Lord Earth Master, you first." He turned to Ming Yi. "My Lord, please answer the questions I'm about to ask properly, and please don't lie."

Ming Yi didn't say anything, and Shi Qingxuan waved dismissively.

"Don't worry. Ming-xiong doesn't even know how to lie."

Xie Lian grinned. "Very well. First question: Who am I?"

Shi Qingxuan was flabbergasted. "Your Highness, what kind of question is that? Aren't you...you? Who else could you be?!"

Ming Yi slowly raised his head and met Xie Lian's eyes. "The Crown Prince of the Kingdom of Xianle, Xie Lian."

Xie Lian nodded, then asked, "Second question. Who's the one sitting next to me?"

Ming Yi paused briefly, then answered, "The lord of Ghost City, Crimson Rain Sought Flower."

Xie Lian then asked, "The last question—who's the one sitting next to you?"

Shi Qingxuan was growing more and more puzzled. "Your Highness, what are you two playing at? Who am I? I'm the Wind Master!"

"Lord Earth Master, please answer," Xie Lian pressed.

This time, Ming Yi didn't reply as quickly.

Because he had run into Venerables of Empty Words on several occasions, Xie Lian had discovered a fascinating quirk of their kind. When Venerables of Empty Words spoke, at least one of every three sentences would be a lie.

This unique quirk could be compared to how a normal human being needs to drink water lest they die from dehydration, no matter how healthy or strong they are otherwise. It was an unchangeable truth regardless of one's ability, unless they ascended and left their humanity behind.

The teleportation array had been drawn by Ming Yi, and he was also the last one out the door. If meddling was afoot, he had the most chances to do it; of course Xie Lian suspected him from the start. But Shi Qingxuan was upset at the time, and if Xie Lian voiced his suspicion, it would no doubt distress Shi Qingxuan even further. This would allow the Reverend of Empty Words to suck more negative emotions from him, fueling its own power. And so, at the time, Xie Lian quickly came up with other possibilities...but he had never given up on the most straightforward one.

The Wind Master and Earth Master had a very good relationship, so it'd be impossible for the Wind Master not to notice if the Reverend of Empty Words was impersonating the Earth Master. But what if the Reverend had covertly possessed Ming Yi?

This was why he'd wanted Hua Cheng to work with him to worm

out Ming Yi's words by way of an ordinary conversation. But Hua Cheng had pointed out that it'd be unnatural for the two of them to try to rope Ming Yi in like that, since they'd never really conversed in the past. Why not use the pretense of a game to create an opportunity? They could make Ming Yi talk and see if they could observe anything of interest without the Wind Master or Earth Master noticing.

But Ming Yi had always been a man of few words; even in a high-energy atmosphere, he spoke sparingly. Xie Lian paid close attention to everything he said earlier in the game, but it was all vague, nothing that could be pinned down as true or false. In the end, he had to use his trump card; he borrowed Hua Cheng's power and secretly controlled the dice to make Ming Yi lose. Presented with those three questions, Ming Yi would have no choice but to answer on the spot.

Because they were playing a game, Shi Qingxuan wouldn't realize anything was amiss; he would assume they were still joking around. Thus, the Reverend of Empty Words couldn't use the opportunity to sneak in and suck out his power. And should Ming Yi answer wrong, Xie Lian would seize him the moment he slipped.

A creature like the Venerable of Empty Words would always lie within three sentences, and Xie Lian had just asked two questions that Ming Yi had answered honestly. If Ming Yi was the Reverend of Empty Words, he would no doubt answer the last question with a lie.

Should he choose, Ming Yi could easily answer vaguely or pretend he was making a joke. However, he'd answered the first two questions simply and succinctly without any such tricks, so the last answer had to be the same—it would otherwise be out of character, which would also prove he was suspect.

Xie Lian and Ming Yi calmly stared at each other. A moment later, Ming Yi finally spoke. His tone was no different from his last two answers.

"One of the five elemental masters, the younger brother of the Water Master Wudu, the Wind Master Qingxuan."

Shi Qingxuan shook his head and sighed. "Why the hell didn't you say 'my best friend'?"

Ming Yi glanced at him. "Who's that?"

Xie Lian silently blew out a breath.

Although the Reverend of Empty Words was called "Reverend," it wasn't a real man of the cloth with any holy spirituality. As long as it remained classified as a nefarious creature, it would never be able to escape the unique quirks of its kind. Three sentences had been spoken, and all three were undoubtedly true. It seemed there was nothing amiss with Ming Yi...unless Shi Wudu and Shi Qingxuan weren't real blood brothers, but such an unbelievably shocking turn of events shouldn't be possible.

Before he fully exhaled, Ming Yi's hand shot out, grabbing straight for Xie Lian's throat!

Xie Lian and Hua Cheng both moved to fend off his hand at the same time; three hands flew as fast as lightning, and the energy was so intense it made Shi Qingxuan leap to his feet.

"Ming-xiong! What are you doing?!"

Ming Yi glared at Xie Lian intently, his voice dark. "You asked three questions, but in the last round I only asked one."

Xie Lian smiled. "Lord Earth Master, please think back on the rules carefully. I never said you could only ask one question per round."

"Very well," Ming Yi said. "Then I'll add to my question. Who are you?"

"Didn't you already answer that question yourself?" Xie Lian asked.

"Perhaps I answered wrong," Ming Yi replied. "If not, will His Highness please explain why he set up this game so suddenly and his reason for asking such strange questions? Lord Ghost King is skilled in the art of luck manipulation, but it seems unnecessary to waste such talent on petty entertainment."

Hua Cheng laughed. "Well, now. If I feel like it, I'll use it however I want."

It must be understood that while Xie Lian and Hua Cheng saw Ming Yi as suspicious, Ming Yi thought them equally suspicious. From the moment Ming Yi struck, they had been speaking aloud rather than using the communication array. Shi Qingxuan didn't know what they were arguing about, but he didn't dare remove his earplugs rashly and could only attempt to intervene.

"Stop, stop, stop, I order you all to stop right now and tell me what happened. Or else...or else I'm gonna butt in too!"

He flashed open his Wind Master fan. Ming Yi shoved him aside.

"Move! Stop adding to the trouble!"

Just then, a blast of sinister wind blew from out of nowhere. The flames of the small campfire they were gathered around quivered and danced wildly with the gust. Silhouettes and shadows twisted and contorted with the firelight, making the two divine statues on the altar appear extremely unsettling: smiling but not, crying but not.

Ming Yi pulled Shi Qingxuan up. "Something's here," he said warily.

He had shoved Shi Qingxuan to the ground without warning, and had pulled him up just as quickly. Shi Qingxuan was dizzy and seeing stars.

"*Ming-xiong!* Can you please be nicer to me?!"

"No time!" Ming Yi said.

Xie Lian had been watching the two statues and urged the others, "Look at their eyes!"

The four looked over and saw that the smiling faces of the two divine statues were streaked with vivid red lines. Their clay eyes streamed bloody tears.

Divine statues which had been sanctified in ceremonies and worshipped by believers possessed a certain power to deter evil. Even if said evil didn't completely retreat, the statues still typically couldn't be defiled by inhuman hands. The Reverend of Empty Words was certainly powerful—Shi Qingxuan was here in the flesh, yet it made the statue of the Wind Master weep bloody tears before the god himself. The tears of blood streamed thicker and heavier, dripping to the ground and gathering into a twisted, complex form.

Shi Qingxuan was bewildered. "What is that thing? Is it...drawing a picture?"

He couldn't figure out what shape was forming no matter how he looked at it. He didn't move closer, but he tried to look at it from various angles to discern the image. Xie Lian snapped out of his shock to realize that it wasn't a drawing—it was an upside-down word!

"Don't look!" he barked. "It's written for you!"

Ming Yi struck out with his palm. *Boom!* The blood-streaked ground and two divine statues were blasted to pieces. Shi Qingxuan's jaw dropped.

"Ming-xiong! You...you, you, you...you can't let my brother know about this, or he'll never forgive you!"

To destroy a heavenly official's divine statue was an act of extreme disrespect. And today, Ming Yi had snapped an establishment plaque in half and then blasted two statues to bits. This was no different than crashing someone's restaurant, smashing their signage, and then soundly slapping the owner in the face. If this got out—specifically, if the person in question found out—they wouldn't sit back and do nothing. Who knew what kind of bloody storm would rise from it?

As Xie Lian idly turned his head, he noticed that the broken plaque they had set aside earlier in the day didn't seem quite right. The establishment plaque was painted blue and had proper golden characters spelling the words "Temple of Wind and Water." But now, the strokes of the characters were twisting into bloody red shapes that appeared to be the beginning of the word "death."

In a flash, he covered Shi Qingxuan's eyes and yelled in the communication array, "Close your eyes!"

"What now?!" Shi Qingxuan shouted back.

"Nothing. It's just that the words on your establishment plaque have changed. The creature knows you can't hear it, so it's trying to write," Xie Lian explained.

"Damn!" Shi Qingxuan exclaimed. "If I can't let myself hear or see anything, then aren't I both deaf and blind?!"

Xie Lian dropped his hands. "Don't worry, just calm down. We're here for you."

Ming Yi grabbed hold of Shi Qingxuan's back collar and dragged him aside. Shi Qingxuan still had his eyes closed, and he put his palms together as if in prayer.

"How reassuring!"

Just as he spoke, an enormously noisy commotion came from outside the rundown temple. Dark blurs darted across Xie Lian's vision, and in the next moment, there was a huge, rowdy crowd of people howling like devils and pouring inside like a pitch-black tide.

It was a mob populated by all kinds of bizarre forms and monstrous shapes. Some had decapitated heads, some were hanged, some had large sabers piercing their skulls, some had their bellies cut open... There were all sorts of violent curiosities. Shi Qingxuan couldn't hear and couldn't see, but he could feel the disorderly, chaotic footsteps all around him; he was even pushed around in the ruckus.

"What's going on?" he asked in the communication array, bewildered. "What's gotten inside? Why are there so many people?!"

"It's nothing major," Xie Lian said. "It's the night parade of the Bloody Fire Social. Let's just get out of here."

In some places, Bloody Fire Socials would hold further entertainment well into the night after the day's parades had ended. Not only did the performers want to get their fill of scaring people, many common folks also had the urge to do the same. And so, they would imitate the Bloody Fire Social's terrifying makeup and use the dark of night to head out and look for people to scare. Unfortunately, the four of them seemed to have run into such a group of night cruisers.

The rowdy crowd of common folk didn't have the same level of realism in their makeup as the proper parade troupes, but they were nevertheless formidable due to sheer numbers and terrifyingly obscured by the darkness of the night—quite the sight to behold. In towns that had such after-hours entertainment during Bloody Fire Socials, locals would lock up their homes tightly and stay indoors. These night cruisers had been wandering around for some time, and they were quite excited when they saw there were people inside the broken shrine, as if they'd spotted prey. Over fifty of them had charged in, overcrowding the small temple.

The four of them were drowned in the pandemonium. Xie Lian kept looking back, but he could only see Hua Cheng, who was still next to him and never more than two steps out of reach. The other two were pushed several meters away.

"Everyone, let's get outside now!" he shouted.

But while some of the night cruisers were purely there for fun, others were small-time merchants there specifically to scam petty change from tourists who had come to watch the Bloody Fire Social.

They blocked them inside, not letting them leave, and began to pester and cajole them.

"Young masters, give us a tip!"

"We worked so hard to dress up! If you had fun tonight, then give us a tip!"

"Yeah, it ain't easy, and this is only a once-a-year thing!"

"If you don't tip us, watch out for the Ol' Ghost Lord who'll come haunt you!"

Since the whole affair had nothing to do with him, Hua Cheng only watched from the sidelines and wasn't the least bit anxious. When he heard them, he laughed out loud.

"I'd like to see what kind of ghost dares come knocking on my door."

As Xie Lian swept a look over the crowd, he saw a pale-faced hanged ghost near the edge of the crowd. It was wrapping a rope around someone's neck while wearing an eerie grin.

It was chaos all around. Everyone was covered in blood, their faces contorted, endlessly playing out games of *"you kill me, I kill you, now you're dead, now I'm dead."* People were constantly howling and falling over. It was hard to differentiate the real from the fake, but Xie Lian's instincts told him that "person" wasn't right, and he threw out his arm. Ruoye flew forth and struck the hanged ghost squarely on the head.

Sure enough, the hanged ghost wailed and turned into a wisp of black smoke, fleeing through a small crack in the ground. No one else noticed, but Xie Lian saw everything clearly.

"Everyone, be careful! Something wicked is mixed in with the crowd!" he warned in the communication array.

There now seemed to be a faint ghost qi wafting within the Temple of Wind and Water. It wasn't from the Reverend of Empty Words, of course, but more likely some little minions that had snuck into the crowd at some point. When people play around and pretend to be ghosts, it doesn't take long to attract real ones. But for them to show up right now really was adding frost to snow. There were too many people and too much chaos in the temple; heads knocked heads, feet stepped on feet, and it was too difficult to determine the exact source of the ghost qi. Xie Lian grabbed Hua Cheng and ran out of the Temple of Wind and Water. He was about to ask after the others but found he couldn't. His spiritual power was almost depleted, and with no power, he couldn't enter the communication array.

In that moment of urgency, he turned to Hua Cheng. "San Lang, lend me a bit of spiritual power—I'll pay you back later!"

Of course, the promise of later payment was nonsense. He was never able to pay back any of the power he borrowed.

"All right," Hua Cheng said, then reached out to hold Xie Lian's hand.

Xie Lian felt a burst of warmth pass into his palm. At that moment, a few bloody individuals came rushing out of the temple in hot pursuit. The one straggling behind that group was dropping innards as he ran and had skin that crawled with *livor mortis*; he also gave off a faint aura of ghost qi. Without thinking, Xie Lian shot a blast from his palm.

A booming sound like an explosion was heard, and a blinding white light flashed. It took a while before Xie Lian realized what had happened.

In the place where the ghost with the cut belly once stood, only a mound of black ash-like residue remained. As for the Temple of Wind and Water, the entire rooftop had been blown away. The rioting night cruisers in the temple had gone still, frozen in shock from the booming sound and blinding light.

"..."

Xie Lian raised his head to look at the Temple of Wind and Water, now missing its roof, then looked down at his own hand. Finally, he slowly turned to look at Hua Cheng, who stood behind him.

Hua Cheng smiled. "Was that enough?"

"...It was," Xie Lian said. "Actually...really, just a little bit would've been fine."

"That *was* a little bit," Hua Cheng assured him. "Do you want more? You can have as much as you want."

Xie Lian quickly shook his head. In the past, he had also borrowed spiritual power from Shi Qingxuan, Nan Feng, and others. They lent very generously, but Xie Lian had never experienced a feeling like this, as if all the blood in his veins had turned into an electrical current that charged through his body. The powers he'd borrowed before had to be economized and saved, only one bite taken at a time for fear of wasting them. Right now, he felt like he could eat a full bowl and dump out ten without a care.

The power Hua Cheng had passed to him was too great; it filled his entire body to bursting. It was to the point where Xie Lian was almost afraid to move, scared that with just a wave of his hand, something else nearby would explode.

Now that their surroundings were temporarily calm, he hurriedly entered the communication array. "Lord Wind Master, where are you? I left the temple, but I don't see you."

"Oh god..." Shi Qingxuan groaned inside the communication array. "Your Highness, why is your voice so loud all of a sudden? I left the Temple of Wind and Water too."

Xie Lian reined in his spiritual powers, then replied, "Sorry, I'm having some trouble controlling this. How did you leave? Are you all right?"

After all, right now Shi Qingxuan had his ears plugged and his eyes closed.

"*Pfft*, how else could I have left? Ming-xiong pulled me out. Thank goodness I wasn't trampled to death by that crowd," Shi Qingxuan said.

A moment later, Ming Yi's voice also sounded in the spiritual communication array. However, his words froze the smile that was just beginning to form on Xie Lian's face.

"That wasn't me!" Ming Yi said.

It wasn't?!

Xie Lian snapped his head around. *Oh no!*

"Lord Wind Master! Just who was it that pulled you away?!"

55
Fight the Reverend, Crown Prince Takes Wind Master's Place

However, Shi Qingxuan did not utter another sound.

Xie Lian knew this was bad news. "Lord Wind Master? What happened to you? Are you still there? What's going on? Why aren't you saying anything?!"

If he had only been pulled away by rowdy night cruisers who were seeking a bit of fun, he wouldn't be so quiet all of a sudden. Had he already met with harm? But his anxiety was useless, since he didn't even know where the Wind Master was right now!

The mob finally quieted down, and Ming Yi was able to push his way out of the Temple of Wind and Water. The Heavenly Realm had a decree to never use spiritual powers on mortals for selfish reasons, nor to appear before them at will. If mortals were harmed or their lives taken, demerits would be imposed. The decree certainly made things difficult for law-abiding heavenly officials—otherwise they would've sent those people flying like that roof with just a wave of their hand. The crowd finally snapped out of their shock and started screaming wildly.

"It—it's appeared! It really appeared!"

"Monsters have come!"

With that, the crowd broke up and dispersed.

"Lord Earth Master!" Xie Lian asked anxiously. "How come you didn't hold on to Lord Wind Master earlier? Have you seen him? When was he lost?"

"Ghosts snuck in and were ambushing people in the middle of all the confusion," Ming Yi explained.

It seemed that he'd seen there were lives on the line and diverted his attention to go save them; he'd fended off the ghost attack, but he lost a friend.

"Let's split up and search!" Xie Lian said. "He shouldn't have gone far."

Suddenly, Shi Qingxuan's voice came over the communication array anew. He was laughing boisterously.

"Ha ha ha ha ha ha ha...."

The laughter was abrupt, but at least there was finally something.

"Lord Wind Master! What happened to you just now? Why did you stop talking all of a sudden?" Xie Lian hurriedly asked. "I thought something happened to you."

"Ha ha ha ha ha ha ha ha ha howcananythinghappen to this Wind Master I was onlytryingtoscareyouall ha ha ha ha ha ha ming-xiongyoubastard howdare younotgrabhold ofme if I die I'mdefinitelyturningintoasupreme to comeandhauntyou ha ha ha ha ha..."

"Stop your *ha ha*-ing. Say something comprehensible!" Ming Yi demanded.

Xie Lian knew that the more anxious and frightened Shi Qingxuan was, the more he would *ha ha ha*. In fact, he'd even forgotten to pause between words.

"You didn't open your mouth to speak, did you?" Xie Lian interrupted. "Your face didn't show any obvious reaction? Have you fought back?"

"I didn't speak. My expression didn't change. I haven't fought back," Shi Qingxuan answered.

Oh dear. He's scared silly. Xie Lian relaxed his tone into something gentler. "Very good. Lord Wind Master, listen to me. Everything's all right, don't be scared. Keep on as you have and pretend you didn't notice anything. If you have something to say, just say it secretly in the communication array. Absolutely do not let the creature notice that you know what it is. Secretly spread your divine aura to form a spiritual circle beneath your feet to protect yourself; that way you can at least ensure you won't trip or fall into a ditch. You'll be able to sense any incoming weapons too."

Shi Qingxuan sounded like he was on the verge of tears. "Okay. And then?"

"And then take deep breaths," Xie Lian said. "That's it. A couple times... Do you feel a little better?"

His tone was very gentle and quite effective at reassuring people.

"Maybe a little bit," Shi Qingxuan said. "Thanks, Your Highness."

Xie Lian then tried probing. "Now...how do you think you would feel if you tried to open your eyes to sneak a peek at the creature pulling you along?"

Would he be able to handle it?

"I'd probably die," Shi Qingxuan said.

"..."

It seemed that if Shi Qingxuan took so much as a glance, his terror would peak the moment he did, and he would turn into a most delicious meal for the Reverend of Empty Words. After that, he would probably lose any capacity for self-defense. Furthermore, if that thing was staring back at him the moment he opened his eyes, the esteemed Wind Master would probably foam at the mouth and crash like a fallen star.

"Why don't you just keep your eyes closed, then," Xie Lian advised.

"What direction did it head in after it took you from the Temple of Wind and Water?" Ming Yi asked.

They urgently needed Shi Qingxuan's location. Shi Qingxuan's eyes were closed and he couldn't see where he was going, but he could approximate his location based on his general bearing and a count of his steps.

And yet Shi Qingxuan replied, "I don't know."

"You don't even know that?!"

Shi Qingxuan was outraged. "Who in their right mind would take note of something like that? And I thought it was you pulling me, didn't I?!"

Hua Cheng was still only observing the proceedings from the sidelines and was already bored to the point that he'd changed back into his red robes. Then he changed to black robes again. Then to white robes. Almost every time Xie Lian looked back, he was sporting a new look, and with every new look there were different hairstyles, different accessories, different boots, and so on. Sometimes playful, sometimes elegant, sometimes deadly, sometimes extravagant. Xie Lian was dazzled by all the colors, but he kept looking back, unable to keep his eyes off Hua Cheng for long. The moment he realized what he was doing, he blinked hard, only just stopping himself from impulsively blurting out, "that outfit's not bad," or "that looks good."

He said instead, "Stop, stop, now's not the time to argue. With every word, Lord Wind Master takes another step, and the farther he wanders the harder he'll be to find."

Shi Qingxuan moaned his grievance. "Is it really that hard for you guys to find me?! It hasn't been more than fifty or sixty steps, I think! It definitely can't be over a hundred; we're going super-duper slow!!"

Not over a hundred steps? Ming Yi swiftly charged to the end of the street and disappeared, then reappeared in an instant in front of the entrance of the Temple of Wind and Water.

"Not there!"

Curses.

"The teleportation array!" Xie Lian cried.

After the Reverend of Empty Words used the mayhem as cover to abduct the Wind Master from the Temple of Wind and Water, it probably cast the teleportation array and sent them both elsewhere. Otherwise, with a radius of only a hundred steps to search, he should've been long since found. If the creature had used that spell, they could be anywhere in the world by now, and searching for the Wind Master would be like hunting for a needle in a haystack!

They couldn't be careless in this affair, so Xie Lian immediately said, "I will report to the Upper Court."

However, Shi Qingxuan hastily stopped him. "Wait! Your Highness, don't go! You promised to keep this a secret. My brother's third Heavenly Tribulation is coming soon. The third one is huge; he can't mess this up!"

"Keep this up, and I'll make *you* go through a tribulation right this minute," Ming Yi said.

Shi Qingxuan was enraged. "I said *no*, and I mean it. Do you have any idea how many eyes are watching my brother? That thing definitely timed this deliberately, but I won't let it have its way! Never! Even if I die and my bones rot, I'll only allow myself to be dug up after my brother's completed his trial!"

A moment later, Ming Yi relented. "Fine. Very well!"

Xie Lian's intuition was sharp, and he sensed a suppressed fury in Ming Yi's tone. Such an intense emotion had never surfaced on him before, and it unsettled Xie Lian. Unwilling to allow any other problems to start, he cut in.

"Lord Wind Master, is the creature still dragging you along?"

"Yeah," Shi Qingxuan replied. "It's gripping my arm right now."

"Is there anything notable about its body? Like a peculiar evil aura, or a certain smell or feel?" Xie Lian asked.

"No. There's nothing."

"What about your surroundings? Is the path under your feet rough or smooth? Have you stepped on anything or hit anything?" Xie Lian wanted to see if he could draw a general perimeter based on the surrounding environment.

"The path is very strange!" Shi Qingxuan said. "Very soft, very light. It's like I'm walking on clouds."

"..." Xie Lian had no response but thought to himself, *You're probably just weak in the knees from terror...*

Two out of five of Shi Qingxuan's senses were already sealed; it was hard enough just to scrape together any clues, and they likely had no more coming. Although Hua Cheng was with them, bored stiff while watching the show, his tagging along was purely for his own entertainment. He had no attachment to Shi Qingxuan whatsoever, and as an entity of the Ghost Realm, he had no reason to help a heavenly official. Furthermore, Xie Lian didn't want to trouble him by always begging for his help, so he steadied himself and voiced his idea.

"Lord Wind Master, I have a plan that might help you escape from the creature in a flash. But I need your permission."

"Okay! I give you permission!" Shi Qingxuan replied without hesitation.

However, Hua Cheng suddenly stiffened. "The Soul-Shifting Spell?"

"What?" asked Shi Qingxuan.

"That's right," Xie Lian responded. "The Soul-Shifting Spell!"

The Soul-Shifting Spell was exactly as its name indicated; it was a spell that let the caster swap souls, to use one's eyes to gaze through another's. The spell wasn't used often, as it brutally burned spiritual power, and very few were willing to give up control of their bodies to begin with.

Hua Cheng's expression grew serious. "Gege, *caution*."

"What're you gonna do if it looks at you?" Shi Qingxuan asked.

"I'm not scared of it, so it doesn't matter," Xie Lian replied.

"Do it," Ming Yi said.

Hua Cheng, however, pressed him again. "Gege, please reconsider."

Suddenly, Shi Qingxuan said, "It stopped moving."

Hearing this, Xie Lian shouted in the communication array, "There's no time to hesitate!"

Shi Qingxuan gritted his teeth. "It's all up to you now, Your Highness!"

"Okay!" Xie Lian said.

He closed his eyes as soon as the words left his mouth. All of a sudden, his body felt feather-light, light enough that it seemed he was floating into the heavens. Then he abruptly became exceedingly heavy, heavy enough that it felt like he was going to plunge deep into the earth. The world whirled around him before his senses gradually returned. He steadied himself, but his eyes remained closed. He could not hear a single sound.

There was a hand gripping his arm, and he was standing still.

Xie Lian opened his eyes. One hand removed the earplugs, and the other twisted to seize the Reverend of Empty Words in a reverse hold. He smiled at the creature.

"Hi there."

Shi Qingxuan's eyes had been closed for a long time, and it was pitch-black all around them. Thus, when Xie Lian opened the eyes of Shi Qingxuan's body, he hadn't adjusted to the darkness and couldn't see anything. But whatever had been grabbing him was now being grabbed *by* him. Ruoye wasn't here, so Xie Lian cast a locking spell to secure that hand like an iron cuff, preventing this creature from escaping with magic.

Shi Qingxuan's voice came over the communication array. "Your Highness! Are you okay? If not, we'll switch back, and I'll take care of it myself after all!"

It seemed Shi Qingxuan had also safely switched to his body. Xie Lian had a firm grip on the Reverend of Empty Words, and he clobbered it with over thirty hard kicks in the span of a second.

"I'm fine!"

Since their souls had only just been switched, they needed time to adjust. As soon as Xie Lian had gotten a chance to get used to this body, his moves would be even more brutal.

"Your Highness, let me tell you the incantation for manipulating my spiritual weapons—use as much of my spiritual power as you need, don't hold back!"

Xie Lian had no sword to wield, so he flashed open the Wind Master fan. "Okay!"

Shi Qingxuan then added, "I'll also tell you the spell for transforming into a woman! I'm stronger in my female form!"

Xie Lian resolutely refused. "No. That's not necessary!"

"Gege, hurry and take a look at your surroundings," Hua Cheng said gravely. "Tell me where you are."

"No," Ming Yi said. "First tell us what you're fighting right now."

During their exchange, Xie Lian's eyes had adjusted to the dark environment. He squinted at the black shadow before him.

However, even though the contours of the surrounding trees and branches could now be distinguished, he just couldn't make out the black shadow's face. It was as if there was a cloud of evil black mist swirling around its figure.

The Wind Master's fan was a first-rate spiritual device; it could blow away evil and cleanse the world. After he received the incantation spell from Shi Qingxuan, Xie Lian recited it in his mind and swept the fan. A whirlwind blew up from the ground, rattling the surrounding woods, and even a few of the small, weaker sprouts were pulled from their roots entirely. It was undeniably powerful, but unfortunately the wind had veered a little off course and didn't hit the right target.

Spiritual devices weren't easy to manipulate. He wasn't the master of the Wind Master fan, after all, and naturally couldn't handle it as smoothly as Shi Qingxuan. The proper angle and power were both difficult to grasp; it was either too strong or too weak, either off course or completely backward. After realizing this, Xie Lian gave up and changed tactics. He snapped the fan shut and used it as a blunt weapon instead, furiously striking at the creature's weak points. He then opened the fan again with another snap. A sheen of spiritual aura generated on the edge of the fan, turning it into a razor-sharp steel blade. It slashed through the air, its glint chilling.

Shi Qingxuan probably figured out what he was doing and cried out despairingly. "Your Highness, what's wrong with you?! That's my spiritual device! I can't believe you're using it as a martial weapon! What a waste of god's gift!"

This was a common flaw when it came to martial gods. Though he was otherwise occupied, Xie Lian spared a moment to say flatly, "It's all the same. Makes no difference!"

"Gege!" Hua Cheng's tone was becoming harsher.

Xie Lian knew what he was pressing for, and as he fought, he rapidly scanned his surroundings. There was picturesque natural scenery, as well as towers and pavilions. However, ultimately nothing stood out that could indicate where he was.

The Reverend of Empty Words noticed his movement and probably guessed his objective. "You're not Shi Qingxuan," it stated.

Xie Lian never paused in his attacks, but his mind rapidly processed the comment. *It shouldn't be this easy to guess that the Soul-Shifting Spell is active. How did it determine I'm not Shi Qingxuan so quickly? Well, whatever. Keep going!*

The way he fought was completely inhumane. The Reverend of Empty Words seemed unable to take the beating anymore, so it spoke. "You'll fall down this instant!"

Sure enough, it had started to direct curses at Xie Lian. However, it was like Xie Lian had heard nothing, and he only pummeled it harder.

The Reverend of Empty Words then said, "You're going to face defeat!"

Xie Lian laughed. "I already faced defeat eight hundred years ago; a few more times means nothing to me. How much more can I be defeated? Just give up! Nothing you say to me will work."

"Gege," Hua Cheng called. "If you can't determine where you are, just launch a whirlwind into the sky with the Wind Master fan, and I'll be able to locate you!"

What a coincidence! Xie Lian had just had the same thought.

"All right!"

Just as he was about to make the move, the Reverend of Empty Words let out a creepy chuckle.

"Someone's coming?"

For some reason, that alarmed Xie Lian. Sure enough, the creature hissed, "Don't worry. The one coming to find you will die before your very eyes!"

Xie Lian couldn't laugh anymore. His heart dropped violently, and his breathing hitched. The next second, he surprisingly yelled out loud, "Shut *up*!"

In a flash, he landed more than fifty heavy kicks on the Reverend of Empty Words, each bashing directly on its head. Though it could barely speak under such an onslaught, it still sighed in deep satisfaction, like it had partaken of some sacred gourmet delight. It then laughed coldly. Xie Lian had accidentally dropped his guard and let it taste what it wanted.

But Xie Lian hadn't the mind to notice, because what it said truly struck a terrible blow on his heart. Even if he knew Hua Cheng wouldn't "die before his very eyes" so easily as the creature said—and to be frank, Hua Cheng was already dead—a deep, uncontrollable panic still manifested in him. He hadn't realized that he couldn't stand to even hear the idea.

Although those in the communication array didn't notice anything amiss, it was as if Hua Cheng had a sixth sense, and he grew audibly alarmed.

"Gege? Is it saying something to you?"

"It's saying nonsense... No! It said nothing," Xie Lian replied.

Hua Cheng immediately understood and let out a curse. "It's seeking its own death! Tell me right now, and I'll come straight to you."

"No need, don't come here," Xie Lian hastily said. "Absolutely do not come!"

"Tell me!" Hua Cheng urged.

"Sorry to interrupt," Shi Qingxuan spoke up. "The two of you really did secretly exchange verbal passwords, right? Your Highness, did you not notice? You're in the wrong array, the wrong array!"

It was only then that Xie Lian realized the problem. Ever since he used the Soul-Shifting Spell, while every word Hua Cheng said to him was passed through their private communication array, he'd been so focused on fighting and his heart was such a mess that he'd been responding in their group spiritual communication array by accident. Now the fact that they had connected in private communication was utterly exposed.

However, this was no time to be embarrassed. "It's nothing," Xie Lian said. "Give me half an incense time. I can take care of this thing!"

After that, he plugged his ears anew and focused only on dealing with the Reverend of Empty Words, unleashing even more brutal attacks. He had no idea that back in the town of Fu Gu, Hua Cheng heard his reassurance, raised his hand, and struck Ming Yi. Ming Yi crashed a meter into the ground from the force of the blow.

Hua Cheng whirled around to address Shi Qingxuan, who had taken over Xie Lian's body. "Switch back."

Shi Qingxuan had already planned on changing back, but after seeing that strike, he hurriedly said, "Crimson Rain Sought Flower, what are you doing?! I'll switch back right now. His Highness is helping me, so it'd make more sense if you hit me; why did you hit Ming-xiong?!"

But the moment he spoke, he realized that he was currently in Xie Lian's body—of course Hua Cheng wouldn't hit him! If he had to hit someone, his only choice was Ming Yi.

Back in the dark forest, Xie Lian's immersion in the fight was disrupted by Shi Qingxuan hollering in the communication array.

"Your Highness, can you please plug my ears and run away? I'm switching back!"

"Lord Wind Master, will you be able to handle it?" Xie Lian asked.

"I can't fight it, but I can still flee from it!" Shi Qingxuan replied.

Xie Lian gave the Reverend of Empty Words one final kick, sending it flying dozens of meters away. He turned around to make a run for it, but then he stopped.

"Wait, you don't need to flee! Let me set up a protection array for you! Lord Wind Master, do you have any protective spiritual devices on your person? If you don't, precious treasures will do!"

Hearing him, Shi Qingxuan hastily replied, "Treasure? I've got that. Feel around my neck—there's a longevity lock.³ Will that do?"

Xie Lian felt around, and sure enough, Shi Qingxuan was wearing a longevity lock on a long golden chain. Its sheen was exquisite and opulent.

"Yes. This is a rare treasure, excellent!" he exclaimed in delight.

"Really?" Shi Qingxuan said. "I've got plenty more: there's the jade belt around my waist, the agate ring on my finger, some pearls on my boots, the sandalwood handle of my whisk that's older than you—oh, apparently the whisk's hairs are also rare, plucked from some spiritual beast..."

He rattled off seven or eight items in one breath, then concluded, "In any case, Your Highness, just take a look and see if you can use anything on me."

"..."

Yes, they could be used—they were all extremely rare treasures! Xie Lian was shocked. As expected of the younger brother of the Water Master, the God of Wealth!

---

3   A longevity lock is a piece of jewelry crafted in the shape of an ancient lock, usually made of gold or silver. It is worn on a chain as a necklace. They are customarily given to newborns to dispel misfortune and therefore "lock" their lives.

"These will work," Xie Lian assured. "I'll find a house nearby to set up an array. When you've switched back, keep the earplugs in and don't look outside. Stay in the house and don't go out. Wait until we come find you!"

Shi Qingxuan was about to break down in tears. "Your Highness, you're just too reliable! Thank you! From today onward, you're my *other* best friend. This Wind Master will never forget you in any good endeavors!"

Xie Lian didn't know whether to laugh or cry, so he responded politely, "Thank you!"

During their exchange, the Reverend of Empty Words was left in the dust. Glancing around, Xie Lian found a small pavilion nearby and hurried inside, then shut and locked all the doors and windows with a wave of his hand. He wrapped the golden longevity lock around the door latch, laid out the other treasures in formation, and bit his finger to draw an array with blood. All of these actions were done in quick succession, and once complete, he sat in the center of the room and closed his eyes.

"One, two, three. Soul-Shifting Spell—*return*!"

He felt violently hurled into the skies again, then plunged downward. After a wave of vertigo, Xie Lian once more felt his feet touch the ground. He swayed and very nearly fell over, but a pair of hands caught and supported him before he could. He heard Hua Cheng's dark, grave voice when he opened his eyes.

"Gege, I think you had better explain yourself."

Xie Lian grabbed his arm to keep steady. Just as he was about to respond, he noticed someone was missing.

"Where's Lord Earth Master?" he asked.

"Don't know," Hua Cheng said dismissively.

Xie Lian was taken aback. "Don't know...?"

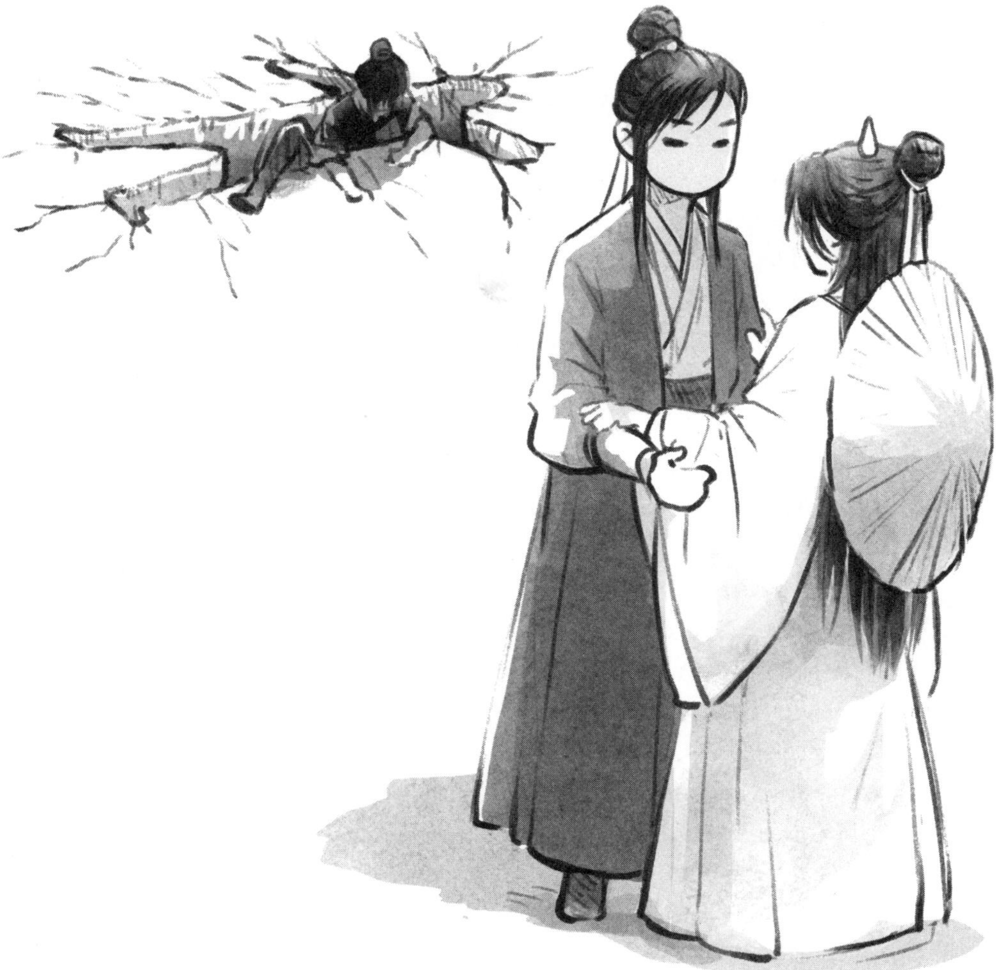

Then he looked to the side. There was a human-shaped crater on the ground, and Ming Yi was slowly crawling out of the hole. Xie Lian was struck momentarily speechless.

Shi Qingxuan's voice came over the communication array. "Huh?"

Xie Lian tensed. "Has it come?"

Since he'd had access to so many of Shi Qingxuan's treasures to form an array, the defense of the house was impenetrable. The Reverend of Empty Words shouldn't be able to intrude so easily; even if it was powerful, it would still take quite a bit of time.

However, Shi Qingxuan said, "No, no, no. Your Highness, this array is impressive, steady as the mountains; it's really secure. I don't think anything could break in for the next three days and nights. It's just...I can't believe I'm *here*."

"Where? Do you recognize it?" Xie Lian asked, amazed.

"Of course I recognize it," Shi Qingxuan replied. "This is the Terrace of Cascading Wine. It's where I ascended."

The Terrace of Cascading Wine? Xie Lian blinked.

Shi Qingxuan seemed to have made a circuit of the room. "That's right," he firmly concluded. "I'm sure of it. I come back here every few decades to check up on it."

No wonder the Reverend of Empty Words could tell he wasn't the real Shi Qingxuan. If he were, he wouldn't have been so disoriented when scanning for nearby landmarks—he would've known they were near the Terrace of Cascading Wine with just one look.

After Ming Yi crawled out of the hole, he squatted on the ground to start drawing an array. But after only drawing a few strokes, he raised his hand and blasted away the array entirely. Hua Cheng's eyes grew cold, and Xie Lian was startled.

"Lord Earth Master, what are you doing?"

Ming Yi rose to his feet. "We can't use the teleportation array anymore. We have to go on foot."

"What do you mean we can't use it?!" Xie Lian exclaimed.

"Someone has just destroyed all teleportation array connection points near the Terrace of Cascading Wine... No, all the connection points in this whole area."

Shi Qingxuan was brought to the Terrace of Cascading Wine via the teleportation array not long ago. It would appear that as soon as Shi Qingxuan hid himself inside the pavilion, the Reverend of Empty Words reacted—it had tampered with the points to intentionally slow the rest of them down. It was like their attempt to cross through a mountain range had been thwarted by their enemy destroying the passes. Now, no one could get close to the Terrace of Cascading Wine using the teleportation array.

"If we leave now, how long will it take before we get there?" Xie Lian asked.

Ming Yi had already turned and set off. "An hour!"

Xie Lian called out to Shi Qingxuan in the communication array. "Lord Wind Master, we're heading to where you are. We'll be there within an hour. Just sit tight until we get there. If anyone or anything knocks, you absolutely must not open the door."

"Yes, yes, yes. That goes without saying," Shi Qingxuan said. "Even if you hadn't said it, I already know *that*. I'm not a toddler who'll open the door to anybody. So then...My Lords, please hurry, okay?!"

Fortunately, the town of Fu Gu and the Terrace of Cascading Wine weren't on opposite ends of the earth but within an acceptable distance of each other. They could still make decent time if they hurried, so the three set off then and there. On the way, Xie Lian casually tested how much power he had left and discovered that the Soul-Shifting Spell had indeed burned out his supply quite aggressively. Of the enormous flood Hua Cheng had poured into him, more than half was already spent.

Hua Cheng noticed his movements. "Gege, do you need more?"

Xie Lian hastily shook his head. "No. Really, San Lang, thank you ever so much for your generosity earlier."

"You're welcome," Hua Cheng said. "I already said, you can take as much as you want." After a pause, he added, half-jokingly, "But when gege pays me back, can I collect some interest?"

Xie Lian softly cleared his throat, thinking it was probably a question of whether he could pay anything back at all. But of course, he still put on a bold front.

"Yeah...sure."

Although they had estimated the journey would take an hour, the three of them weren't mortal and it was a dire situation, so naturally they arrived sooner than expected. When they reached the Terrace of Cascading Wine, Xie Lian took a look around—sure enough, it was the same place he'd seen before. They were surrounded by the chaotic mess created by his misuse of the Wind Master fan; it had refused his control and blown over trees and bushes. Xie Lian felt a little embarrassed by the sight.

"Your Highness, in which building did you set up the spiritual array? Do you remember?" Ming Yi asked.

Of course Xie Lian remembered, and he was searching for it as well. Soon, his eyes lit up and he pointed.

"It's that small pavilion."

The three headed toward the pavilion; the nearer they got, the more relaxed they became, as if they had finally seen a ray of hope. But when they were close, Xie Lian's pupils shrank.

The doors to the small pavilion were open. They creaked eerily as they swung back and forth in the cold night air.

56
From a Designed Prison, Doors Open to Greet the Ghost

"WHERE IS HE?" Xie Lian asked.

The three entered the small pavilion, but there was no one within. The spiritual devices and treasures were set up exactly as they had been before, but since the doors had been opened, they were now useless.

"Lord Wind Master? Where are you?!" Xie Lian shouted in the communication array.

They had been focused on rushing here, and Shi Qingxuan had been so distraught that Xie Lian had proposed that he meditate to calm down—to stop thinking and saying nonsense and scaring himself. Shi Qingxuan had thought the suggestion was very sensible and gradually stopped talking, so the lack of chatter on the way over didn't seem like cause for concern. That was why Xie Lian hadn't noticed anything amiss, but now, no matter how he yelled, there was no answer. A sense of foreboding spread within his mind. In a situation like this, there could only be two possibilities: either Shi Qingxuan deliberately wasn't responding, or he had lost consciousness.

Every single one of the dozens of spiritual devices and treasures on the Wind Master's person was a rare and precious item, and Xie Lian had used all of them to set the formation of the array. Nothing should've been able to break through so easily—even if it could be done, it would take at least three days and nights, just as

Shi Qingxuan himself had said. What's more, it would be impossible not to leave evidence of a break-in. But from the look of things, the pavilion's doors and windows were all intact, and there were no tunnels or ladders to be found. Xie Lian returned to the entrance and collected the golden lock from the ground to inspect it.

"He really did open the doors himself."

Why would he welcome in his own doom when he knew reinforcements would arrive at any moment? Xie Lian couldn't understand it.

"He said he wouldn't open the doors to anyone other than us. So why did he do just that?"

"Maybe he thought we *were* the ones at the door?" Ming Yi said gravely.

A grim scene played out in Xie Lian's mind when he heard this theory. He pictured three individuals, one wearing his face, one wearing Hua Cheng's, and one wearing Ming Yi's. They knocked on the pavilion's doors, and an overjoyed Shi Qingxuan rushed to welcome them inside. Then the three "people" surrounded him, their smiles eerie. The golden lock in Shi Qingxuan's hand fell to the ground by his feet, never to be picked up.

Xie Lian shook his head. "That's impossible. I've never heard that the Reverend of Empty Words has the ability to disguise itself."

"Maybe it called for helpers," Ming Yi said.

Xie Lian considered this but dismissed it. "Everything we ran into today was sudden and unforeseen. We hadn't predicted we would need an array to protect the Wind Master, so it shouldn't have been able to round up ghosts to help on such short notice. And didn't we tell Lord Wind Master that we'd call to him with the communication array when we got here? It should've been easy to figure out who was outside, and whether they were real or fake, by just asking us in the group array. How could he be so easily deceived?"

Xie Lian came to an abrupt halt. "Unless he was told to open the doors by someone he knew..." he mumbled.

"Someone he knew?" Ming Yi questioned. "How so?"

"His ears were plugged. He couldn't hear," Hua Cheng pointed out just then.

Xie Lian seized his arm and exclaimed, "Well said, San Lang! It was exactly for that reason I determined it must be someone he knew. Because Lord Wind Master had his ears plugged, he wouldn't have been able to hear anything from the outside! Unless he removed the earplugs, but would he do that? No—he was so terrified, he'd die first. And so there was only one way he could've been deceived into opening the door..."

The private communication array!

Xie Lian started to pace. "Which means that while we were on our way over, someone secretly connected with Lord Wind Master and told him something that made him open up. And it had to be someone he was close with, because otherwise they wouldn't know Lord Wind Master's verbal password. Heavenly officials' verbal passwords are strictly guarded secrets, not to be shared freely with just anyone—and especially not with nefarious creatures like the Reverend of Empty Words. Furthermore, it must have been someone he trusted deeply, or else he wouldn't have opened the doors so carelessly."

"Or," Hua Cheng offered, "he didn't know the person, but the person knew him. And when they came knocking, they came bearing something that gave him no choice but to open the doors."

Xie Lian gave serious consideration to that possibility. "Theoretically, we can send messages to Lord Wind Master as long as we have his verbal password. But wouldn't Lord Wind Master find it odd if a stranger's voice started speaking to him out of nowhere? He would've told us in the communication array the moment he heard… unless this mysterious individual who sent the private communication paralyzed him with their very first message. But what kind of message could possibly do that?"

"A threat?" Ming Yi wondered.

"How? 'If you don't come out, I'll tell your brother I've returned to harass you'?" Xie Lian dismissed the thought. "Not likely."

The Reverend of Empty Words wasn't necessarily aware of Shi Qingxuan's worries. And furthermore, it wasn't a heavenly official— how could it even contact the Water Master to announce its existence? Reinforcements were arriving within the hour, but Shi Qingxuan couldn't even wait that long.

Whether the creature even stood a chance against the Water Master was another matter entirely. It was worth remembering that it had never harassed Shi Wudu; its eyes were dead set on Shi Qingxuan, specifically picking the lower-hanging fruit. It was clear that the Reverend was very wary of the Water Master, so it wouldn't directly provoke him.

"Search for another hour, one last time," Ming Yi said.

Xie Lian understood what he meant and nodded. "Okay. If we still can't find him after an hour, Lord Water Master must be informed of the situation, no matter how much Lord Wind Master protests. Let's split up! We'll search over here, and Lord Earth Master, please search over there."

Ming Yi turned around and left without a word. Xie Lian searched the area on fleet feet, and all the while he never gave up calling for Shi Qingxuan in the communication array. However, there was nothing but dead silence on the other line.

"How goes it?" Hua Cheng asked.

Xie Lian shook his head. "No response whatsoever."

His sense of foreboding was growing stronger. He searched every room of every pavilion and had gone through almost every building in the surrounding area—but there was no trace of Shi Qingxuan at all.

Soon, the two came to the tallest pavilion around. This pavilion was obviously the star of the surrounding buildings, the centerpiece. It had been renovated multiple times and stood in impressive magnificence, with a number of poetry verses written on the walls. Xie Lian raised his head to look at the establishment plaque, which read *"The Terrace of Cascading Wine."*

"Is it referring to the 'Young Lord Who Poured Wine'?" he wondered out loud.

"That's right," Hua Cheng confirmed. "This is indeed where the tale of 'The Young Lord Who Poured Wine' took place."

Xie Lian looked at him. "So it really *is* all related?"

"Mhm," Hua Cheng replied, then briefly gave an account.

As the tale went, when Shi Qingxuan was still mortal, he would often come to this place after training to lounge on the terrace and drink. He was happy, carefree, and always quite inebriated. One day, a wicked crook came along; the crook often bullied the good people of the nearby village. When Shi Qingxuan spotted him from his perch on the terrace high above, he cast a little spell and then leisurely poured down wine from his cup. The wine spilled onto the crook's head and knocked him out in an instant. After Shi Wudu appointed him a deputy general, Shi Qingxuan still loved the Mortal Realm, and he continued to drink at this place as he had before—and he ascended while he was doing just that.

Ascending while knocking back cups sounded a bit absurd, but it actually wasn't *that* silly; sometimes chance arrives without any rhyme or reason. For example, Xie Lian himself was fast asleep and dreaming strange dreams when his ascension happened. Perhaps in the future someone's bathroom break would be interrupted by their own ascension—that would certainly be quite the sight.

In any case, scholars and poets always loved visiting places that served as the settings for historical legends and tales. Such spots would always inspire intellectuals to raise their brushes and express their longing for such a heavenly lifestyle. Xie Lian now understood that this was one of those landmarks. There were no tourists in the middle of the night, but there would surely be many the next day—and they would be met with the astonishing sight of blown-away houses and trees, and would surely cry that the Wind Master had paid a visit.

Nevertheless, the renowned tale of the Young Lord Who Poured Wine was slightly different from what Xie Lian had imagined.

Just then, he heard Hua Cheng say darkly, "Gege, I need to go take care of something. A trifle. Please be careful, I won't be long."

Take care of what? Xie Lian wondered. When he recalled Hua Cheng's angry tone in the private communication array and now saw his unfriendly demeanor, he asked, "Are you going to seek out the Reverend of Empty Words?"

Hua Cheng paused for a moment, then replied, "No."

Since it wasn't that, then it wasn't his place to press further. Xie Lian nodded.

"You were only here for fun anyway. Since something's come up, just go. Please take care of yourself too."

"I will," Hua Cheng said. After a pause, he added, "When I come back, I'll tell you something."

Xie Lian blinked. "Tell me what?"

But Hua Cheng had already disappeared.

After an hour, there was still nothing, and Xie Lian called out to Ming Yi in the communication array.

"Lord Earth Master! How are things on your end? I haven't found him here, so I'm coming back."

"Nothing!" Ming Yi answered.

"This won't do. I can't hold my tongue any longer," Xie Lian said. "Let's meet up at the center of the Terrace of Cascading Wine. I'm going to report to Lord Water Master right now."

With that, he mentally recited the verbal password to Ling Wen's private communication array.

"Ling Wen, are you there? Can you find Lord Water Master? Please tell him to meet us at the Terrace of Cascading Wine at his soonest convenience. It's urgent!"

The clear voice of a man rang next to his ear; it sounded like Ling Wen was in his male form at the moment.

"Your Highness? Lord Water Master is here with me right now. He's not someone who likes heading out and about, so he probably won't descend. What business do you have with him? I can pass on the message."

Xie Lian had almost reached the main building of the Terrace of Cascading Wine, and he spotted something hanging from one of the balconies. It looked like a white cloth ceaselessly fluttering in the night breeze.

Xie Lian was stricken. *Was there something there before...?*

When he walked closer, he finally saw what it was. Wasn't that Shi Qingxuan's outer robe?!

Ming Yi's voice came roaring over the communication array. "Your Highness, come to the tallest pavilion of the Terrace of Cascading Wine! Hurry!"

Xie Lian jolted. On the other end of the communication array, Ling Wen asked him, "Your Highness? Are you still there?"

"Please have Lord Water Master descend as soon as possible!" Xie Lian exclaimed. "Something happened to Lord Wind Master!"

After shouting that last message, he charged up the pavilion. There were no more sounds from the other end of the line; Ling Wen was probably shocked by his message and was reporting the situation to Shi Wudu. When Xie Lian made it to the highest floor, a person was sprawled out in the middle of the room.

It was Shi Qingxuan.

Shi Qingxuan's eyes were shut tight. He had no external injuries, nor were there traces of blood. Ming Yi helped him upright, and as he tugged at Shi Qingxuan's unconscious body, something clattered to the ground from where it had been resting on his chest. As Xie Lian looked closer at that fallen item, he felt his heart tighten—it was the Wind Master's fan, and it had been snapped in half. This absolute jewel of a spiritual device could only be chanced upon; one could spend centuries attempting to forge something like it and still not succeed. It was the Wind Master's primary spiritual device, and yet it had been easily destroyed!

"When we looked in here earlier, there was no one!" Xie Lian exclaimed.

But as he spoke, he noticed something amiss that he hadn't spotted before. When he and Hua Cheng had searched this chamber, the room's walls showcased dozens of poetry verses that had been left by scholarly tourists; some graceful and flowing, some wild and arrogant, others proper and focused. But now, they were all gone, as if someone had wiped them clean.

The only thing left behind was a phrase that hadn't been there before, written in large, crimson script that seemed to drip like blood.

"WRETCHED BEGINNING, WRETCHED END."

That was the very same curse the Reverend of Empty Words bestowed on Shi Qingxuan when he was born!

"Your Highness, where's the one who was with you?" Ming Yi asked suddenly.

Xie Lian began to fret. *Oh no! San Lang left at such an inopportune moment!*

The moment Hua Cheng left his side, something happened to Shi Qingxuan. This really couldn't be explained away easily. However, Xie Lian did not allow his distress to show.

"I asked him to go search for the Reverend of Empty Words," he explained solemnly.

"When did he leave?" Ming Yi asked.

Xie Lian replied without batting an eye. "Just now. I don't think he's been gone for even half an incense time."

The truth was, it was much longer ago than that. But Xie Lian himself never doubted Hua Cheng, so he naturally wouldn't allow anyone a chance to suspect him. It prevented any issues that might arise from such a misunderstanding.

Thunder rolled in waves in the skies overhead. An eight-wheeled golden carriage broke through the clouds and drove toward them menacingly.

As he'd been unable to reach the Terrace of Cascading Wine using the teleportation array, it seemed Shi Wudu had gone straight for a golden carriage. It must be said that riding forth from the heavens driving a golden carriage pulled by burnished metal horses was a rather huge fanfare. There would doubtless be an uproar in the Mortal Realm if he was spotted by anyone out stargazing at this hour. The Water Tyrant really wasn't afraid of anything.

The golden carriage bore down on them threateningly, and Xie Lian made an urgent request of Ming Yi.

"Lord Earth Master, if any heavenly officials should ask, please don't say a word about Hua-chengzhu. Many of those in the

Heavenly Court like to exaggerate and fabricate stories. This case has nothing to do with him, so there's no need to complicate things."

Ming Yi gave him a look. "Very well."

He agreed surprisingly easily, then looked down to keep an eye on Shi Qingxuan's condition. Xie Lian let out a sigh of relief, but seeing the unmoving Wind Master, his heart sank once more.

The golden carriage roared closer and closer, trailing propitious clouds behind it, and finally landed. A small team of junior heavenly officials stood at the ready outside the carriage, and three grand heavenly officials exited the vehicle: Shi Wudu, Pei Ming, and Ling Wen. Three of the Mid-Autumn Banquet's top ten had come at once. Of course, Xie Lian had long since forgotten that he himself was the first of that top ten...

With a flick of his sleeves, Shi Wudu disembarked the carriage wearing a frown and deeply knitted brows. Water Master fan in hand, he entered the pavilion with Pei Ming and Ling Wen following behind. The moment he saw his younger brother lying on the ground like a corpse, his expression changed and he rushed over.

"Qingxuan? *Qingxuan!* What happened?"

"Lord Wind Master ran into the Reverend of Empty Words," Xie Lian succinctly explained.

"...What did you say?" Shi Wudu exclaimed in disbelief. "The Reverend of Empty Words?"

At the sound of that name, it wasn't only Shi Wudu's face that dropped but Pei Ming's and Ling Wen's as well. It seemed they'd long known of Shi Wudu's scourge. Watching them, Xie Lian couldn't determine if anyone was faking or secretly delighted; they were all acting naturally. Especially Shi Wudu—there was no way *he* was acting.

Ling Wen retrieved a collection of bottles and vials from his sleeve. "Try feeding him these one by one."

Pei Ming simply remarked, "It's you again, Your Highness."

"An unlucky coincidence," Xie Lian replied. "There are only so many of us milling around in the heavens."

"It seems that every time we see you, the *other* one is involved somehow. I wonder if that's true this time too?"

"No, no. Of course not," Xie Lian replied coolly.

He was lying through his teeth, but Ming Yi surprisingly kept his promise and didn't say a word on the matter. Pei Ming stopped talking, and with a wave of his hand, he led the officials under his command in a search of the premises.

Given the situation, it was actually better that Hua Cheng had left. At least he wasn't caught at the scene of the crime.

Shi Wudu couldn't wake Shi Qingxuan, but he inadvertently glanced at the giant, bloody words scrawled on the snow-white wall, and his face twisted at the sight of them. He paled whiter than the wall, and his entire body began to shake with fury.

"Who wrote this? Who wrote it?!"

Even though he was shouting, his voice was trembling.

Just then, Ling Wen exclaimed, "Lord Wind Master is awake!"

Xie Lian instantly bent down. "Lord Wind Master?"

Shi Qingxuan's eyes slowly blinked open. Shi Wudu shoved everyone aside and exclaimed, "Qingxuan? Are you all right? Do you feel pain anywhere? Who hurt you?!"

Shi Qingxuan was dazed for a good while before he gradually came around. When he fully regained consciousness, the first thing he saw was Shi Wudu. And then something happened that no one could have expected—Shi Qingxuan shoved Shi Wudu away, clutched his own head, and screamed.

"Aaaaaaaaaaaaaah—!"

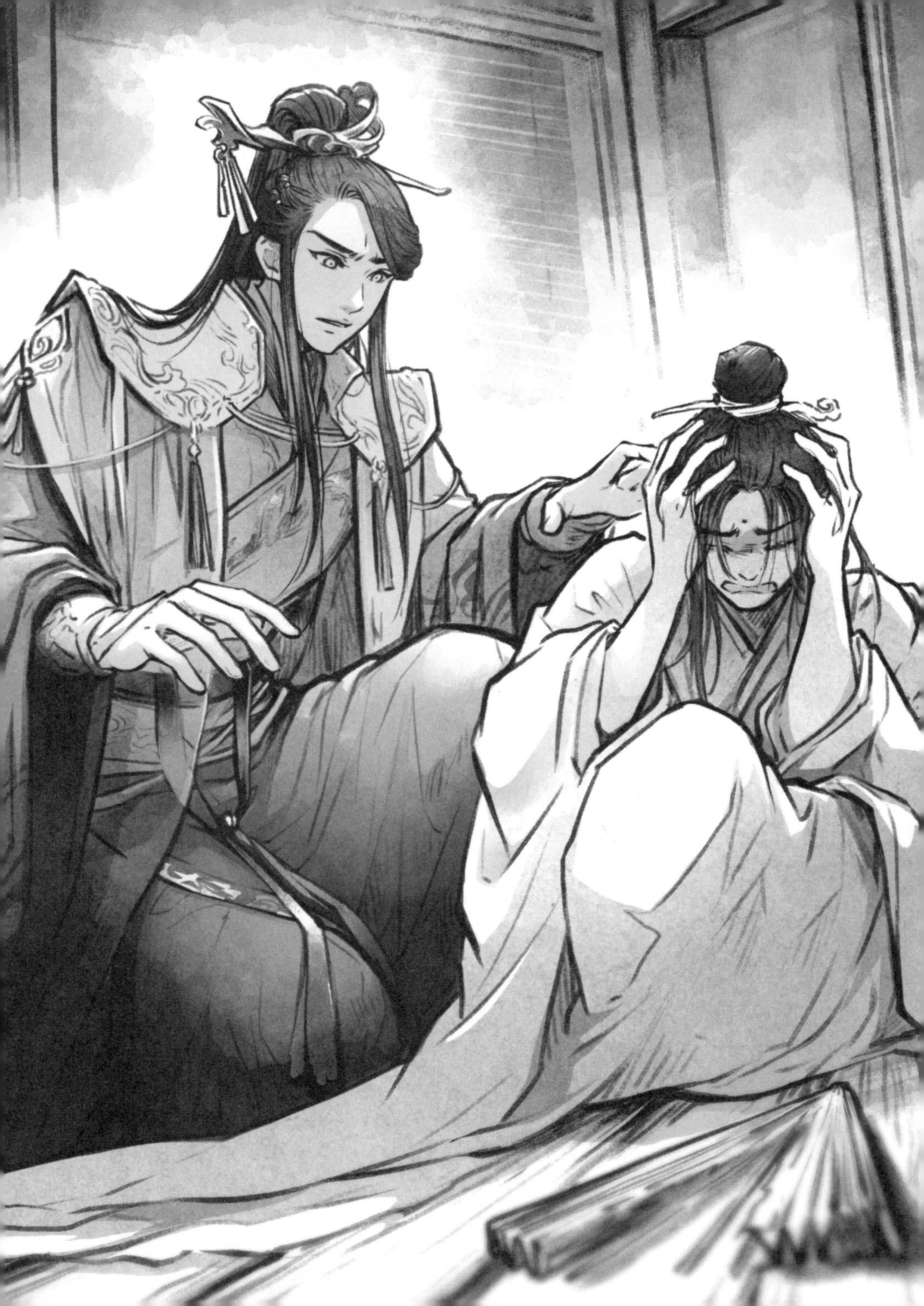

57
Teasing Words Befuddle Me and Also My Dear

THE ESTEEMED WATER MASTER almost tumbled backward with the force of that shove. He spent a few moments in that sorry state, completely dumbfounded, before he called out to his brother once more.

"Qingxuan, it's gege."

"I know it's you!" Shi Qingxuan roared.

So he knew it was Shi Wudu; he wasn't delusional and unable to recognize people. Why such a reaction, then?

Shi Wudu reached for him again. "Everything's all right now..."

Shi Qingxuan slapped his hand away. "'All right,' my ass! How can anything be all right?! Just stop talking! *Ahh!* I can't take this!"

The moment he said that, it wasn't just Shi Wudu's face that changed color but Ling Wen's as well—and as he returned from giving out directives to his subordinates, Pei Ming's.

"Qingxuan, stop making a scene. Talking to your brother like that is no different from slapping him in the face and pouring poison on his heart."

When Shi Qingxuan heard Pei Ming speak, he usually couldn't resist biting back at least a little. But now, he ignored him completely as he clutched his head and muttered like he was possessed.

"I don't want to hear anything. You stop talking too. Let me cool down for a minute. Just go. Just get out of here!"

Shi Wudu couldn't stand it any longer. "What nonsense are you spouting?!" he barked.

"Lord Wind Master," Ling Wen also chided, "if there's something the matter, just tell us. Then we'll know what we can do to address it..."

"Do you not understand the words coming out of my mouth?!" Shi Qingxuan roared, enraged. "Get out of here! Can you all *please* just get the hell out of here?! *Aaaah! Aaaaaaaaaaaaaah!*"

He was growling like he was unhinged, and he screamed and screamed until he sputtered out a mouthful of blood.

"Lord Wind Master!" Xie Lian exclaimed.

Shi Wudu seized his wrist to check his pulse. After feeling it, his expression turned more terrifying than a ghost's, like he was going to cough up blood on the spot too.

"Lord Water Master, what's wrong with Lord Wind Master?" Xie Lian asked.

He reached out to check for the pulse as well, but Shi Wudu forcefully slapped his hand away, like he couldn't allow Xie Lian to discover the details of Shi Qingxuan's condition. Shi Wudu glared at him with raw fury, but he soon redirected his attention to his younger brother.

"You're ill. You're deranged from fright. I'm taking you back for treatment. You'll heal up just fine."

Shi Qingxuan stared at him squarely. "I am not ill," he stated, putting emphasis on each word. "*You* should know best whether I'm ill! Don't write me off as crazy; I'm very aware. I've never been so aware in my life!"

Shi Wudu grabbed hold of him, then began to drag him to the carriage, yelling as he went. "You don't understand anything! Don't speak nonsense!"

"Ming-xiong!" Shi Qingxuan wailed. "Ming-xiong, save me! Your Highness! Save me!"

He reached out to them with both arms, grabbing on to one with each hand. Xie Lian and Ming Yi both held on to the hands he extended, but Shi Wudu ruthlessly yanked him away again.

"Let's go. Everything's all right. Gege is here."

Shi Qingxuan was still screaming, and Pei Ming and Ling Wen went over to help Shi Wudu hold him down.

"Your brother doesn't want to go back with you!" Ming Yi shouted.

"The Reverend of Empty Words hasn't been dealt with yet!" Xie Lian exclaimed as well. "Lord Water Master, what do you plan on..."

Shi Wudu cut him off sharply. "What Reverend of Empty Words? I have no idea what you're talking about. He's ill. His mind is addled. That is all!"

"But Lord Wind Master..." Xie Lian tried once more.

Shi Wudu cut him off again. "He's my brother; don't you think I have his best interests at heart? This is a family matter—there's no need to trouble outsiders! Also, would the two lords *kindly* not spread word of this around? Just mind your own business!"

Then he raised his hand in front of Shi Qingxuan and swept it down, sending the Wind Master into unconsciousness. Then Shi Wudu forced him into the golden carriage.

While his words were unpleasant, they gave Xie Lian pause. He wasn't wrong—Shi Wudu was Shi Qingxuan's brother by blood, so how could he intend to harm him? And with two other heavenly officials accompanying them, sending Shi Qingxuan back with their party truly was the safest option. When family showed up, how could outsiders continue to interfere?

The Wind Master fan lay broken in two on the ground, ignored by everyone. Ling Wen finally collected it as he addressed Xie Lian and Ming Yi.

"Your Highness, Lord Earth Master, please don't be offended. Lord Water Master is only losing his head because he's so worried. This affair is personal, and personal scandals shouldn't be publicized, so pray My Lords keep this to yourselves. He will surely make amends once this is settled."

After the perfunctory niceties were said, Ling Wen also hastily boarded the carriage. The golden carriage rose in the air, rumbling, and then flew off. As Xie Lian watched the stream of propitious clouds gradually disappear in the night sky, it finally hit him—the Water Master really did take the Wind Master away, just like that. And after they'd run around all night, they were really left behind, just like that.

Ming Yi was about to leave when Xie Lian snapped out of it.

"Lord Earth Master!" he called to him.

Ming Yi paused in his step. He turned his head and gave him a long, meaningful look. "Relax. I won't say anything about Hua Cheng."

Xie Lian sighed a breath of relief. "Thank you. Are you going to go check up on Lord Wind Master?"

Ming Yi nodded once, then turned back to continue on his way.

Although Xie Lian was also very worried about the Wind Master, the medical heavenly officials in the Upper Court would be much more help than him. Besides, Shi Wudu would most certainly not want any outsiders to witness his brother's madness; given that, it wasn't the right time to pay a visit. Hua Cheng's sudden departure was a bigger concern, so after weighing his options, Xie Lian decided to go find Hua Cheng first. With his mind made up, Xie Lian left the Terrace of Cascading Wine and swiftly began his overnight journey.

Unable to use the teleportation array, and without a golden carriage drawn by burnished metal horses, Xie Lian could only depend on his legs to carry him through the mountain paths.

What kind of situation did San Lang run off to handle? Xie Lian wondered as he sprinted. *His expression and tone of voice made it seem like it was something serious. Hopefully I'll be able to give him a hand this time.*

An incense time hadn't even passed before he noticed that the roads ahead of him were thick with evil qi, the haze of it blurring visibility. Xie Lian unconsciously slowed his pace.

No way. What is it now?

He stood on the side of the road to quietly observe and play it by ear. A long moment later, he heard a bizarre work song from the thick of the evil qi ahead:

"Hey-hey-ho!

"Hey-hey-ho!"

An enormous, hazy silhouette appeared at the end of the road ahead. It was large, with some parts floating about, but Xie Lian couldn't tell what it was. He had never seen anything with such a shape, but it was certainly quite massive. He reflexively took a step back in alarm; Ruoye was coiled on his left arm and ready to attack, and he rested his right hand on Fangxin's hilt.

Soon, the giant thing emerged from the mist and showed its true form. Xie Lian's eyes widened.

It was a glamorous and exceedingly extravagant step-litter. Exquisite, featherlight satin veils cascaded from its golden canopy—anyone enthroned within would be obscured by the expanse of enchanting crimson drapes and leave much to the imagination of anyone marveling from the outside. Four golden skeletons with abnormally large bone structures served as porters, carrying the step-litter along as they hollered their work song. Small ghost fires twirled and floated next to each skeleton's skull. These little ghost fires were likely used for illumination, as they burned brighter whenever they passed through a darker section of the road.

The sight was so strange, and had such an air of evil, that Xie Lian couldn't help but gape, wondering if he'd run into some ghost lady out to meet a lover on a date. He hurriedly backed onto the side of the road to give way. Unexpectedly, the four golden skeletons carrying the extravagant step-litter stopped in front of him and turned their skulls in his direction.

One of the golden skeletons clattered its jawbone up and down, and out came a sound from who knew where. It addressed him with a shuddering voice:

"Lord Chengzhu sent us to receive the Crown Prince of Xianle. Is that you, My Lord?"

"..."

Lord Chengzhu... That had to be Hua Cheng. Xie Lian removed his hand from the hilt of his sword.

"That's me."

Clatter clatter. The skeletons seemed to rejoice, and they lowered the step-litter.

"Please board. Let's go!"

Could these four golden skeletons wish to carry him to Hua Cheng? "Would that...be too much trouble?" Xie Lian bold-facedly ventured.

"Nothing of the sort. It's no trouble at all, this is our job."

"Your Highness, please board! Lord Chengzhu awaits your arrival."

Thus, Xie Lian cautiously stepped onto the platform, lifted the veil, and seated himself within.

"Thanks for your help."

The golden skeletons were ecstatic, clattering away something incomprehensible. They picked up the step-litter and started bumping along the mountain paths.

Within the step-litter was a soft chair lined with brocade, exceedingly comfortable. Xie Lian sat with poise at the center of the chair, though he thought it was a bit big for just one person. The way the skeletons were carrying the vehicle made it look like a very bumpy and wobbly ride, but when he actually sat down, it was quite steady. They moved extremely fast, swifter even than flying on a sword. And other than the bizarre work song those golden skeletons enjoyed chanting, it was practically silent—much quieter than a rumbling golden carriage with burnished metal horses, and even more mysterious in appearance.

When Xie Lian was still a crown prince, he would sometimes ride a step-litter when he went out. He was much younger back then and sat on the lap of either his father or mother. The step-litter was carried by specially chosen palace attendants who escorted them with fanfare. It made for a mighty and impressive sight. When he got older, he didn't enjoy it as much anymore. Still, this was his first time being transported by creatures such as these, so he couldn't help but find it curious.

After traveling for a while, he sensed a band of green ghost fires ahead. Their wispy light shimmered through the veils, and hushed whispers could be heard in the night air.

"Who goes there? Shouldn't ya be leavin' somethin' behind, crossin' through this burial ground?"

It seemed they'd run into some wild ghosts blocking the road.

They were crooks doing crooks dirty, ghosts devouring ghosts—but the very idea of them challenging Hua Cheng made those skeletons laugh and clatter their jaws.

"What do you want us to leave behind?"

Xie Lian was mulling over whether he should go out to help deal with this when he heard those tiny voices shriek.

"Oh gosh, oh lord, *forgive us*! Our damned eyes be blind; we didn't realize this was the step-litter of our venerable Hua-chengzhu! Git back to the burials, git back! M'lords, please pass as ya will. M'lords are magnanimous, please pass as ya will!"

"Too late, too late, Lord Chengzhu gave clear instructions that the Highness seated in this step-litter shall not be offended," the golden skeletons said. "So what shall we do with you now that His Highness has been delayed?"

Hellish wails howled all around. Xie Lian couldn't just sit and watch anymore—he had to intervene.

"Um, don't worry about it. Since we're in a rush, let's just let this go."

"As His Highness orders, I suppose we shall let them go," the skeletons said. "Y'all got off easy!"

"However, remember not to block the roads and not to harm travelers," Xie Lian added.

The wild ghosts were jubilant. "No, no, no, we swear we've never! Thank you, m'lord!"

"We're off!" the skeletons hollered.

As they passed through the blockade, Xie Lian faintly heard the curious gossip of female ghosts.

"Hey, who do you think the Highness who's sitting in there is? I've never heard of Hua-chengzhu's golden step-litter carrying anyone but him."

"If it were a lady, it'd be easy to guess. But it's a man. How very strange."

What's so strange about it? Xie Lian wondered.

Then he heard the female ghost say, "Yeah. And here I was so sure the golden step-litter was carrying his honored wife!"

As he rode in the step-litter, Xie Lian began to feel drowsy from the long days he'd spent running around. With one hand propping up his cheek, he dozed off. A long while later, he felt the step-litter stop again.

"What is it...?" he mumbled groggily.

He thought they had run into another gang of road-blocking wild ghosts. But as soon as he spoke, he felt the step-litter dip. Another person had gotten on.

The man lifted the veil and called out softly, "Gege?"

Xie Lian rubbed his eyes and squinted, gazing out at the voice. "San Lang?"

The one who'd come was, naturally, Hua Cheng. Greeted by the sight of Xie Lian's bleary half-awake state, he was a little stunned. Xie Lian sat up and cleared his throat, feeling a bit embarrassed.

"I accidentally fell asleep."

Hua Cheng smiled and climbed up to sit as well. "Gege is exhausted. I hope gege won't mind if I squeeze in."

Xie Lian nodded and tried to shuffle to the right, wanting to give Hua Cheng more space. However, Hua Cheng wound his arm around his right shoulder, pulling him back.

"No need. There's plenty of room."

Truthfully, there wasn't. This step-litter was too craftily made;

too big for one person, too cramped for two. It would not be a perfect fit for a pair unless one employed the method from Xie Lian's younger years: that is, one sitting on the lap of the other.

"You left just in time earlier. Three heavenly officials from the Upper Court descended at once."

Hua Cheng humphed. "Was it the Three Tumors? I'd expected that."

"Was that why you ran off?" Xie Lian teased.

Hua Cheng gave a joking reply as well. "No, I went to hail a ride. So how is it, gege? Isn't my Infernal Ghost Carriage much more fun than those Upper Court officials' golden carriages?"

"Yes, very much so!" Xie Lian laughed. But when he was reminded of Wind Master's odd state, he couldn't laugh anymore and became solemn. "By the way, San Lang, what was it you wanted to tell me before?"

Their eyes met inadvertently. Hua Cheng still hadn't let go of Xie Lian's right shoulder, as if he was holding him in an embrace. Looking from the outside, two overlapping silhouettes could be seen through the step-litter's veils, curled together into one inseparable whole. Inside those red curtains, Hua Cheng smiled.

"Gege, want to get married?"

"..."

Xie Lian was struck dumb. "...Huh?"

Such an intent gaze, such words; they were in such close quarters with nowhere to run. Colors exploded in Xie Lian's vision, and his mind went completely blank. His entire body was frozen, stiffer than a corpse.

Seeing his reaction, Hua Cheng withdrew his arm and let out a snicker. "It's a joke. Did I shock gege?"

"..." Xie Lian only snapped out of it with concerted effort. "...You're too much. How can you joke about something like that?"

It wasn't just shock. He was so rattled by that question that his heart had almost stopped. And though he did not quite understand why, he also felt a trace of hurt.

"My bad," Hua Cheng laughed.

He stretched out his long legs and crossed them, settling them at the front of the step-litter and wiggling his feet. The silver chains on his boots clinked against each other, jingling crisply. Playful, indeed. Before tonight, Xie Lian would have thought his boyish heart was fun—adorable, even. But now, for some reason, the jingling noise disrupted his calm, and an unexplained frustration filled his mind.

He was dismayed for a good while and couldn't help but say it again in his mind: *How can you joke about something like that...?*

However, when he thought about it, there wasn't anything wrong with Hua Cheng saying what he'd said. It was *because* it didn't mean anything that he could joke about it.

Hua Cheng noticed his odd expression and promptly sat up straight. "Your Highness, please don't take it to heart. I was in the wrong just now. I won't joke about it ever again."

Seeing him apologize so solemnly, Xie Lian felt guilty. *Am I stupid? It was only a joke, nothing serious. Besides, San Lang only said, "Want to get married?" He didn't specify to whom, so where did my mind wander off to? Get ahold of yourself! This instant! Right now!*

He mentally slapped himself a few times and steadied his spirit before he smiled.

"No, no, no, how are you in the wrong? Don't misunderstand— I was just thinking about Lord Wind Master, so I looked a bit serious."

"Oh?" Hua Cheng said. "Since the Water Tyrant descended, that affair should be taken care of, right?"

They cooperated very well in changing the subject. Xie Lian gave serious thought to the idea, then lightly shook his head.

"San Lang, do you really think this is all over? Somehow, I think it's only the beginning."

Shi Qingxuan had always admired and respected his older brother, but he'd reacted so intensely when he escaped danger and awoke to the sight of his brother's face. A frightening thought sprouted in Xie Lian's mind—could Shi Wudu have been the one who cajoled Shi Qingxuan into opening the doors?

Although Shi Wudu should've been in the company of Ling Wen and General Pei at the time, it wasn't difficult for powerful heavenly officials to create clones and send them off on errands.

He was just about to tell Hua Cheng of his suspicions when Hua Cheng stated, "No. This matter is done and over with."

His tone was so firm that Xie Lian was stunned in spite of himself. "San Lang?"

Hua Cheng stared at him intently. "Gege, do you trust me?"

Xie Lian met his eyes and was equally firm in his response. "I do."

"Then believe me." Hua Cheng continued slowly, "Stay far away from the Wind Master, the Water Master, the Earth Master, Ling Wen, and Pei Ming. The farther away, the better."

After that exchange, thoughts weighed down Xie Lian's mind for the rest of the journey. He tried prodding for more information, but every response Hua Cheng gave him seemed to indicate he had already said all he was willing to say on the subject. And so Xie Lian didn't push.

Upon their return to Puqi Shrine, dawn had not yet broken. As he pushed the door open, Xie Lian could see that the dishes had been cleaned and put away. Lang Ying, Guzi, and Qi Rong were all inside, tucked under a blanket and soundly asleep. It seemed that there really was someone who had attended to things here while he was gone, and they had already silently left.

This time, when Xie Lian returned, there was a large stack of prayers waiting for him.

Puqi Shrine had never received so many prayers before, but he didn't think it had anything to do with the wealthy merchant spreading the good word—yes, the wealthy merchant who lived in town finally stopped by to fulfill his vow.

However, even if he had stopped by, he either didn't notice or purposely ignored the very obvious sign Xie Lian had placed out front. He also didn't donate as much money as he promised he would. The most important purpose of his visit was to gift a silk pennant, and he enthusiastically presented it to Xie Lian in front of all the villagers. Xie Lian rolled it open unsuspectingly, then promptly folded it closed. The giant words on the pennant were still burned into his mind: *"Return Babes through Miraculous Hands."*[4]

Xie Lian had been struck speechless.

Remembering sending the wealthy merchant off, he exhaled a long sigh. He worried every day, wondering when the shack would finally collapse; he really didn't know when he'd be able to have it repaired.

4   [妙手回胎] *"Return Babes through Miraculous Hands"* is a play on the idiom [妙手回春] *"Return Spring through Miraculous Hands,"* which is a compliment for doctors who are so skilled they can bring the dying back to life.

Hua Cheng was leaning against the shrine's door and seemed to have guessed what he was sighing over.

"I've been wanting to ask," Hua Cheng said. "If gege doesn't feel secure living here, why not move somewhere else?"

Xie Lian shook his head. "That's easy for you to say, San Lang. Where would I move?"

Hua Cheng smiled. "Why not move in with me?"

Xie Lian knew that those words couldn't be as nonchalant as they sounded. But that "joke" the other night had somehow traumatized him, and he no longer dared respond to anything Hua Cheng said using that "joking" tone. He'd only acknowledge him with a brief smile and a tilt of his head.

As for the prayers he'd received, they were all quite mundane requests—the old ox broke his leg and couldn't haul the plow, or the wife in the house got pregnant and couldn't help in the fields. But they were prayers nevertheless, and he had to treat all worshippers equally. So after taking a few days to rest, Xie Lian responded to them by heading into the village to help plow and plant the fields.

Since Hua Cheng was staying with him, naturally he tagged along to play. Xie Lian hadn't wanted him to take up such hard manual labor, but he refused to be dissuaded. And so the two changed into coarse clothing, rolled up their sleeves and trouser legs, and entered the waters of the rice paddy fields.

Bustling farmers scattered the expanse of lush green rice paddies, and among them, two silhouettes were particularly conspicuous.

Hua Cheng's impressive air could hardly be hidden away so easily, even when he was dressed in Xie Lian's gritty clothing. Rather, the ragged outfit only seemed to accentuate his face and figure. The two of them were fair-skinned, with beautiful arms and long straight legs, and they were brilliantly eye-catching amidst a field of muddy farmers. The village girls were used to being surrounded by boors, and the sight of such a pair made their hearts race and cheeks redden. They kept sneaking glances as they planted seedlings, and soon their grafts veered so far off course that they became the targets of the day's teasing.

Hua Cheng's blanched skin was a color devoid of blood, while Xie Lian's luminously pale skin had rosy undertones. Due to Xie Lian's natural physique, the more he sweated, the more his skin glowed like white jade. With the blazing sun overhead as they worked, he flushed as white as powder in no time at all. The dry heat was intolerable, and he wiped at the beads of sweat rolling down his collarbone.

A sudden thought struck him—ghosts were creatures of the shadows and disliked the sun, so Hua Cheng must be even more irritated than he was. Xie Lian turned his head to look. Sure enough, he saw Hua Cheng straighten up languidly as well, his eyes squinting as he used one hand to block out the sun. Though partially hidden under the shadow of his hand, his eyes were gazing in Xie Lian's direction.

Xie Lian walked over and pressed his bamboo hat onto Hua Cheng's head. "Here."

Hua Cheng seemed somewhat surprised by the action, but his eyes soon squinted into a smile. "Okay."

Although Hua Cheng had said he was only going to work the fields for the fun of it, when he actually got down to business, he was much faster than Xie Lian. He was quick and proper and incredibly skilled. An hour later, Xie Lian finished transplanting his paddies, but he was already sore and achy. He straightened up and knocked his fist against his lower back for some relief, and Hua Cheng instantly came over to help him out. Xie Lian took a look at Hua Cheng's section, and he was shocked to see that he'd quietly finished a large patch of field all by himself in only an hour. Each green rice stalk stood neat and orderly in the watery paddies, and it was a sight most pleasing to the eye.

"San Lang, you really do learn fast," Xie Lian marveled earnestly. "You don't need to help me. Go sit and rest, and drink some water or something."

As Xie Lian wished, Hua Cheng went to the field ridges to retrieve water. The village chief had been watching from the sidelines for some time, and he gave a thumbs-up.

"Daozhang, which house does that lad belong to? He's so diligent! So amazing! Just one of him is as good as ten men! If any girl catches his eye, it'll be her good fortune!"

Xie Lian snorted a laugh, but it wasn't long before a few others crept over to inquire as well.

"Hey, hey, Daozhang, where does the lad staying at your shrine hail from? Is he married yet? He hasn't got a wife at home, right?"

"Surely not! He's so young!"

Xie Lian didn't know whether to laugh or cry, and answered vaguely. "Um...I guess not? He's young, so it's not time to consider anything yet."

"Well, that's not right," the villagers countered. "It's precisely because he's young that the matter has to be settled quickly!"

"Daozhang, you gotta talk to him. Men gotta get settled early before they can mature. Gotta start a family before anything else."

"That's right! Young people got those raging hormones and all! They can't endure too many lonely nights!"

All these villagers were from households with daughters and were clearly there to dig for information. Just as Xie Lian courteously turned them away, Hua Cheng strolled over with a bamboo water bottle dangling from his hand.

"I'm married. There's a wife at home."

When the villagers heard this, they were greatly disappointed but still unrelenting.

"Whose daughter is it? Won't you tell us, little fella?"

"You're not lying to us, are you?"

"She must be virtuous and beautiful."

Hua Cheng raised his brows. "Mmm, that's right. Virtuous and beautiful. A real noble, gracious special someone who I've liked ever since I was young. I had a crush for many years and pursued it nonstop until I managed to win my special someone over."

He spoke with such a straight face, without a hint of falsehood, that the villagers felt they had no chance. They could only disperse, their disappointment apparent.

Xie Lian was lost in thought at his words when Hua Cheng handed him a cloth and water bottle.

"Water?"

Xie Lian took the cloth and wiped his muddy hands before drinking a few swallows from the water bottle, then he passed the bottle back over. Without realizing it, he had bunched the cloth in his hands into a messy ball, and he patted himself with it here and there.

He tried to hold in the question for a while, but in the end he still couldn't help but ask, "...Is it true?"

Hua Cheng took the bamboo bottle back and drank from it himself, his Adam's apple rolling up and down once with the motion of his throat.

"Hmm? Is what true?" he asked, lowering his head.

Xie Lian wiped a bit of sweat from his forehead with his sleeve. He wondered if the sun was a little too bright today, because his forehead and his cheeks were burning up. He smiled and tried his best to sound casual.

"That there's a wife at home, virtuous and beautiful, a real noble, gracious, special someone. You had a crush since you were young, and pursued it nonstop until you won that person over."

"Oh," Hua Cheng said. "That's a lie."

Xie Lian let out a sigh of relief, though he didn't notice. This time, his smile was genuine, and he copied Hua Cheng's tone from before. "You liar."

Hua Cheng grinned and added, "But it wasn't all a lie. I just haven't won that person over yet."

Xie Lian was dumbstruck by this. But Hua Cheng had already turned around to continue laboring in the fields.

Xie Lian stood where he was in a daze for a bit before eventually bending down and getting back to work. For some reason, he felt a little unhappy. Soon after, he discovered that a row of his grafts was off course, and he quickly pulled his mind back to earth.

As he worked the fields, he tried connecting with the Wind Master through the private communication array. Although Hua Cheng had warned him about getting close to the Wind Master and his coterie, Xie Lian couldn't help it. He'd made multiple attempts over the past few days, but not once did he succeed; he recited the password over and over and was met with nothing but silence on the other side. Thus, he changed tactics and reached out to Ling Wen instead.

"Ling Wen, how is Lord Wind Master doing?"

Ling Wen connected promptly, and her voice sounded next to Xie Lian's ear. "Lord Wind Master? I think he's a little better."

Xie Lian's instincts told him she wasn't telling the truth, but he didn't push. However, it did help him make up his mind to go up fairly soon to investigate.

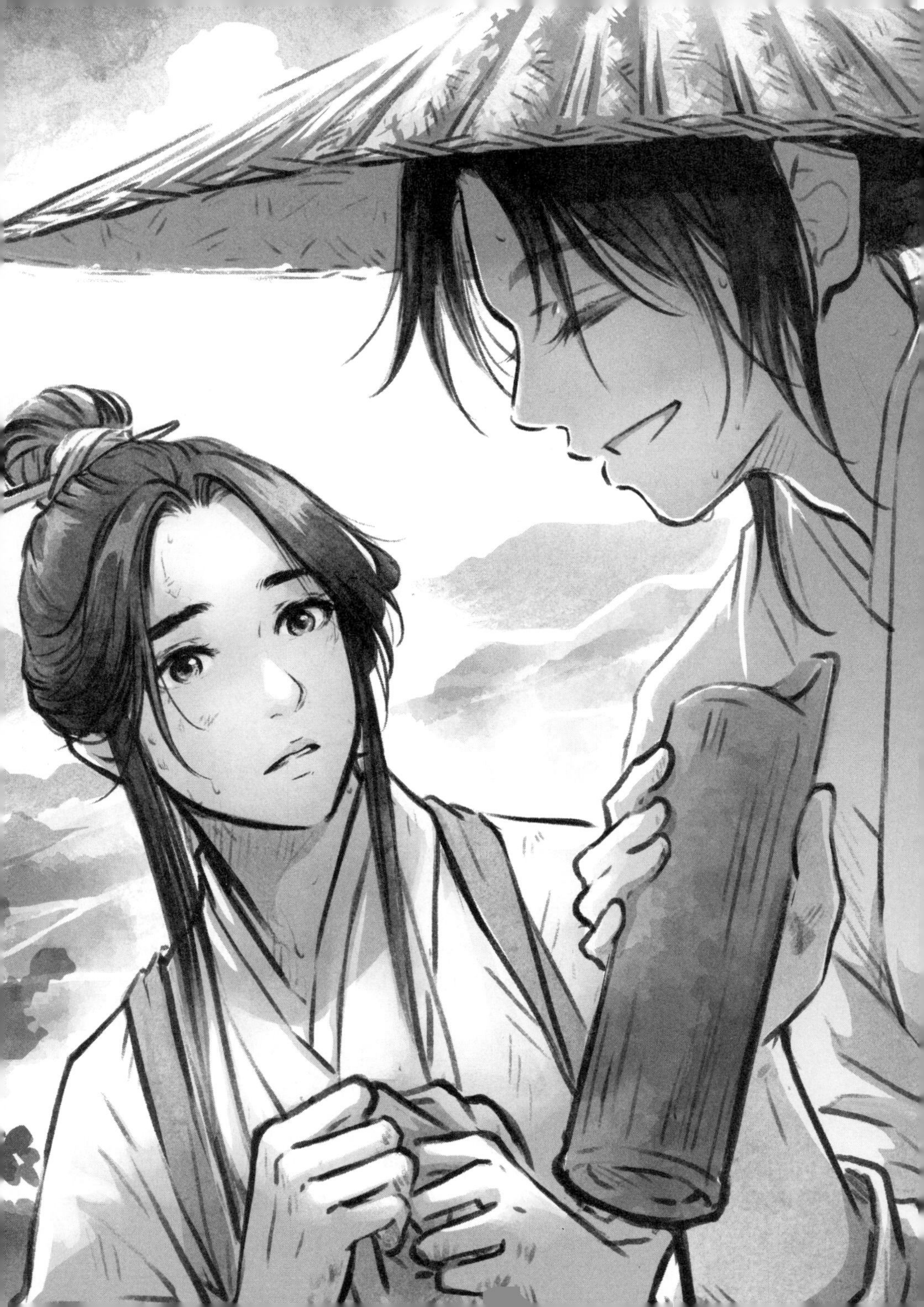

"By the way, Lord Water Master sent a gift to you, and it has already arrived," Ling Wen added. "Please remember to take a look, Your Highness."

Xie Lian was perplexed. "A gift? That isn't necessary; I haven't done anything deserving of a reward."

"There's no need to be modest," Ling Wen said. "When Lord Wind Master gets impulsive, he drags anyone nearby along with him. You went through so much trouble for so long while in his company. In any manner of speaking, there is no shame in accepting the gift. Lord Water Master said it was nothing but a small show of gratitude, so just take it."

Xie Lian still didn't think it appropriate and kept it tucked at the back of his mind.

Once work was done and they cleaned up, Hua Cheng went over to the village chief's house to help repair his plow, and Xie Lian returned to Puqi Shrine. After moving the three "good-for-nothings," as Hua Cheng had called them, behind the shrine, Xie Lian searched all over his small abode.

Where's the gift? he wondered.

Thinking it might have fallen in the cracks behind the donation box, he rolled up his sleeves to lift and move the box aside. It unexpectedly refused when he tried—it was excessively heavy, like it had grown roots into the ground. Perplexed, Xie Lian dug out the key and opened the box. The moment he did, he was nearly blinded by bright golden light.

The donation box was packed to bursting with gold bars. Even with just a cursory glance, there were clearly enough to exchange for a million merits minimum!

Xie Lian instantly threw the cover shut, pressing it down with both hands. *"Nothing but a small show of gratitude"?!*

To give such a hefty gift for no reason—was this a bribe to keep his mouth shut? He had initially thought that if it really was just a small gift, such as a jade pendant that contained a supply of spiritual power, then it might be best to accept it. After all, returning a gift might injure the Water Master's face; the Water Master was proud, so it wouldn't be a nice thing to do. But now...well, all right. As expected from the God of Wealth. A chest this big, filled to the brim with gold bars! Now he *had* to return it.

It just so happened he'd already been planning on making a trip to the heavens to check on the Wind Master. He figured Hua Cheng wouldn't be back soon enough to let him know in person, so he left a note and then hoisted the oppressively heavy donation box onto his back before taking off.

Unexpectedly, there was mayhem in the Heavenly Capital when he arrived. Xie Lian stood there, bug-eyed and gaping at the destruction around him. The once perfectly tidy Grand Avenue of Divine Might was completely wrecked; potholes, cracks, and craters marred the street. A team of junior heavenly officials was running around in circles attending to this and that, while Ling Wen was squatting next to a deep crater massaging her throbbing temples.

Xie Lian approached her. "Zhenjun, what happened?"

Ling Wen looked up and was flummoxed by the giant donation box on his back.

"Your Highness, what are you doing carrying such a big donation box up here?! As for what happened...don't even ask." Ling Wen sighed. "General Nan Yang and General Xuan Zhen got into a fight and destroyed each other's palaces."

Feng Xin and Mu Qing? Xie Lian was amazed.

"Why were the two of them fighting again?"

"What could it be but that business with the fetus spirit?" Ling Wen explained. "A few martial gods met up to debate how to deal with the ghost mother and son. General Nan Yang suggested bringing the fetus spirit to the refinery to dissolve it, since it did murder many people. But Xuan Zhen wouldn't let him. His tone wasn't the nicest, as you'd expect, so Nan Yang said, 'As if you've ever been so benevolent! Maybe you have a guilty conscience!' And other such things.

"Your Highness, you know how it is. They didn't say much before they went off with their fists, just like that. Look—look around. Look at the state of this place. You martial gods really don't have a good culture. This year's repair expenses are terrifying. I only ran the numbers halfway and now I've forgotten everything again. Honestly..."

She really did look like she had quite the headache.

"Then...I'll leave you to it," Xie Lian said. "I'll go check up on Lord Wind Master."

Ling Wen looked up. "Visit Lord Wind Master? Don't bother, Your Highness. Lord Wind Master isn't seeing visitors right now."

"Didn't you say he was a bit better?" Xie Lian asked.

"That's what Lord Water Master said," Ling Wen replied. "But Lord Wind Master not seeing visitors was also a statement from Lord Water Master. Not even I can see Lord Wind Master right now, so he probably needs more time to recuperate. You'd best not go, Your Highness. Speaking of, isn't your donation box too..."

Wham! Xie Lian dropped the donation box to the ground.

"Then will you please help me return this to Lord Water Master? I haven't done anything deserving of such a reward. And even if he didn't give me anything, I would never say anything that shouldn't be said."

He felt relieved after throwing the box down and left with haste. Ling Wen called after him, but upon receiving no response, she let it go and continued to stare at the deep crater with a throbbing head.

Although Xie Lian did leave, of course he wouldn't descend to the Mortal Realm so easily. Instead, he snuck over to the esteemed Palace of the Wind and Water Masters in the Heavenly Capital.

The palace was swarming with guards both inside and out, but a small thing like that couldn't stop Xie Lian. Shi Qingxuan had brought him here in the past, so he had a general idea of where the Wind Master's bedchambers were located. He flipped over the wall and alternated between stealthily running across rooftops and slinking around the grounds until he arrived at his destination. It took him no time at all. His only concern was the possibility that the Wind Master had been moved elsewhere by his brother and wasn't in the building at all.

Fortunately, this wasn't the case. He climbed onto the roof and found a blind spot where no one could see him, then he hooked his legs onto the eaves and flipped himself upside down to peek into the bedchamber.

What he saw shocked him.

Shi Qingxuan was tightly trussed up, tied to his own bed with ropes that bound his hands and legs. Even so, he still struggled non-stop. Meanwhile, Shi Wudu was pacing back and forth next to his bed with a bowl full of an unknown black substance in his hands. He paused for a moment before suddenly walking over to the head of the bed.

And then he forced the bowl's contents down Shi Qingxuan's throat.

58
Traversing Through Tunnels, Sword Hanging Above

SHI QINGXUAN VIOLENTLY CHOKED as Shi Wudu squeezed his jaw and force-fed him the contents of the bowl. He spat and sputtered out more than half the stuff, dirtying the front of his robes. Screaming, he slammed his head into the bowl to knock it from his brother's hands. Shi Wudu fumed.

"Go ahead! Keep breaking them!" he yelled. "There's plenty of medicine where that came from. Break one bowl and I'll bring twenty more! I'll keep forcing it down your throat until you drink it all!"

"*Aaaaaah!* Can't you just leave me alone?! Just let me die!" Shi Qingxuan screamed.

"I'm your brother!" Shi Wudu snapped. "If I don't take care of you, who will?!"

Shi Qingxuan ceased his screams and settled for twisting his head away. Shi Wudu sat down on the side of the bed and softened his tone.

"I'll have your fan fixed."

"I don't want it anymore," Shi Qingxuan said.

The Wind Master loved that rare spiritual device of his, his Wind Master fan; he'd often bring it out just to play with. Even at the height of winter with snow choking the skies, he would flutter that fan undaunted. But now he'd said he didn't want it anymore. Xie Lian was only growing more and more curious.

"If you don't want it, that's fine as well. We'll use the opportunity to forge you a new spiritual device."

Shi Qingxuan turned his head back to look at his brother. "I don't want a new one either! Just let me descend."

Shi Wudu peered at him. "Descend? Descend where?"

"Descend to the Mortal Realm," Shi Qingxuan replied. "I don't want to stay in the Upper Court anymore. I don't want to be a god anymore!"

Veins bulged on Shi Wudu's fair brow. "What a joke! Throw away your godhood and return to the Mortal Realm? Do you think the Mortal Realm is some kind of *wonderful* place? Stop embarrassing yourself! I don't think you understand just how many people in the world want to ascend or how many officials in the Middle Court would die to join the Upper Court!"

"That's right! I don't know!" Shi Qingxuan shouted, his anger obvious. "I just want to be a carefree drifting vagabond! Is that so wrong?!"

"I won't permit it!" Shi Wudu snapped. "A carefree drifting vagabond? Dream on! I..."

The color of his face changed abruptly; it seemed he'd received a private message that passed on worrisome news. With two fingers pressed against his temple, Shi Wudu rose to his feet at once and listened intently. His face grew more and more serious, and he turned to Shi Qingxuan.

"Stop adding to my troubles. I've been busy, I've no time to mind you! Once I return from my third Heavenly Tribulation, you won't be able to act out like this any longer!"

Then, with a whirl of his sleeves, he swiftly left the bedchamber.

Once it was clear that he was gone, Xie Lian silently flipped down. He pushed at the window, hoping to sneak in, but it wouldn't budge.

Some sort of seal of restriction must have been cast on it. He dared not force it open, lest he trip any alarms associated with that spell.

And so he could only call out in a quiet voice: "Lord Wind Master. Lord Wind Master?"

Shi Qingxuan jerked on the bed. He turned his head, joy clear on his face. "Your Highness?!"

"It's me," Xie Lian responded. "What happened to you? I can't open this window. May I try coming in another way?"

When confronted with a window that couldn't be opened by normal means, it was easy to guess the entry method a martial god would choose.

"Don't, don't, don't! Don't destroy anything!" Shi Qingxuan said hurriedly. "There are spells on all the windows and doors. If you force your way in, the whole Palace of Wind and Water will know someone's here. They can only be opened from the inside, unless you're me or my brother."

"But you're all tied up," Xie Lian pointed out.

Shi Qingxuan started to struggle like mad. "Your Highness, wait a sec! Watch me flex these ropes right off..."

"..."

Xie Lian watched as he rolled around the bed in an immense struggle to break free, alternating between curling up like a shrimp and straightening out like an iron board. Xie Lian softly cheered him on.

"Keep at it, My Lord!"

He could tell with a cursory glance that the rope binding Shi Qingxuan wasn't a spiritual device. With Lord Wind Master's considerable power, it should've snapped with but a hook of his finger. Why was he having such trouble? Was Shi Qingxuan really so seriously hurt that he couldn't break free of simple bindings?

All of a sudden, an odd movement came from under Shi Qingxuan's bed, and a hand stretched out from below. Xie Lian was startled, and his heart raced in alarm.

"Lord Wind Master, watch out! Someone's hiding underneath your bed!"

Shi Qingxuan's expression also changed. "What?!"

Just as he spoke, a black figure swiftly crawled from under the bed.

Staring down commandingly at him from above was a man dressed in black and wearing a ghost mask. It was hard to tell how long he'd been hiding there or what he was about to do. Shi Qingxuan writhed desperately, unable to escape his bonds, and Xie Lian remained locked outside—it was truly a dire situation. But before Xie Lian could put his thoughts of smashing the window into action, he saw the man push up his ghost mask.

"Shut up!" he hissed in a hushed voice.

Shi Qingxuan's eyes widened. "Ming-xiong? Ming-xiong! My god, Ming-xiong, my good pal, quick! Help me loosen these ropes!"

With just one hand, Ming Yi snapped the rope that bound Shi Qingxuan. Shi Qingxuan worked out the kinks in his limbs, then crawled out of bed and rushed over to the window. He clutched Xie Lian's hands and shook them in earnest gratitude.

"Your Highness! Thank you for remembering me!"

Xie Lian patted his shoulders and then hopped into the bed-chamber with nimble feather lightness.

"Wasn't there a restriction seal on the chamber? How did Lord Earth Master get in?"

"It was hardly a feat, considering my profession," Ming Yi said.

After saying this, he seemed to notice something amiss. He picked up the rope on the ground and inspected it before asking Shi Qingxuan, "Why couldn't you break free of something as trivial as this?"

Xie Lian looked closely as well. This was a completely ordinary rope. With such strong spiritual power at his command, why did the Wind Master remain bound for so long by nothing but coarse twine?

Shi Qingxuan's face froze, and Ming Yi grabbed his left wrist. As he felt his pulse, his expression turned grim.

"What's going on?!"

Xie Lian reached out and took hold of Shi Qingxuan's right wrist. After a moment, his discovery dumbfounded him.

"Lord Wind Master, how did this happen?"

There was not a trace of spiritual power in Shi Qingxuan's body!

"Was it that bowl of medicine?" Xie Lian guessed.

Recalling the bowl of medicine Shi Wudu was trying to force down Shi Qingxuan's throat earlier, Xie Lian crouched to check the spillage.

However, Shi Qingxuan replied, "No."

It truly wasn't the medicine. Xie Lian was somewhat familiar with the healing arts; judging by its smell, the medicinal broth was likely an anesthetic meant to calm him. At most, it might cause drowsiness. Thinking back to the Terrace of Cascading Wine and the frightening look that crossed his face, Shi Wudu must have noticed his younger brother's condition when he grabbed his wrist. He was likely making his brother drink such a broth for his own good, so why was Shi Qingxuan so adamant in refusing it?

No wonder Shi Qingxuan wasn't answering any private communications. With all his spiritual power completely gone, he was no different from a mortal.

"Lord Wind Master, you've been banished?" Xie Lian blurted without thinking.

How else could this have happened? But there were no cursed shackles on him, and there was no way a banishment could be kept under wraps. The Upper and Middle Courts would've caught wind of it in no time. Shi Qingxuan's face was pale, and he seemed unable to stand any longer.

Xie Lian helped support him. "Why did Lord Water Master tie you up?"

Only then did Shi Qingxuan snap out of it. "Right. My brother. Let's hurry out of here while he's still gone. Let's talk after we've escaped!"

Then he dropped to the floor and crawled under the bed. Xie Lian bent down and called after him.

"Lord Wind Master!"

There was actually a hole under the bed, leading to somewhere unknown. Shi Qingxuan disappeared into it, and Ming Yi lowered himself down as well, ready to follow him. After a moment of thought, Xie Lian decided to follow them too. However, Ming Yi came back out.

"Your Highness, don't involve yourself anymore."

Xie Lian was taken aback by his rebuff. "Lord Wind Master has given me generous assistance on many occasions. Now that he's in trouble, I can't just sit back and watch."

"He's generous to everyone. But when there's real trouble, most people don't return the favor," Ming Yi said.

"How others behave has nothing to do with me," Xie Lian stated. "After we've figured out what's going on, I will of course take my leave if my assistance is unnecessary."

Shi Qingxuan's voice came from under the bed. "Are you two coming? The hole is closing!"

Sure enough, the hole under the bed was gradually growing smaller. Seeing this, Ming Yi leapt inside, and Xie Lian followed. As they crawled through the tunnel Ming Yi dug, Xie Lian looked back to find that the entrance to the hole had closed on its own. How absolutely magical.

"Lord Earth Master, how did you dig this out?" he asked in a hushed voice. "I thought it was impossible to burrow beneath the Heavenly Capital."

It must be known that the foundation of the Heavenly Capital was not the same as the earth of the Mortal Realm.

In response to Xie Lian's question, he learned the Earth Master Ming Yi was a skilled tradesman prior to his ascension. In his mortal lifetime, he repaired bridges, fixed roads, opened mountain paths, constructed houses, and bestowed prosperity to countless common folk—these astounding feats of service were what allowed him to ascend. Before any major construction projects began in the Mortal Realm, before any earth was broken, the people first prayed to the Earth Master for the blessing of successful labor.

After ascension, he forged a spiritual device: a shovel in the shape of a crescent moon. Rumor had it that there was no mountain this sacred shovel could not flatten, no tunnel that could not be dug, and no building that could not be entered. This was extremely useful for spying operations in Ghost City—if he wished to enter a secret chamber, he could simply dig his way in, and his tracks would cover themselves. Maybe he could've escaped on his own using his treasured shovel if Hua Cheng hadn't beaten him to a pulp and significantly damaged his spiritual powers.

The Earth Master had never tried using his shovel to tunnel beneath the residence of any heavenly official; he didn't really show the thing off in general. He usually kept it in storage, which was probably for the best—spiritual devices of Upper Court officials were generally elegant and beautiful, like books and brushes, swords and fans, and guqin and flutes. It would completely ruin the court's image if among them was a heavenly official who hauled a shovel around all day.

Once he heard the explanation, Xie Lian couldn't help but wonder: if he wanted his Puqi Shrine to be renovated, maybe he should pray to the Earth Master too?

After crawling for a while, ahead of him, Xie Lian heard Ming Yi ask a question of Shi Qingxuan.

"Was it the Reverend of Empty Words?"

Xie Lian also wanted to know the answer. If the Reverend of Empty Words had injured Shi Qingxuan like this, and if news of the incident got out, it would shake up the Heavenly Realm and cause a huge panic. To think that a monster could rob a heavenly official of their powers in such a short time, and that it could cause them to fall and become mortal! It wasn't hard to imagine the mayhem that would create.

It was such a serious affair, but after a few moments of silence, Shi Qingxuan replied with a simple statement.

"No matter who did it, this whole thing is over and done with."

His reaction was extremely questionable. He shouldn't have been acting so flippant if he was caught in a trap designed to drain him of his power. Shi Qingxuan wasn't a sucker who'd take a beating lying down.

A sudden dreadful idea dawned upon Xie Lian. Although awful to consider, it would explain everything.

Just then, Ming Yi ordered, "Silence."

They all held their breaths, and Xie Lian and Shi Qingxuan looked at him. Ming Yi ignited a palm torch, and the flickering flames illuminated their immediate surroundings.

Ming Yi seemed to want to communicate via the spiritual array, but Shi Qingxuan's power was gone and he couldn't communicate with his mind alone. Thus, Ming Yi changed tactics and used his finger to write words in the air. Wherever his fingertips traced, a black streak trailed behind like drops of thick ink diffusing in clear water.

The other two read what he wrote:

"Don't speak and don't move. Wait."

He waited for everyone to finish reading, then puffed a soundless breath that dispersed those words into the air. Xie Lian still had some spiritual power left, so he raised his hand and replied in writing as well:

"Wait for what? For how long?"

Ming Yi wrote: *"Wait until the person above leaves."*

Xie Lian and Shi Qingxuan both looked up at the same time. It seemed this underground tunnel Ming Yi had dug burrowed beneath some heavenly residences and temples. A heavenly official probably just happened to be above their heads at that very moment.

Listening intently, they could hear the sound of steady footsteps pacing back and forth in the chamber above. Judging by those footsteps, Xie Lian determined that it had to be a martial god. Martial gods' senses were sharp; if the three of them weren't careful and made any suspicious noises, they might be discovered.

Shi Qingxuan couldn't use the communication array nor write with ink in the air; all he could do was move his lips silently to express his accusations. Xie Lian watched him repeat the phrase twice before he could understand what he said.

"Ming-xiong, why didn't you avoid temples and palaces?! Couldn't you have dug under the Grand Avenue of Divine Might instead?!"

Ming Yi indifferently wrote, *"There wasn't anyone in this palace before. The Grand Avenue of Divine Might is full of holes right now."*

Xie Lian wrote, *"That's right. I saw it on the way over earlier. The avenue is full of holes and craters. Some are even a few meters deep.*

If we dug into one of those by accident, we might come face-to-face with someone above."

And so the three remained as silent as dull rocks, waiting patiently for the heavenly official above them to leave. After waiting for a while, Shi Qingxuan moved his lips again.

"Are they gone?"

Ming Yi shook his head. Veins popped on Shi Qingxuan's temple, and his angry expression was almost the same as it had been when he was arguing with his brother earlier. He mouthed soundlessly:

"Who the hell is dilly-dallying like this? It's not even the proper hour for sleeping! And what heavenly official needs to sleep, for that matter? Are we under their bathroom or what?!"

Strictly speaking, heavenly officials didn't need to go to the bathroom either. As Shi Qingxuan's lips formed the word "bathroom," Xie Lian felt the hair on the back of his neck stand. In one fluid motion, he shoved the two in front of him down while he backstepped and tumbled away.

A sharp blade penetrated the tunnel from above, bearing down threateningly and roiling with murderous intent—and it stabbed into the ground right between Xie Lian's legs.

59
Eve of the Last Day of Autumn, an Unscrupulous Substitution

ALTHOUGH XIE LIAN DID INDEED live his days passing himself off as impotent, pretending not to have the thing was still fundamentally different than truly losing the thing forever. It shocked a sheen of cold sweat into covering his body.

"Dodge!" he barked.

The blade was pulled out of the ground just as he spoke. Xie Lian seized the chance to move forward, but then he immediately yanked Shi Qingxuan back.

"Watch out!"

The blade plunged down again and stabbed right in front of Shi Qingxuan, practically scraping past his head; if Xie Lian hadn't pulled him back in time, he would've been nailed to the ground on the spot.

"That was close!" he exclaimed, terrified. "How did you know where it would attack?"

"Don't know! I guessed!" Xie Lian said.

It was pure instinct. When it came to facing down an enemy with murderous intent, he had trained to the point where he could react without thinking. A second, a third, and a fourth blade came plunging down, the glare of each blade blocking the way forward and back. *Boom!* A huge explosion followed shortly after. Violent tremors shook the tunnel, raining down dust and debris.

"They've opened fire from above!"

Each boom got progressively louder, and the tremors grew in strength—their source was obviously coming closer and closer. Sharp swords blocked them from the front and back, all young, keen blades. Fangxin was a senior, so Xie Lian wasn't sure that it could fight them head-on. Ming Yi retrieved his crescent shovel from somewhere and began to dig into a wall of the confined tunnel with great difficulty. Next to him, Shi Qingxuan was so distressed that his soul was about to leave his body.

"Ming-xiong, can you even do this? Ming-xiong, can you hurry up? It's your fault for not using that thing for such a long time! You gotta spend more time with your devices, all right? Get intimate. Look how stiff and rusty it's gotten!"

To be fair, allowing it to become rusty was forgivable. After all, aside from Xie Lian, there wasn't a single heavenly official who could carry around a shovel every day with a straight face.

Veins popped on Ming Yi's forehead. "Shut up!"

Xie Lian hastily intervened. "Don't be mad, don't be mad. The tunnel's been dug!"

It was as he said. The moment Ming Yi put pressure on his shovel, a hole opened up before them. Raising his shovel high, he burrowed crazily ahead while Shi Qingxuan cheered him on crazily from the middle. As the only non-crazy person, Xie Lian brought up the rear. The shovel of the Earth Master was truly magical—it dug out a few dozen meters ahead with only a few strokes, and when he looked back, the hole behind was gradually closing up on its own.

However, thin light leaked from above the place where they'd just been trapped.

"They're drilling through!" Xie Lian alerted them urgently.

Ming Yi picked up the pace and burrowed even crazier. But suddenly, his movements stopped and he looked up. Xie Lian reacted the same way, because they both sensed the same thing: it was completely silent above them. They could detect no movement. There was likely an empty palace above them.

Since their tunnel had already been discovered, they needed to get out before trying anything else. Ming Yi changed course and started digging upward.

"Are you two sure there's nobody here who'll spot us when we get out?!" Shi Qingxuan asked.

"Haven't heard anything. Unless they're sleeping," Ming Yi replied.

Of course, that shouldn't be a possibility—heavenly officials usually didn't need to sleep at all, never mind in the middle of the day. Ming Yi's shovel broke through and all three poked their heads out to take a gasp of fresh air. However, before they even had the chance to exhale, they saw someone on the bed across from them. It was a young man, and he was soundly asleep with his arms and legs sprawled out like a starfish.

Xie Lian was baffled. It seemed there really *were* heavenly officials who slept in the middle of the day!

Roused by the hubbub, the youth rolled over and sat up. His curly hair was a frightful mess from his slumber, and he watched the three strange heads with sleepy eyes. He furrowed his brows and scratched his head, clearly confused as to why such things had appeared in his palace. The three of them pretended that nothing was wrong and hastily clambered out of the hole. But just when Shi Qingxuan was almost out, he gave a cry of alarm. Xie Lian looked back and saw that a hand had caught his ankle.

That hand's owner was Pei Ming. He maintained exceptional manners even while stuffed into a tunnel.

"I'd wondered what little mouse was scurrying under my palace. Qingxuan, why are you out and about? Where are you going? You know how your brother gets when he's mad. Hurry back before he finds out."

Ruoye flew forth to strike his hand away, and Pei Ming leapt out of the hole.

"Your Highness, Lord Earth Master, don't you have anything better to do? It's quite preposterous that you're encouraging the Wind Master to run away from home for no reason, isn't it?"

"General Pei, while Lord Wind Master is Lord Water Master's younger brother, he has still been a heavenly official for centuries. Please don't talk about him like he's a three-year-old toddler," Xie Lian said. "If we're going to talk about *reasons*, Lord Water Master imprisoned a heavenly colleague with no justification. No matter how you want to spin it, wouldn't you say *he's* the one being preposterous?"

If his theory on the matter was right, then the Wind Master really couldn't stay in the Upper Court any longer.

The figure in bed sat up—it was Quan Yizhen. He stayed where he was, watching them with a glassy look. He still seemed confused about the whole situation.

Pei Ming raised his sword. "Qi Ying, stop staring and come give me a hand," he said sternly. "Apprehend them."

After giving it some thought, Quan Yizhen decided to assist. He rolled off the bed, picked up that same bed he had just been sleeping on, and hurled it at Pei Ming.

He indeed gave a hand, but to help Xie Lian and company. The bed crashed into the unsuspecting Pei Ming.

"Qi Ying! Why did you hit me?!" he said, flabbergasted.

Quan Yizhen waved at Xie Lian, gesturing for them to hurry and leave. Xie Lian and company stood bewildered for a moment before hastily making their exit.

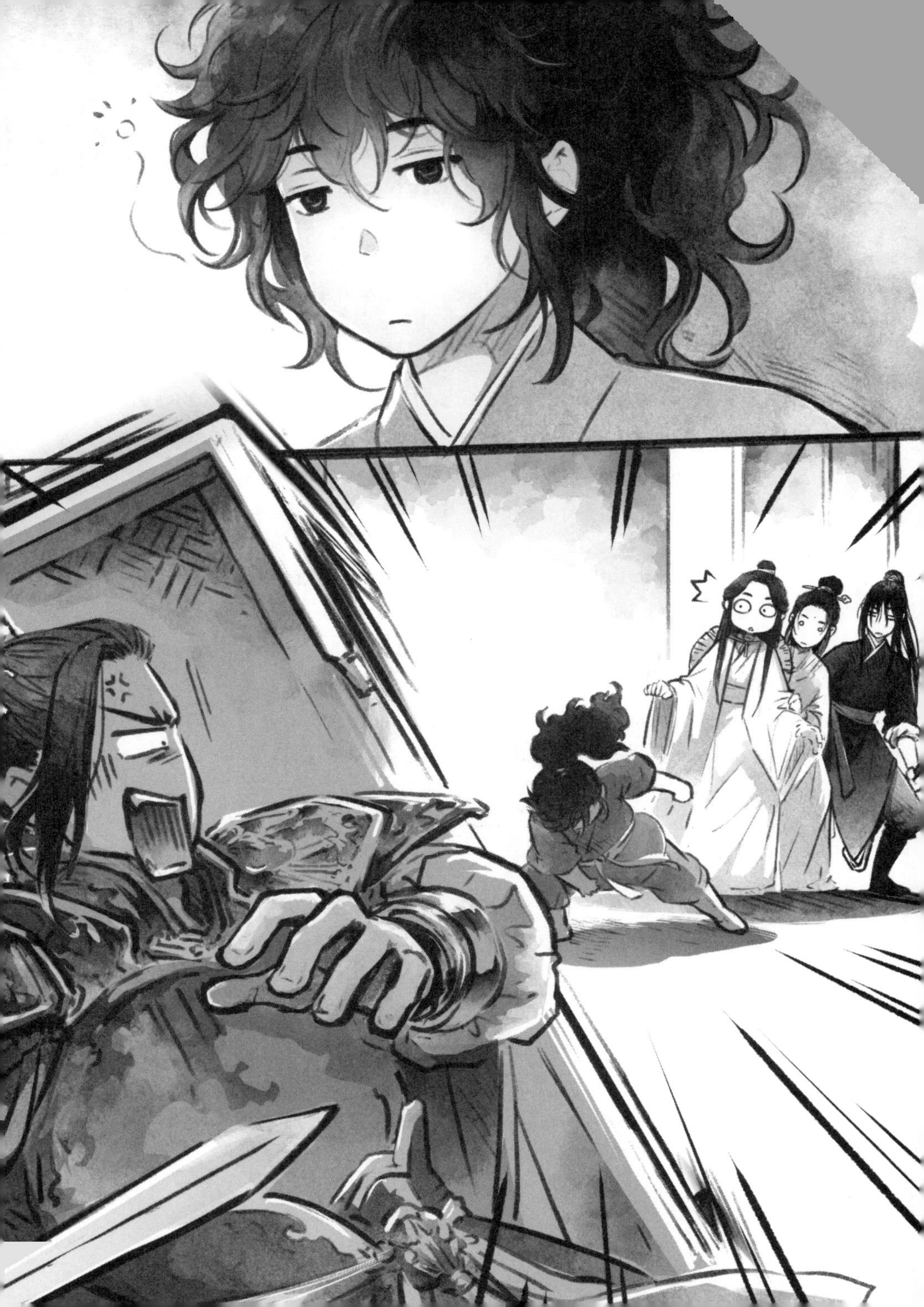

haps he was drained because of his injury, but Shi Qingxuan ...gged a few steps before his face turned pale. Xie Lian moved to help him along, but Ming Yi immediately yanked him over and lifted him up onto his back. Xie Lian placed his hand on the door and dug out two dice, then called out behind him.

"Thanks so much!"

Quan Yizhen was still in the process of pummeling Pei Ming, his moves vicious and aggressive and without method. If it wasn't for Pei Ming's own skills—if anyone else took such a thrashing—he would've been beaten bloody by now.

Veins popped on Pei Ming's forehead. "Guards! Stop them!" he yelled.

Before he could finish calling for the guards, Xie Lian had already tossed the dice, opened the door, and gotten the hell out of heaven. But as he closed the door and turned around, he never could've expected the sight that would greet him.

Hua Cheng was fully nude from the waist up. He had one foot up on a new donation box and was wiping away his sweat.

"..."

"..."

"..."

Xie Lian felt like he was going to suffocate. His run-down, tiny little Puqi Shrine couldn't possibly hold so many great idols.

There was also a certain possessed individual who was completely oblivious howling and making a terrible racket outside.

"GUZI~! COME GIVE DADDY'S LEGS A LI'L MASSAGE CHOP~!"

It took a moment for Hua Cheng to toss Eming aside, which he had been using to carve wood. He arched an eyebrow.

"...?"

The color of his skin and the contours of his bare upper half were exceedingly beautiful, extremely eye-catching—so much so that Xie Lian's eyes were about to fall out of their sockets. Even if he hadn't caught all the details, he still couldn't stop the blood from rushing to his head and making his vision go dark. Xie Lian fumbled and stumbled over to Hua Cheng and opened his arms wide, blocking him from Ming Yi and Shi Qingxuan's view.

"Close your eyes! Quick! *Close your eyes!*"

Their expressions stiffened. They stared at Xie Lian and Hua Cheng, clearly perplexed.

Hua Cheng placed his hand on Xie Lian's shoulder. "...Gege. Why are you so nervous?" he asked, sounding amused.

Only then did Xie Lian snap out of it. Yes, why *was* he so nervous? Hua Cheng wasn't a woman; who cared if he decided to work half-naked? He still didn't drop his arms, doing his best to cover Hua Cheng completely.

"Either way, just...just put on some clothes first."

Hua Cheng shrugged. "Okay. As gege wishes."

He then calmly grabbed a shirt and took his time putting it on.

Watching him move so fluidly and with such perfect composure, Shi Qingxuan said awkwardly, "Um, sorry for the intrusion. I didn't think you guys...ha ha ha, you two are pretty much...ha ha ha. Anyway, just...ha ha ha."

"...My Lord, if you have something to say, say it out loud so I can explain any misunderstandings. Don't just ha-ha it away, okay...?" Xie Lian said.

They were pressed for time. Pei Ming might pursue them to Puqi Shrine at any moment, so they couldn't stay for long. Ming Yi set down Shi Qingxuan and started drawing the teleportation array on the ground. Xie Lian was just about to ask where they were going when he heard Hua Cheng sigh behind him.

Xie Lian then remembered his advice not to get close to the Wind Master and company. He turned to him in spite of himself. "Sorry about all this, San Lang."

Hua Cheng was dressed by then. "I already knew you wouldn't just sit back and watch." After a pause, he smiled. "But why is gege apologizing to me? You remember what I said a few days ago. But did you forget what I told you before that?"

Xie Lian was slightly taken aback and wondered, *What?*

He then recalled what Hua Cheng had told him that night at the Green Ghost's lair: *"Just focus on doing what you want to do."*

Xie Lian blinked. He didn't know what to say; he only knew that he suddenly really wanted to do something for Hua Cheng. But at that moment, there really wasn't anything he *could* do. He was stuck in place—until he noticed an issue with Hua Cheng's collar.

"Wait!"

He hurried over to help Hua Cheng fix his collar, which hadn't been properly flipped out after he shrugged the robes on. Having fixed it, Xie Lian inspected him for a moment and then smiled.

"There."

Hua Cheng smiled too. "Thanks."

A small voice inside Xie Lian replied, *I'm the one who should be thanking you.*

The other two seemed unable to look at them anymore, and Ming Yi's hand even seemed incapable of drawing a perfectly round circle. Once he finished drawing the array and the door opened again, Xie Lian thought he would see either a gloomy cave or some majestic palace. Instead, there was a large expanse of farmland. Lush green bamboo groves and mountains could be seen in the distance, and farmers were hard at work in the fields. There was also a burly, glossy black ox pulling a plow.

The scenery almost made Xie Lian think they were still in Puqi Village, and he was briefly stunned. Ming Yi had already walked out carrying Shi Qingxuan on his back, and Hua Cheng had also stepped through before Xie Lian managed to collect himself.

The four walked along the field ridge. Maybe it was all in his mind, but the black ox seemed to be staring at them the whole way. After walking for a while, they found a small cottage and went inside to sit down. Shi Qingxuan blew out a long breath.

"Are we not fleeing any further?" Xie Lian asked. "What if General Pei chases us here?"

Hua Cheng stared outside for a while—focusing especially on the black ox—before finally closing the door.

"Don't worry. He wouldn't dare provoke the master of this land," he said nonchalantly. "He wouldn't have an easy time if he tried. The Water Tyrant won't do anything rash either."

Xie Lian contemplated that for a moment and couldn't help but voice his thoughts. "San Lang, this whole thing is a mess. It probably involves many in the Heavenly Court. It might be best if you don't hang around."

Hua Cheng only chuckled at that. "What goes on in the Upper Court has nothing to do with me. I'm only here to sightsee by your side."

All of a sudden, Shi Qingxuan stated, "You should *all* stop hanging around."

The others in the cottage looked at him.

"His Highness is right. This whole thing is a mess, and there are too many involved," Shi Qingxuan continued. "I'm going to stay here. My friends, there's no need to help any more. Let's end it here."

"Lord Wind Master, it isn't up to you whether things end here," Xie Lian said slowly. "It's up to Lord Water Master and the Reverend of Empty Words."

Hearing this, Shi Qingxuan's expression stiffened.

"Lord Wind Master, I have a question. I hope you won't mind," Xie Lian added.

"What?"

"Is the Reverend of Empty Words holding something over your and Lord Water Master's heads?"

Shi Qingxuan turned slightly pale.

That night at the Terrace of Cascading Wine, Xie Lian had set up an extremely secure protection array. As long as Shi Qingxuan hadn't opened the door, he wouldn't have been harmed. So why would he choose to do just that?!

Unless someone connected to his private communication array, and the first thing that they uttered was blackmail. That would give Shi Qingxuan no chance to fight back nor raise the alarm, and he could only do as instructed.

Xie Lian sat down by the table. "I'm more inclined to think it's blackmail against Lord Water Master, since I don't believe you knew the full story. At least not at first."

This would explain why his reaction was so strong after learning whatever it was. The knowledge had provoked such a sharp revulsion toward the Upper Court that he would rather descend and become a drifting immortal or a wandering cultivator than stay in the heavens as a god.

Ming Yi frowned. "Blackmail?"

Shi Qingxuan wasn't a fool. If he fell victim to a plot and lost his powers, his normal reaction should've been extreme rage or retaliation directed at the culprit, or a drive to investigate the matter. But there was none of that to be seen. There was rage, but it wasn't directed at the Reverend of Empty Words—it was directed at his own older brother. And to everyone else, he only declared that this would all end then and there.

This was entirely abnormal—unless Shi Qingxuan's ascension wasn't normal to begin with!

It was outrageously audacious to defy the heavens and alter fate. It was treacherous heresy to raise someone who couldn't ascend upon the divine altar. Xie Lian had never heard of anything like it. Such a revelation, if true, would surely raise a tidal wave of chaos if it got out. Just think: everyone wanted to ascend, but wouldn't the very laws of the universe be rendered irrelevant and worthless if someone could do so using that kind of method?

The conjecture seemed absurd, but the more he considered it, the more it made sense. The Reverend of Empty Words had harassed Shi Qingxuan since birth, and the only way to escape was to ascend. And miraculously, he did just that. In the span of just a few years, a pair of blood brothers ascended in succession—what a grand, fine tale. But also, what a grand coincidence.

Xie Lian didn't want to question Shi Qingxuan's ascension, but if the Wind Master was deified naturally, why was it so easy to rob him of his powers? If a monster could turn a god into a human so effortlessly, surely there would be many past cases of heavenly officials who fell victim.

Unless Shi Qingxuan should have been mortal in the first place. Unless the Water Master did something underhanded to make the Wind Master ascend.

It wasn't out of line to use rare treasures and devices to aid in cultivation. Nor was it out of line to ascend by way of massacre and war during unstable periods in the Mortal Realm. After all, that was the way of the world: honor is accompanied by blood, and the slate is cleaned after ascension. With that said, it would be a completely different matter if a mortal or heavenly official used crooked means and conducted wicked rituals to harm others' lives for the sake of becoming a god. Some things were forbidden.

"Lord Wind Master, the night you ascended, was it the eve of Hanlu?" Xie Lian asked in a low voice.

A few moments later, Shi Qingxuan drew a deep breath.

"Yes."

After a pause, Shi Qingxuan explained.

"When we were in the town of Fu Gu, that same thing crossed my mind. 'The eve of Hanlu—wasn't that the same day I ascended?' I wanted to ask you guys about it, to see if it might be a clue or related somehow, or if it was just a coincidence. But I wasn't sure, so I didn't bring it up. Well, now you know whether it's related."

It was related. It was *very* related.

Why did the Reverend of Empty Words choose that day to send Shi Qingxuan to the town of Fu Gu to watch the exciting performance during the Bloody Fire Social parade, then whisk him off to the Terrace of Cascading Wine and maim him there? It wouldn't go to such lengths if it didn't have a reason.

Xie Lian connected the timing and the two places together. Centuries ago, a mortal called Scholar He broke down and murdered countless people in the town of Fu Gu on the eve of Hanlu. Centuries ago, Shi Qingxuan ascended at the Terrace of Cascading Wine on the eve of Hanlu.

It was obvious what the Reverend of Empty Words wanted to

say: *"Shi Qingxuan, your ascension is directly tied to the death of the hero of the Bloody Fire Social!"*

This was Xie Lian's dreadful but logical theory.

To rescue Shi Qingxuan from the Reverend of Empty Words, after Shi Wudu ascended, he secretly found a mortal who matched the requirements of birth and name. He then conducted some sort of wicked ritual to make that man take on Shi Qingxuan's misfortune. That man was no doubt Scholar He—the man who was exceptionally clever, exceedingly impoverished, and endlessly unlucky to the point where his entire family was ruined.

Scholar He took on Shi Qingxuan's fate, and the Reverend of Empty Words was deceived. That meant *his* original fate was taken by Shi Qingxuan. On that same Hanlu eve, one experienced a taste of hell on earth, and the other successfully ascended under immensely powerful protection.

But their two fates were originally the complete opposite!

60
Gods Appointing Gods is Beneath Ghosts Devouring Ghosts

"My theory is that Scholar He has the given name 'Xuan,'" Xie Lian continued, "and that his birth details are exactly the same as My Lord's."

It was no easy task to deceive the heavens and commit such fraud. And furthermore, not just any target would do—there were certain requirements that needed to be met.

From the three questions the Reverend of Empty Words had asked when it encountered the young Shi Qingxuan in the woods, it was clear that it knew two things: first, that its prey's name contained the word "Xuan," and second, its prey's birth details. However, it couldn't recognize its prey's face and had needed Shi Qingxuan to approach for it to see. The Reverend probably knew nothing besides those two facts, thanks to the Shi family's speedy response to the original incident.

In order for someone to take Shi Qingxuan's place and take on his misfortunes, two things had to be true. The target had to be male and share the same birth details—the same year, same month, same day, same time—and their name had to contain the word "Xuan."

How difficult it must have been to find a scapegoat! The world is vast, but even if Shi Wudu searched every corner of it, he might not have found a single individual who satisfied the conditions to the letter. Using the power and influence of his great Water Master status, he cast the net wide and actually landed a perfect catch.

Furthermore, it was one who possessed the potential to ascend, and who was about to go through his first Heavenly Tribulation!

How could he let this chance slip the line? This was a convenient shortcut to arduous cultivation. If he let him go, he might not find another opportunity ever again!

At this point, Ming Yi's increasingly dark expression indicated that he had arrived at the same conclusion. Though Shi Qingxuan nodded at first, something seemed to have struck him, and he looked to where Hua Cheng stood leaning against the door. This wasn't something that should be discussed before a ghost, after all. However, Hua Cheng only chuckled and crossed his arms.

"No need to look at me, Lord Wind Master. I'm not the one you should worry about; I have nothing to do with this whole business. Why don't you concern yourself with whether anyone else in the Upper Court has caught wind of your brother's dirty little secret?"

"You really *do* have spies in the heavens," Ming Yi accused darkly.

"Didn't you already know that?" Hua Cheng replied lazily.

Lord Earth Master was originally sent to Ghost City to investigate that very topic, but he came back empty-handed after over a decade of undercover work. It seemed the spy was planted deep, and their identity was never uncovered. Hua Cheng said this business had nothing to do with him, so naturally Xie Lian believed him and didn't think any more of it. But Hua Cheng had also mentioned that Shi Qingxuan should instead worry about others in the Upper Court, which reminded Xie Lian of something else.

"Lord Wind Master, why did you open the door and disrupt the protection array that night at the Terrace of Cascading Wine? Did someone call out to you? Who was it?"

"Yeah," Shi Qingxuan replied. "It was the Reverend of Empty Words. It said..."

Xie Lian crossed his hands into his sleeves. "How did it know your verbal password?"

"..." Ming Yi made an annoyed face. "Isn't it because he's always prancing around trying to make friends? He yaps nonstop whether others are free or not! He talks too much!"

Shi Qingxuan was aggrieved. "Ming-xiong, you can't say it like that. Everyone who chats with me is an Upper Court official! I've never given anything personal to that creature!"

"If the Reverend of Empty Words could so easily uncover Lord Water Master's...secret...after returning from its long dormancy, then getting Lord Wind Master's verbal password wouldn't have been difficult either," Xie Lian said. "Someone must've leaked your verbal password. It's worth investigating, whether it was intentional or not."

"So? Did you see what it looked like? What did it do after calling you out?" Ming Yi asked.

"..." Shi Qingxuan's head seemed to start throbbing. "I don't know what it looks like. It cast a spell; I couldn't see clearly."

This vague answer didn't elaborate on what he *did* see. Ming Yi's tone was becoming sullener by the minute. Xie Lian considered the possibility that it had emulated some gory scene from the Bloody Fire Social, which was certainly difficult to describe. A moment later, Shi Qingxuan sighed.

"I'm the useless one. If I could've ascended on my own, none of this would have happened."

Shi Qingxuan's original fate was probably quite good by mortal standards, otherwise the Reverend of Empty Words wouldn't have set its sights on him. Even so, ascension still might have been a long way away. Those who could ascend were protected by spiritual auras, and inhuman creatures had a hard time doing anything to them. And what nefarious creature would risk messing with a future heavenly official?

A person's ability to ascend didn't depend on how smart they were. Intelligence and effort might not matter at all, and all the rare treasures and devices in the world certainly wouldn't increase one's chances. Sometimes, it was just that vexing—ten years of study couldn't compare to natural wit and talent, and a century of bloody struggle couldn't compare to a moment's enlightenment.

If it wasn't written in fate, then it wasn't written in fate. The Water Master could invest all the power and treasure he wanted in his younger brother, but without a fate to match, Shi Qingxuan would remain in the Middle Court as nothing more than the bellwether of the lower ranked officials. It had only been possible for him to reach such a glorious position because his older brother robbed another of what was originally theirs and secured it for him instead. If he had even a shred of conscience or pride, it wasn't hard to imagine how he must feel after having learned the truth.

If that exchange of fates had never happened, the man who should have ascended would surely be supremely glorious today.

Having thought this far, something struck Xie Lian.

"No," he said. "Lord Wind Master, the one who called to you wasn't the Reverend of Empty Words."

Shi Qingxuan raised his bowed head. "Huh? The voice definitely was; I couldn't have mistaken it."

"No, no. While that was its voice, it doesn't mean it was the same *body*," Xie Lian said. "Everyone, do you remember? Each of the Reverend of Empty Words' targets died by way of suicide...except for one."

After a pause, he continued, "How did Scholar He die? How was it portrayed at the Bloody Fire Social? Was it suicide?"

Shi Qingxuan's eyes grew wide. "It wasn't suicide. It was..."

"Exhaustion," Ming Yi answered.

"That's right!" Xie Lian exclaimed. "Even though he was hounded by misfortune, never once did Scholar He think of killing himself.

"Think about it. He had abnormally strong determination," Xie Lian continued somberly. "He was ground down by so much unfairness, so much injustice. A typical person would've given up or ended everything. Yet he always fought back; he never yielded. Perhaps, once the Reverend of Empty Words found him, it never managed to suck out what it wanted: fear. The cause of his death wasn't suicide due to fear and despair. When the Reverend of Empty Words clung to him, it didn't bite down on sweet fruit but rather an iron plate. In the end, it broke its teeth and lost thoroughly."

Shi Qingxuan shook his head as he listened. He sighed in earnest. "...I really am nothing compared to that man."

"He died filled with murderous intent and resentment," Xie Lian pointed out. "I don't think a soul hammered into shape by such means would easily rest in peace. Instead, he'd thirst for revenge.

"So, Lord Wind Master, I believe the current 'Reverend of Empty Words' is quite possibly not the same one that hunted you from birth. Instead, it's Scholar He himself—or rather, He Xuan—who stubbornly fought till the end, then bit back at the Reverend."

Shi Qingxuan and Ming Yi were both left stupefied by his claim.

"Ghosts devouring ghosts," Hua Cheng added coolly.

When humans devour humans, they fill their stomachs at most. When ghosts devour ghosts, with the right method, the devourer can absorb the devoured's powers for their own use.

"This could also explain why the 'Reverend of Empty Words' knew so many of the details of this whole affair," Xie Lian said. "A monster like that should be simpleminded and strange in its logic.

It shouldn't be so intelligent. However, the one that's currently pursuing you two is a..."

He wanted to say "hybrid," but it didn't feel accurate.

"Enhanced entity," Hua Cheng offered.

"Right," Xie Lian said. "After Scholar He devoured the Reverend of Empty Words, his consciousness took complete control. Right now, he is not only intelligent, but he's also able to curse. And he bears endless resentment toward you and your brother."

This explained why it didn't send a death curse directly through Shi Qingxuan's private spiritual communication array, despite knowing his verbal password. Instead, it tightened the snare gradually—it forced Shi Qingxuan to plug his own ears, shut his own eyes, and lock himself in an empty room. Like a cat that caught a mouse, it wouldn't kill him quickly. It would play and play until the mouse died of its own terror.

Moments later, Ming Yi said, "Now that it's come to this, what will you do?"

Everyone looked at Shi Qingxuan, whose hair was a frightful mess from his unconscious head-scratching.

"...Well, don't look at me!" he responded bemusedly. "I...I don't know what to do either! I just...I just don't know how to look at my brother right now..."

They were brothers by blood, after all, and Shi Wudu had committed this heinous crime and harmed the life of another for Shi Qingxuan's sake. It was understandable that he didn't know what to do.

"But I must beg everyone here to keep this a secret! Don't say anything yet! Just for now. Only for now," Shi Qingxuan pleaded. "Give me time to think properly...about what is to be done. Even though I've been thinking for days now and still came up empty... Anyway, let me cool my head first..."

Toward the end he was rambling, and his eyes were unfocused.

Shi Wudu kept claiming that Shi Qingxuan needed to be treated for his "illness," but what illness was there to treat? It was simply that he had fallen from divine grace and had transformed back into a mortal. That "illness" could only be cured if his fate was changed again and he ascended once more. It'd be difficult to find another qualified candidate, but who knew what other evil spell Shi Wudu would come up with? No wonder Shi Qingxuan was so desperate to flee and kept ranting about becoming mortal and abandoning his godhood.

As for that error-filled scroll about the Reverend of Empty Words, no doubt it was made to mislead Shi Qingxuan and ensure he didn't discover the truth. While its author could have been either Shi Wudu or Ling Wen, Shi Wudu would have needed help from the Palace of Ling Wen at the start to cast the net for a qualifying candidate. Did Ling Wen really know nothing of this? If a single heavenly official had ascended this way, could there perhaps be a second, or a third, or even more who ascended using the same method?

If that were the case, it'd be horrifying; the world would be turned upside down. This incident had to be treated with the utmost gravity. Everyone in the little cottage was filled with gloom and doom, as if a great enemy was about to descend upon them—everyone except Hua Cheng, of course, who had no horse in this race and was visibly enjoying himself.

Just then, there was a sudden commotion outside the cottage. Oxen lowed furiously, and farmers started shouting.

"Stop! Stop!"

"Such murderous intent! What do you want?!"

Xie Lian moved to the door and peeked out through the crack. "It's General Pei."

Pei Ming had just taken a beating from Quan Yizhen, yet he still appeared to be in one piece. There was a leaning stone slab that marked the land's boundary, and Pei Ming seemed rather wary of it, not daring to enter rashly. He remained standing at the boundary marker, sword in hand. The farmers gripped their pickaxes and sickles, and their faces were written with unwelcoming expressions.

The black ox in the paddy blew a few heavy breaths from its nostrils, then suddenly stood on its hind legs. An instant later, it transformed into a large, strapping man. He was rather handsome and wore a small iron nose ring.

"Well I'll be, is that General Pei?" the ox laughed. "What a rare guest. What winds blew My Lord over today? Lemme say this first: we've got nothing to do with your Little Pei's situation."

Xie Lian looked thoughtful. He'd already had a vague suspicion when he saw the black ox out in the paddies. After all, this was Mount Yulong, the home of the Rain Master, and this very Ox-xiong had lent Xie Lian the Rain Master Hat to create rain long ago. Centuries had passed, and yet the ox was impressive as always. He still plowed the fields diligently and with great strength.

Shi Qingxuan squeezed over to the crack in the door and explained the sight to Xie Lian. "The ox is from the Rain Master's household. He's a good guy."

Pei Ming had once suffered a loss at the hands of the Rain Master, so for the time being he was maintaining a perfectly polite mien, neither haughty nor humble.

"Please, no need to flatter me. Pei didn't come to seek the Ruler of Yushi. May I inquire if Lord Wind Master has stopped by your esteemed country?"

61
Pass the Heavenly Tribulation, Waves Surge in the East Sea

"HEH, I DIDN'T OFFER ANY FLATTERY," the ox said. "We're busy planting the fields; nobody saw anyone."

"If that's the case..." Pei Ming took a step forward.

The farmers raised their pickaxes at once and began to shout at him. "Trampled! He trampled it!"

Pei Ming frowned. "Trampled what?"

"You trampled the crops that they so painstakingly planted," the ox stated. "You'd best apologize."

Pei Ming looked down. "Aren't these just weeds, if I'm not mistaken?" he asked patiently.

The ox gave him a puzzled look. "What would a belligerent general like *you* know? We're the ones who do the planting. Wouldn't we know better than you whether those are crops or weeds?"

Xie Lian could tell the people of Yushi Country were giving Pei Ming a hard time on purpose, but he too couldn't help but wonder whether those were crops or weeds.

Pei Ming was the esteemed Martial God of the North—why would he apologize to a bunch of farmers for such a nonsensical reason? He ignored them and took a few more steps over the boundary, then raised his voice to call toward the cottage.

"Qingxuan, come out! Your brother is going through his Heavenly Tribulation right now, and things aren't looking good. Something bad is going to happen!"

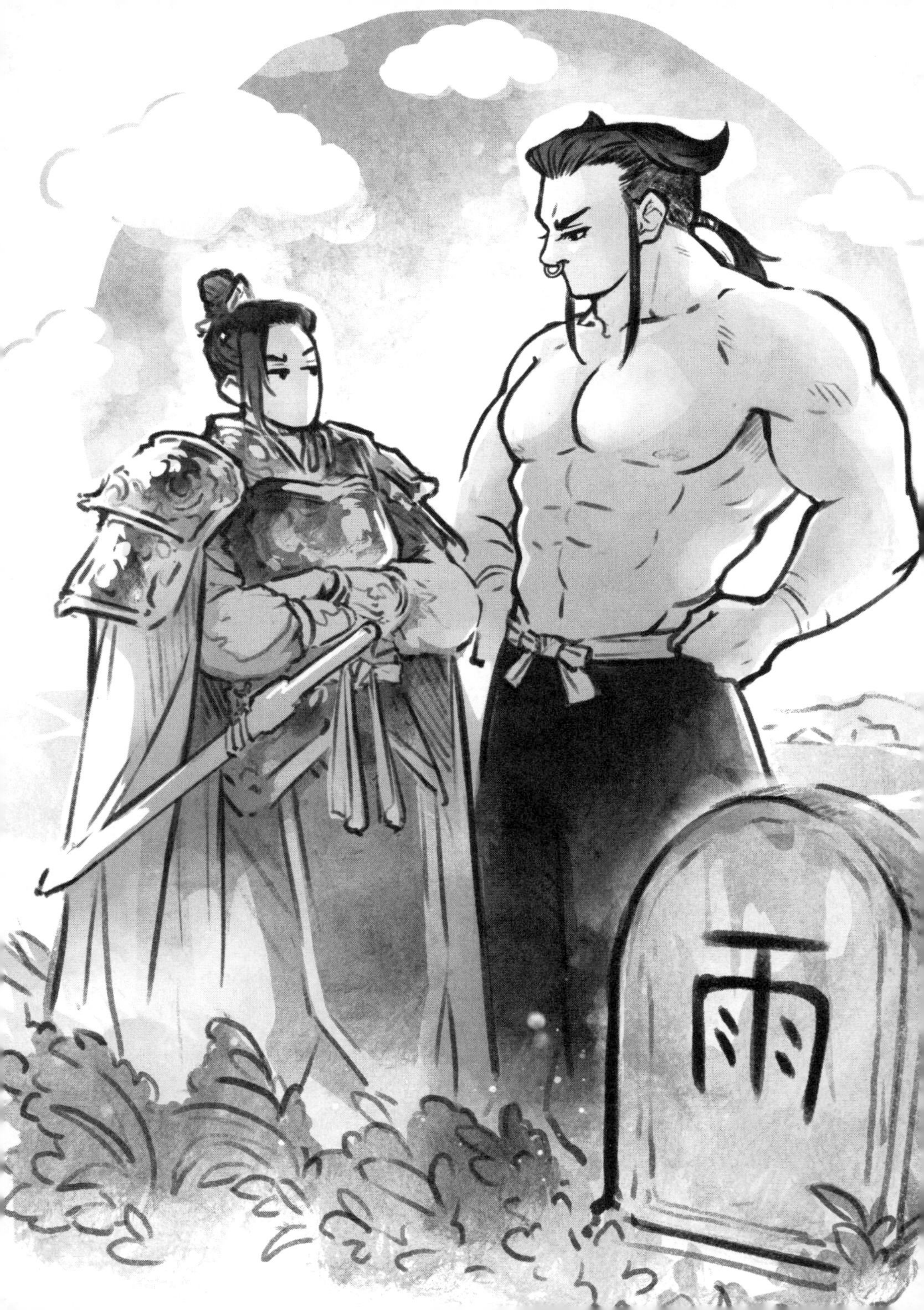
雨

"..."

Shi Qingxuan had decided to hide in the cottage, as he knew Pei Ming wouldn't dare break in. However, the moment he heard this he rushed outside.

"What?!"

Pei Ming gave the ox a look, then said to Shi Qingxuan, "I knew you'd come running here!"

Shi Qingxuan was dumbstruck but snapped out of it and leapt back. "Y-y-y-you can't fool me! How could it have come so fast? It's too sudden! I thought he'd have at least another few months!"

But at the Heavenly Capital, the Water Master had indeed departed in a hurry, like he had left to take care of something critical. Shi Qingxuan immediately brought two fingers to his temple. That was the hand seal for connecting to the spiritual communication array, and he belatedly remembered he had lost his powers. There was no time to be depressed, so he frantically grabbed on to Xie Lian.

"Your Highness, help me ask, is it true?"

Xie Lian and Ming Yi both entered the spiritual communication array. Sure enough, inside the array it was as utterly confused as a pot of stew and full of upset. Many of the heavenly officials were watching a display projecting the action taking place in the East Sea and mumbling to themselves.

"My heavens...this battle stance... As expected of the Water Tyrant!"

"B-b-but will he pass successfully...?"

The stronger the powers of a heavenly official, and the more Heavenly Tribulations they had passed, the more perilous their next trials would be. Shi Wudu reigned over the waters, dominated the path of wealth, and this was his third Tribulation. It was easy to imagine how things would proceed from here.

"It's true," Xie Lian confirmed.

The ox was still blocking the path, and Pei Ming couldn't force himself through. He called out from afar:

"You're not a child anymore! Who would lie to you about something like this?! Passing a Heavenly Tribulation isn't like planning a dinner where you can pick a date and change into new robes. It comes as it wills—and without warning! He's currently above the East Sea and the waters are surging. No one can enter, and no one can escape. He was battling the waves when someone reported that you ran away, so how can he possibly focus on passing his trial?!"

"Then why don't you tell him I'm in Yushi Country?!" Shi Qingxuan responded.

Xie Lian listened to the direct relay of the situation in the communication array. "It's no use. A frenzied spiritual field has been released over the entire area where Lord Water Master is undergoing the trial. He's probably in turmoil right now—no one can reach him!"

Shi Qingxuan charged toward Pei Ming. "Take me to him!"

Pei Ming extended his hand. "Come!"

However, Ming Yi raced over and blocked Shi Qingxuan's way, his expression dark.

"Ming-xiong, what is it?" Shi Qingxuan asked.

Ming Yi remained silent, his brows locked into a furrow. Xie Lian could guess what he was probably thinking—why he felt that he had to stop Shi Qingxuan.

Was helping Shi Wudu pass his Heavenly Tribulation really the right thing to do?

If the fate-changing had occurred, the Water Master must receive an equally grave punishment. Was it really appropriate to help him climb to a new level of power before investigating the matter?

Xie Lian could guess such a thing because he was pondering the very same question. Shi Qingxuan hesitated for a moment but eventually exhaled a long breath.

"...Ming-xiong, I...thank you. But no matter what, that's still... I'm still worried, so let's just focus on passing this trial first!"

He rushed to Pei Ming's side and turned his head to call to the rest.

"Thank you, Your Highness! Thank you, Lord Rain Master! Thank you, Ox! Thanks, everyone! I'll repay this one day!"

They hurried away. Ming Yi stayed where he was for a moment before following after them. Xie Lian watched their retreating backs, but he didn't move. Hua Cheng leisurely stepped out of the cottage.

"Gege's not going?"

After some thought, Xie Lian shook his head. "This matter is beyond me. I can't help," he said slowly. "Let's see how they resolve this themselves first."

Shi Qingxuan was the central figure of this mess, but he still couldn't figure out what he should do and was troubled by his own indecision. Although Xie Lian could understand why Shi Wudu did what he did, he still didn't agree with the method. The ideal resolution would be for Shi Wudu to admit to his crimes and turn himself in to receive punishment. Ming Yi probably hoped for the same thing, which was why he had stopped Shi Qingxuan. However, considering the Water Master's imperious, arrogant personality, this scenario was most likely impossible. After sitting in such a high position for so many years, no one would willingly step down.

If this were anyone else, Xie Lian would probably report the affair to the Heavenly Court straightaway. But he keenly remembered the Wind Master's warmhearted friendship, and Xie Lian couldn't turn his back on Shi Qingxuan when his older brother was facing such a dire situation. He couldn't kick a person when they were already down, couldn't disregard past affections. The only thing he could do was sit back and see how they would take care of this themselves. However, if their chosen course of action was untoward...

Having thought to that point, he turned to Hua Cheng. "San Lang, your advice from before was probably right," he said in a self-deprecating tone. "Gosh, what a mess this is."

Hua Cheng smiled and was about to speak, but Xie Lian's expression changed at the sound of Ling Wen's distressed voice within the spiritual communication array.

"What?! Hundreds of fishermen's boats got dragged in?! Did this have to happen right now?!"

Xie Lian was aghast. "Fishermen? Dragged in where? The East Sea?" he responded anxiously.

If the communication array had been as confusing as a pot of stew earlier, the stew had now just toppled onto the ground and fed the dogs. Ling Wen didn't even have time to respond to him anymore, though her voice remained considerably collected.

"Excuse me, which martial god is on duty? Ol' Pei?"

Pei Ming responded in the communication array. "Don't worry. I have Qingxuan with me, and we're rushing over. Lord Earth Master is here too. First, figure out how many people got pulled into the storm so we can bring them all back. We'll try not to lose a single one."

"Thanks for your trouble," Ling Wen said. "Since Lord Water Master has explosively released the spiritual field, forbidding others to enter the perimeter of his trial, any Middle Court officials will be blown to smithereens if they attempt to enter. Upper Court officials can perhaps still try to break through the barrier, though. There were probably over two hundred individuals pulled in, so just the two of you might not be enough. We'll need another martial god.

Which highness is present right now? General Nan Yang? General Xuan Zhen?"

"Weren't those two generals placed in confinement for tearing up the Heavenly Capital?" someone responded. "They won't be able to heed the call..."

"What about Tai Hua? Has His Highness Tai Hua returned?"

"No! He's been assigned out!"

"Qi Ying?"

"Who knows where he ran off to?! He blocks all messages and listens to no one; you already know that!"

Other than those few, there weren't any other martial gods worth a dime. Although he was anxious, Xie Lian couldn't help but feel a little woeful. Was his Scrap God aura so strong that everyone forgot he came from a martial god background?

"Me! I'm present!" he responded hastily. "Let me go. It's just rescuing the fisherman in the East Sea, right?"

"Your Highness, the winds and waves of the East Sea are perilous, and your spiritual power only works occasionally. What if—"

"It's fine," Xie Lian said. "I've fished in all four seas, and every single time it was storming. I've often drifted on the waters for half a month at a time, so I'm very used to it."

"..."

All the officials couldn't help but wonder, *You've done that too?! Just what else have you done?!*

The situation was dire and didn't allow room for more thought, so Ling Wen acquiesced. "Very well. Thank you for the trouble. General Pei, get coordinated!"

"Sure thing!" Pei Ming responded.

Xie Lian closed the communication array and turned to Hua Cheng. "San Lang, in the East Sea..."

When he turned his head, he saw that Hua Cheng had unexpectedly already changed into a refreshing fisherman getup. He tossed up a die and caught it as it fell. His other hand was on the door.

"Let's go!" he said simply.

Xie Lian was briefly stunned, but soon smiled and hurried to his side. "All right!"

When the door opened, it wasn't the interior of a cottage that greeted them but an expansive, gloomy seashore.

The two emerged from a small fisherman's shed on the beach; this little shed was one of the most-used connection points for the teleportation array on the East Sea. Beyond the beach was the boundless ocean, stretching to the ends of the horizon. The beach was gray not because the sand was gray but because the skies and sea were both that steely color. Gloom pressed down, and black clouds rolled; the malaise was oppressive and suffocating.

Giant waves surged and collapsed in the distant sea like magnificent fortress walls that rose from flat ground before crumbling in an instant. Water pillars resembling dragons roared into the sky and thrashed like tornados before hurtling back into the depths. Ominous lightning crawled across the skies, twisted and savage.

A large, newly built ship was berthed by the beach. There had to be a place for them to stand on the open sea; if they attempted to fly, they might get struck by lightning, so a seafaring vessel was needed to carry them out. Naturally, this wasn't an ordinary ship. Shi Qingxuan, Pei Ming, and Ming Yi were already on board, and the moment they saw Hua Cheng and Xie Lian exit the fisherman shed, Pei Ming called out.

"Your Highness!"

Shi Qingxuan sighed. "Your Highness, you...! Sorry for the trouble. I truly am."

Xie Lian boarded the ship. "Only doing my duty. How do we start the ship?"

Pei Ming noticed Hua Cheng, who had his arms crossed and appeared quite at home. "Nonessential individuals must leave. This tempest isn't a joke," he warned.

Hua Cheng was dressed in plain, patched clothes and looked like a winsome little fisherman. Nonetheless, nothing could hide away his bright handsomeness.

"I'm not nonessential. I'm just following My Highness," he laughed.

"He's from my palace," Xie Lian explained.

But Pei Ming had already flashed an inch of his blade from its sheath. "Stand down," he stated, unrelenting and determined.

Xie Lian hadn't yet responded when Hua Cheng answered with unusual firmness. "No. I have to go with you on this trip."

Both sides were only in a stalemate for a moment, but Shi Qingxuan was living seconds as if they were seasons. He turned to Pei Ming.

"General Pei, this man is fine. Let's just go!"

During their exchange, lightning violently struck the surface of the sea. The current coursed through the waters and crackled outward, brightening the sea to an aqua color. It looked like a giant heart that had suddenly started pulsating and breathing. It was a spectacular sight but also terrifying. Pei Ming didn't want to wait any longer and barked an order to leave.

"*Start!*"

The ship gave a violent shudder. With the rumbling sounds of shafts whirling, the ship steered itself without any manual control. It left the beach and sailed out with great speed. As lightning flashed and thunder roared, the ship opened a path between crashing waves.

The storm was huge, but Xie Lian, Hua Cheng, Pei Ming, and Ming Yi all stood steadily. As for Shi Qingxuan, it was only thanks to Ming Yi's support that he hadn't fallen over.

"Can the ship hold out against this storm?!" Xie Lian yelled.

"It's manageable right now, but it'll be hard to say as we move forward!" Pei Ming replied.

The ship was already moving at an extremely fast pace, spearing through the waves and creating huge splashes of its own in its wake. Yet Shi Qingxuan still asked, "Can't this thing go any faster?!"

"Running this ship burns spiritual power; this is already the fastest it can go!" Pei Ming replied.

Shi Qingxuan clenched his right fist. That was the hand he used to hold the Wind Master fan. With just one swing, it could've provided a tailwind and made the ship go at least four times faster. Yet now, that hand was empty. He couldn't help but exhale another long sigh.

Hua Cheng tapped Xie Lian lightly and whispered, "Gege."

Xie Lian turned his head, and his eyes widened. About thirty meters out, there was a small fishing boat spinning in the waves. He could vaguely see a few figures that seemed to be calling for help, but their cries were being swallowed by the noise of the waves.

The fishermen in distress!

This was why he was here. Ruoye shot out and wrapped around the fishermen's midsections, then hauled them in. Their legs almost gave out the moment their feet touched the ship's deck. Pei Ming immediately opened the door of one of the cabins and threw them inside. When the fishermen opened the door again, they would find themselves back on shore.

Hua Cheng and Xie Lian fished up thirty or forty fishermen. While they were doing so, the ship was carried by the turbulent waters closer and closer to the center of the tempest. Right now, there were surely many heavenly officials watching this frightening scene from afar, and there were surely many mortals staring in awe and terror at the might of heaven. The lightning struck at the ship with increasing frequency—attracted to sources of spiritual power, it would pursue and strike at those who stood out. This was why other officials generally stayed far away when someone was undergoing a Heavenly Tribulation, lest they fall victim.

Shi Qingxuan was mortal right now, Xie Lian only had enough power to communicate through the array, and Hua Cheng's powers were tucked away neatly, as he had no need to use them. Thus, the lightning focused on Pei Ming alone. He frequently needed to strike bolts back with his sword, though he managed it with considerable ease. Xie Lian was rather impressed by his show of skill. This was why Middle Court officials were not permitted to come—if they were present, they'd surely be chased away with lightning hot on their tails, and they certainly wouldn't be able to strike back.

After crossing through the barrier, Shi Qingxuan yelled, "Ge!"

Xie Lian looked upward. Sure enough, Shi Wudu floated there in the skies, surrounded by seven or eight roaring water dragon pillars. His hands formed a battle hand-seal, and his white robes whipped wildly in the wind.

Although he was still suppressing the great waves, he seemed somewhat unfocused and his control was unsteady. The frenzied water dragons stalked him relentlessly and seized upon every chance to get closer and devour him whole. Each time, he only barely dodged. The ship was dozens of meters away from him; if the Wind Master fan was still usable, Shi Qingxuan could've pushed the waves down a notch. In his current mortal body, even his voice couldn't reach very far, and he could only watch in distress.

When Pei Ming spoke, his voice was broadcast powerfully and widely.

"Water Master-xiong! We've found Qingxuan!"

As soon as he spoke, Shi Wudu opened his eyes.

Another giant wave surged to the skies and crashed back down. The ship was thrown high into the air, but it didn't keep up with the speed of the collapsing waters. It hung there for a brief second before falling rapidly. Xie Lian used the Thousand-Pound Weight spell to steady himself and grabbed Hua Cheng's hand tightly.

"Watch out!"

It was a funny feeling. Hua Cheng was clearly taller than him, and it took him no effort to carry Xie Lian with one hand. But Xie Lian always felt that Hua Cheng was light as a feather—like if he didn't pay attention, he would disappear. And so Xie Lian held him firmly, and Hua Cheng clutched his hand in turn.

"Water Master-xiong, focus!" Pei Ming called out. "If you don't push those waves of yours down, you'll drown your little brother!"

Shi Wudu saw the ship in the distance and heard his words. Anger flashed across his face. His hand seal changed, and a spiritual shield burst from around him. It struck the water dragons that had been circling him, and they exploded into a deluge of water that crashed soundly into the sea.

The raindrops hurtled like rocks against the deck and pelted their bodies painfully. However, after this assault, the storm slowed and calmed somewhat. Shi Wudu carefully descended and landed on the ship. Everyone was drenched from head to toe like drowned dogs.

Shi Qingxuan wiped his face and mumbled with trepidation, "...Ge."

Shi Wudu's face was still dark, and he approached in large strides. "I told you to stay put, but you had to run away! Will you finally be satisfied if I'm angered to death?!"

Shi Qingxuan really didn't know what to say to that. When he couldn't see his brother, he'd worry, but now that he had seen him, he could only think about that whole awful business. His heart just couldn't get over it.

"...I'm only just... I..." In the end, he scratched his head and sighed. "As long as you passed your trial, that's all that matters. I think, I still think..."

Shi Wudu cut him off. "Who said my trial is over?"

Shi Qingxuan was taken aback. "Wasn't that it?"

Pei Ming made use of the water to slick back his hair. "Don't relax so soon. This is your brother's third Heavenly Tribulation, so it's not gonna be that easy. It'll take at least seven days and seven nights. What you just saw was only the opening act."

Truth be told, even if it were his first Heavenly Tribulation, it wouldn't be so easy. The "Heavenly Tribulation" that prompted Shi Qingxuan's ascension was heavily diluted compared to everyone else's. He must've come to that conclusion as well, and his face grew glum.

Xie Lian's primary concern was the original goal of this journey, so he asked in the spiritual communication array, "Ling Wen? We've entered the area where Lord Water Master's Heavenly Tribulation is taking place. Can you tell us the location of the fishermen who were dragged into the storm?"

"Please wait a moment," Ling Wen replied. After a pause, she said, "This is troublesome. Today, two hundred and sixty-one fishermen were pulled into the perimeter of the Heavenly Tribulation, and they're scattered all over the place..."

Her voice started to break up, and Xie Lian couldn't really understand her anymore.

"What's wrong? Ling Wen?"

He thought his powers were low again, but when he looked up and saw Pei Ming's face, it was obvious that he was experiencing the same thing. Before they could discuss the matter, Xie Lian saw more little broken boats not far away from them.

"Maybe the aftershocks of the opening round were too great and affected spiritual communication. It might improve in a bit. Ling Wen said two hundred and sixty-one fishermen were scattered by the waves, so let's just save as many as we can."

Naturally, no one objected.

"Water Master-xiong, why don't you go inside and rest for a bit?" Pei Ming suggested. "Your trial only just started, and who knows when the next round will come. You're pretty unlucky to have dragged in so many mortals this time."

Shi Wudu did appear somewhat tired. He nodded, pushed open the door of another cabin, and went inside to meditate. Shi Qingxuan looked like he wanted to say something serious to him, but since his Heavenly Tribulation wasn't over, he couldn't bring himself to speak. He could only swallow his words and mope off to the side with Ming Yi.

However, Shi Wudu opened his eyes again and said sharply, "Don't go running around. Come and sit right here."

And so, Shi Qingxuan could only crouch down next to Shi Wudu.

More than half a day passed thus. As the night darkened, the ship floated farther into the deeper part of the East Sea.

Although spiritual communication still only worked sporadically, they managed. Xie Lian and company rescued over two hundred fishermen during this period. The fishermen had gone to sea to fish as always, but stormy winds and waves suddenly surged, and they were pulled too far out. It would've been impossible to drift back on their own if help hadn't come—and if left to drift, they would've floated endlessly until they died from starvation or dehydration, their corpses desiccated under the sun. They were understandably overjoyed at this miraculous ray of hope that saved them from the brink of death.

Who knew how many days and nights it'd take for all the drifting fishermen to be rescued from open water? And Shi Wudu's third Heavenly Tribulation had still not officially started. Danger could rear its head at any moment, but even at a time like this, Pei Ming still acted as he always did. In the evening, they came upon a few terrified fisher-girls needing rescue, their faces smeared with tears. He held them in his embrace and soothed them with gentle words. It was a true show of honey-sweet romance, an affectionate, charming display. Only after he charmed the girls did he send them off to the cabin, and the girls were all reluctant to leave, clearly hoping that when they opened the door, he would still be there.

Shi Wudu cracked open his eyes. He'd been meditating for a while now, and his complexion looked better.

"Don't you usually have high standards?"

Although the fisher-girls were in the full bloom of youth, they were still only average; they were nowhere near the standard of targets Pei Ming usually hunted.

Now that he'd held some women, Pei Ming's face was glowing. He rubbed his chin as he laughed. "After rescuing so many old, scraggly-bearded fishermen, any woman looks like an outstanding beauty in comparison."

Upon hearing this, both Shi Qingxuan and Ming Yi didn't want to look at him anymore. Xie Lian actually found it rather funny and shook his head. He and Hua Cheng sat down next to each other at the side of the ship, and he felt the emptiness of his stomach a moment later.

Everyone else on the ship didn't need to eat. Shi Qingxuan was a mortal right now, but Xie Lian suspected Shi Wudu must've given him some sort of holy pill, the kind that could fill a stomach for a few days; even now Shi Qingxuan didn't show any sign of hunger. This ship wasn't built in the Mortal Realm, so it wouldn't carry any rations. Xie Lian was about to get up and try catching some fish when Hua Cheng passed something over. Xie Lian looked down to find that it was a soft, snow-white steamed bun.

He sat back down and whispered, "Thank you, San Lang."

"Take this for now, gege," Hua Cheng whispered back. "It'll get better soon."

They split the steamed bun in half to share, and the two sat together to slowly munch on it. Pei Ming heard them whispering to each other from where he stood on the other end of the ship. He slicked his hair back again.

"Have you two discovered something? Why don't you leave your little world for a moment and share with the rest of us?"

Xie Lian was about to say something to put him off but frowned instead. "Don't you all sense something strange?"

Ming Yi frowned as well and looked up. "Yes."

Xie Lian rose to his feet. "The ship seems to be going much slower. Is it running out of power?"

"How could that be?" Pei Ming said. "The ship's stores of spiritual power should allow it to run for several more days at sea."

Xie Lian approached the side and set his hands on the railing. "But I keep getting the sense that the ship got heavier..."

He abruptly stopped mid-sentence. Shi Wudu and the others gathered where he stood.

"What is it?"

But there was no need to ask—with just a glance, they understood. Despite the darkened sky, the draft of this ship's hull was visibly abnormal; the hull was much lower in the water than before, and the waterline was still climbing!

"Is the hull leaking?!" Xie Lian asked. "Did we hit a shoal? Is there something in the water that tore a hole?"

"That's impossible!" Pei Ming exclaimed. "How would we not notice hitting a shoal? And this isn't some ordinary ship, nothing should be able to pierce the hull, unless..."

He choked as though he had abruptly realized something.

"Unless what?" Ming Yi demanded.

"Oh no," Pei Ming said.

"What do you mean, 'oh no'?" Shi Qingxuan demanded.

Pei Ming whirled around. "Ships immediately sink in ghosts' territories. We've drifted into the Black Water Demon Lair."

62
Ships in the Lair of Ghosts Shall Sink

"One of the four supremes, Ship-Sinking Black Water?" Xie Lian asked.

"Four Calamities, not four supremes."

"..."

Only then did Xie Lian realize that he had subconsciously removed Qi Rong from the calamity ranks. This was likely because there was no way he could put Night-Touring Green Lantern on the same level as the other three.

As someone who had dutifully crammed with informative scrolls, Xie Lian knew a bit about Ship-Sinking Black Water. According to legend, he was a great and powerful water ghost who lurked in the outer seas. Like Crimson Rain Sought Flower, he slaughtered his way out of Mount Tonglu. Although he tended to keep a low profile, that profile was only low in the Mortal and Heavenly Realms—he had devoured over five hundred infamous nefarious creatures across the land, about four hundred of which were other high-level water ghosts. The Black Water Demon Lair was his personal domain.

Just as Ghost City was under Hua Cheng's jurisdiction alone, lawlessness reigned within these boundaries. When one stepped foot into a supreme's domain, they had the final say. There was a widespread saying in the Ghost Realm: *"Crimson rules the land; Black masters the waters."* "Crimson" obviously referred to Crimson

Rain Sought Flower, who was known for his signature red clothing. "Black" was none other than Black Water Demon Xuan.

"Water Master-xiong, you're *really* unlucky this time," Pei Ming said. "But Demon Xuan isn't like the Green Ghost; he's not the type to look for trouble. Thankfully we haven't strayed too far, so let's steer back quickly before we're discovered."

The others stared at him. "Well, why don't you change course then? Aren't you the one in charge of this ship?"

Pei Ming was equally confused. "Did it not change course yet? The ship should follow my command on its own, it shouldn't require physical control..."

But the rudder didn't budge. With no other options, Pei Ming resorted to manual steering. But when his hand landed on the rudder, he furrowed his brows. Xie Lian went over as well.

"It won't move?"

It was impossible that Pei Ming lacked the strength for it. Xie Lian was fairly confident in his own strength, and yet he wasn't able to move it either.

After examining the situation at hand, Ming Yi announced, "It must've gotten caught on something. I'll go down to take a look."

Shi Qingxuan chimed in. "I'll go with you, Ming-xiong!"

"Come back here!" Shi Wudu said sternly. "Don't go running around."

Shi Qingxuan didn't dare disobey, knowing that his brother shouldn't be distracted or emotionally agitated while he was undergoing his trial. He returned to Shi Wudu's side shamefaced, leaving Ming Yi to investigate under the deck alone. Xie Lian wanted to help, but he knew he wasn't as capable as the Earth Master when it came to building and repairs—even if he went, he wouldn't be able to do much.

As he gazed into the pitch-black sea that surrounded them, Xie Lian remembered something more important. "Did any fishermen end up around here?"

Hua Cheng had extremely good eyesight and had been working alongside Xie Lian in the search and rescue efforts. He was the one who had discovered many of the stranded fishermen. He did a quick survey around them.

"There shouldn't be," Hua Cheng concluded. "Black Water Demon Lair is in the South Sea; they wouldn't drift this far. And the area here has a barrier, so ordinary folk can't enter, barring special circumstances. Even if they did, they're beyond saving. Basically everything that drifts here sinks."

The South Sea. He hadn't realized they'd drifted so far. Xie Lian tested his spiritual communication array, and sure enough, the connection was down. Their connection before had been spotty but still usable; now, there was complete silence. Although the sea currently looked peaceful, there could be danger lurking in the abyssal depths. The sky was growing darker, and Xie Lian felt uneasy.

"Since there aren't any stranded fishermen in these parts, if Lord Earth Master can't repair it, why don't we abandon ship and head ashore? Lord Water Master can return to the East Sea for his trial, and we can continue the search and rescue as well," he suggested.

"That works," Pei Ming agreed and opened the cabin door.

Yet when he pulled open the door, instead of dry land, he was met with the interior of an empty cabin. His face changed at the sight.

"The teleportation array lost its power?!"

Hua Cheng laughed. "Isn't that obvious? If you can't use the spiritual communication array, why would the teleportation array work any better?"

Pei Ming sent a sidelong glance at him. "Little friend, you seem quite calm for someone so young. Not worried at all, are you?" he commented flatly.

"The ship drifted into ghost territory and is sinking as we speak," Xie Lian interrupted. "We can't leave even if we want to. Let's solve the problem at hand first."

Shi Qingxuan called under the deck. "Ming-xiong, how's the situation looking down there? Can you fix it?"

Ming Yi's voice came from below. "Nothing's broken! The ship isn't caught on anything either. Something else made the ship lose power."

"That would be Demon Xuan's spiritual field," Pei Ming stated gravely.

As he was speaking, the ship dipped violently again. Xie Lian saw that water had already swallowed over half the ship. A normal boat would've given way to the waves by now, but this one still resisted and fought to stay afloat due to its divine provenance.

"There must be exceptions. It's impossible that everything sinks here," he insisted. "There must be *something* that won't sink."

"There is," Hua Cheng said.

All attention fell on him. With his arms folded, he elaborated lazily, "There is one type of wood that will not sink in the Black Water Demon Lair."

Xie Lian guessed at several common special varieties of wood. "Sandalwood? Agarwood? Elm?"

"Coffin wood," Hua Cheng answered.

"Coffin wood?!"

"Yup." Hua Cheng said. "No one has returned alive after stumbling into the Black Water Demon Lair...except for one individual. He was traveling home with the corpse of a family member. After his boat sank, he rode the coffin and drifted back to shore."

Pei Ming raised his brow. "You sure know a lot, little friend."

Hua Cheng mirrored his expression. "Nah. You just know too little, that's all."

Shi Wudu remained in his meditation position and his hands maintained their seal, but he turned his attention to Hua Cheng and narrowed his eyes.

"Pei-xiong, I've been meaning to ask—who exactly is this? Where is he from? Why is he with you?"

"I'm afraid you'll have to ask His Highness about that," Pei Ming explained. "After all, he's someone from *his* palace."

"All right, all right," Shi Qingxuan interrupted. "Enough of that 'who knows how much' talk. Now that spells have lost their power, where do we get a coffin around here?"

"That's easy," Pei Ming answered. "Come. Gege will build one for you right now. I'll show you what it means to take things into your own hands and live well without anyone's help."

"..."

"That won't work," Hua Cheng pointed out. "It has to be a coffin that's carried a corpse."

That was that, then. It wasn't like they could build a coffin and then kill a person in the group to fill it. As they discussed the topic, the boat dipped again. The deck where they stood tilted and was almost level with the water's surface, and Shi Wudu nearly toppled out of his prim-and-proper meditation pose.

"Forget it! Let me handle this," he said coldly.

He produced his fan and tapped it lightly against the center of his forehead, then fanned it out to reveal the character for "water" on the front and a wave pictogram made up of three curving lines on the back. He lifted his arm and issued a command.

"Water, come forth!"

Xie Lian felt the ship spring upward. The deck rose almost a meter above the waterline, and some sense of safety returned.

"The Water Master fan even controls the waters of the Black Water Demon Lair?" he asked in surprise.

"Not the water here," Hua Cheng corrected. "He channeled it from elsewhere."

As it turned out, they hadn't ventured too far past the boundary of the Black Water Demon Lair, so Shi Wudu was still able to call forth nearby waters to lift the ship from underneath.

"Beautifully done, Water Master-xiong!" Pei Ming praised. "Now that the rudder is useless, the boat can't turn around. Quick, use the current to haul the ship back!"

Before Shi Wudu could reply, the ship dipped once again. The Demon Lair's water refused to concede defeat and clashed with the current from the outside seas. The dip was ruthless this time, and the deck tilted even more. Losing balance, the crew slid to the bow of the ship. Although Shi Wudu was born with gentlemanly, handsome looks, his personality was extremely imperious, and he refused to retreat. Sensing that something dared to oppose him, anger flashed across his face. He snapped his fan shut, and when he opened it again, the three wave lines had grown larger, and the outer current doubled in force. The ship was yanked up once again.

With one force relentlessly dragging the boat down and another stubbornly forcing it to rise, the ups and downs made it seem like a giant game of tug-of-war. The ship sailed onward, then jolted to a stop, and it sank and rose with the motion. Waves crashed wildly around them, making seawater roll across the deck and into the ship. It was an incredibly vexing situation. If ordinary folk were on board, they would be scared witless by now. Xie Lian gripped the ledge tightly with one hand while he held on to Hua Cheng tightly with the other.

"What's happening? The ship is turning!" he exclaimed.

It was just as he said—the ship had started spinning. The faster it spun, the lower it sank. Xie Lian abruptly realized that the ship had been dragged into a giant maelstrom and was being sucked into its vortex!

"Everyone, be careful!" he warned. "The two forces of water are clashing!"

In the end, this was not Shi Wudu's home turf. While the current he'd summoned from the outer seas was mighty, it weakened after crossing the boundary. It was at a slight disadvantage in the fight against the tides of the Demon Lair.

As expected, as soon as Xie Lian spoke, the ship was sucked into the vortex. Xie Lian tossed out Fangxin at the last second and pulled Hua Cheng close. The two stepped onto the sword and flew up and away!

At first he was worried that Fangxin wouldn't have the strength, but he let out a sigh of relief the moment they left the deck—although it was shaky, at least the sword could still fly. They looked down from above to see that the whole area was painted a deep, terrifying black. Below them were two massive currents of obviously different colors, and it was their pursuit of and clash with each other that had formed the colossal maelstrom. As the vortex swallowed the ship whole, the two water currents quickly separated; however, their battle was far from over. They continued to snap at each other like two venomous vipers, and each collision stirred angry waves.

Xie Lian looked around. "Lord Wind Master? Lord Earth Master? General Pei? Is everyone still here?"

Shi Qingxuan's voice came from dozens of meters behind him. "Your Highness! We're over here!"

"Did you hop on your sword as well..."

Xie Lian turned, and the scene that greeted him left him speechless.

Ming Yi stood atop of the handle of a crescent shovel. Shi Qingxuan was seated on the head of the same shovel and was waving at Xie Lian.

They didn't ride forth on a sword, but...a shovel. The sight was unbearable to witness!

Pei Ming's voice also called to them from nearby. "Where's Water Master-xiong?"

Seeing that Pei Ming was on his sword alone and there was no sign of the Water Master, Shi Qingxuan cried out, "Ge? Ge?!"

"No need to panic; the Water Master is the God of Water, he can't have gone under," Xie Lian reassured him. But when he recalled the power of the whirlpool, he didn't dare underestimate its might. He turned to Hua Cheng. "San Lang, hold on tight to my waist—don't lose your grip and fall."

Hua Cheng very obediently did so. "Mmm, okay. But, gege, there's something I have to tell you."

"What is it?" Xie Lian asked.

"You can't fly in the Black Water Demon Lair. It'll attract things."

Not a moment later, a long, sharp cry pierced the air. A behemoth white creature broke through the water's surface and headed straight for Pei Ming.

Pei Ming was a master swordsman, and he reflexively reached for his sword the moment he saw a monster attacking—only to belatedly realize said sword was under his feet. Luckily, his reaction was swift; he leapt into the air, grabbed his sword, and sliced the incoming creature in half. Before gravity could take hold, he flipped back onto the sword without a single hair out of place.

He steadily flew upward and asked in a rather calm tone, "What was that?"

After it was cleaved in half, the creature crashed back into sea with a mournful wail. Xie Lian squinted to get a better look at the creature floating on the water's surface.

"Fish?"

It was certainly a fish, but this wasn't your average sea creature. It was a skeletal fish over fifteen meters in length and half a dozen meters wide! This "fish" had neither flesh nor scales, only stark white bones that connected to a mouth filled with sharp teeth. He couldn't immediately determine if it was venomous, but its bite would surely be a pain in the butt regardless.

Pei Ming flew higher. "Be careful, there's definitely more than one of those things!" he warned.

Sure enough, the moment he mentioned "more than one," a second skeletal fish shot out from the depths. This time, it headed straight for Ming Yi and Shi Qingxuan!

Unfortunately, the Earth Master wasn't a martial god and had little fighting power, and the Wind Master was now in mortal flesh. On top of all this, Ming Yi was rusty when it came to...shovel-riding. Even though the two didn't get bitten, they were still knocked off balance and sent tumbling down to the waters below. As they fell, Shi Qingxuan cried out in despair.

"Ming-xiong! After today, make sure to use your spiritual device more, okay—"

"Screw off," Ming Yi snapped at him.

Pei Ming sighed and rushed over to rescue the two. Seeing his skilled form, Xie Lian knew that he would be able to handle it on his own.

It's really not Earth Master's fault, he thought. *A shovel as a spiritual device...no heavenly official with any sense of shame would want to bring it out...*

Just then, a chill ran down his spine. Xie Lian regained his focus and said temperately, "San Lang, hang on tight and watch out. Something's coming our way."

"Okay." His arms tightened around his waist.

Not long after, four watery walls shot up from the depths and surrounded them. Four giant bonefish rose from the sea.

Rather than "fish," the ghastly behemoth skeletons were more like dragons. Sharp, jagged horns protruded from their skulls, balls of inextinguishable ghost fire burned in their empty eye sockets like giant lanterns, and the four legs each one had were tipped with claws. Their bodies were as thick as water vats and at least a few dozen meters long—their upper halves breached the water's surface, but it was impossible to guess the length of the rest that lurked beneath the waves. The creatures circled Xie Lian and Hua Cheng as they hung there in the air, leaving no room for escape. The pair couldn't fly upward; this was as high as Fangxin could go. If they descended, the deathly silent ocean would greet them.

Xie Lian sighed. "All right...who's first?" After a moment of consideration, he clasped his hands. "Together it is."

Soon after, the bone dragon to the east took the initiative. It shrieked and charged forward. Xie Lian raised his hand and jabbed a finger in its direction.

The bone dragon froze on the spot.

It was a massive creature, but it was frozen in place by one sword, one man, and one finger! No matter how it struggled, it couldn't move another inch forward. Its tail and hind claws thrashed and raised walls of waves.

The other three dragons lunged forward as well. Xie Lian curled his fingers into a claw, grabbed the frozen bone dragon by the horn, and lashed its body out like a whip. A loud *whoosh* tore through the sky. The three incoming dragons were skewered by the one Xie Lian thrashed out, and they howled as they collapsed into the sea in a mess of bones. Xie Lian watched the broken bones drift with the movement of the waves as he dusted off his hands and let out a breath. He turned around.

"San Lang, are you okay?"

Hua Cheng smiled happily at him. "Under gege's protection, how could anything happen to me?"

His response made Xie Lian feel embarrassed. Now that he thought about it, dealing with this sort of thing was also an easy task for Hua Cheng—how could he be anything but perfectly fine? So it sounded like Xie Lian was intentionally asking for praise.

Just then, the sword unexpectedly dipped. Before Xie Lian could even register what had happened, they were already falling rapidly— an instant later, they plunged headfirst into the icy cold water.

They weren't dragged down by anything; Fangxin was simply too old and couldn't hold out anymore. It needed to rest after straining itself for so long!

The bone-chilling seawater rushed in from all directions. Xie Lian choked on water a few times, then quickly shut his mouth tight and tried to swim upward. But the Black Water Demon Lair was as wicked as described. Though Xie Lian considered himself a fairly good swimmer, his body felt like a block of lead in these waters. No matter what he did, he couldn't float. He opened his eyes, but the water was as black as the world behind his eyelids, and he couldn't find Hua Cheng. He groped around with his hands, but he only managed to grab hold of the sinking Fangxin, not the person he sought. He started to grow anxious. The more anxious he was, the more sluggish his movements became, and the faster he sank.

Thankfully, it wasn't long before a hand suddenly parted the fog. Xie Lian's eyes lit up. In the next second, someone grasped his hand, hugged his waist, and tugged him upward. They ascended rapidly through the waters and broke the surface, and Xie Lian sucked in a few breaths. When he wiped his face, he found that he'd been brought up from the depths by none other than Hua Cheng.

It was quite strange. Technically, Hua Cheng was dead. As the saying goes, the dead are heavier—deadweight, so to speak—so he should've sunk faster than Xie Lian. But he floated lightly and effortlessly in the water.

He lowered his head to look at Xie Lian. "Are you all right?"

Xie Lian nodded. But this scene felt quite familiar and brought with it memories of a similar situation that had happened not so long ago. It made him blush.

With one arm wrapped around Xie Lian, Hua Cheng used his free arm to leisurely glide through the water.

"Hang on tight to me, gege. You'll sink if you let go."

At a loss for words, Xie Lian blankly nodded several times. Not far from them, the water stirred, and several sharp horns broke through the surface, like the fins of a school of sharks. The horns rushed toward them with incredible speed. The four bone dragons that Xie Lian had knocked out were back for revenge.

The bone dragons circled them, eyeing them with predatory gazes, but soon they could hold themselves back no longer and ferociously dove in. Xie Lian gripped Fangxin tightly, but as he waited for the right moment to strike, he heard Hua Cheng click his tongue in annoyance.

The bone dragons were already within arm's reach and ready to tear them apart, but upon hearing that sound, their killing intent immediately vanished. The fanged mouth that had been ready to snap Xie Lian's throat instead inched forward and nudged at Fangxin, as if pecking it with tiny kisses.

Xie Lian was utterly confused.

He remained dumbfounded as the four bone dragons scampered away like they were scared, tails between their legs. Xie Lian was left speechless, and he floated there in sheer bewilderment, but Hua Cheng had already continued swimming.

"Gege, you see that? If you plan on raising pets in the future, definitely don't consider those things. They're useless trash."

"…"

Pets?!

"No, I don't need any pets…" Xie Lian replied weakly.

All of a sudden, a water dragon hurtled up from under the water's surface and shot into the sky. Xie Lian looked up and saw Shi Wudu seated on top of the creature's head. His hands were clasped together in an aggressive attack hand seal, and his face was dark with hostility, as if he was fighting vigorously against some unseen force. The once-calm, once-peaceful sea was now tossing and turning.

Xie Lian called out, "Lord Wind Master! Lord Earth Master! General Pei! Where are you?!"

Borrowing the moonlight, he was able to scan his surroundings. Instead of finding his comrades, he found himself engulfed by a huge shadow. Xie Lian turned his head sharply, and his eyes widened. It was an enormous wave, as tall as a city wall. It engulfed the skies as it lunged his way.

In the next moment, he was awash in complete darkness.

◇ ◈ ◇

He drifted with the ebb and flow of the ocean for a long time.

Xie Lian finally opened his eyes. While he didn't sit up, he could feel beneath him that he'd arrived on land. As he lay there regaining his strength, he lifted an arm and saw that his hand had become wrinkled from the prolonged soak.

He felt something hard under his waist, and when he tilted his head to look, he realized that the object was Hua Cheng's arm. Hua Cheng was lying right next to him. By the look of things, he had never once let go.

Surprisingly, even though Xie Lian had woken up, Hua Cheng had not. His eyes were tightly shut. Xie Lian quickly sat up and nudged him gently.

"San Lang? San Lang?"

Hua Cheng didn't respond. Xie Lian nudged him again while surveying their surroundings. They were on land, but it was a densely forested island with no signs of civilization in sight. No docks, no people at all. It seemed like an isolated island, not the mainland. The most surprising thing of all was that it was already daylight—they must've floated all night! Where had they ended up?

Even after repeated nudging, Hua Cheng was still deep asleep and hadn't moved an inch. Ghosts couldn't drown, so Xie Lian trusted that Hua Cheng had not done so. But there was no guarantee that he hadn't been secretly wounded by something else—such as those barbed, poisonous bonefish. Xie Lian patted Hua Cheng down to check for wounds, feeling up his chest, his arms, and all the way down his legs. But other than coming to the conclusion that Hua Cheng had a truly fine body, he made no notable finds.

Xie Lian blanked for a bit, then began to panic a little. "San Lang, don't joke around," he mumbled.

No response.

In a moment of panic, Xie Lian pressed his head against Hua Cheng's chest to search for a heartbeat before he remembered that ghosts had no such thing. To his surprise, he actually heard a steady thump. Taken aback, a thought came to him. Hua Cheng shouldn't be able to drown in his true form, but he was presently in the form of a seventeen- or eighteen-year-old human youth—so did the same rules apply?

Although he still didn't think that Hua Cheng was the sort to overlook such things, there was really no other option at hand. He couldn't be roused even after Xie Lian pressed his chest a number of times. After a brief moment of hesitation, Xie Lian slowly reached out and cupped Hua Cheng's face with gentle hands.

He was excessively good-looking. With his eyes closed, his sharp features softened into something gentler. He held Hua Cheng like this; he gazed at him and thought about what he was about to do next.

It made it extremely difficult for Xie Lian to calm his heart.

He debated for a long time, then looked around. There was no one there.

He looked back at Hua Cheng. Still unconscious.

In the end, he made up his mind. Gritting his teeth, he whispered a simple phrase.

"...I apologize in advance."

His voice was practically shaking as he said it. He clapped his hands together in silent prayer and then bent down. With his eyes shut tight, he pressed his lips against Hua Cheng's.

Hua Cheng's eyes snapped open.

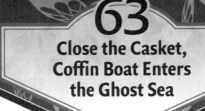

63
Close the Casket, Coffin Boat Enters the Ghost Sea

HOWEVER, since Xie Lian was feeling both overly nervous and overly guilty, his eyes were shut tight and he remained completely unaware.

The last time they had exchanged air, it was Hua Cheng who initiated it. He was domineering, and the kiss was deep. Xie Lian didn't dare recall the event after the fact, only remembering that his lips had been swollen and numb. This time he was taking the lead, and he was very cautious—he placed his lips very softly upon Hua Cheng's, as if he was afraid he'd accidentally wake him if he used too much force. But in retrospect, wasn't waking Hua Cheng his exact goal? If his kiss was too light and air leaked out between their lips, then wouldn't this be for naught?

Xie Lian kept his eyes closed and silently rattled off excerpts from *Dao De Jing* as he pulled away to take a breath, then pressed his lips against Hua Cheng's once more.

This time, the kiss was much deeper. Xie Lian fully captured Hua Cheng's thin, cool lips and gently blew in air.

His eyes were closed through the whole process, not daring to look. After delivering five or six breaths, he thought he should push down on Hua Cheng's chest a few times—but the moment he opened his eyes, he found himself staring squarely into Hua Cheng's own widened ones.

"..."

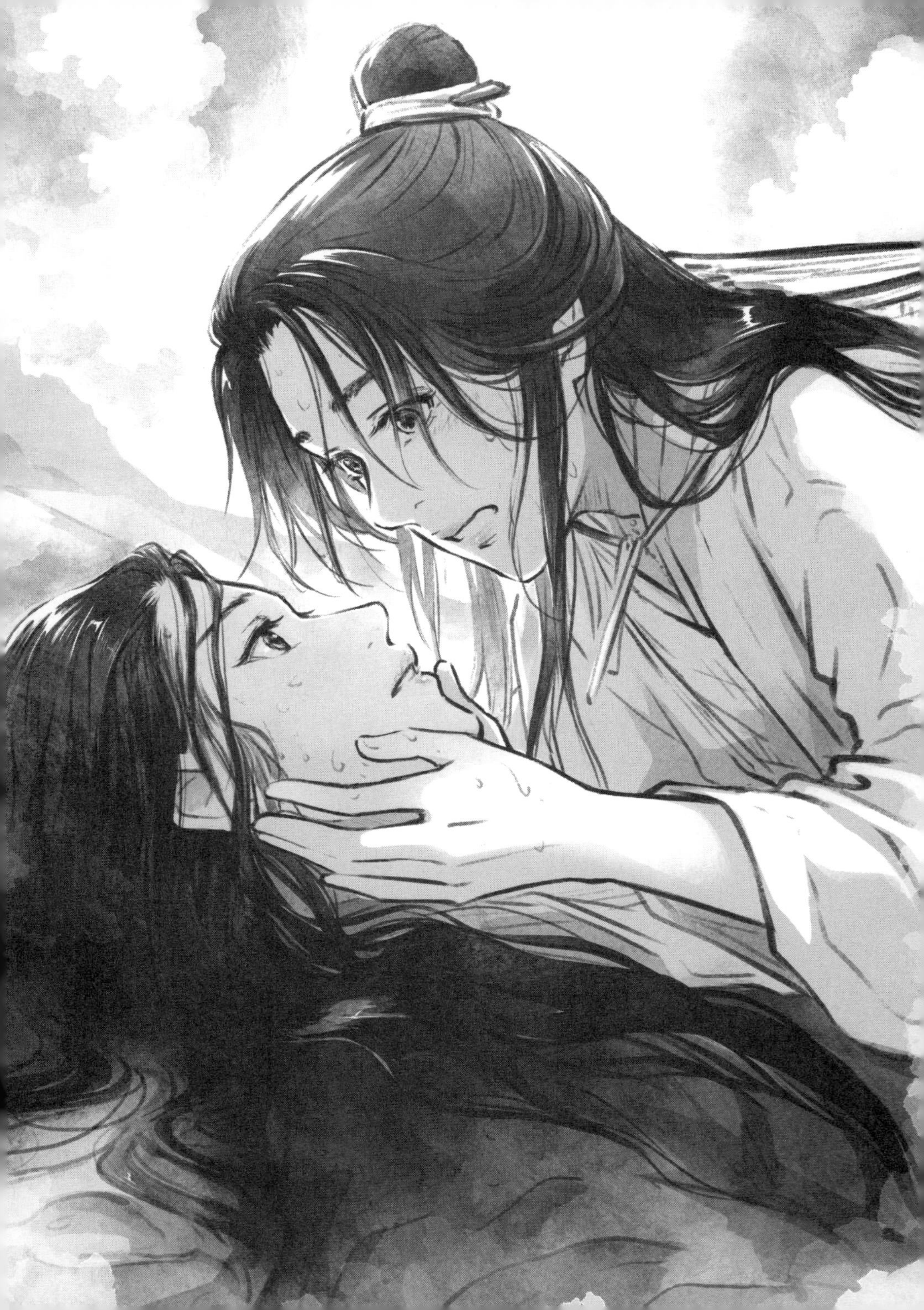

"..."

Xie Lian's hands still cupped Hua Cheng's cheeks, and their mouths had only just parted; soft, gentle numbness still remained on their lips. It was like the two had turned into stone statues, as if they would shatter with an errant breeze. Xie Lian's petrification was expected. But Hua Cheng, who always stayed carefree when faced with all manner of things, was equally stunned.

Xie Lian didn't know how he managed not to drop dead on the spot from all the blood rushing to his head. It took him a good moment to say, "San Lang, you're awake."

Hua Cheng didn't speak.

Xie Lian dropped his hands from Hua Cheng's cheeks at once and leapt meters back.

"...No, no, no no, no no no! *No, no, no, no, no!* It's not what you think! I just wanted to..."

To what? Deliver air?! Did ghosts need air?! If he said that out loud, even Xie Lian himself wouldn't believe it!

Xie Lian was stumped. Hua Cheng quickly pushed himself up and extended a hand toward him, looking as though he was also forcing himself to keep steady.

"...Your Highness, you...just calm down first."

Xie Lian clutched his head. He was a mess from head to toe. Finally, he put his hands together as if in prayer and gave Hua Cheng a deep, abrupt bow.

"I'm sorry I'm sorry I'm sorry I'm sorry!"

Having shouted his apologies, he turned around and bolted, fleeing the scene. Hua Cheng finally snapped out of it and scrambled to his feet to chase after him, shouting as he did.

"Your Highness!"

Xie Lian covered his ears and screamed his penitence as he ran. "I'm *sorry!*"

Die! Just die! If I can't die, just dig a hole somewhere and pretend to be dead!

His mad dash carried him into the depths of the forest. As he ran, something resembling a sharp arrow came flying at him. Xie Lian might have been rattled to the core, but his skill did not suffer for it. With a sweep of his hand, he caught a bone spur. He came to an abrupt stop and looked to where the attack had come from— but there was nothing there, only rustling shrubs. With danger lurking in the bushes, he calmed at once and whirled around to hurry back.

"San Lang!"

Hua Cheng had been trailing close behind, and Xie Lian's sudden change of direction almost sent him right into his arms. Xie Lian grabbed Hua Cheng's hand and dashed out of the woods.

"Run—there's something in the forest!"

Hua Cheng had at first been chasing after him, and he was now being dragged back where they came. Once they made it back to the beach, Xie Lian let out a breath of relief.

"We weren't followed, *phew.* Thank goodness."

"Mmm. There are some little things on this island, but don't worry, they won't follow us here," Hua Cheng commented.

Hearing this, Xie Lian suddenly realized: how could Hua Cheng possibly be afraid of those things? He looked down and found that he was still clutching his companion's hand. Xie Lian froze once more, then hurriedly let go and jumped away.

Now that there was some distance between them, they fell silent for a moment. Then, Hua Cheng sighed and tugged at his collar.

"Thank goodness gege rescued me earlier. Human bodies really are quite inconvenient. I end up choking down mouthfuls of salty water just from taking a dip in the sea. Disgusting."

Xie Lian wasn't that stupid—he *knew* Hua Cheng was giving him an easy way out—but he went along with it, of course. "It's nothing, don't worry about it," he mumbled vaguely, head bowed.

After a pause, Hua Cheng added, "But gege didn't do it correctly."

Flustered, Xie Lian asked awkwardly, "Did I not? I...I thought I only needed to blow in some air."

"Yeah. That's not the correct method," Hua Cheng replied. "Don't do this to anyone else in the future, otherwise..."

Otherwise, not only wouldn't he save a life, but he might just *end* a life. Hua Cheng spoke so seriously that Xie Lian felt rather ashamed. Good thing he'd never tried doing this before or else he really would have committed a sin.

"I won't, I won't," he hurriedly swore.

Hua Cheng nodded, then grinned. Although Xie Lian really wanted to ask Hua Cheng for instructions on how it should be done, he dared not dwell any longer on the subject and made a mental note of it instead. He looked around.

"Is this island really deserted? No trace of humans at all?"

"Of course," Hua Cheng replied. "This is Black Water Island, at the heart of the Black Water Demon Lair."

He stated that with complete confidence. Crimson Rain Sought Flower and Ship-Sinking Black Water...the two supremes seemed to know each other.

"San Lang, have you been here before?" Xie Lian asked.

Hua Cheng shook his head. "Never. But I know of this island."

Xie Lian knitted his brows. "I wonder where Lord Wind Master and the others drifted. Perhaps they're here as well."

This was the Black Water Demon Lair located in the South Sea; it was someone else's territory. Pei Ming's main domain was in the north, the Earth Master wasn't a martial god, and there was no need to elaborate on the Wind Master's condition. If anything happened and they incurred the ire of Black Water Demon Xuan, the only one who could fight back was the Water Master...and there was no knowing when Shi Wudu's Heavenly Tribulation would hit. The current situation wasn't looking good.

"San Lang, does Black Water Demon Xuan have a temper?" Xie Lian asked. "What would he do if heavenly officials accidentally intruded on his domain and entered his home?"

"Hard to say," Hua Cheng said. "But gege has surely heard the saying, 'Crimson rules the land; Black masters the waters.' Even I have to watch my step in the Black Water Demon Lair."

This wasn't simply because it was the heart of Black Water's domain but also because they were both supremes—it was best for Hua Cheng to give his fellow ghost king some face so they could remain cordial.

"Then we'd best leave as quickly as possible," Xie Lian said.

Though they didn't reenter the forest, they did a circuit of the island's edge. Xie Lian called out a few times, but he didn't hear any response from the Wind Master or anyone else.

"They probably didn't drift here," Hua Cheng surmised.

The two returned to the beach. The surface of the sea was still heavy with gloom. Xie Lian picked up a piece of wood and threw it far into the distance. The wood should've floated, yet it instantly sank upon impact with the water.

Xie Lian looked back at the dense forest. "It seems like it'd be useless to build a boat. The teleportation array won't work here either. How are we going to leave the island?"

"Who says it would be useless?" Hua Cheng said.

"But only coffin wood that's housed the deceased can float in the Black Water Demon Lair..."

He trailed off when he realized it. Coffin wood. There were trees everywhere, and there was a deceased person right before his eyes.

Sure enough, Hua Cheng smiled. "Won't it work fine once I settle inside?"

Although he smiled, Xie Lian's heart was squeezed strangely by the statement.

Hua Cheng flattened his palm, and the scimitar Eming appeared in his hand. Having committed to the endeavor, they went straight to work collecting materials. They didn't venture deep into the woods, so they didn't encounter anything hiding in the shadows. It took no time at all for them to chop down a number of trees. A whole day of labor went by in the blink of an eye, and the sky grew dimmer overhead. The two divided the work but competed with each other to scoop up more tasks, so their efficiency was amazingly high. By evening, the coffin was essentially complete.

Xie Lian had only eaten half a steamed bun during this entire journey and was bitterly starving. But the sooner the coffin was made, the sooner they could leave, so he only excused himself to catch some fish after the coffin had taken basic shape. Yet how could there be fish within the waters of the Black Water Demon Lair? Returning empty-handed, Xie Lian instead went to the edge of the forest and picked some wild fruit from the safer areas. But to his surprise, by the time he got back, Hua Cheng had already started a small campfire; he sat by the fire with one hand supporting his cheek and the other holding a stick with a wild hare forked on it, which he was roasting over the fire.

He'd already cleaned the wild hare, and it was roasted per-fectly—dripping with juice, crisp and golden, the smell fragrant and

alluring. Once he noticed Xie Lian, Hua Cheng smiled d the stick over. Xie Lian traded him some wild fruit for it. are all edible."

Both were still wet and dripping; they were soaked in seawater and sweat. However, there was a tacit understanding between them, and neither even suggested stripping out of their clothes to dry them.

The meat of the wild hare was crispy on the outside but tender on the inside; Xie Lian could feel the lingering heat from the fire in his teeth as he took a tentative bite but quickly found that he couldn't stop eating. He savored the flavor that lingered on his lips. Even as he stuffed himself, Xie Lian conscientiously divided the meat in half and gave Hua Cheng his due portion.

"San Lang has such amazing skills," he sighed in awe.

Hua Cheng laughed. "Really? I thank gege for the compliment."

"It's true," Xie Lian said. "I've never met anyone better than you at anything, whether it's carpentry or cooking. That noble, gracious, special someone really lucked out."

As he said that, he acted like he was very focused on eating, though there wasn't any response from Hua Cheng. It was a while before Hua Cheng replied quietly.

"That I got to meet that person...I'm the one who lucked out."

"..."

Xie Lian didn't know what to say and tried to focus even harder on eating. Only after several minutes did he register that Hua Cheng was calling him.

"Gege, gege."

Dazed, Xie Lian replied, "Huh?"

Hua Cheng passed him a handkerchief, and Xie Lian suddenly realized he'd been chomping too hard on the meat—his mouth and chin were covered in grease, and he looked extremely silly. He felt quite embarrassed as he took the handkerchief to wipe himself clean.

Hua Cheng passed him the other half of the roast hare as well.

"Gege must be starving. Don't rush yourself."

Xie Lian took it. Though he was a little dismayed, he still broached the subject in the end.

"San Lang, just what kind of person is your special someone?" he asked. "Why haven't you won them over yet?"

He genuinely believed that if Hua Cheng wanted someone, there was no one on earth who could resist his advances. But that day, Hua Cheng had said he hadn't won them over yet. Xie Lian couldn't help but feel rather glum, and an odd feeling grew toward this individual the ghost king fancied. It was probably because he thought the other party lacked taste. Or perhaps he thought they were taking Hua Cheng for granted.

"It's all right if gege finds it funny," Hua Cheng replied. "But, truth is, I'm afraid."

Whether it was out of a sense of injustice or a fear that Hua Cheng was putting himself down, Xie Lian responded in a serious tone. "What's there to be afraid of? You're the Supreme Ghost King, Crimson Rain Sought Flower."

Hua Cheng laughed out loud. "What a shitty 'Ghost King.' If I was really that formidable, I wouldn't have been so powerless when people strung me up and beat me centuries ago, ha ha ha ha..."

"You shouldn't say it like that," Xie Lian said. "Everyone has to go through trials to grow up..."

But even as he said that, he realized that he'd never experienced humiliation of that sort before his first ascension. He cleared his throat lightly.

"That person saw me at my worst," Hua Cheng said.

"Then I'm very envious of that," Xie Lian replied.

Hearing him say so, Hua Cheng gazed over.

Xie Lian stopped eating and said gently, "But I can sort of understand...your feelings."

After a pause, he continued, "There was a period in my own life that wasn't easy. Back then, I'd always think about how wonderful it would be if someone could still love me for who I was, even if they saw me rolling in the dirt and couldn't get up. Though I don't know if there's anyone out there like that. And I'm scared of showing that part of myself too.

"But if it's someone San Lang yearns for...I think that even if they saw you at your worst, they wouldn't say something like, 'ah, you're not so great after all.'"

His face grew solemn.

"To me, the one basking in infinite glory is you; the one fallen from grace is also you. What matters is *you*, not the state of you.

"I...admire San Lang very much. I want to understand your everything, so I'm very envious that someone has already met that version of you so early on. That kind of affinity can only come by chance; it can't be begged for. And whether that bond should live on is three parts fate and seven parts courage!"

The campfire crackled, and the two remained silent for a good while. Xie Lian softly cleared his throat as he rubbed his forehead.

"Have I said too much? How embarrassing."

"No, what you said was good. Very right," Hua Cheng replied.

Xie Lian let out a breath of relief and quickly returned to eating the meat.

"It's not just that. There are many other reasons," Hua Cheng added.

Despite Hua Cheng's assurance, Xie Lian felt he'd said far too much and wanted to stop discussing this subject immediately.

He couldn't understand it—why did he ramble on like that, and why did he encourage Hua Cheng to bravely pursue his beloved? It wasn't like he was the heavenly official who presided over marriage. He could only give a mumble as a reply.

"Mmm…"

After his speech, the air between the two seemed rather delicate, and they quickly finished eating to continue their labor. Soon, the coffin was officially complete.

Hua Cheng pushed the newly constructed coffin into the water and hopped in to sit inside. Although it was a long, heavy chunk of wood, it really did float, not sink. They didn't make the coffin particularly wide, and as Xie Lian lifted his robes to step in, he felt like there wasn't enough space to sit.

Muffled roars of thunder boomed above them, and steely clouds rolled. Violet flashes of lightning streaked from the skies, and their explosive noise startled the ears. Thin threads of rain began to fall, and the downpour only grew heavier by the minute. It seemed a storm was approaching.

Fortunately, the two didn't slack off while building and had crafted a cover for the coffin as well. Otherwise, it wouldn't have taken long for it to flood with rainwater and sink into the depths.

The two met eyes, and Xie Lian softly mumbled, "Sorry."

Hua Cheng didn't say anything more and lay down inside the coffin. Xie Lian climbed in fully and pulled the cover over them. As if a candle had been blown out, they sank into darkness.

The coffin floated into open water and drifted errantly for a while. Pouring rain beat down on the cover, and the two spoke not a word inside. Their bodies were pressed hard against one another, but it couldn't be helped—they were squished into such a narrow space. The waves pushed and pulled them, flipped and flopped them.

Xie Lian used one hand to push against the edge of the coffin to steady himself, trying his best to make more room. His head knocked lightly against the wood with the motion, and Hua Cheng reached out to cradle the back of his head with one hand, shielding it from further bumps. He rested the other hand on his back and pressed him to his chest. Xie Lian didn't even dare to breathe harshly.

"San Lang...how about we switch it up?"

"Switch what?" Hua Cheng asked.

"...You on top and me on the bottom," Xie Lian replied.

"Top, bottom; isn't it all the same?" Hua Cheng asked.

Xie Lian was afraid he was too heavy. "Our journey will take at least a day. Your body is only seventeen or eighteen right now, isn't it? And I'm a martial god; I'm very heavy..." Before he could finish his sentence, he was forced to exclaim, "San Lang, don't...don't just suddenly turn big!"

Although it was hard to see in the dark, they were pressed together so tightly that Xie Lian could feel Hua Cheng's body transform. While the change was minute, he still sensed it and assumed Hua Cheng had probably transformed back to his true form. Sure enough, when Hua Cheng spoke again, his laugh was deeper; truly his real voice. Xie Lian lay helplessly on his chest, but after the change, the nebulous awkwardness lightened a bit. Hoping to shift his body and change position, he raised his leg slightly, but Hua Cheng abruptly stopped laughing.

"Don't move," he said grimly.

Xie Lian froze. There was a loud noise, and the coffin sank violently.

Xie Lian was bewildered. "What's going on?!"

Soon after, there was another roaring sound, and the two were forcibly tossed around inside the coffin. It seemed their vessel had rolled over. Thank goodness there weren't any leaks, but u. couldn't be guaranteed if they were attacked again.

Hua Cheng pressed him down. "Something's got its eye on this coffin boat."

As soon as he spoke, the two felt a familiar weightlessness, and their positions abruptly changed from lying to upright—the coffin boat rose up, then swiftly plunged, flipping over once more!

Hua Cheng's arms were locked in a vice grip around Xie Lian's waist, with one hand still shielding his head. "Hold on tight to me!" he shouted.

If they were in an open space, Xie Lian could manage even if the spinning were three times as violent; the problem was they were trapped inside a narrow, tight space. They couldn't stretch out their limbs, and they had no idea what was happening outside.

All he could do was tense in alert while anxiety roiled within. "What if the coffin breaks?" Xie Lian wondered.

"Don't worry. Even if it breaks, I'm here. You won't sink," Hua Cheng reassured.

They were firmly pressed against each other, and Hua Cheng nearly brushed his lips against his hair when he spoke. Xie Lian could even feel the slight tremble of his Adam's apple. It made his mind start to wander, but his attention was stolen again by another wave of violent rolling. The boat was like a toy being jostled about by a toddler, and it shook and swung ceaselessly. With no other choice, Xie Lian embraced Hua Cheng tightly with one hand, bracing the other on the coffin wall.

Through the chaos, the two were hoisted and dropped, flipped and flopped into who-knows-how-many different positions. Their bodies collided and rubbed together in countless ways. Even though Hua Cheng had the appearance of a young man, only after this tumble did

Xie Lian realize that Hua Cheng was solid and hard from top to bottom. Xie Lian was seeing stars from the torment. When the shaking finally eased for a moment, he found that Hua Cheng was now on top of him. He pressed down heavily and crushed the breath out of him.

Xie Lian managed to raise his hand and grabbed on to the strong forearm beside his body that Hua Cheng was using to prop himself up. His head spun, and he groaned softly. "Is it over yet..."

For some reason, Hua Cheng didn't respond. Before Xie Lian finished his thought, his breathing hitched. He had very suddenly noticed that a certain part of his body had experienced a somewhat unusual shift.

"..."

In that split second, Xie Lian felt more incredulous than if he'd seen an iron tree bloom[5]—and at least his mind wouldn't be so blank in such a scenario.

Mortifying shame and embarrassment battered him more violently than the tempest battering the coffin outside. Xie Lian closed his knees in panic, but that didn't appear to be the right move; it seemed he'd touched something he shouldn't have, and it elicited a brusque grunt from Hua Cheng.

"Don't move!"

The grunt was deep and sharp, and Xie Lian hurriedly flattened his legs again. If he didn't close his knees, he was scared Hua Cheng might notice his body's reaction—in which case he might as well just smash his head against the coffin and die. He could've explained it away as an "unavoidable natural reaction," but there was already that awkward incident on the island. He could say it was unintentional once or twice, but how could he possibly explain himself after the third or fourth time?!

---

5   An idiom that means a very rare occurrence, or something extremely difficult to achieve.

Trapped in such a dire situation, Xie Lian blurted, "No! San Lang, don't...don't touch me!"

There was a brief silence, then Hua Cheng said gravely, "Very well. Let's break out of here."

It was like he had been absolved. Xie Lian cried, "Go!"

With another vicious attack of weightlessness, the coffin that contained the two was thrust into the air!

Just as it was, Hua Cheng and Xie Lian smacked their palms on either side of the coffin in unison, and it shattered instantly. The two broke free and leapt out under the moonlight. Xie Lian looked back and saw a giant water dragon dangling the broken pieces of the coffin from its mouth. It let out a roar beneath the pouring rain, baring its sharp teeth as if raging at the empty coffin it had presumed was full of food. This water dragon must've been thrashing the coffin boat about with its mouth, snapping it here and twisting it there.

The coffin boat had drifted at sea for a while, but the water dragon had dragged it back inland. The two landed back on Black Water Island. There were two new figures on the beach—Water Master Wudu and General Pei. Shi Wudu's hands were still in a seal, and he faced the storm like he was trying to call the water dragon over. Pei Ming patted his shoulder.

"Water Master-xiong! Just take it easy, will you? This round is over, but who knows when the next will come? Save your energy for now."

Turned out, the sudden pouring rain was the accompaniment to Shi Wudu's Heavenly Tribulation. The storm was calming down, and Shi Wudu whirled around with a flick of his sleeves to regard Hua Cheng and Xie Lian.

"What's with you two?" he questioned.

"..."

Pei Ming just had to give his input as well. "Yeah, Your Highness. Why don't you two explain yourselves? What's going on? What were you two doing in there?"

When the coffin boat exploded, their tight embrace was put on display for all to see. Xie Lian blinked. He was about to speak when he abruptly realized that after tumbling around inside the narrow coffin boat, their hair was mussed and their clothes were disheveled. The two of them looked as improper as one could imagine. Xie Lian wiped the rain off his face and found that his cheeks were burning.

Hua Cheng took a step forward to shield him. A moment later, Xie Lian softly cleared his throat.

"...Nothing's going on. Just...the coffin was too small."

Shi Wudu was puzzled. "I wasn't asking about that."

Pei Ming pointed at all the leftover wood pieces they left behind on the beach. "You made that coffin yourselves, right? Why didn't you build a bigger one?"

"..."

The coffin boat was designed by both Hua Cheng and Xie Lian, and it seemed neither of them had considered making it bigger at the time. Xie Lian could only laugh awkwardly.

"You're right. Ha ha, ha ha. Did My Lords only just drift to this island?"

"Yes," Pei Ming replied. "Water Master-xiong battled the current of the Black Water Demon Lair, and we only just made it here. Didn't expect to see a coffin sailing the waters of the Black Water Demon Lair; what a curious sight."

Xie Lian could feel himself tense, and he forced a smile. "Curious indeed."

"You." Shi Wudu turned to Hua Cheng and narrowed his eyes. "On the ship, didn't you say that the only thing that doesn't sink in the Black Water Demon Lair is wood that has carried the dead?"

Pei Ming drew his sword. "Yeah," he said leisurely. "There's the wood, but where's the dead?"

Hua Cheng smiled too. "If you're so concerned with who's dead here, I suggest you go kill yourself."

Pei Ming pointed his blade at him. "Such arrogance. As expected of Crimson Rain Sought Flower!"

As suspected, he had already guessed. Hua Cheng burst out laughing, and seeing that a fight was about to start, Xie Lian stepped protectively in front of Hua Cheng.

"My Lords, please calm yourselves. You can be completely assured that San Lang is on this journey out of generosity alone."

"'San Lang'?" Pei Ming wondered. "I've never heard of Lord Crimson Rain Sought Flower ranking among the boys of some house. And *generosity*? Your Highness, are you sure that's the word to describe his intentions?"

Shi Wudu had to stand in the spotlight at all times, so he pushed Pei Ming aside. "Are you the one who's been meddling this entire trip?" he demanded sharply. "What is your intention in luring us here to the Black Water Demon Lair? Where's Qingxuan?"

"This is someone else's territory. Do you think I *want* to be here?" Hua Cheng answered.

Xie Lian was already used to these kinds of situations and changed the subject with practiced ease. "Has Lord Wind Master not been found yet? Didn't General Pei go looking for him and the Earth Master?"

Pei Ming shrugged. "I almost fished them up, but one of Water Master-xiong's waves came along and washed them away."

"Mind your misleading tongue, Pei-xiong," Shi Wudu snapped. "If I didn't raise waves and simply allowed those things in the water to keep attacking over and over, you wouldn't have been able to find them in the first place!"

"Calm down, calm down," Xie Lian soothed quickly. "Um...Lord Wind Master is with Lord Earth Master, so there shouldn't be any need to worry."

Shi Wudu humphed. "Earth Master? What good is that Earth Master?! Mediocre and unaccomplished. He's not a martial god either, and his spiritual powers aren't as strong as Qingxuan's..."

He trailed off when he seemed to remember that Shi Qingxuan no longer possessed any spiritual powers. His face fell, and he grew silent.

Every profession has its experts, Xie Lian thought. Although Ming Yi wasn't a martial god and his spiritual powers weren't terribly strong, he wasn't as bad as the Water Master described. Besides, the skills the Earth Master demonstrated at Banyue Pass weren't bad at all. Even if he wasn't the best, he wasn't the worst either.

"Don't worry too much yet," Pei Ming assured as well. "Lord Earth Master should be able to take care of things as long as they don't run into Demon Xuan."

Hua Cheng laughed. "Your Heavenly Tribulation has pursued you all the way to the Black Water Demon Lair. You guys have already made a huge mess of his territory. Do you really think the master of the domain hasn't noticed?"

Shi Wudu's face twitched, and he retrieved a golden longevity lock pendant from underneath the collar of his robes.

"Water Master-xiong, did something happen?" Pei Ming asked.

The golden longevity lock vibrated in Shi Wudu's palm. "Qingxuan is close by...and he's injured!"

Xie Lian took a look at the golden pendant. It looked exactly the same as the one Shi Qingxuan had been wearing that day—the one he removed to build the protection array and left behind in the end.

"Is Lord Wind Master still wearing his longevity lock? I remember he removed it before."

"I picked it up and put it on him again," Shi Wudu said.

The two longevity locks had been forged by the brothers' golden essence. When they were near one another and one was hurt, the locks would call out to each other; the closer they were, the stronger the resonance. This was a natural attribute of the locks and not a spell, so it was unaffected by the Demon Lair's spiritual field. Shi Wudu removed the longevity lock pendant from his neck and dangled the chain from his hand. He held his arm out straight and slowly turned in a circle. When he faced a certain direction, the vibration of the golden lock abruptly grew stronger.

It was calling them into the forest—toward the unfathomably deep heart of the lonely island.

"Looks like Qingxuan is here," Shi Wudu said grimly.

With that, he strode into the forest with large strides. Naturally, Pei Ming followed along. Xie Lian thought about their present situation. Since the Wind and Earth Masters were both on the island and the Wind Master seemed to be injured, finding them should be their priority. They could worry about the rest later.

"My Lords, there are little ghost minions hiding in the forest. Be careful of ambushes."

Hua Cheng came along as well. Xie Lian wanted to grab his hand, but he remembered his disgraceful state in the coffin boat, and his outstretched hand shrank back in spite of himself. In the end, he tugged a corner of Hua Cheng's sleeve, not daring to look at his face. Pei Ming, however, looked back frequently and appeared to be very interested.

"Your Highness and Crimson Rain Sought Flower—the two of you sure are stuck together like glue. A ghost king like yourself, following us so openly—aren't you even going to try to avoid suspicion?"

"What is General Pei saying?" Xie Lian replied easily. "Under these circumstances, it's much less suspicious if he comes along. If My Lords run into any danger, you may suspect him—how else can he hope to clear his name?"

"He made it to the rank of supreme, so what difference does it make if he's with us or not? Wouldn't it be easy for him to create a clone?" Pei Ming said.

He had just spoken when a sharp sound tore through the air. Pei Ming raised his hand and caught an arrow.

"So there *is* something. That was close! Water Master-xiong, be careful..."

Before he could finish, there were more swishing sounds, and several more arrows came flying toward him. *Cling clang.*

Pei Ming swept his sword and wondered, "What the heck?"

Shi Wudu laughed out loud. "Pei-xiong, I think you'd best watch yourself instead!" Then he quickened his pace.

An ambush of arrows was nothing to be afraid of; it was simply an annoyance. Pei Ming irritably flattened a patch of shrubbery and soon plucked out a few more little minions.

"You guys got guts!"

The ghosts were scrawny and sallow-skinned, the lowest of lackeys. They were terrified of the general and cowered in little balls as they hung from his hand, begging for mercy nonstop. They were gatekeepers after all, so attacking intruders was what they had to do. Pei Ming let them go after a few threats.

When they ran into more cunning and vicious minions later on, Pei Ming squashed those ghoulies into a ball and dribbled it as they made their way. The four of them brushed away branches and pushed their way through bushes, hiking through the dense forest for what seemed like ages. As they walked, the resonant cries of the golden lock in Shi Wudu's hand grew louder and louder.

Finally, they reached a large clearing at the heart of the forest. At the center of it was a lake, and the four walked toward it.

Suddenly, Pei Ming spoke up. "Crimson Rain Sought Flower, if you continue with these pranks, I won't tolerate you much longer."

Both Hua Cheng and Xie Lian looked at him, then at each other. Pei Ming frowned.

"If you want to fight, then challenge me like a man. I'm not like those thirty-three heavenly officials; I'm not afraid of you. Shoving me around is pointless."

Hua Cheng arched his brows. "Gege, you have to believe me. I've got nothing to do with this."

Xie Lian intervened. "General Pei, he doesn't play meaningless pranks like that."

Pei Ming was doubtful. "Really?"

Xie Lian grew alarmed. "Be careful, something else on this island might be stirring up trouble."

Pei Ming stopped talking. Right then, Shi Wudu slowed his pace. "It's here."

The golden longevity lock seemed to cry hardest here, meaning Shi Qingxuan was somewhere close. But this area was open with nowhere to hide—there was nothing here besides the lake.

"Could there be an underground palace?" Pei Ming wondered.

Shi Wudu stared at the surface of the water, and Xie Lian said, "Or it could be at the bottom of the lake."

But a lake on Black Water Island shouldn't be entered carelessly, lest one never come up again. The surface of the lake was calm and unrippled. It looked like a giant mirror, reflecting the blanched moon that hung high in the starless, cloudless night sky. The four circled the edge of the lake. Xie Lian was still weighing options about how to investigate the lake bottom when a terrified scream ripped through the night air.

Shi Wudu was leading the group, and Pei Ming was bringing up the rear. The three in front looked back to see that the screamer was the little ghost that Pei Ming had captured on the road. Its scrawny, bony body stood in place, but its head was gone, and black blood spurted almost three meters from its neck. Its head was flying through the air, screeching.

"General Pei, why did you kill it so suddenly?" Xie Lian asked.

Pei Ming, however, exclaimed, "No!"

Before he could explain, his body crumpled, and he dropped to one knee.

Hua Cheng laughed. "There's no need for such a grand apology."

Pei Ming's expression was stark bewilderment. "Water Master-xiong, watch out!" he shouted.

Watch out for what, though? Other than the four of them by the lake, there was nothing here!

It was as if Pei Ming had been bound by something invisible. Shi Wudu was rushing over to help when a chilling light flashed in front of him. He dodged just in time, though the attack still managed to draw a trail of blood across one of his cheeks. He wiped it with his hand, and his face changed.

Xie Lian stood firm in front of Hua Cheng to shield him. "An invisibility spell?!"

Pei Ming finally broke free of his formless constraints. "Gather around! Don't split up!" he shouted.

But Shi Wudu didn't care. The moment he heard the longevity lock start crying again, he charged around the lake, frantically calling out for his brother.

"Qingxuan! *Qingxuan!*"

It was mayhem, but amidst the ruckus Xie Lian noticed something quite peculiar.

The area along the lakeshore was open and empty, with no notable landmarks to be seen. But the shore reflected on the lake's surface showed a different story.

In the reflection, a charcoal-black building loomed on the edge of the water. The building was cold and sinister, more like a prison than a place where someone lived. It had no door, only a set of windows set high in the walls and sealed by unforgiving iron bars. A pale white hand reached from between those iron bars, waving desperately like it was begging for help.

Xie Lian's head shot up, and he looked to the shore opposite him; there was nothing there aside from Shi Wudu darting around with the longevity lock. When he looked down again, the reflection clearly showed a sinister iron prison. Shi Wudu was right in front of the building, but he couldn't see it.

"My Lords!" Xie Lian blurted out. "I found it! Look..."

Just then, his pupils shrank. Something new was reflected within Black Water Lake.

A shadowy figure had appeared soundlessly behind him and Hua Cheng.

64
In the Nether Water Manor, Black Robes, White Bones

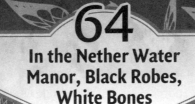

YET ON THE SHORE, there was still not a single soul behind them!

Xie Lian had kept Fangxin at hand during their entire trek, and the moment he saw the reflection, he stabbed behind him. But while his attack had clearly pierced the black shadow, it felt like he had stabbed a ball of water that broke up into ripples and disappeared on the spot. Hua Cheng cocked his head and knitted his brows as he stared in the direction where the black shadow had disappeared.

Soon after, more and more shadowy figures appeared in the water's reflection. Their stark, ghastly pale faces and hands were the only illumination that the black night offered.

Xie Lian kept up the assault with his sword and shouted, "General Pei! Go to the water! Look at the reflection! The water can reveal the creatures!"

Those little ghosts normally wouldn't be able to even approach a heavenly official, but things were different in the Demon Lair. Pei Ming hadn't been able to see the enemy, but now that he understood what was happening, he stared at the water's surface and easily felled all the ghostly shadows surrounding him with but two swings of his sword.

Shi Wudu also finally noticed the strange reflection, and he knelt by the water to shout into the lake. "Qingxuan?! Are you there?!"

The black water and black iron prison blurred together, making it hard to make out details aside from that single white hand. Suddenly, a face appeared between the iron bars—it was Shi Qingxuan!

He didn't seem able to see Shi Wudu kneeling outside the prison, and his expression was one of absolute terror. He clutched onto the iron bars with both hands and desperately tried to squeeze his head out. It looked like he was crying for help, yet not a single sound passed through. And his pleas were short-lived—several wizened hands grabbed at him, seized his head, his face, his neck, his shoulders, and then forcibly dragged him down!

Shi Wudu cursed at the sight. Pei Ming pulled him back before he could leap into the water himself.

"Water Master-xiong, you can't! How do you know this isn't a trap? You can't manipulate the waters of the South Sea. Even as a Water God, you're at someone else's mercy when you enter their water territory!"

Shi Wudu patted his shoulder and said simply, "Then help me by standing guard out here."

With that, he pushed him away and leapt into Black Water Lake!

Once he submerged, he did not resurface.

"Water Master-xiong!" Pei Ming called out.

But he couldn't follow. He knew there was most likely a "boundary" at the bottom of this lake. Much like mechanisms in ancient tombs, outsiders could open the gates and intrude, but once they were inside, the doors would slam shut. They couldn't be opened from within, and the graverobbers would be trapped and left to die. It was hard to say whether this boundary worked in a similar manner.

"General Pei! Don't go after him!" Xie Lian called out. "There's a corpse right by your feet. Take it and hurry back to the beach! Use it to build a coffin and prepare for evacuation. I'll go myself!"

"Your Highness? Are you in fighting shape?!" Pei Ming asked.

"This place has sealed off nearly all of your spiritual powers; we're about the same now. And I have more experience than you when it comes to fighting with bare fists!"

Pei Ming glanced at Hua Cheng, who was standing next to Xie Lian, and recalled that he could float on the water's surface. The two of them would be much more useful than him in this situation, so without further argument, he picked up the little ghost's corpse and rushed back into the woods.

Xie Lian turned to Hua Cheng. "San Lang, will you lend me a little spiritual power again...just a little! Just a little, tiny bit is enough!"

Without a word of complaint, Hua Cheng gently patted the small of Xie Lian's back. A giant beam of white light sprung forth from Fangxin, and when Xie Lian swung, every little ghost surrounding the lake was killed by the sweep. Xie Lian was speechless for a moment, then simply sheathed his sword.

"I'm off!"

The two jumped into the water together. There wasn't anything strange at the bottom of Black Water Lake besides abnormally cold lake water. In fact, this water was much more normal than the strange, ship-sinking waters of the Black Water Demon Lair; one could float in it no differently than in an ordinary lake. Puzzled, Xie Lian kept swimming downward. It didn't take long for him to reach the bottom, but there weren't any strange mechanisms, and he didn't see Lord Wind Master or Lord Water Master. Brows knitted, he mused on the matter for a moment before swimming back up.

Upon surfacing, he gasped a few breaths and wiped his face. Once his sight was clear, he noticed that a different shore stretched out before him!

An iron prison loomed over Black Water Lake. It was the same one that had been reflected in the lake's waters.

Other than the prison, everything on the shore was exactly the same as he remembered. The oppressive quiet made the atmosphere all the more haunting. Shi Wudu was already ashore, angrily smashing the giant lock on the prison gates with a big rock. He was the heavenly official who controlled water, but he had entered the domain of another water master and couldn't call forth the water he ruled. He was like a ferocious beast that had been defanged and declawed.

The moment Shi Wudu saw Xie Lian and Hua Cheng climb ashore, his eyes lit up and he raised his hand to beckon them over.

"A martial god! Perfect timing! Quick, use your martial god ways to take care of this!"

"..."

Maybe now everyone will understand the benefits of having a martial god around? Xie Lian thought. He approached wordlessly and unleashed a kick, which nearly cracked the lock in two. Another kick, and the prison gates opened.

Shi Wudu rushed inside, crying out, "Qing—"

Before he even made it through the door, a mob came rushing out, wailing and howling hellishly.

"Ohhhh—ahhhh—woooo—wahhhh—!"

The people were disheveled and unkempt, emaciated and gaunt; their ragged clothes covered nothing and revealed rows of ribs. They were so filthy it was like they hadn't bathed in over a decade. Their eyes were glazed as they stomped their feet, swung their hands randomly, and grabbed and beat at their own chests. They roared and cried incoherently, creating an exceedingly horrifying scene as they streamed out like a wave of polluted water. Shi Wudu was left petrified in shock.

However, they were simply trying to escape; they didn't stick around to harass anyone. Even if Shi Wudu was momentarily stunned, he didn't actually care about what they did and continued his charge into the building.

"*Qing—!*"

Before he could even make it a few steps, he staggered so hard that he almost fell—the ground was extremely slippery! There was an indescribable putrid smell emanating from within the iron prison; Xie Lian could even smell it from outside, and he held his breath. Shi Wudu covered his nose and mouth with his sleeve and continued his charge inside, finally able to yell the full name.

"*Qingxuan?!*"

It was pitch-black within the prison, and from all around them came the sound of weeping and strange whispered murmurs. Moments later, a weak voice came.

"...*ge...*"

In the deepest part of the iron prison, Shi Qingxuan was slumped against the only wall with a high window. The moonlight leaking through it illuminated him and blanched him white as a sheet. He was surrounded by a group of filthy wretches. Some had festering sores covering their entire bodies. Some were snorting like pigs, and some were pecking for grain like chickens. Some were hugging Shi Qingxuan, wailing and declaring him their baby. All of them were clearly insane.

Shi Qingxuan had once been an esteemed heavenly official. Never before had he fallen to such a state.

Shi Wudu stormed forward and shot a blast from his hand. "Get lost! What in hell are these ghosts?!"

Though he and Shi Qingxuan resembled each other, their bearing was completely different. Shi Wudu's spiritual powers might be greatly diminished right now, but that only doubled his overpowering presence, and it made the madmen scramble away in fear.

Xie Lian couldn't help but feel sympathy, and Shi Qingxuan also chided, "Ge, don't attack them! They're not ghosts. They're...living humans!"

This was true. Although they looked more ghostly than ghosts, they were all human. Xie Lian was shocked by the sight.

Why would Black Water Demon Xuan lock all these people up here? he wondered.

Shi Wudu, however, had no such regard for their suffering. Clutching the longevity lock pendant in one hand, he grabbed hold of Shi Qingxuan's arm with the other.

"How did you get here? Where are you hurt?"

Shi Qingxuan was certainly dirty, but he didn't seem injured aside from a cut on his leg that was bleeding a bit. "I don't know how we got here. A wave surged and knocked us out. When we woke up, we were already imprisoned. This is just a scratch; it's nothing serious! Ming-xiong's injuries are more severe."

Only then did the others notice that Ming Yi was lying on the ground nearby. He looked ashen, but not from displeasure. Patches of purple and blue mottled his face.

"What happened to Lord Earth Master?" Xie Lian asked.

"I think he was bitten by those creatures in the sea," Shi Qingxuan replied. "Those bonefish have green moss growing on their teeth and spikes, and they're poisonous! I applied all the medicine I had to him, but...*sigh*."

Xie Lian crouched to take a closer look at him, but the disgusting stench that permeated the air almost knocked him out. He looked around. There were wooden buckets filled with swill placed around the prison, and they emanated a musty, putrid smell. There was also the rotten stink of sores and blood and the horrifying odor of chamber pots that Xie Lian suspected hadn't been emptied for months.

Shi Wudu's tolerance had run dry. "Such revoltingly bad taste. It seems this Ship-Sinking Black Water has little class to speak of. Qingxuan, let's go!"

He pulled Shi Qingxuan to his feet and started to drag him out, but Shi Qingxuan spoke up.

"I'm fine, no need to assist me."

He then helped Ming Yi upright and supported him as they slowly exited the iron prison.

However, it was easier to come than go. The boundary passage in Black Water Lake was sealed shut. They dove into the waters and surfaced a few times, but the scenery never changed—proving that they were being held inside the boundary of Black Water Lake, unable to leave.

"Where's General Pei?" Shi Qingxuan asked.

"I had Pei-xiong stay on the other side. He should be trying to think of a way in as well," Shi Wudu replied.

"I told General Pei to build a coffin boat, so once we're out, we can evacuate then and there," Xie Lian said.

"If he finishes the boat, he could also go back to report on the situation and then return for us," Shi Wudu said.

However, Ming Yi was wounded—they might not be able to wait that long. While they weren't sure how powerful the poison was, it would still be better to leave as soon as possible.

After some contemplation, Xie Lian said, "Black Water Demon Xuan might live in seclusion out here, but surely he must leave sometimes? He wouldn't want to cross the entire Black Water Demon Lair every time he wants to go out, right?"

"Yes, that's a very good point," Shi Wudu said. "There must be a spot on this island where one can cast the teleportation array."

Shi Wudu hadn't particularly cared for Xie Lian at first, but he looked at him differently now that they were shouldering hardships together and he'd seen Xie Lian save Shi Qingxuan time and time again. Thus, he agreed to Xie Lian's suggestion without argument.

Ming Yi weakly raised his hand, and Shi Qingxuan asked, "Ming-xiong? Is there something you want to say?"

Ming Yi didn't speak, only raised his hand higher. It seemed like he was trying to conserve his strength. The others looked in the direction he was pointing and saw a gloomy black building standing in the depths of the forest.

Ming Yi dropped his arm and said, voice raspy, "That place... what's it for? Do you know?"

"No," Xie Lian said. "We didn't see it on the way here."

Shi Wudu squinted. "That must be the Nether Water Manor of Black Water Demon Xuan." That was the rumored name of Black Water Demon Xuan's residence. That conclusion made, he declared, "Let's go."

He started toward the manor, shockingly fearless of any retribution. Although it seemed impetuous and rude, what other choice did they have under the current circumstances? One could say they had been going around in circles in someone's backyard, and now they were about to break into their home through the front door.

"San Lang, you don't need to come along if this is awkward for you," Xie Lian whispered to Hua Cheng.

Hua Cheng's face was serious as he replied, "Quicken your pace, gege. Get out of here as soon as possible."

Xie Lian nodded and didn't say any more. Hua Cheng seemed wary, but not about the master of this land—Xie Lian could tell it was something else. He kept feeling that something was off, and the thought of all the little questions they'd accumulated made him uneasy.

The group hiked through the forest, paying no mind to the band of madmen that was now running wild and free. Finally, they arrived at the haunting black building.

They only noticed upon their arrival that the Nether Water Manor was actually a large, majestic palace—in fact, its build was very similar to the peerlessly splendid Palaces of Wind and Water. The group ascended the countless steps and stood before the tightly shut gates.

Xie Lian knocked. "Pardon the intrusion!" he brightly called out. "It is purely by accident that we have most bluntly offended you by our indiscretion. We deeply apologize."

No one answered. Collecting himself, Xie Lian carefully pushed open the palace doors.

Xie Lian knew from years of experience that, even if there was something waiting for them inside, it wouldn't pop out and "greet" them the moment the door was opened. But it seemed today he would have to eat his own words—the first thing he saw was something petrifying.

Sitting at the center of the grand, spacious entrance hall was someone dressed all in black, their face snow-white...

It was a skeleton!

Wham! Xie Lian immediately shut the door. *Did I perhaps open it incorrectly? Something like that usually doesn't show itself so quickly...?*

He wanted to start over and try his greeting again, but Shi Wudu had already walked past him and pushed open the doors with a humph.

"We're already here, so what does it matter if he doesn't welcome us?"

The group slowly stepped into the palace and cautiously approached the skeleton dressed in black. Xie Lian examined it carefully. *To whom do these bones belong? Why are they enshrined here?*

Ming Yi knitted his brows. "...Wasn't...General Pei...left behind? It's not him, is it?"

It was possible. Shi Wudu was slightly rattled and looked the skeleton over a few more times before he could refute the idea.

"I don't believe so. The bone structure is flatter than General Pei's."

"Wait," Shi Qingxuan said all of a sudden.

The group looked at him, and Shi Qingxuan continued, "Isn't it obvious? This is the Nether Water Manor. Naturally, the only one that could be worshipped inside the Nether Water Manor is..."

Xie Lian understood what he was trying to say, but he dismissed the idea just as quickly. "Black Water Demon Xuan? That's impossible."

Xie Lian gazed at Hua Cheng. "For those in the Ghost Realm, their ashes are their life source—and also their fatal weakness. Why would he put something so important on display?"

Hua Cheng had told him this when they first met. While he stated the fact quite seriously, for some reason his mind unconsciously wandered to the other thing Hua Cheng had said about ashes.

Hua Cheng was watching him intently, and Xie Lian lost himself for a moment. He twisted his gaze away and softly cleared his throat.

"Then...who could these bones belong to?" Shi Qingxuan wondered.

The group surrounded the eerie skeleton to investigate it, and Xie Lian was the first to voice his findings.

"First, it's a man."

"We see that," the group said.

"Second, the man's hands and feet must've been fairly dexterous. Particularly his fingers," Xie Lian continued. "He likely practiced some sort of martial art, but his skill may not have been strong. Exceptional martial artists start training at a young age, and their bone structures wouldn't look like this."

In contrast, Shi Wudu only gave the skeleton a cursory look before he turned away. "As long as it's not in our way, it doesn't matter who it was. Lord Earth Master, where do you think we can cast the Teleportation..."

Before he could finish, the skeleton raised its head and lunged at him without warning!

Fortunately, Xie Lian reacted swiftly and felled it with a single chop of his hand. The skeleton clattered to the ground in a heap of shattered bones.

"Ge!" Shi Qingxuan exclaimed.

Of the five present, Xie Lian was the only martial god. And Hua Cheng would never help or protect anyone aside from Xie Lian, so Xie Lian had now become quite important. Although Shi Wudu had just been attacked, he remained fairly collected; he had only taken a single step back even after an attempt was made on his life.

"What's with this skeleton? Does it still have a soul lingering within?"

Xie Lian crouched to rifle through and inspect the bones, then shook his head. "That's weird."

"What's weird?" Shi Wudu asked.

Xie Lian rose to his feet. "It doesn't have a single breath of its soul left. If it did, we would have noticed strange disturbances when we approached."

"If that's the case, then how did it manage to pounce at me?" Shi Wudu asked.

Humming for a moment, Xie Lian answered, "I think it's terminal lucidity."

Shi Qingxuan was puzzled. "Terminal lucidity? Doesn't that only happen to the living? Those on the verge of death...are still alive, I guess."

"The dead experience it as well," Xie Lian explained. "The Seventh Day is a form of terminal lucidity, when the souls of the deceased return to greet family. In fact, it's the same for anyone—the living, dead, and all in between. I think Lord Water Master must've provoked it, which was why it gathered the last of its strength and made a move."

Because his theories made sense, Shi Wudu valued his words more and more. "Then in the opinion of Your Highness, what was that provocation?"

"It was either something you said or something on your person," Xie Lian said.

"What did I say?" Shi Wudu wondered.

Ming Yi blew out a breath. "...'As long as it's not in our way, it doesn't matter who it was.'"

Shi Qingxuan scratched his head, puzzled. "Was there something wrong with that...? Could our friend here have a violent temper?"

Nothing conclusive could come from further discussion, so Xie Lian said, "In any event, the soul has dissipated. Let's drop the matter."

He collected the remains of the bones and settled them upon the altar anew, then clapped his hands together in prayer and bowed a few times. Shi Qingxuan came over as well and randomly bowed a few times, following his lead.

After that was settled, the five of them wandered the Nether Water Manor. There wasn't anyone around—it seemed the legendary Black Water Demon Xuan wasn't home. The water manor's structure was complex, with many branching side chambers both big and small. However, there was one that was particularly hidden and cramped. There were strange spells scrawled upon its doors—traces left over from the use of the teleportation array.

It would appear there *was* a place where the teleportation array could be used on Black Water Island, and that place was this tiny side chamber. Setting up a room to serve as a dedicated connection point drained a lot less spiritual power than drawing a completely new array every time.

Considering they didn't have much spiritual power available at the moment, this was perfect.

Ming Yi was the expert, and he was able to grasp the chamber's specifics with a glance. "This array only allows one-way transport."

Xie Lian understood. "Meaning that it can only send forth; one cannot come here from elsewhere, correct?"

Ming Yi nodded. "It further reduces the spiritual power required."

"Isn't that exactly what we need?" Shi Qingxuan said. "We just want to leave, so this is great! Let's get outta here before the master of Black Water discovers us."

Hauling the Earth Master along with one arm, Shi Qingxuan moved to push open the doors with his other hand.

"Stop! There's a trap!" Ming Yi exclaimed sharply.

Shi Qingxuan stumbled back a meter when he heard this. "What trap?!"

Ming Yi was dragged along with him, stunned speechless for a moment. He gestured for Shi Qingxuan to help him approach again, and they walked to the door once more. There, Ming Yi thoroughly inspected the spells scrawled upon it.

"It's a trap," he stated firmly. "Arrays drawn in this chamber can send only one person away at a time."

"That's a thing?!" Shi Qingxuan exclaimed. "Then what happens if two people go together?!"

"You'll find they've been crushed into one person upon reaching their destination," Ming Yi answered coldly.

"..."

Among those present, only Ming Yi had advanced knowledge on this topic. The rest of the group consisted of one water god, one wind god, and one martial god, none of them particularly knowledgeable in this subject. Xie Lian's first reaction was to look at Hua Cheng—he was intently staring at the array, but he didn't voice any objections. It seemed Ming Yi wasn't lying.

Xie Lian hummed. "If that's really the case, then any ignorant intruders attempting to activate this array to escape would have an... atrocious end. A trap, indeed."

The skies rumbled outside. Twisted lightning crawled across the gloomy clouds and flashed white and blue upon the faces inside the Nether Water Manor. They looked like a congregation of menacing ghosts. The group exchanged looks of dismay.

"Ge, it's another..." Shi Qingxuan said.

Shi Wudu's face darkened, and he did not respond. But everyone knew this was his Heavenly Tribulation in pursuit of him again. Pei Ming's unintentionally ominous words faintly echoed in Xie Lian's mind again: *Water Master-xiong, you're really unlucky this time...*

"Since we can use the teleportation array, let's hurry and get out of here," Shi Qingxuan urged. "If Heavenly Lightning struck here and destroyed the water manor, then..."

Then they'd only elicit greater animosity. Dismantling a heavenly official's temple was an attack on their brand, and they would surely develop a deep hatred for the culprit. It was unclear whether the Ghost Realm had the same taboo, but surely *no one* would like it if their house was demolished for no reason.

Ming Yi dipped his fingers into the blood from his wounds and stood with some difficulty to prepare the array. "Where to? And who is going first?"

"Lord Earth Master, you have to go first. You're wounded," Xie Lian said.

However, Ming Yi shook his head. "The array needs to be redrawn after each use. None of you know how to draw it, so I have to stay behind."

"Then Ming-xiong, I'll stay with you and go second to last," Shi Qingxuan said.

"What are you saying?" Shi Wudu snapped. "Right now, you're... Even if you stay, you'll be of no use. Leave first, *right now*, and go to the East Sea!"

"Right now, everyone is equally useless—so what does it matter?!" Shi Qingxuan countered. "This whole thing had nothing to do with Ming-xiong, but he had to suffer like this. I..." He sighed. "I feel really bad."

"We're all being sent to the same place anyway; it won't take long. What are you afraid of?" Shi Wudu persisted.

In the past, Shi Wudu would lecture a word or two at most, and Shi Qingxuan would always listen. Things were different now, and Shi Qingxuan wasn't listening anymore; he pushed against each of Shi Wudu's demands.

"If we leave like this, what about General Pei? Won't he be left behind?"

Shi Wudu also noticed that his little brother wasn't as obedient as he once was, and his expression grew complicated. A moment later, he replied, "It's fine, Pei-xiong's stubborn and resilient. He'll be able to hang on until we get reinforcements from heaven."

"..." Xie Lian didn't know whether to laugh or cry. Although his instincts told him the Water Master was right and didn't mean any harm by his words, he still felt sorry for Pei Ming.

After a pause, he said, "Hold on a minute."

The group looked at him.

"Lord Earth Master, are you sure this chamber can really be used for the teleportation array?" Xie Lian asked. "Could there be any unforeseen issues? I don't think it's wise to rush in so carelessly. Why don't we test it first?"

At that, Ming Yi's hand really did pause. "How? We'll still need a volunteer to test it."

Shi Qingxuan raised his hand. "Then I volunteer!"

Hua Cheng hadn't spoken throughout the whole conversation, but now he crossed his arms and announced his thoughts. "Sorry to interrupt. Have none of you realized the problem with that?"

"And what is My Lord's expert opinion?" Ming Yi asked.

"How will you know if the volunteer arrives at the intended destination?" Hua Cheng pointed out.

Xie Lian blinked. "That's true... Lord Earth Master did say this array only goes one way."

Which meant the person would not be able to return after being sent out and couldn't let the others know if they'd safely arrived at their proper destination. They'd forgotten to consider this matter—this deserted island was isolated from the outside world, and the spiritual communication array was blocked. It would appear they'd come to a dead end.

"So. Further discussion is meaningless," Hua Cheng concluded. "It's one simple decision: go, or leave. Get this over with quickly. Scared? Then stay."

Although Hua Cheng was smiling, Xie Lian could sense he was uneasy—like he wanted to leave this place as soon as possible. He'd been anxious ever since they were brought back to the island by the dragon Shi Wudu summoned, and it was only getting worse.

Shi Wudu also didn't want to wait any longer; Heavenly Thunder was crashing in his ears, it would strike sooner or later if he didn't leave, and *that* would be an unpleasant time for everyone. So he stormed into the side chamber and slammed the door behind him. Ming Yi quickly finished drawing the array, and when they opened the door once more, faint smoke wafted from inside the empty chamber.

"Done," Ming Yi said. "Next."

"Then, Your Highness..." Shi Qingxuan began to speak.

Before he could finish, Ming Yi grabbed him and stuffed him inside the chamber. He slammed the door shut and completed the array. The second time he opened the door, Ming Yi looked at the remaining two.

"San Lang, why don't you go first?" Xie Lian offered.

However, Hua Cheng pulled him along into the chamber. "Gege, we go together," he said darkly.

Xie Lian was confused. "But doesn't this array only allow for one at a time..."

"I'm not a living human, don't worry," Hua Cheng said.

Xie Lian still felt there was something worrisome afoot, but he couldn't put his finger on what it might be. Hua Cheng brought him inside the chamber and gave a curt order to Ming Yi.

"Puqi Shrine."

Ming Yi nodded in silent reply. The door slowly closed in front of Xie Lian, and through the closing gap, he could see Ming Yi's ashen expression.

In spite of himself, he wondered, *Can Lord Earth Master really make it through this?*

Hua Cheng pulled the door fully shut himself, waited for a moment, and then reopened it.

They were greeted by the interior of Puqi Shrine. It was the middle of the night, and Qi Rong's snores roared like thunder. He was sprawled out like he'd been violently murdered and was hogging the blanket. Guzi used to have a proper sleeping posture, but his cheap dad's bad influence had taken its toll. Presently, he was draped over Qi Rong's stomach like a dead fish. In contrast, Lang Ying was curled properly in a corner, using a few shirts as covers. Xie Lian lifted the blanket covering Qi Rong, suppressed the urge to smother him with it, and instead covered the two small children.

"We're...back?" he whispered.

Hua Cheng closed the door behind him. "Yes. It's over."

"Not yet, I don't think," Xie Lian said. "We don't know if Lord Wind Master and the others are safe."

Pushing the door open very lightly, he walked outside. Only then did he raise his voice to call out in the spiritual communication array they'd set up earlier.

"Lord Earth Master? Is everyone back?"

There was no response. Xie Lian thought that perhaps Ming Yi might not have made it back quickly, so he entered the communication array of the Upper Court. He had no way of knowing before he entered, but it was complete chaos inside. He jumped in surprise at the noise. Every heavenly official was yelling, and even Ling Wen was throwing a fit.

"Don't throw every bit of useless information my way—how much do you think I have to go through every day?! Don't any of you know how to use your brains before asking me?!"

"Ling Wen!" Xie Lian called out hastily. "Have Lord Water Master and the others not returned?!"

Ling Wen instantly caught hold of him, and she seemed to change into a completely different person. "Your Highness! Why is your voice so loud...? Have you returned from the East Sea? Where did Lord Water Master and General Pei go? Why haven't we heard from them?"

"I came back from the South Sea," Xie Lian said.

"The *South* Sea?"

"The South Sea. Specifically, the Black Water Demon Lair."

Ling Wen was dumbfounded. "But...how did you end up there?! We never go near that place. Are Ol' Pei and the others still there?"

"It's a long story," Xie Lian said. "While Lord Water Master was facing his Tribulation, we accidentally stumbled into the Black Water Demon Lair. We just escaped. He and Lord Wind Master left before I did, so they should've reached the East Sea by now. Have you not seen them?"

"No!" Ling Wen said. "The East Sea calmed down a while ago, and those two-hundred-something fishermen have all been rescued. But there's no trace of those two on the shores or in the sea!"

"How can that be?!" Xie Lian exclaimed. "Unless..." Unless what?

"Unless what?" Ling Wen asked anxiously. "Your Highness? Your Highness...do you have something else to say? Should we send heavenly officials to the South Sea right now?"

"It's too late," Xie Lian muttered. He shut down the communication array and whirled around. "San Lang."

Hua Cheng seemed like he'd already anticipated his question. His hands were clasped behind his back as he gazed at him in solemn silence.

"Did the two of you reach some sort of agreement a long time ago?" Xie Lian asked.

Hua Cheng didn't immediately respond. Just as he began to move his lips, Xie Lian quickly assured him of his intent.

"No, no, no, don't tell me! You don't have to answer. If you had a prior arrangement with someone, don't go back on your word on my account. I wouldn't want that. It's my fault for asking so suddenly; I didn't mean to put you in a difficult position."

"I'm sorry, Your Highness," Hua Cheng murmured.

Xie Lian shook his head. "Don't apologize. I should've thought of this before. That arrangement must have prevented you from interfering, and from directly telling me the truth."

Hua Cheng had tried to talk him out of it, but he hadn't interfered with Xie Lian's wishes. He accompanied and protected him the whole way, with an escape plan already prepared—except at every turn, something always came up that dragged Xie Lian deeper into the heart of the affair.

"I should be thanking you," Xie Lian said.

"You've figured everything out?" Hua Cheng asked.

Xie Lian nodded. "Pretty much. In fact, I should've figured this out a long time ago. He really is incredible. I'd often overthink it and dismiss my own suspicions, and I wound up overlooking the most straightforward possibility."

After a pause, he continued, "And he really did give you face. He put in considerable effort to send me away peacefully and wasted a lot of time on the detour."

"Your Highness," Hua Cheng said, "this whole thing ends here. It's over."

Xie Lian sighed. "I wish that was the case. But he might have crossed the line."

There was a moment of silence, and then Hua Cheng said gently, "Let them take care of their own affairs. You made it home, and there's no way for you to get back to the Demon Lair anyway."

"Don't be so sure," Xie Lian said.

Hua Cheng froze upon hearing this.

"I have an idea. It only came to me just now. I have a way to connect with Lord Wind Master," Xie Lian said.

He started forming a hand seal.

"So, I'm sorry, San Lang. I have to go back for a little while."

Hua Cheng caught on the moment he saw that hand seal. He clearly hadn't expected this move, and his eye widened.

"Gege...?"

Xie Lian said, loud and clear: *"Soul...Shifting...Spell!"*

As he closed his eyes, a familiar weightless sensation seized him—like his soul was yanked out and hurled high into the air before plunging back down. When he opened his eyes again, the sight before him wasn't Hua Cheng's face. He found himself fleeing through mountainous woods under an endless, starless night sky. Xie Lian could hear harsh breathing coming from his mouth and the violent pounding of his heart.

Success!

The Soul-Shifting Spell wasn't used often, and it burned a great deal of spiritual power. It was stronger than spiritual communication and considered pretty questionable, so its use was fairly rare. The blocking parameters of spiritual barriers usually didn't take it into consideration.

He and Shi Qingxuan had used the Soul-Shifting Spell that fateful night, and Shi Qingxuan hadn't had the chance to seal his spiritual consciousness before he lost his powers and became mortal. To explain further, it was like the two of them had exchanged the keys to each other's houses and made use of each other's home. After they switched back, Shi Qingxuan should've changed the locks on his door so Xie Lian couldn't reenter. Because he didn't, Xie Lian could still use the key from before. However, Shi Qingxuan could no longer open Xie Lian's door, so the two were now using the same body. Xie Lian's own body probably had gone limp and collapsed... Perhaps Hua Cheng had caught him before he hit the ground?

Shi Qingxuan was out of breath and completely overwhelmed with terror. It seemed he was fleeing from pursuit. Xie Lian listened intently and heard the sound of hellish wailing from behind them—it was the band of madmen that had been locked up in the iron prison. They seemed very fond of Shi Qingxuan—even to the point of yearning for him. They pursued him relentlessly, with their eyes rolled back and their tongues lolling from their mouths. Shi Qingxuan's ribs and lungs were burning with the strain of his flight. He was on the verge of tears, and he wanted to scream but had no voice to do so. Xie Lian could tell that he was running without mind or method; he wouldn't last much longer like this. So he assumed direct control of his body.

"Lord Wind Master!"

He used Shi Qingxuan's mouth to speak, and Shi Qingxuan was so surprised he almost bit his tongue.

"Who?! Who's in my body?!"

"My Lord, please calm down!" Xie Lian said. "I've come to you using the Soul-Shifting Spell! Give me your body—I'll help you run."

Xie Lian felt two lines of hot tears fly from Shi Qingxuan's eyes. "Your Highness?! How reassuring! You're so dependable! Thank you!"

"No need for thanks!" Xie Lian said. "Listen to me, Lord Wind Master! Run away!"

"Aren't I already running?!" Shi Qingxuan exclaimed.

"I don't mean like this," Xie Lian explained. "I mean you need to escape..."

As he spoke, several filthy madmen leapt from the woods and lunged at Shi Qingxuan. Xie Lian cracked his knuckles and vaulted into the air to unleash thirty rounds of power kicks. The madmen were knocked to the ground, left crying and unable to get back up. Shi Qingxuan's jaw dropped.

"Did I do that? That's amazing. Martial gods are so awesome! I want to be a martial god too now."

Xie Lian, however, earnestly killed his joy. "My Lord, you can't. Your physique isn't made for the martial path..."

The two talked using the same body, as if one person were asking and answering their own questions. From an outside perspective, it was truly bizarre.

"Lord Wind Master, where's Lord Water Master?" Xie Lian asked.

Shi Qingxuan scanned the area. "I don't know where Ming-xiong or my brother went. When I opened the door, I was still in the Nether Water Manor; I was only sent to a different room. I don't know where things went wrong..."

Without warning, Xie Lian rolled from the balls of his feet onto his tiptoes and leapt into a tree. Shi Qingxuan didn't understand this change of route, but having his body spring about and move so freely was a curious feeling, so he allowed Xie Lian to control him as he willed. They lightly and nimbly shimmied onto a tree branch.

"Your Highness, why did you suddenly…"

Before Shi Qingxuan could finish, Xie Lian covered his mouth… which was also his own mouth. Xie Lian quickly crept to the tip of the branch and kept himself low to hide in the dense leaves.

At the end of the road, a slender shadow stumbled into view. Upon closer inspection, it was Ming Yi. He still looked tragic, which gave a dead air to his good looks, though he could still manage to walk. Shi Qingxuan was overjoyed and dropped his hand to call out to him, but Xie Lian immediately raised his hands to cover his mouth again. This time he used both hands, smothering himself so firmly he could hardly breathe. Shi Qingxuan wasn't a rash person and knew that Xie Lian must be doing this for a reason, so he didn't fight it, simply watched as Ming Yi walked past them down that little path. Once he was gone, Xie Lian loosened his grip and stealthily slipped out of the tree, then snuck back into the dense woods.

After they'd run for a while, Shi Qingxuan glanced back and whispered, "Your Highness, why didn't you let me call out to Ming-xiong earlier?"

Xie Lian's only response was to bring their mad sprint to a dead stop. Shi Qingxuan glanced ahead, and his pupils shrank in an instant.

Ming Yi clearly should have been far behind at this point, but here he was, standing right in front of him. Or rather, them.

Ming Yi supported himself with a nearby tree and frowned at the sight of Shi Qingxuan. "Why are you here too?"

"I…" Shi Qingxuan blurted.

Xie Lian didn't speak but instead moved a hand behind his back and waved—a sign not to let anyone know there was a third "person" present. Shi Qingxuan understood, but the furrow of Ming Yi's brow only deepened.

"What're you doing with your hand behind your back? Are you hiding something?"

Shi Qingxuan urgently shoved both hands forward, palms open, to show him. "No!"

Xie Lian could feel his blood run cold and waves of numbness run down his spine. Although Shi Qingxuan considered Ming Yi very dependable, it seemed his abrupt appearance also gave him quite a fright.

Ming Yi looked bewildered. "I didn't mean I actually wanted you to show me."

His expression was one of disdain, but it was also incredibly familiar. Shi Qingxuan sighed in relief, and the goosebumps that had raised on half his body began to fade. In contrast, Xie Lian was immensely anxious, but he didn't dare to speak rashly and remained silent.

"Where's Lord Water Master?" Ming Yi asked.

"You haven't seen my brother either?" Shi Qingxuan replied. "I've been looking for him everywhere. Didn't you say you could send us off Black Water Island? How come His Highness made it back, but we're still here?"

Xie Lian listened and grew more apprehensive with each word spoken between them. While he did his best to suppress Shi Qingxuan's involuntary reflex to giggle when nervous, it wasn't like Shi Qingxuan to speak so seriously. Thus, he furiously tugged at his own hair and pointed at Ming Yi, yelling accusations.

"Ming-xiong! Didn't I tell you to practice more in your free time?! Did you draw the array wrong again because you're rusty?!"

The act was a bit exaggerated but rather effective all the same. Sure enough, Ming Yi's face dropped.

"Screw off! Draw it yourself if you have the skill."

He said that, but he walked over nevertheless—evidently, he hadn't noticed anything amiss. Shi Qingxuan was still frozen in place, so Xie Lian hurriedly moved on his behalf. He went over and put his arm under Ming Yi's shoulders, assisting him.

"Ming-xiong, how are your injuries? The poison isn't getting worse, is it?"

Ming Yi shook his head. "It's fine. Let's find Lord Water Master first."

Shi Qingxuan nodded, and the two slowly made their way along the forest path. Xie Lian groaned with frustration, unable to find a chance to warn Shi Qingxuan of his suspicions. Suddenly, he felt his mouth fall open—Shi Qingxuan was soundlessly moving his lips. Xie Lian paid eager attention to the shapes he was forming.

"Just what exactly is going on?" he said.

Ming Yi was so close to them and would surely notice. For fear of being discovered, Xie Lian lowered Shi Qingxuan's head slightly and responded with his lips as well.

"He's fake."

The moment the words fell from his lips, Xie Lian could feel goosebumps spring up on his arms.

Shi Qingxuan's eyes bulged. *"Fake?! Then who is he?!"* he mouthed to him.

Xie Lian gave his soundless answer.

"The Reverend of Empty Words," he said.

Shi Qingxuan drew in a sharp breath.

Ming Yi's voice came from ahead. "What is it?"

Shi Qingxuan inhaled that sharp breath completely, then exhaled. His voice trembled as he replied. "I'm scared."

Ming Yi was quiet for a moment, then said, "It's too early to be scared."

In the past, such a response would no doubt have been interpreted as a twisted form of comfort. But right now, it sounded like a threat, and the words radiated an unspeakable chill.

Shi Qingxuan lowered his head and mouthed to Xie Lian, *"No way. The Reverend of Empty Words can't shapeshift!"*

Truthfully, Xie Lian had felt "Reverend of Empty Words" wasn't quite appropriate even as the words left his mouth. It was too disrespectful, too impertinent. A few days ago, the Reverend of Empty Words that Shi Qingxuan had bumped into was no more than a minion, a pathetic clone, some leftover crumbs of the real thing.

And so, he gave a second answer.

"Black Water Demon Xuan."

Shi Qingxuan tripped.

"What's with you now?" Ming Yi demanded.

Shi Qingxuan's teeth were chattering. "I want to die..."

"Dream on," Ming Yi responded coldly.

There it was again, that familiar frosty tone of voice and those equally icy, cruel words. It was the same as it had always been, but now it took on a completely different meaning. This was far from over.

Xie Lian soundlessly gave a third name.

"He Xuan."

Shi Qingxuan seemed unable to take it anymore, as Xie Lian could feel his heart pounding like a drum.

Coincidentally, they were just crossing a small creek. Making a decision on the spot, Xie Lian said through Shi Qingxuan's mouth, "Ming-xiong, I think you'd better rest a little before we continue searching!"

"You think we have time to rest right now?" Ming Yi replied.

"You're poisoned. The more you move, the more the poison will circulate," Xie Lian said for Shi Qingxuan. "Even if you don't want to rest, mortals like me have to. Sit down, I'll go get some water."

He forced Ming Yi to sit on the grass, trying his best to keep their hands and feet steady and to stop any visible shivering. He went to the creek alone, and once he got there, Xie Lian used the noise of the current to cover their hushed conversation.

Shi Qingxuan cupped a palmful of water and splashed it on his face to calm down. "Your Highness, what are you saying?!" he hissed. "Who exactly is the person behind me?! Did one of those three shapeshift into Ming-xiong?! Or did they all possess him at once?!"

"Lord Wind Master, calm down!" Xie Lian said. "It's not them, it's *him*! There's only one person next to you right now. It's *always* been that same person, right from the start. No one shapeshifted. No one was possessed!"

"But...but Ming-xiong, he..." Shi Qingxuan mumbled.

"Don't call him Ming-xiong anymore. The real Ming-xiong is long dead!" Xie Lian said.

"How do you know? Did you see?" Shi Qingxuan pressed him.

"I wasn't the only one who saw," Xie Lian said. "You did too. The real Lord Earth Master was the skeleton worshipped inside the Nether Water Manor! Why do you think *he* couldn't properly control the Earth Master's crescent shovel? It's because it didn't belong to *him* in the first place! The one behind you...his original name, given centuries ago, was He Xuan. After cultivating into a supreme, his name became Black Water Demon Xuan. He devoured the real Reverend of Empty Words and had it chase you. He imprisoned and murdered the real Earth Master. He took on the Earth Master's name long ago and assumed his position in the heavens!"

Just as he finished, he froze.

A hand had tapped his shoulder without warning.

65

End the Deadlock, Water Master Battles Demon Xuan

MING YI'S VOICE CAME from behind. "What are you grumbling about all alone?"

Shi Qingxuan's body stiffened. "I...I...I..."

Xie Lian wanted to help him respond, but Shi Qingxuan's tongue was refusing his control. It couldn't be helped; his most trusted, beloved friend had turned out to be the one he feared the most, hiding right beside him all this time. Now that there was no one around to help, there was no telling what he planned to do. Who wouldn't be scared?

Suddenly, Ming Yi's fingers dug in. Pain flared in Shi Qingxuan's shoulder as he was pushed to the ground.

At the same time, a ghastly pale white hand lunged from the creek and groped the empty space that Shi Qingxuan's neck had occupied just moments before.

A water ghost!

The hand's attack missed thanks to Ming Yi's timely push, and Ming Yi parried with a palm blast. Screams came from beneath the water—whatever creature lurked beneath was probably obliterated by that strike. Shi Qingxuan still lay sprawled on the ground where he'd been shoved, and Ming Yi pulled him up.

"What were you thinking, using some random water in the Black Water Demon Lair to wash your face?!"

"..."

Shi Qingxuan had just washed his face with the water of a creek that was contaminated with the putrefying corpses of water ghosts. He should have felt disgusted, but he had no mind right now to notice such details. His face and hair were still dripping wet. He was as drenched as a drowned dog and looked equally as lost and forlorn. Mind completely blank, he let "Ming Yi" pull him up and followed along behind him.

Truthfully, everything about "Ming-xiong" had always smelled a bit fishy if he thought about it.

He was the Earth Master, so he drew every teleportation array waypoint along the journey. The technique should've been his specialty, but he ran into problems at every juncture. The four of them were inexplicably sent from Puqi Shrine to the town of Fu Gu. And then, when it came time to transport the Wind and Water Masters from Black Water Island, there was another hiccup.

Was it because the transportation chamber was in disrepair? Was it something else causing ghostly mischief? Was the mastermind omnipotent?

Why overthink the issue? The simplest answer was the most likely—Ming Yi had been meddling all along!

When the Wind Master was taken away by the "Reverend of Empty Words," it was "Ming Yi" who had allowed it by losing sight of him; he'd also been the one to discover the Wind Master after he had been robbed of his powers. He had always stayed by Shi Qingxuan's side and knew his fears and tendencies like the back of his hand, and he was certainly close enough to the Wind Master to know his verbal password. Wielding his command of the "Reverend of Empty Words," he was also the one who coerced Shi Qingxuan into opening the doors to the protection array at the Terrace of Cascading Wine.

At the Temple of Wind and Water, he cracked that establishment plaque with his own hands without a hint of remorse. Perhaps it was a necessarily evil...or perhaps it was an entirely purposeful one. What audacious arrogance to openly dismantle his enemy's establishment plaque with such a chivalrous excuse—and his enemy had to be grateful for it!

It wasn't like Xie Lian hadn't been suspicious at times with so many odd little coincidences. He'd tried to probe by asking those three questions, but he'd never imagined that something this inconceivable, this audacious, could happen—that a ghost had impersonated a heavenly official and hidden among them for so long!

Ship-Sinking Black Water kept a "low profile"?

Of course he did, since a low profile was a necessity for someone existing under a different identity for so many years!

"Ming Yi" had devoured the Reverend of Empty Words, and its powers were devoured along with it; he was able to command it as his minion and wield its might as his own. His responses to Xie Lian's three questions were flawless because a Supreme Ghost King would hardly be burdened by the unique quirks of a minion's species. If he wanted to speak the truth, then he could speak the truth. If he wanted to deceive, he could lie as he willed.

And then there was that skeleton. Its dexterous hands and feet matched the expected physique of the Earth Master. Why worship it in the Nether Water Manor? Because those were the remains of a heavenly official. If they weren't treated with solemn respect and were buried carelessly, the bones wouldn't rest in peace. No coffin would hold. And so he was forced to worship it with grand ceremony within his own halls.

With all that said, there was something else that tipped Xie Lian off to his real identity. It was the skeleton's lunge.

The Water Master had asked why the skeleton would experience terminal lucidity, and Ming Yi quickly tried to brush it off by claiming it was reacting to his flippant statement, *"As long as it's not in our way, it doesn't matter who it was."* But that wasn't what had provoked the real Ming Yi at all. It was the part that came after: *"Lord Earth Master"*! He was the real Earth Master, and his impersonator was standing right before him, deliberately and nonchalantly leading the rest of them astray!

He hadn't only meddled all this time. To escape suspicion, "Ming Yi" would sometimes do just the opposite and nudge them back on the right track. He once said to Hua Cheng, *"You really do have spies in the heavens."* As if he wasn't that very spy! That, of course, also explained Hua Cheng's sarcastic response, *"Don't you already know that?"* He'd been mocking this game of pretend.

However, the word "spy" was probably inaccurate. It was more likely an agreement between those two—specifically, an agreement about the exchange of information.

The two Supreme Ghost Kings cooperated for their mutual benefit—wasn't that a win-win? Black Water infiltrated the Upper Court and observed all movement in the Heavenly Realm, big and small. Hua Cheng took root in the Mortal Realm, increasing the number of worshippers. It remained to be seen whether they cooperated in other matters.

When Jun Wu sent the "Earth Master" to infiltrate Ghost City, it was no different from attempting to flood the oceanic Temple of the Dragon King or sending thieves to raid a bandit's lair—completely futile.

It seemed that only two major accidents occurred while he was undercover. The first was that Ascending Fire Dragon spell—an impostor obviously wouldn't instigate such a pointless charade.

Xie Lian was more inclined to think that the real Ming Yi had cast the Ascending Fire Dragon spell during a botched escape attempt.

In order to sneak into the Upper Court in the guise of a total stranger, one must have a thorough understanding of the person being impersonated. Therefore, the impersonated individual must be kept alive to pry out details as they become relevant over the years—information about their life experience, their skills, their methods of manipulating their spiritual device, and so on. The fake Ming Yi likely kidnapped and imprisoned the real Ming Yi right after he passed his Heavenly Tribulation but before his ascension; an impostor would've been easily detected if the real Ming Yi had already known other heavenly officials.

The escape and the subsequent spell were accidents, which was why when Hua Cheng received the news, he had to leave to help his collaborator clean up the mess. And right at that time, Xie Lian received the Ghost City rescue mission from Jun Wu.

While he hadn't thought so at the time, in hindsight, he realized that the operation had gone a little too smoothly. Xie Lian rescued the "Earth Master" from the dungeons of Paradise Manor, but how did he discover said dungeon? He had spotted a cursed shackle on the wrist of Hua Cheng's ghost-masked subordinate and then saw him sneaking around Paradise Manor.

A cursed shackle was a mark of humiliation; when heavenly officials were banished, they would normally hide their shackles from the eyes of others. But the ghost-masked man wore it openly on his wrist. Why did he hide it again on Xie Lian's subsequent Ghost City visits? If it wasn't simple carelessness, the only other explanation was that it was done intentionally to grab Xie Lian's attention and lead him to the "imprisoned" fake Earth Master. The real Ming Yi, the one who'd really set off the distress signal, was likely killed after that. It was impossible to completely destroy his remains and remove all evidence, but keeping the flesh intact would be too great a risk to the masquerade—so it was dissolved until he was nothing but white bones.

The second accident was Shi Qingxuan seeking Xie Lian's help after getting spooked by the return of the Reverend of Empty Words.

It was obvious that Hua Cheng didn't want Xie Lian to be pulled into this affair, which was why Ming Yi declared at Puqi Shrine that *"Coming here was not my will!"* While they searched for Shi Qingxuan at the Terrace of Cascading Wine, Hua Cheng likely left to rendezvous with Ming Yi and demand an explanation for what was happening.

Xie Lian had no opening to explain any of this to Shi Qingxuan, but Shi Qingxuan was clearly thinking through each detail on his own. The hands hidden within his sleeves trembled nonstop.

As the two walked side by side, Xie Lian's mind was churning. Where in the world had Shi Wudu gone?

Shi Wudu was first to leave via the array, and "Ming Yi" was last. He shouldn't have been able to jump over Shi Qingxuan to do anything to Shi Wudu, which meant there were three possibilities. First, Shi Wudu was sent elsewhere. Second, something was waiting wherever Shi Wudu had been sent, and he had become its victim. Third, Shi Wudu left on his own.

If it were the first or second possibility, there was no reason for "Ming Yi" to keep up this act of searching for Shi Wudu in front of Shi Qingxuan.

Having thought that far, Xie Lian heard "Ming Yi" ask, "Where's your golden pendant?"

Shi Qingxuan still hadn't recovered, but Xie Lian was filled with dread. "Ming Yi" had to ask the question a few times before Shi Qingxuan managed a "Huh?"

"Didn't you say that you and your brother used your golden essences to forge those longevity locks?" "Ming Yi" said gruffly. "And that they'll cry out if their masters are hurt?"

"..."

Shi Qingxuan told "Ming Yi" everything, so he of course also knew how this particular spiritual device worked. Which meant he was going to use the golden pendant to find Shi Wudu!

"But...but my scratches healed!" Shi Qingxuan objected.

"That's easy to solve," Ming Yi said coldly, raising his hand.

Is he going to hurt Lord Wind Master?! Xie Lian tensed, ready to go on the defensive. But unexpectedly, Ming Yi squeezed the clotted-over gash on his own arm. It began to ooze blood again.

"Give me the pendant, I'll wear it," he said.

"..."

Xie Lian couldn't help but be awed at the scene playing out before him. Even if this was an act, his ability to take it this far was astounding. He now understood why Shi Qingxuan thought so highly of Ming Yi. Someone like this would truly be worth befriending, if not for the malicious, murderous intent lurking beneath the surface!

Shi Qingxuan was still hesitant, too scared to move. The moment he handed over the longevity lock, the two golden necklaces would cry out for each other. Shi Wudu would surely come find him when he noticed.

"Ming Yi" furrowed his brow. "Are you scared stupid?"

"No...!" Shi Qingxuan said. "Actually, this...this lock, did I never tell you? It only works if I'm the one wearing it."

"Ming Yi" looked doubtful. "Really?"

Shi Qingxuan clutched his longevity lock with a death grip and gave a hard nod. "That's right!"

"Ming Yi" stared at him for a moment but ultimately seemed to abandon the idea. He glanced at the reopened gash on his own arm and didn't say another word.

Just then, the longevity lock around Shi Qingxuan's neck started vibrating. Color drained from Shi Qingxuan's face. "Ming Yi" reacted immediately and started moving in the direction the longevity lock pointed.

"Lord Water Master is over there."

The golden lock's resonance meant that Shi Wudu was wounded. He'd been perfectly well when he entered the array, so what had hurt him since then?

Xie Lian could sense that Shi Qingxuan was torn; he was anxious to go, but at the same time very reluctant to do so. They were trapped in Black Water Lake's illusion, and there was no one else on the island who could help. Pei Ming was building a coffin boat outside the illusion and waiting for their return, and Shi Qingxuan was currently mortal. If Shi Wudu was injured, they'd have nowhere to turn for help. How could they possibly escape if they delivered themselves right to the master's doorstep?

They hurried to follow in the lock's wake. Shi Qingxuan tried speaking up. "Ming...xiong, I think it's a trap. It's probably best not to go!"

"What trap?" "Ming Yi" asked.

To answer him, Shi Qingxuan spun a bold-faced lie. "How could my brother possibly get hurt? It can't be him over there."

Unfortunately, unlike Shi Qingxuan, "Ming Yi" still had a firm hold on logic. "We're in a Supreme Ghost King's territory. Lord Water Master might not have what it takes to protect himself. Let's go there and take a look first."

Shi Qingxuan couldn't think of a reason not to go, and Xie Lian was equally stumped. He watched in silence, planning to play it by ear.

They followed the longevity lock, using its vibration as a guide to grow closer and closer to the target—until finally, they found Shi Wudu curled in on himself on the ground. He was holding his stomach, and he looked distressed and in immense pain.

"Ge!" Shi Qingxuan cried.

He rushed over with Ming Yi trailing close behind. However, when they approached Shi Wudu, the prone figure leapt to his feet and erupted into maniacal laughter as he pulled Shi Qingxuan into a hug. Shi Qingxuan was utterly bewildered as he stood enveloped in those arms, and he only belatedly realized how twisted the man's face was. This wasn't Shi Wudu; it was only a madman dressed in his robes and wearing his golden lock pendant!

Shi Qingxuan hadn't even opened his mouth to speak when "Ming Yi" abruptly collapsed next to him. His chest now had a hole in it the size of a fist, and his blood spilled upon the ground.

A figure in white leapt from a tree, grabbed Shi Qingxuan, and dragged him along as he fled. *"Run!"*

Upon closer inspection, Xie Lian saw that it was the real Shi Wudu!

"Ge?!" Shi Qingxuan exclaimed.

"Don't talk, just come with me! He's no good!" Shi Wudu ordered in a hushed, urgent voice.

In a flash, Xie Lian understood what had happened. As it turned out, Shi Wudu wasn't one to be underestimated. He knew something was off the moment he walked out of the transportation array's chamber and saw he was still in the Nether Water Manor. Shi Wudu didn't overthink things like Xie Lian, and he was much sharper. He immediately suspected Ming Yi, so he hid in the shadows to watch and determine what he was up to. He and Shi Qingxuan were probably sent to different locations, otherwise he would've brought Shi Qingxuan along to hide.

After spotting Ming Yi and Shi Qingxuan together, Shi Wudu had seized a madman and dressed him in his outer robes and golden lock pendant, then hit him with a blast to wound him. It was all bait to lure in Ming Yi and distract him from the ambush he had planned. It was a ruthless move. There wasn't any solid proof that Ming Yi had actually tampered with anything, but Shi Wudu had still shot to kill!

Shi Qingxuan couldn't help but look back. When he did, he saw "Ming Yi" lying as still as a corpse. And then he sat up. The blast had pierced right through his heart. He stoically looked down to stare at the gory hole, then slowly rose to his feet.

Shi Qingxuan's blood ran cold, and Xie Lian could feel it in his own heart. Even a heavenly official shouldn't be able to move so easily after being wounded this severely—he had to be something inhuman!

As the two brothers continued their flight, suddenly the hairs on the back of Xie Lian's neck stood all at once.

"Watch out!" he shouted.

He yanked at the Water Master. A sharp noise whistled by, leaving a chilling light in its wake. The Water Master would've lost his head if not for Xie Lian's tug.

Those invisible creatures from the water's reflection had returned!

Shi Wudu cursed, then he flipped the Water Master fan open backward and swung. Several long, thin water arrows shot from the waves painted on the surface of his fan, and they encircled their bodies to form a protective shield. The invisible creatures couldn't do anything to breach the barrier, and the two brothers continued to run.

Shi Qingxuan couldn't help but look back again. This time, *he* could feel his hair stand on end.

"He...he's catching up!"

Sure enough, "Ming Yi" was about seventy meters behind, following them at a heavy, dolorous pace. Although his steps appeared slow, the distance between him and the two brothers grew significantly shorter with each one he took. It looked as though, in just a few more steps, he'd be able to touch the hems of their robes.

Shi Wudu never looked back. With another swing of his fan, twenty or thirty more dragon-shaped water arrows shot forth. With one more swing, their numbers doubled. He fluttered the fan rapidly, and the hundreds of razor-sharp water arrows hurtled toward "Ming Yi" and barraged him from all sides. Though they were made of water, they slashed through the air like steel blades. If he took a single misstep, his body would be riddled with holes—and yet "Ming Yi" caught the very first water arrow with his bare hands. He yanked like it was the end of a rope, and with that motion, the Water Master fan was snatched from Shi Wudu's hand!

The water dragon arrows dancing wildly in the skies dissolved the moment the fan left his hand, and a weak drizzle rained upon them. Shi Wudu abruptly stopped in his tracks and looked at his hand in disbelief. Over his centuries-long tenure, no one had ever been able to seize the Water Master fan from his hand. He now knew he couldn't escape and finally looked back.

"Ming Yi" was still stalking steadily toward them with his hands clasped behind his back. He was going through an intricate full-body transformation. With every step, a change occurred. His already-blanched face became even paler until it resembled Hua Cheng's bloodless translucence. His forehead grew sharper, his brow deeper, and these shifts made him appear even more somber.

Upon his black robes, subtle patterns of waves appeared on the once-unremarkable corners of the hems, woven with thin threads and shimmering with a mysterious silver glow. By the time he arrived before the Wind and Water Masters, although his face was mostly the same, he was clearly a completely different person.

The Earth Master wasn't a martial god, so he had no talent for martial arts and his spiritual powers were only average. However, neither of these points applied to the one before them now.

"What, exactly, are you?" Shi Wudu cautiously demanded.

"Ming Yi" seemed to find the question funny. He squinted in amusement. "You're standing in my territory, yet you still need to ask?"

"...Black Water Demon Xuan?" Shi Wudu ventured.

"Ming Yi" turned his gaze to Shi Qingxuan, but Shi Qingxuan didn't react.

"You've always been the Earth Master? Or..." Shi Wudu trailed off and seemed to come to a conclusion similar to Xie Lian's. "I see."

But he had only realized that Black Water Demon Xuan had infiltrated the heavens.

"You and I have always minded our own business. Well water doesn't interfere with that of rivers, and we've likewise ruled over our own domains," Shi Wudu said. "It was not my intent to intrude in your territory, so why don't we both take a step back?"

"Well, well, Water Tyrant. It seems there *are* times when you dare not be tyrannical," Ming Yi mused aloud.

Shi Wudu was proud by nature, and displeasure flashed across his face at this comment. Since they were under someone else's roof and his younger brother was by his side, he had to lower his head—but he still wasn't willing to back down.

"I would have no reason to fear you, were it not the wrong place and time."

"Ming Yi" took another step forward. "Shi Wudu, look at my face," he said icily. "Do you know who I am?"

Shi Wudu stared at him, a frown creasing his mouth. He had seen the Earth Master a few times, so he didn't understand what he was trying to say.

"Who do you *want* me to say you are?" He paused for a moment, thinking "Ming Yi" was hinting that his identity must not be revealed. He offered, "It doesn't matter who you are. I swear on my Water Master title, as long as you don't involve me or my brother, nothing you do will concern me..."

"Ming Yi" frigidly cut him off before he could finish.

"Men of importance truly have short memories. Water Tyrant, how many mortal names and mortal births did you so arduously flip through to find me? It hasn't even been—what, a few hundred years? And you've already forgotten what I look like?"

Shi Wudu's face contorted by degrees as he listened to this. There was a mortal idiom for manifested terror, "You look as though you've seen a ghost." For the first time in his life, Shi Wudu showed that very expression on his face. His pupils shrank to pinpricks.

"You're still alive?!" he blurted.

"I'm *dead*!" He Xuan coldly corrected him.

With four fingers pressed together, he swung his palm upward. Xie Lian felt a sudden pain surge through his skull. It seemed He Xuan's spiritual field had affected Shi Qingxuan's body, and they fainted.

An unknown amount of time passed before Xie Lian and Shi Qingxuan slowly regained consciousness together. Xie Lian could feel something rubbing back and forth against him. As he sluggishly opened his eyes, he saw that he was being nuzzled by several foul-smelling, hairy heads. A mob of madmen surrounded him, giggling and looking shy as they felt him all over. Xie Lian remained fairly calm at the sight, as he'd determined that their peculiar attention wasn't life-threatening; the madmen were just a little dirty, not a threat. However, Shi Qingxuan was appalled. He wanted to push them away immediately, but loud *clings* and *clangs* sounded with each attempt. There was coldness around his hands and feet, and he couldn't move an inch. When he looked up, he realized that he was cuffed to the wall by iron chains as thick as wooden clubs. His arms were raised up high.

From the look of the floors and ceiling, he was probably back at the Nether Water Manor. Xie Lian could feel exactly what Shi Qingxuan was feeling, which at the moment was a deep, searing pain in his head. He tried to bid the Lord Wind Master to be calm, to assure him that he would teach him how to break free from cuffs such as these, but he abruptly realized that he couldn't make a single sound!

Perplexed, Xie Lian quickly took stock of his own condition and found that a large portion of his spiritual power had been lost. His soul was still able to stay in Shi Qingxuan's body, but he could no longer manipulate him or even speak to warn him.

Could the spiritual powers he'd borrowed from Hua Cheng have run dry? Impossible. Hua Cheng knew exactly how much spiritual power it took to perform the Soul-Shifting Spell, and he had given him an extremely generous loan of significantly more than what was needed and not a bit less. And Xie Lian could sense the powers draining away with each passing moment. It was making him both leery and anxious.

A raspy voice called out from across the room. "Qingxuan!"

Shi Qingxuan's vision was blurry, but when he focused his eyes in the voice's direction, he could see that it was Shi Wudu calling him.

Shi Wudu wasn't fettered by iron shackles, but he was kneeling on the ground. His white robes were filthy and in wild disarray. Relief visibly washed over his face when he saw Shi Qingxuan wake up, and he seemed to want to come over. However, his attempt was thwarted—he was kicked down by the one standing next to him and forced to kneel anew.

The man standing there wore a cruel, sinister expression, and his hands were clasped behind him. His skin was so pale it sent shivers down one's spine. This was Black Water Demon Xuan—or rather, He Xuan.

There was an altar behind him. Four smooth, obsidian-black urns sat serenely upon it. Two shredded fans were discarded on the floor—the Wind Master fan and the Water Master fan.

Father, mother, sister, fiancée.

"Kowtow," He Xuan ordered.

Shi Wudu kept his eyes on Shi Qingxuan. He gave a single word in response: "Fine."

With that, surprisingly, he heeded. He moved to kneel before the altar and kowtowed before the urns over a dozen times. *Thud, thud, thud.* After this, he attempted to raise his head, but He Xuan's foot came down heavily and stomped his skull back in place.

"Did I permit you to rise?" he coldly asked.

This brutal move pinned Shi Wudu's face to the floor. Shi Wudu answered through gritted teeth, blood running from every orifice.

"...No."

His elder brother was once so proud that his head never bowed, but now, his face was being stomped into the dirt. Although Shi Qingxuan knew he deserved retribution ten times worse for what he'd done, blood was thicker than water. Ultimately, he couldn't bear to see him like this.

"Ge..."

He Xuan's attention was drawn by the sound of Shi Qingxuan's voice, and he was now the focus of that chilling glare. Even though he couldn't raise his head, Shi Wudu knew that meek cry would do nothing but provoke their captor.

"Be quiet!" he barked at once.

After a moment's thought, He Xuan removed his boot from his head. Shi Wudu was filled with trepidation but had no strength to drag himself up.

"Qingxuan!" he groaned.

He Xuan languidly approached the wall. The madmen scampered away whimpering; they were obviously terrified of him. However, they still sneaked glimpses at Shi Qingxuan, as if there was something on him that they coveted.

Shi Qingxuan watched from where he was chained as He Xuan came closer, step by step. The ever-so-familiar face that Shi Qingxuan once knew was now dreadfully foreign.

He Xuan crouched in front of him. He was quiet for a moment before he asked, "Is the Reverend of Empty Words scary?"

Though his tone was smooth and calm, Shi Qingxuan was bug-eyed with fear. He couldn't speak a word in response through his quivering lips.

The Reverend of Empty Words of the past was already extremely horrifying. The person looking at him now had *swallowed* the Reverend of Empty Words. He was ten times, a hundred times more terrifying than the nightmare of his younger years.

But that terror was something Shi Qingxuan should've endured from the start.

"He Xuan," Shi Wudu called to him. "A man must answer alone for what he has done. It was my idea to use you to ward off his misfortune; this has nothing to do with my little brother."

He Xuan sneered. "Nothing to do with him?"

Without blinking once, he stared at Shi Qingxuan and spoke each word with clear enunciation and intent.

"Your little brother, an ordinary, *common* mortal, obtained the ability to ascend. His endless glory was plundered from my fate; he enjoyed *my* divinity. And you tell me that this has nothing to do with him?"

Every word was a knife, and every cut stabbed the heart. This was said for Shi Qingxuan to hear, and though he knew it all by now, he still bowed his head and felt like he could never hold it high again.

"You...you've always been by his side, so you should know very well that I'm not lying to you," Shi Wudu said with forced calm. "He's not one to hide anything; from start to finish, he genuinely did not know!"

"That's precisely why he's so detestable!" He Xuan interrupted sharply. "Why was he allowed to know nothing?!"

Shi Qingxuan's head bowed even lower.

What right did he have to suck another's blood and trample another's bones to reach the skies, all the while maintaining his peace of mind? To enjoy such luxuries without any sense of burden?

"He didn't know then, but is he still so ignorant?!" He Xuan added.

Shi Qingxuan looked up. His voice trembled. "Ming-xiong, I..."

"Shut up!" He Xuan shouted.

When Shi Qingxuan saw his near-savage expression, he shuddered and went silent. He Xuan whirled around and started pacing the hall of the Nether Water Manor, growling as he walked.

"I gave you so many chances!"

Shi Qingxuan closed his eyes and clenched his fists. Xie Lian recalled that excessively furious *"Fine. Very well!"* back when they were in the town of Fu Gu. He remembered how "Ming Yi" had tried to stop Shi Qingxuan from following Pei Ming to the East Sea.

But each time, Shi Qingxuan had chosen to help Shi Wudu.

"...I'm sorry," Shi Qingxuan whispered.

He Xuan stopped in his tracks. "And what good is your apology?" he demanded.

The four urns had been placed directly in Shi Qingxuan's field of view, and it seemed as if they too jeered at his featherlight sorry. Misery pierced his heart and scorched his insides as if his words meant nothing no matter what he said.

"...I know it's futile, but I..." Shi Qingxuan pleaded.

"But you *what*?" He Xuan's tone returned to its cold indifference. "You know it's futile, but you still want to express your utmost sincerity? Are you hoping you can move me? Make me let go of this grudge and allow my resentment to dissolve?"

"No! No! That's not what I meant!" Shi Qingxuan said hastily. "It's just... It's just, I...I really am very sorry that I wronged you. Really. Ming...He...He-gongzi. I know that both my brother and I are in the wrong. There's no remedying the situation at this point, so..."

He Xuan was listening intently. "So?"

At this point, any further words would only sound feeble and pathetic. Shi Qingxuan tried desperately to come up with something, but he drew a blank and was unable to continue.

"Well, talk. Why did you stop?" He Xuan asked coldly. "So are you willing to die for your sins?"

Shi Qingxuan was shocked. Shi Wudu couldn't listen anymore and shouted, "*He Xuan!* The offense was mine—mine and the Reverend of Empty Words'! Qingxuan's sin doesn't merit a death sentence, you..."

"And who in my family sinned?" He Xuan countered. "Who in my family deserved death?"

Shi Wudu choked.

"Go on. Tell me," He Xuan continued. "Are you willing?"

"...I am," Shi Qingxuan whispered.

He Xuan sneered at this. Since Shi Qingxuan had his head bowed, Xie Lian couldn't see his expression, but he probably wouldn't be able to discern what he was feeling even if he saw.

He Xuan stalked away with his hands clasped behind him. That group of madmen saw him leave and came to surround Shi Qingxuan once more, hugging his arms and thighs and refusing to let go. Some tugged at his hair, some draped themselves around his neck. Each of them had a ravenous glint in his eyes, like he wanted to eat him alive. Xie Lian had lived among the homeless in the past, but even he felt his hair stand on end. *Just who are these people? Why did Demon Xuan gather a bunch of madmen here?*

Shi Qingxuan silently endured the pushing and shoving of the madmen, tolerating their pulling and dragging, too frightened to make a sound. He Xuan observed detachedly for a while before he spoke.

"Do you know who these people are?"

Emaciated, claw-like fingers felt all over Shi Qingxuan's face and body. He didn't even dare to breathe, much less ponder who those people were, so he shook his head.

"Rotten fates. Contemptuous fortunes. Lives lower than an animal's. Fates that can drive a man mad," He Xuan explained.

"..."

Cold dread washed over Xie Lian. He had an inkling of what He Xuan planned to do. Shi Wudu understood at once, his eyes bulging.

"You...?!"

He Xuan stood between Shi Wudu and Shi Qingxuan.

"I'm giving you two options."

He pointed at Shi Wudu.

"Option one. Pick one individual from this crowd and exchange your brother's fate with theirs. And then, go make yourself scarce in the Mortal Realm."

Shi Wudu's eyes grew bloodshot, and his shoulders started to shake.

"Since you enjoy switching fates so much, you must be quite skilled at it," He Xuan commented. "No need for me to guide you through the process."

If the motives behind this punishment were disregarded, then it was truly vicious. Although Shi Qingxuan's original fate wasn't good enough to ascend, it was still a life filled with peaceful luxury and leisure. The madmen, on the other hand, were racked with disease and rotten sores and had been driven to madness by adversity. It was clear that every single one of them was ensnared by an absolutely wretched, miserable fortune. If Shi Qingxuan exchanged fates with any of them, wouldn't that mean he would fall into the same tragic state? Such fates would drive one to madness in and of themselves. He would suffer endless agony and torment from then after.

Faced with this disaster, it was obvious Shi Wudu now had no chance of passing his Heavenly Tribulation. Furthermore, he would no doubt be banished now that the affair with the Reverend of Empty Words had been revealed. Once banished to the Mortal Realm, he would no longer be able to switch Shi Qingxuan's fate to a better one. A common mortal with his powers stripped away and a common mortal suffering the most wretched of fortunes—how could they possibly keep living?

Shi Wudu huffed a breath and gritted his teeth. "And the second option?"

"The second option," He Xuan continued. "You."

This time, he eyed Shi Qingxuan. Each word was spoken slowly and clearly.

"I won't touch your fate. Chop off your brother's head. Right here."

Clang!

He threw a rusty knife to the floor. Shi Qingxuan stared at it, his eyes wide.

"And then never show yourself to me again. In return, I will pretend you never existed."

His bones had steeped in the brine of hatred for centuries, and it had boiled over all at once. Anyone could see the fervent madness that burned in his eyes. Anyone could see that he wasn't bluffing.

After a moment of silence, Shi Wudu croaked, "...I'll kill myself. Let me do it to myself."

"You have no right to bargain with me," He Xuan stated.

Shi Wudu glanced at Shi Qingxuan. "You're asking for our lives..." he mumbled miserably.

Shi Qingxuan, however, hadn't succumbed to despair just yet. "Ge! *Ge!* Let's...let's choose the first option. The first one," he said hurriedly.

A moment later, Shi Wudu regained control of himself. "No. I choose the second one."

"..." Shi Qingxuan was dumbfounded. "Why the second option? Can't we both live? Ge, let's go with the first one, I really can't do the second..."

"Quiet!" Shi Wudu furiously snapped. "Don't you know me? You think *I* can do it—lose everything and be forced to watch you become a filthy wretch?! You might as well infuriate me to death!"

"Ge!" Shi Qingxuan exclaimed. "Let it go... Clinging to life is still better than a good death. Besides, really, if you think about it, we've... we've lived for centuries now, it's time to...it's time to..."

As he spoke, he seemed to remember just how well he had lived the past few hundred years, and he was so ashamed he didn't dare continue.

He Xuan was still watching them coldly. Shi Wudu arduously crawled to his feet. He grabbed the rust-mottled knife and stumbled to the wall, then grasped his younger brother's shoulder.

"Come!" Then he whispered harshly, "...Go find General Pei. Ask him to take care of you."

The blade was terrifyingly heavy and covered in rust; it'd be difficult to even kill a chicken with it, never mind a man. Both the executioner and the target would suffer greatly if it was used to cut off someone's head. Shi Qingxuan was so horrified he couldn't keep hold of it and kept dropping it on the ground.

"Forget it, ge, forget it! Haven't you always told me that everyone only cares for themselves, and that there's no reason anyone would look out for us? Haven't we always taken care of ourselves? Don't give this thing to me, *don't give it to me!*"

"Qingxuan! Don't be so immature!" Shi Wudu barked. Then he smiled wryly. "...Your brother's nicknamed the Water Tyrant. It's not like you don't know that. Over all these years, I've raised so many waves that have shaken the world—there have been at least eight hundred, if not a thousand. I have nothing but enemies from heaven to hell. It'll be easier if I die. If I die, then nothing else will happen to you. But if I survive while losing everything, that's a fate worse than death. If I'm not the Water God, I can't take care of you; I won't even be able to protect myself. We probably won't last two days out there... *Take it!*"

Shi Qingxuan was so scared he was going to weep. "No! I can't I can't I can't, ge, I can't, I really can't!" he exclaimed uncontrollably. "Don't force me! *Don't give it to me!* Help, help, *help*!"

He started screaming with every fiber of his being, wailing until he was hoarse, crying desperately to be saved.

"It's all right!" Shi Wudu exclaimed. "Don't be scared, Qingxuan, this won't hurt as much as exchanging fates or stripping away spiritual power..."

He Xuan had been infinitely patient up to this point, but now he lashed out with a kick. Shi Wudu sputtered a mouthful of blood as he was knocked over, and he hit the ground hard, unable to get up.

Shi Qingxuan, still bound to the wall, screamed in distress. "Ge!"

"Quiet! Enough of this revolting brotherly love act," He Xuan said chillingly. "No one here will be moved by you."

Shi Wudu coughed up a large amount of blood. Suddenly, he flipped onto his back and leapt to his feet—and then seized Shi Qingxuan by the neck. Xie Lian was shocked. He felt his lungs cease to draw breath and blood rush to his head.

"...Ge?" Shi Qingxuan gasped.

"Qingxuan! I can't leave you alone like this!" Shi Wudu bit out through his bloodied mouth. "There's no way you'll survive in the world if I die, so you might as well come with gege!"

He squeezed harder. Shi Qingxuan's sight was going dark, and a death rattle escaped his throat. Xie Lian was shocked to the core. Was Lord Water Master really going to strangle Lord Wind Master to death?!

It didn't take long for the pressure on his throat to disappear. Fresh air poured in as Shi Qingxuan gasped and coughed uncontrollably, then finally caught his breath as the choking stopped. He Xuan stood next to them. He had ripped off both of Shi Wudu's arms at the elbows, halting the attempt to wring Shi Qingxuan's neck.

"Did I give you a third path?" he said coldly.

Blood pulsed like a fountain from Shi Wudu's mangled arms, yet he began to laugh uproariously. He Xuan tossed the forearms aside like they were trash.

"What are you laughing about?"

Shi Wudu waved his long, empty, blood-soaked sleeves. "I'm laughing at *you*! I'm laughing at how you think you've got the upper hand! Do you think you've finally gotten your revenge after so many years of waiting? Does it feel *good*?"

"It *does* feel good, seeing you on the brink of death like this," He Xuan confirmed.

"Is that right?" Shi Wudu laughed. "Then let me tell you something. I feel good too!"

He "caught" He Xuan's collar with his profusely bleeding, mutilated arms.

"Because I see you right now—so filled with rage, so filled with suffering, so filled with hate. You're grinding your teeth so hard you're crushing them. And yet you're still powerless to bring your family back! You're still nothing more than a ghost of the gutters. Be as angry as you want, they're *long* gone! But me and my brother, we've lived for ages, we've been heavenly officials for centuries. Even if he can't be one anymore, even if he can't live anymore, he still profited. I still won! And so I feel even better than you! *Ha ha ha ha ha ha...*"

The longer he listened, the more He Xuan's pale face dropped. His expression was like a frozen, barren land had been set ablaze with ghost-fire. The air in the chamber grew suddenly freezing cold.

Shi Qingxuan was terrified to the core. "...Ge, don't talk anymore," he croaked hoarsely. "Can you please stop? Ge, my god, what are you saying? What nonsense are you spewing..."

He Xuan's hand shot out and seized Shi Wudu's neck. "You! Have you no remorse?!"

Shi Wudu laughed maniacally. "Remorse? *Hmph!* What a joke! Ship-Sinking Black Water, to think you're a Supreme Ghost King! You want to talk to me about remorse?! Let me tell you, *there is no such thing!*"

Shi Qingxuan wailed. Shi Wudu continued with his head held high.

"Everything I have today, I fought for! I will fight for what I don't have. I will change my fortune if fate denies me! *My fate is up to me and not the heavens!*"[6]

This was the first time Xie Lian had heard such an interpretation of that proverb—not simply rejecting fate but forcibly altering it—and he was blown away even through the chills that washed over him. He Xuan also burst out laughing, sounding like his eyes had been opened to a brand-new world by Shi Wudu's unshakable tenacity in refusing to admit his own wrongs. His expression grew more and more frightening, and Shi Qingxuan broke down.

"...Gege, please I beg you, *please.* Please stop talking, please shut up. *Help...*"

---

6 A Daoist proverb: [我命由我不由天] / "My fate is up to me and not the heavens." Generally used by those who refuse to bow down to the heavens and accept their fate.

However, Shi Wudu's smug arrogance was undaunted. "Qingxuan, gege will go first. I will wait for you down below. Ha ha ha ha ha ha..."

Before he finished his sentence, He Xuan placed his hand on his head and gripped his hair. Shi Qingxuan's soul was going to leave his body; the iron chains banged and clanged wildly against the wall.

"Ming-xiong! Ming-xiong! I'm sorry, I'm sorry I'm sorry I'm sorry I'm sorry I'm sorry I'm sorry! We're the ones who sinned! We're the ones in the wrong! It's my fault—my brother only did what he did because of me! My brother's gone mad—he's gone crazy, can't you see?! I...I...you...you..."

He wanted to beg for forgiveness, for mercy, but he couldn't. All he could do was kowtow endlessly with his eyes. He Xuan slowly turned his gaze on him. For a fleeting moment, he seemed to have remembered something. He calmed and stopped.

The sight of this was like a ray of hope, and Shi Qingxuan let out a breath of relief. The tears welling in his eyes finally rolled down his cheeks. But before he could speak, he heard He Xuan's cruel reply.

"You called for the wrong person."

In one swift movement, he wrenched Shi Wudu's head from his neck!

"Aaaaaaaaaaaaaaaah—!"

Blood erupted from the uneven stump of Shi Wudu's neck as his head was yanked from his body. The far-reaching spray coated Shi Qingxuan's body and face. Shi Qingxuan could finally endure it no longer and started screaming as if he had just lost his own mind as well.

The madmen found it incredibly interesting to see a headless corpse stand without collapsing, and they went wild with delight. They spun around him in circles, clapping and cheering, their bare feet smearing bloody footprints across the floor.

"Oh my, oh my! He's dead, he's dead!"

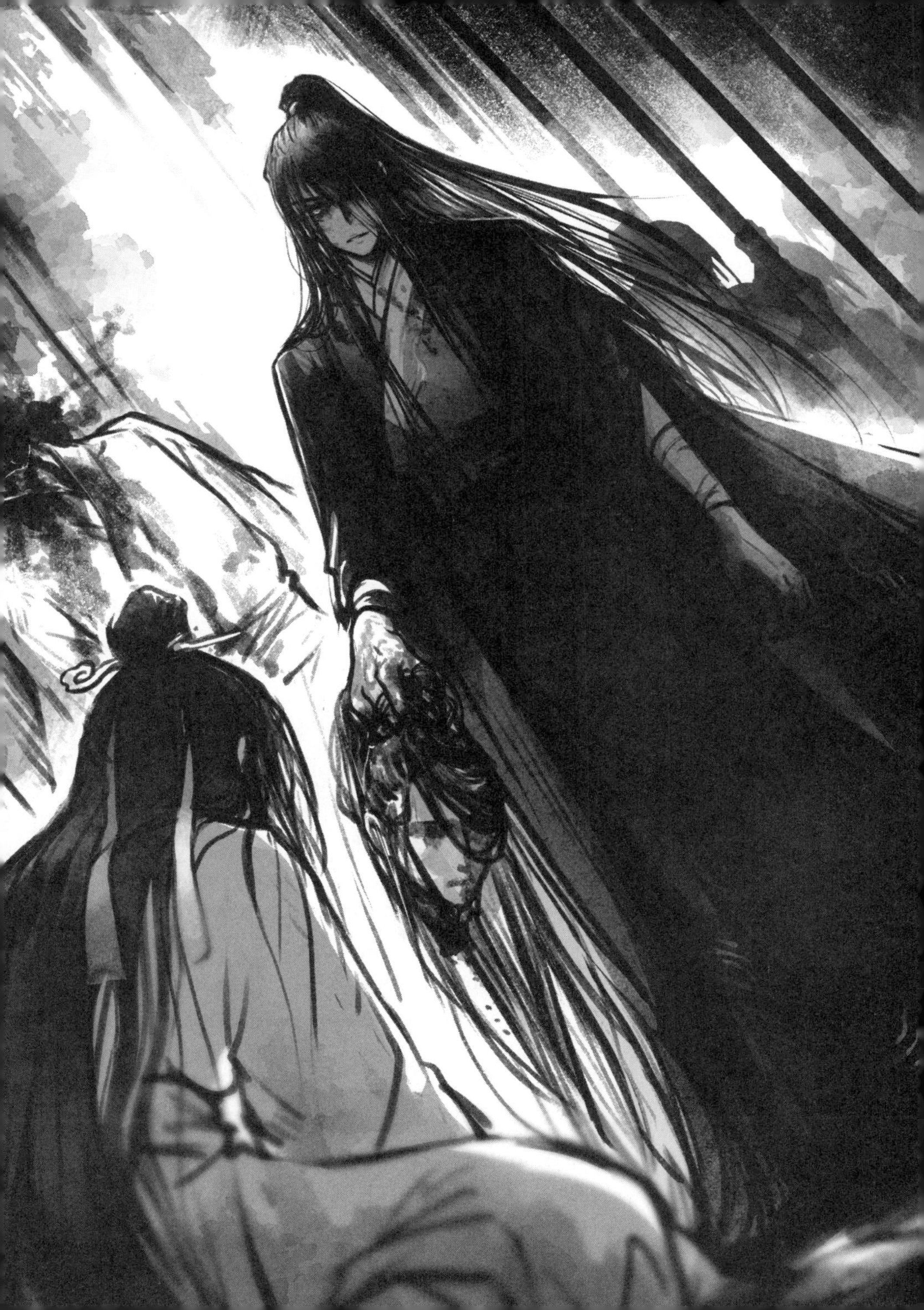

"Dead, *dead*! Hee hee hee!"

Shi Qingxuan screamed for who knew how long, screamed until it felt like his soul and spirit had fled his body, and as the screaming finally ceased, he didn't even remember stopping. When he regained his awareness at last, he had collapsed into a lifeless heap on the blood-soaked floor for an unknown amount of time.

He Xuan stood not far from him. He was staring commandingly down at Shi Qingxuan from above. Shi Wudu's head dangled from his hand, eyes still round and wide.

A moment later, He Xuan asked in monotone, "Do you have anything else you want to say?"

"..."

Shi Qingxuan's eyes were lifeless. His gaze was unfocused as he stared at the row of urns atop the altar before him and at those two shredded fans on the ground.

It was a long time before he mumbled, "...I want to die."

"Dream on," He Xuan responded coldly.

He Xuan extended a hand toward him, and Shi Qingxuan closed his eyes.

At the same moment, Xie Lian's soul was suddenly yanked out and thrust upward!

When he fell back down and reopened his eyes, he found that a red-clad man was embracing his limp body. Hua Cheng was kissing him deeply, with one hand gently holding his chin in place. No wonder the spiritual power supporting the Soul-Shifting Spell had been slipping away so rapidly—Hua Cheng had used the fastest and most effective way to suck out the powers he had lent, and he'd successfully called Xie Lian's soul back into his body.

Seeing Xie Lian wake up, Hua Cheng parted his lips and began to pull away. But under such dire circumstances, Xie Lian had no further mind for propriety. He circled both arms around Hua Cheng's neck and hauled him down to suck back the spiritual powers that Hua Cheng had sucked from him.

Hua Cheng clearly hadn't expected him to do this, and in his moment of carelessness, his reclaimed spiritual powers flowed back the other way. Afraid he was going to break away, Xie Lian cupped his face and then flipped their bodies over to pin Hua Cheng to the ground. He felt a coolness pour into his body; it streamed down his throat and spilled warmth into his stomach.

Just then, the little wooden door of Puqi Shrine creaked open. A giant green figure crawled outside like a caterpillar.

"Fucking hell, which son of a bitch is this bold?! Has some thieving punk dared to come to *my* house to steal and to disturb *my* slumber?! *Achoo!* This ancestor's gonna show you a thing or..."

He trailed off when he saw the two entwined figures outside the shrine, apparently wrapped in each other's arms and kissing with fervent passion. One red, one white—who *else* could they be?

"YIIIEEEEEAAAAAAAAAAH!" he shrieked.

Hua Cheng had raised his hand to grab for Xie Lian's shoulder, but he turned his wrist at the sound of Qi Rong's racket. Qi Rong yelped as he was thrown back inside, and the door slammed shut behind him with a *wham*! Only then did Hua Cheng roll them over again and pin Xie Lian beneath him. He pulled back slightly to gasp harshly for breath. His eye was flickering, its glint dark.

"Your Highness!"

Xie Lian didn't have the time to explain; he wound one arm around Hua Cheng's neck again to pull him down once more.

After he'd sucked down enough spiritual power, he choked out a cough, then cried aloud, *"S-Soul-Shifting Spell!"*

But this time it was like there was a wall blocking him before that upward swing, and his soul rebounded heavily back into his own body. Opening his eyes with a shocked gasp, he found that the scenery above him was still the same starry night sky and Hua Cheng's anxious face.

Xie Lian sat up and hugged his head. "...I can't pass through anymore," he murmured.

Was Shi Qingxuan dead? Did Black Water Demon Xuan reinforce his barrier? No matter the reason, he couldn't return to Shi Qingxuan's body. Even if he rushed to the South Sea that very moment, he'd almost certainly be too late.

Seeing how disconcerted Xie Lian was by this development, Hua Cheng said, "Your Highness, I'm sorry."

Xie Lian looked at him.

"But outsiders shouldn't interfere in this affair," Hua Cheng added.

Xie Lian waved dismissively. "...You don't need to apologize. Honestly, I wouldn't be able to do much even if I were there."

The Soul-Shifting Spell only allowed him to enter Shi Qingxuan's body, and Shi Qingxuan was now nothing more than mortal. Even if Xie Lian could help him break free of those shackles, how could he possibly fight against the master of the Black Water Demon Lair? Escape was impossible.

After swiftly composing himself, Xie Lian reentered the heavenly communication array.

"Ling Wen, have you guys headed out yet?"

"Your Highness!" Ling Wen exclaimed. "Why did you go silent for so long all of a sudden? We've already dispatched a number of heavenly officials to the South Sea. His Highness Qi Ying returned, so he'll head out soon too. But it's not easy to enter the Black Water Demon Lair; who knows when we'll find them."

"Wait, I'll go with you all," Xie Lian croaked. "Maybe I'll still remember the way. But I'll need to trouble you to send someone to pick me up from Puqi Shrine."

"Very well. He just arrived," Ling Wen said.

Slightly confused, Xie Lian turned his head to look. Hua Cheng had disappeared, but he spotted two junior officials walking toward the shrine from the direction of Puqi Village. Behind them was a tall young man with curly raven locks—it was Quan Yizhen.

Xie Lian inclined his head to greet him. Quan Yizhen didn't understand that he should return the courtesy, but Xie Lian hardly minded. He looked around. He didn't see any trace of Hua Cheng anywhere, and Xie Lian knew that he was giving him space to deal with this affair.

The two of them, accompanied by the junior officials, left for the South Sea. At Xie Lian's suggestion, they went out of their way to gather dozens of hefty coffins that had carried the dead to prepare for any unexpected situations. After they had raced over the waters for about six hours, they happened upon a bizarre sight.

The corpses of a number of giant bonefish floated lifelessly on the sea's surface, and their remains knocked into the ship as they sailed along. Many of the heavenly officials were alarmed.

"Are we there?!"

"We can't be," Xie Lian said. "If we had entered the Black Water Demon Lair, the ship wouldn't still be afloat or moving this quickly."

That said, they were clearly sailing through the aftermath of General Pei and the Water Master's battle from the previous night. As they sailed, Quan Yizhen perched on his heels on the ship's railing, maintaining the high-difficulty position with ease. Suddenly, he asked a question.

"There's a black island ahead. Is that the one?"

Xie Lian squinted to look, and sure enough, there was a shadowy landmass not too far away—and it did resemble Black Water Island!

Xie Lian frowned slightly. "It does look like it. But how have we found it so easily? And the ship didn't sink either... Please remain vigilant, everyone. This might be a trap."

But as soon as he spoke, he realized it wasn't. This was because he'd spotted a figure on the beach slashing at logs with a sacred sword that was meant for battle. The figure was building coffins underneath the hot sun; there were already three completed ones set to the side, and a fourth was in progress. Xie Lian started waving.

"*General Pei!* It's General Pei! That's the right island, without a doubt!"

The ship immediately changed tack and sailed swiftly to their new destination. When Pei Ming saw that reinforcements had arrived, he didn't appear particularly delighted; instead he stabbed the sword into the ground and rubbed at his nose.

"What the heck? You had to show up just as I finished making these," he said, sounding grim.

"It's amazing that anyone showed up at all," Quan Yizhen said. "When they heard it was to save you, suddenly no one had time."

"..." Pei Ming's expression seemed to indicate that he couldn't be bothered with children, and he turned to Xie Lian. "Your Highness, you went back first? How did you manage to get this ship to float on the water of the Demon Lair?"

"I don't think it's the ship," Xie Lian said. "The Black Water Demon Lair's curse has dispersed."

Still perplexed, Pei Ming tested this theory—sure enough, he felled a thicket of large trees with just one swing of his sword. His spiritual powers had returned. Speechless for a moment, Pei Ming shook his head.

"Had I known, I wouldn't have worked so hard to build these coffins."

It was true; he'd labored tirelessly all night for nothing. He made coffins for four, but three of them were now useless.

The team of heavenly officials disembarked the ship and ran straight for the heart of the forest. The little ghosts lurking in the woods had never seen a sight like this, and they scampered away in fright. There were no invisible creatures lying in wait when they reached Black Water Lake and no spiritual fields to disrupt their powers. After some examination, they dispersed the illusion cast upon the waters. The iron prison and the Nether Water Manor appeared before their eyes.

Xie Lian collected the remains of the black-robed skeleton when they entered the Nether Water Manor and carried the bundle with him while he frantically searched the palace. Soon, they found the great hall. Two bloody shackles hung empty on the mottled wall. A headless corpse lay sprawled on the floor in the middle of the chamber. Its blood had already run dry, and a group of madmen were throwing random objects at it. The moment the heavenly officials entered, the madmen grew even more excited.

Pei Ming was stunned for a good while before he dared to recognize that corpse. Shaken, he exclaimed, "...Water Master-xiong!"

Of course, Xie Lian already knew that this had happened, and he issued instructions to those around him. "Will everyone please search the manor and the island proper for Lord Wind Master...or his remains."

However, no matter where they looked, there was no trace of Shi Qingxuan on the island.

Had Black Water Demon Xuan taken the Wind Master away? Or perhaps he'd murdered the Wind Master then and there and thrown his corpse into the sea for his flesh to be devoured by fish?

Shi Wudu had gone berserk and provoked He Xuan to violence; he was dead, but he hadn't been killed by Shi Qingxuan's hand. Would He Xuan still go through with his threat to switch Wind Master's fate?

After chasing away the pesky madmen, Pei Ming half crouched on the floor and was lost in thought for a long time. At last, he sighed.

"Water Master-xiong. You were proud your whole life, but it ended like this. I don't even know if your eyes are closed.[7] Truly, the higher you climb, the harder you fall. Life's misfortunes are inescapable. Even as gods, we cannot be spared in the end."

Quan Yizhen, on the other hand, didn't share such deep sentiments. He ran around the Nether Water Manor, his footsteps pitter-pattering everywhere, and wandered into the chamber where they stood for a look. He gave a cursory glance to the dead body and thought it strange.

"Where's his head?"

"It was taken by Black Water Demon Xuan," Xie Lian replied.

"What grudge, what resentment did the Demon Lair Master hold against him?" Pei Ming lamented. "And where's Qingxuan? Or the Earth Master? Did three of the elemental officials perish—Earth, Water, and Wind alike?"

"It was a great grudge indeed, and a great resentment," Xie Lian said. "As for Lord Earth Master, it depends on who you're asking after. The real one is in my hands. The fake one took Lord Water Master's head."

"What?!"

Xie Lian eyed him. "General Pei probably didn't know, right?" he asked softly. "Black Water Demon Xuan's real surname was He. His name is Xuan."

---

7   "To die with eyes closed" means "to rest in peace."

Pei Ming's face changed slightly at the name. It seemed that Pei Ming and Ling Wen weren't completely in the dark regarding what Shi Wudu had done, though the extent of their knowledge couldn't be determined so easily.

Everything that had to be reported was reported, everything that needed to be dealt with was dealt with. When Xie Lian finally returned to Puqi Village, an entire day had come and gone. Xie Lian's steps dragged with exhaustion. When he returned to Puqi Shrine and opened the door, he could hear Qi Rong barking and yelling.

"DOG HUA CHENG! DOG-FUCKED XIE LIAN! Have you two no shame?! AAAAAH, FUCK! What the hell was that in the middle of the night; I'm fucking horrified! My eyes are fucking blinded, you fucking owe me!"

Nothing but vulgarities and profanities spewed from his mouth. Xie Lian was struck by the frightful memory of the night before, when he and Hua Cheng had taken turns pinning each other to the ground, sucking power back and forth. He'd been too panicked to think it embarrassing at the time, but now he had nothing to distract him from keen awareness. He almost threw the door shut and fled.

Hua Cheng had been leaning back in his chair with his boots crossed and propped on the table, but the moment he heard Xie Lian enter, he put his legs down and casually struck the back of Qi Rong's head to knock him out. He then rose to his feet to greet him.

"Gege."

Xie Lian nodded and closed the door behind him. Qi Rong lay prone and bound like a little green worm, and Xie Lian stepped over him to sit down at the table.

"Did Guzi and Lang Ying go out to play?"

"Yeah, I let them out. You've worked hard," Hua Cheng said.

"No, you're the one who worked hard," Xie Lian said.

Hua Cheng flashed a brief smile. Then he said, "I thought gege would blame me."

Xie Lian shook his head. "San Lang doesn't need to overthink things. I really don't blame you. In fact, you were right about this whole thing. Outsiders really...can't possibly interfere."

After some thought, he still asked, "San Lang, what do you think Black Water Demon Xuan will do to Lord Wind Master?"

Hua Cheng was briefly silent before he answered. "I don't know either. Black Water is rather eccentric; he languished alone in misery for far too long. No one can understand what he's thinking."

"No one can understand what he's thinking." Xie Lian remembered that this was similar to remarks many of the heavenly officials in the Upper Court had made about Crimson Rain Sought Flower.

Ship-Sinking Black Water had emerged from Mount Tonglu after slaughtering millions of ghosts, and Crimson Rain Sought Flower had done the same. He Xuan had suffered alone for ages, and Hua Cheng couldn't have suffered any fewer years of solitude.

Hatred was what made Ship-Sinking Black Water. Then what about Crimson Rain Sought Flower?

What made Hua Cheng *Hua Cheng*?

Myriad ideas flashed through Xie Lian's mind in the span of an instant. He shook his head to will away the phantom of that "noble, gracious special someone," and organized his thoughts.

"San Lang, there's something I don't understand. This whole business with the Water Master's fraud must've been done quite covertly, and he deceived everyone for so long. How did Black Water learn the truth? If it'll make things difficult for you to answer, you don't have to respond."

"He fled, moved his domain, and even dropped the heavenly official act. What's left to be difficult at this point?" Hua Cheng replied. "It's simple, actually. The night Black Water died, Shi Wudu personally went to confirm his death."

"Because the Reverend of Empty Words only moves to a new target when the previous is dead?" Xie Lian hypothesized.

"Yeah. Black Water didn't know who he was, but he remembered his face. Later on, when he became a ghost and learned more of the affairs of heaven and earth, he discovered that man was the Water God."

No wonder he remembered, for it was very strange indeed. Why would the esteemed Water God go to observe the death of a random mortal?

"But that alone shouldn't have made him suspect a change of fate had occurred," Xie Lian stated.

"That's why he impersonated the real Earth Master and infiltrated the heavens to investigate," Hua Cheng replied. "Pretty brave, if I must say so myself."

"Worthy to be called brave and astute, indeed... If only he hadn't killed the real Earth Master and dragged over two hundred fishermen into his mess."

However, Hua Cheng had to correct him on this point. "Gege, I don't know if he's the one who killed the real Earth Master. But I'm afraid someone else dragged those fishermen into the storm on the East Sea."

66

Ache of Separation, the Agitated Heart Sends the Path of Ink Astray

XIE LIAN WAS TAKEN ABACK. "Then who could it be? Generally speaking, storms like that shouldn't involve more than fifty people."

"I suspect it may be the same person who sent that empty-shelled cultivator during the Banyue Pass incident."

Now that he mentioned it... It did seem like there was a hand pushing him to the heart of every case every time.

Feeling a little baffled, Xie Lian wondered, "What could that person possibly be after?"

Hua Cheng shook his head, but he also seemed pensive. Suddenly, the sounds of children laughing and playing were heard from outside, and his eyes shot to the window. Following his cutting gaze, Xie Lian saw only two small children—Guzi was riding atop of Lang Ying's shoulders looking completely untroubled and carefree.

The Water Master audaciously deceived the heavens and committed a criminal substitution. The Wind Master was a fake, and the Earth Master was an impostor. On top of all that, the Water Master's severed head was nowhere to be found. Four cases, each a bolt from the blue, and each a burst of explosive thunder that rocked the heavens. Each one was more deafening than the last. This naturally raised a tidal wave that flooded the Upper and Middle Courts.

Everyone was so shaken that they had no idea what to say about the matter, and only crickets could be heard in the Palace of Divine

Might. Even Jun Wu's hand didn't seem able to prop up his head anymore.

Ming Yi had never really gone out of his way to befriend anyone, and barely anyone was close to him aside from Shi Qingxuan—and *he* enjoyed pestering others and assumed everyone was his friend from the moment they met. However, the shock was truly too great when they realized that one of their own colleagues was a legendary Supreme Ghost King.

Over the past centuries, that ghost king had worked with dedication and diligence to properly play the role of the Earth Master. He had amassed a large number of worshippers in the Mortal Realm, and he even managed to make it into the top ten during the Battle of the Lanterns at the Mid-Autumn Festival Banquet. It was honestly frightening, just as expected of a Supreme Ghost King.

Now, even if someone announced that Hua Cheng was among them or had planted a spy in the Upper Court, no further news could surprise them.

There was no question that the one who murdered the real Earth Master Yi was Black Water Demon Xuan, even without mentioning the grudge he held against Water Master Wudu. The Upper Court thus released an official warrant for his arrest, but everyone knew that a Supreme Ghost King who wanted to stay hidden wouldn't be so easily found.

As the saying goes, "All will tread on a man when he falls." The Wind and Water Masters once stood in greatness and glory with hundreds who would answer their call. Shi Wudu was extolled and celebrated every time he appeared, yet after his violent death, his supporters cowered, not daring to breathe a single breath too loud. Shi Qingxuan loved making friends and was generous to all, but now those "good friends" were nowhere to be found. Pei Ming collected

Shi Wudu's headless corpse from the Nether Water Manor, and the ceremony he hosted was quiet and sparsely attended on the day of his burial. There were barely any heavenly officials in attendance besides Xie Lian and Ling Wen.

Xie Lian thought of how in recent days, bands of people had already started to burn down and desecrate Temples of Wind and Water. He couldn't bear the sight of it and tried on several occasions to stop them, but he knew the acts of aggression would only grow worse as time passed and people discovered their prayers were no longer being answered. He could stop them once, but he couldn't stop them forever. In ten years, or perhaps in only three or four, people would completely forget the heavenly officials of Wind and Water who used to rule at the summit of heaven. Xie Lian couldn't help but feel melancholy.

Once the funeral was over, Xie Lian turned to Ling Wen.

"The whereabouts of Lord Wind Master...of *Qingxuan* is now in your hands. We're counting on you."

Ling Wen looked solemn. She hadn't smiled in days. "Even without Your Highness's appeal, I would still do my utmost in this duty."

"Your Highness, why not talk to that Crimson Rain Sought Flower of yours, instead of waiting around while the Palace of Ling Wen drags their feet like an old ox pulling a broken cart?" Pei Ming asked. "Can't you have him ask that mad ghost Black Water where he's taken Qingxuan? He already took Water Master-xiong's head—what more does he want?"

Xie Lian shook his head. "General Pei, please don't assume such things are doable," he replied helplessly. "Does one Supreme Ghost King need to keep the other informed on whatever he wants to do?"

With that, Pei Ming didn't say anything more.

When Xie Lian returned to Puqi Shrine, many of the villagers were milling around the shrine whispering amongst themselves. Xie Lian didn't need to ask to know what was happening thanks to the clearly audible yowling coming from within his shrine. The village chief was visibly scared and nervously tugged at him.

"Daozhang, your mad little cousin, h-h-he, he's…"

The excuse Xie Lian had given the world was that Qi Rong was his insane younger cousin, family he'd taken in out of obligation after he'd been rejected and left without anyone willing to care for him. On some level, this was not entirely a lie.

"Is he throwing a fit again? Don't worry, he's properly locked up. He won't escape. Everyone can go home," Xie Lian said.

"Oh," the villagers murmured amongst themselves and dispersed.

Before the group fully broke up, the village chief gave Xie Lian a basket of eggs. "Um, Daozhang, your Xiao-Hua…"

Xie Lian was confused at first. "…Xiao-Hua?" Then it dawned on him. "Oh, San Lang?"

To the outside world, Hua Cheng was currently posing as Xie Lian's younger blood brother who had run away from home and come to visit for fun. Xie Lian couldn't help but feel a little flustered.

"Yeah! Lemme tell ya, your Xiao-Hua helped us repair some stuff again today, so you'll have to reward him well tonight," the village head said.

"Yeah! Add some supplements to his meal, make him big and strong. He'll do an even better job!"

Xie Lian couldn't help but chuckle. "I will, I will. For sure, for sure."

When he opened the door, Lang Ying was already curled up in a corner and fast asleep. Qi Rong, meanwhile, was lying on the ground like a corpse and wailing as though his innards were on fire. Guzi was massaging his shoulders and back.

"Dad, do you feel any better?"

"..."

Xie Lian removed the bamboo hat from his head and put the eggs down. "What's with you? Ate something bad?"

"As long as you don't fucking cook me anything, I won't suffer stomachaches even if I lick shit and grime off the ground!" Qi Rong spat.

Listening to him exaggerate, Xie Lian crossed his hands in his sleeves. "Then why don't you try licking those things to test your theory?"

"Gross, gross, gross!" Qi Rong spat again. "What the fuck did I say? You're exposing your dark side again! Trying to torture me in all sorts of ways! *Mmm yesss*, my good son, that's good, that's good, now chop this side. Hee hee hee hee~! Augh, fuck, what the fuck's going on? I've been so agitated lately, yowling like a fucking tomcat in rut. Am I sick?! Cousin Crown Prince! *I'm sick!* I must be sick 'cause you've been torturing me! You goddamn snow lotus, you're out for blood!"

Xie Lian crouched and felt his forehead. "Are you running a fever?" After a pause, he dropped his hand and frowned. "You aren't. You're not faking this, are you?"

Qi Rong was going to start cussing again. Guzi explained pitifully, "Daozhang, my dad didn't lie to you. He hasn't been feeling well—he's been crying in misery for a long time now."

Watching Qi Rong squirm around on the floor, Xie Lian shook his head and rose to his feet. He was about to look for the medicine box when he noticed that the donation box was heavy—Hua Cheng had only recently built it, so it shouldn't have anything inside. Puzzled, Xie Lian took the key out to open it, and his jaw dropped when he was greeted by the blinding sight of densely packed, glimmering gold bars.

Wham! Xie Lian quickly shut the donation box again.

He had already returned the gold bars that the Water Master had given him. Did someone else send them back?! It couldn't be Hua Cheng; he wouldn't do something as simple and crass as stuffing him full of gold bars.

Xie Lian turned his head. "Qi Rong, did someone come by?" he asked.

Qi Rong jabbed his finger at him and cussed. "Hey, what's wrong with you?! Do you take me for your guard dog?! Do you think you're a supreme?! Even a supreme isn't this shameless! Not even that stinkin' Black Water or that goddamn Hua Cheng would dare take me for a guard dog!"

BANG!

Someone kicked open the door of Puqi Shrine, and that someone was Hua Cheng. Qi Rong went mute the moment he saw him and silently wriggled to a corner of the shrine, not daring to say anything more about what he saw that night.

"San Lang, you're back," Xie Lian said.

Hua Cheng smiled cheerfully. "Yeah."

"Thanks for your hard work," Xie Lian said. "The village chief wanted me to give you these gifts as a reward. We'll have something nice to eat tonight."

"Sounds good," Hua Cheng said. "But, gege, do you want to come to my place tonight?"

"Ghost City?" Xie Lian asked.

"Mmm. And take that *thing* along too," Hua Cheng said, pointing at Qi Rong. "We'll see if there's any way to pull his soul out."

Xie Lian hummed for a moment. "That's probably a good idea," he acquiesced.

They shouldn't keep dragging their feet about this. Of course, the most important reason was that Qi Rong ate too much, and Puqi Shrine could no longer provide.

When Qi Rong heard they were going to send him to Ghost City, his face drained of color, and he objected as hard as he could. But his objections all fell on deaf ears. With a puff of smoke, Hua Cheng turned him into a green budaoweng, and Guzi carried him in his arms as they left for Ghost City.

As he strolled down the main street, Xie Lian saw that Ghost City was as bustling as always. The ghosts remembered Xie Lian, and they all shouted greetings when they saw that he had come to visit.

"Grand-uncle! Ah, no...Chengzhu's Lord Friend, you've come again!"

"Quack! Is it because you miss our specialty street food, quack?!"

Xie Lian had brought the basket of eggs along, and he gave them away as souvenirs from the Mortal Realm. Those he bestowed an egg upon danced with joy; some declared that they would eat it stewed in their own blood, and some proclaimed that they would hatch a twenty-five-meter-tall yao beast from it.

Hua Cheng released the spell on Qi Rong. With another blast of green smoke, the man possessed by Qi Rong appeared on the street. He was crouched low, clutching his head defensively and not saying a word. However, some of the ghosts caught his scent.

"Hmm? Ain't that the Green Ghost we smell?!" they exclaimed.

The crowd of ghosts approached and surrounded him. After taking a good sniff, they cackled at their findings.

"Ha ha ha ha ha ha ha, it really *is* the Green Ghost! The dumbass is here again! *Ha ha ha ha ha ha ha!*"

"Didn't you catch enough of a beating last time?! Ha ha ha ha ha ha, you seriously came back?!"

"Watch over the little one," Hua Cheng said. "As for the big one, think of a way to drag him out of the body without hurting the flesh."

"Yessir, My Lord!"

Several lovely female ghosts picked up Guzi and hummed a little lullaby to put him to sleep. The rest of the nefarious creatures started playing tag with Qi Rong—or rather, it was some game where the latter fled screaming from the former group's relentless pursuit. Hua Cheng and Xie Lian watched the show for a while before heading inside Thousand Lights Temple.

The two leisurely stepped into the hall and approached the altar, which was still stocked with brushes, ink, and paper. Xie Lian's heart has been heavy lately, and at the sight of that stationery, he decided to relax the mood.

He smiled softly. "Back when I taught you, I said you'd need to practice when you had the time. But I suppose you haven't lately."

Hua Cheng cleared his throat. "Gege, you gave my reward away to other people. What will I eat tonight?"

Xie Lian arched his brows in an imitation of Hua Cheng. "Don't change the subject."

"I can practice the sword but not calligraphy," Hua Cheng said. "If gege isn't at my side to tutor me, I'll go astray while I practice all alone and get worse the more I write."

Xie Lian's brows arched higher. "San Lang is so smart—how can there be anything he's no good at?"

Looking very humble, Hua Cheng picked up a brush and dipped it in a bit of ink. "It's true. Pray gege teach me."

Xie Lian sighed. "Why don't you write something first?"

Thus, Hua Cheng very seriously wrote two verses. Xie Lian watched for a bit, then couldn't bear to anymore.

"...Stop, stop. You'd...better stop after all."

Don't waste good paper and ink.

"Oh," Hua Cheng said obediently, and he really did stop, putting the brush away.

Xie Lian shook his head. "San Lang, don't...don't tell anyone that I taught you how to write, okay?"

"Gege, I really tried my best," Hua Cheng pouted.

The way he spoke sounded almost *aggrieved*. Here was a perfectly splendid Supreme Ghost King whose name made all three realms shiver in fright, and he was standing there at that moment like a young student, obediently attentive to Xie Lian's critique. After lecturing him on a few crucial points, Xie Lian held his hand just as he had last time.

"Let's try again. Be serious this time."

"Okay," Hua Cheng said.

They immersed themselves in composition. After they had practiced for a while, Xie Lian asked casually, "Why is it still *Ache of Separation*?"

Hua Cheng answered casually. "I like this poem."

"I like it too," Xie Lian said. "But does San Lang have any other poems he likes? Once you're familiar with transcribing this one, you can try copying others."

The poem only had so many words. The two of them had written it over a dozen times, so it should be time to change it up.

However, Hua Cheng was adamant. "This one is fine."

Setting the brush down, he blew gently at the ink and smiled. "If I like something, then my heart has no room for anything else. I'll always treasure it. A thousand times, a million times, my feelings won't change no matter how many years pass. And so I won't tire of this poem."

"..." Xie Lian gave a small smile. "Is that right?"

"Mmm," Hua Cheng replied.

"..." Xie Lian released his hand and quietly cleared his throat. "That's a good thing. It's nice that San Lang is such a sentimental man... Oh, why don't you practice some more by yourself? Ah, that's right. Qi Rong said he was feeling unwell lately..."

Hua Cheng settled the paper on the altar and picked up the brush again. "Unwell how?"

Xie Lian turned around, his back now facing Hua Cheng. "He said that he felt agitated all over, but I looked him over and it didn't seem to be a problem with his host's body. It can't be because of the bad weather...?"

Behind him, Hua Cheng asked, "When did this start?"

"Within the past few days, I think," Xie Lian replied. "Today was especially bad..."

Before he could finish his sentence, a sense of foreboding suddenly sprouted in his mind. Just then, he heard a soft noise behind him, like an object had fallen to the ground.

Xie Lian whirled around. "San Lang?!"

The brush in Hua Cheng's hand had dropped onto the snow-white paper and slashed a long, erratic trail of ink. Hua Cheng's expression was vaguely grim, and he was swaying slightly on his feet. He clutched the edge of the altar with one hand to hold himself upright, while the other one covered his right eye.

67
Mount Tonglu Reopens, the Agitation of Ghosts

JUDGING FROM HUA CHENG'S EXPRESSION, it seemed his right eye was throbbing with unbearable pain. Xie Lian rushed forward.

"Are you all right?!"

The corner of Hua Cheng's mouth twitched, but he forced back any words he wished to say. The silver eye engraved on Eming's hilt snapped open, and the eyeball started to spin wildly. Veins bulged under the skin of the hand that Hua Cheng had planted atop the altar. That hand seemed ready to flip the table at any second.

Xie Lian reached out, wanting to touch him, but Hua Cheng only growled, "Stay back!"

Seeing Xie Lian freeze, Hua Cheng gritted a plea through his teeth. "...Your Highness, please. Get away from me, hurry. I might..."

Xie Lian cut him off. "How can you tell me to leave when you're like this?!"

Hua Cheng sounded harried. "If you stay here any longer, I—"

Just then, waves of hellish howls and cries sounded from outside Thousand Lights Temple. Ghosts were doubling over on the street, bawling their eyes out as they clutched their heads and wailed. They sounded like their skulls were splitting open, like they were on the verge of death.

Qi Rong, however, was still dashing ahead at incredible speed. Although the flesh vessel had stifled his powers, his possession of a human body also acted as a protective barrier, so any attacks aimed specifically at ghosts were weakened. This was the only reason Qi Rong was still able to be up and about, and he seized this chance to flee. The female ghosts who had been cradling Guzi had fallen to the ground, mewling in pain from their headaches, and were unable to continue singing their hypnotic melody. Guzi groggily woke up to see Qi Rong bolting away like a madman, and he stumbled upright to chase after him.

"Dad! Dad! Wait for me!" he yelled.

As he ran, Qi Rong turned his head, stuck out his tongue, and rolled his eyes. "PBBBBBBBBHT! GOOD BOY, DADDY'S OFF! HA HA HA HA HA HA HA HA HA!"

Guzi chased after him relentlessly on his short little legs, but when he saw that the distance between them was only growing bigger, he burst into tears.

"*Waaah!* Dad! Please don't throw me away! Dad, take me with you!"

"GET LOST! GET LOST! Don't follow me, you nuisance!" Qi Rong began spitting at the boy.

His spit flew so far that it hit Guzi on the forehead and knocked him onto his butt. He cried even harder, as if his heart were going to break and his lungs were going to burst. Xie Lian couldn't bear it any longer, and he furiously stormed out of Thousand Lights Temple.

"Qi Rong!"

The moment Qi Rong saw Xie Lian blocking the path in front of him, he spun around in fear and ran back the way he came. Along the way, he scooped Guzi off the ground and yelled threats behind him.

"Don't come after me! Do it and I'll bite off this little dead-weight's head to show you!! My good son; you're gonna become your ol' dad's meal, how filial! Dad'll cook you tomorrow. Braised or steamed, take your pick! HA HA HA HA HA HA!"

Xie Lian wasn't fazed by the threat in the slightest, but just as he was about to give chase, a loud crash sounded behind him. As if struck by a sudden fury, Hua Cheng had swept all the stationery off the table and flung it to the ground. Left with absolutely no choice and no time to deal with Qi Rong, Xie Lian rushed back inside.

"San Lang…"

And then, Hua Cheng caught him in a tight embrace. His voice trembled.

"I lied. Don't leave me."

Xie Lian stood as still as an iron board, locked within those arms. "San Lang? Do you recognize me?"

It seemed like he had lost his senses and couldn't recognize the one in front of him. He clutched Xie Lian even tighter in his arms and muttered over and over, "…I lied, don't leave me…"

Xie Lian's eyes widened. Outside the temple, Qi Rong broke out in smug laughter while Guzi wailed uncontrollably.

"BAH HA HA! Hua Cheng, you fucker! That'll teach you to look down on me all the time!" he cackled. "Look at you, so cocky all day! Down for the count, aren't you? That's karma!"

The ghosts howling on the streets were exhausted by their misery, but upon hearing this, they cursed back with vigor.

"Green Ghost! You useless piece of crap, ya dare mouth off to our Chengzhu?!"

The annoying ruckus going on around them seemed to further provoke Hua Cheng's fury. Driven to the edge of his tolerance, he raised his hand to blast them to pieces. Xie Lian hastily returned the hug to hold his arm down.

"Okay, okay," he soothed. "I won't leave. I won't leave you."

With a flick of Xie Lian's hand, Thousand Lights Temple's grand doors shut by themselves. To prevent Qi Rong from busting into the temple under these circumstances, Xie Lian hurled threats to shoo him away.

"If you're gonna go, then go! I don't have time for you! Careful—if you don't get lost, I just might...*ah!*"

To his surprise, Hua Cheng was unsatisfied with a shallow embrace. He roughly pinned Xie Lian down on top of the jade table, scattering ink, paper, and brushes across the floor. Caught up in the struggle, Xie Lian's hand accidentally skimmed past the cinnabar dish stationed on the table, smearing crimson marks across the paper underneath him. On *Ache of Separation*'s line *"Scattered from the peak of Mount Wu, there are no other clouds,"* the two characters of "the peak" were now stained with alluring streaks of vivid red. It was an endlessly bewitching sight.

"San..." Xie Lian started.

Before he could utter another word, Hua Cheng grabbed him by the shoulders and leaned down into a kiss.

Qi Rong had undoubtedly heard something that didn't sound right. He laughed uproariously. "Cousin Crown Prince, you'd better be careful! That damn Hua Cheng is probably rabid right now—he'll bite whoever he sees! I'll help you spread the news personally. There are plenty of monks and cultivators out there who are enemies with that damn Hua Cheng, so they should take this chance to hurry here and get even with him! HO HO HO, HA HA HA HA..."

Xie Lian tensed as Qi Rong's laughter faded into the distance. If Qi Rong really did call forth a large band of cultivators who Hua Cheng had wronged, and they came to shoot a ghost while he was down, how could the ghosts of Ghost City escape harm in their current condition?

But Hua Cheng wasn't allowing him even a moment to think. He was clearly not a living person and should have no warmth in his body, yet at this moment he was searing hot, as if he had been stricken by a burning fever. With their lips pressed so tightly together, Xie Lian was forced to take in the waves of heat flowing into him. The hands that had intended to push Hua Cheng away instead dug into the folds of red fabric at his shoulders.

Maybe it was because Hua Cheng's spiritual power was too potent, but Xie Lian felt filled to bursting by the warmth flowing down his throat, through his chest, and all the way into his stomach—so much that it was unbearable. If he was forced to keep enduring this, he was going to burst from the sheer amount of power that Hua Cheng was pouring into him. His jaw tightened, and he struck heavily with his palm. Although the blow did land, he couldn't bring himself to hit Hua Cheng in earnest, so all he'd done was tap his shoulder with inconsequential strength. Unfazed, Hua Cheng seized his wrist, held it down, and continued to press his heat directly into Xie Lian's mouth.

If this continued, he really would be crushed. This time, Xie Lian used both his hands to push Hua Cheng away, then fled in panic to the other side of the altar, panting for breath. With his eye bloodshot, Hua Cheng hounded him, followed him, and pinned him down against the altar.

"San Lang!" Xie Lian cried.

"..."

Perhaps his voice reached him, for Hua Cheng stared at his face for a long time before abruptly wrapping him in a crushing hug.

Seeing that Hua Cheng listened and stopped forcefully pumping spiritual power into him, Xie Lian sighed a breath of relief. However, as he stood in Hua Cheng's embrace, he could sense the energy inside Hua Cheng going berserk. No wonder Hua Cheng had kissed him the moment he caught him. With such wretched turbulence within him, he had to find an outlet to expel it. Bloodletting would be necessary for him to fully regain his senses. But Hua Cheng wasn't alive—how could he have any blood to let?

After much consideration, Xie Lian made a decision.

"...Forgive me."

He cupped Hua Cheng's cheeks and captured his lips with his own. Xie Lian then began to gently guide the turbulent flow of heat into his own body, helping ease Hua Cheng's pain and agitation. Hua Cheng looped his arm around Xie Lian's waist, eliciting a small shiver from him. In the next moment, the two tumbled down and sprawled atop the altar.

It really wasn't fair. Xie Lian didn't dare touch anywhere on Hua Cheng that was even slightly dangerous. But in his confused state of mind, Hua Cheng's hands roamed over every inch of his body without restraint, causing Xie Lian unspeakable torment. This altar was originally a place to worship the divine, but presented there this evening instead was a ghost and a god entangled in a fervent, inseparable embrace, their tongues entwined. It was absurd and strange, and yet a sight of breathtaking loveliness.

The first few times they had committed this sort of act, they had been more or less clearheaded. There was a proper justification every time and some measure of control—nothing beyond lips covering lips. But this time, one was confused and the other caught off guard, and these fevered kisses had crossed the line. Through the fog that clouded his mind, Xie Lian finally accepted something. Although every time this happened was out of his control and he never had a choice...the truth was, he couldn't resist his feelings. Every time.

He was tormented thus for half the night before the agit
within Hua Cheng finally began to calm. The arms that embr___
Xie Lian gradually slackened, and Xie Lian flipped over and sat up.
He gazed at Hua Cheng's slumbering face, then breathed a sigh.

Eming had been thrown to the side, and its eyeball was still frantically spinning. Xie Lian picked up the scimitar, and it was only
after an extended petting session that Eming's eye finally relaxed
into a smiling crescent, as if it was finally satisfied. Not long after,
Hua Cheng shot upright from where he had been sleeping.

"...Your Highness?!"

Xie Lian quickly adjusted his expression into a beaming smile,
then turned to Hua Cheng. "You're awake? Everything's fine now."

Hua Cheng scanned the room. Thousand Lights Temple was an
enormous mess. His face was uncharacteristically distraught, as if he
couldn't remember what had happened the night before. Xie Lian
jumped at the chance to speak, sounding calm and easy.

"What happened last night? All your subordinates were suddenly
struck with fevers and terrible headaches. Everyone was restless. You
were too—you had quite the temper!"

"Besides that?" Hua Cheng demanded.

Xie Lian blinked. "Besides what? Nothing else happened."

Hua Cheng stared at him hard. "There really was nothing? Then
how did I calm down?"

Xie Lian cleared his throat softly, as if he was slightly embarrassed.
"San Lang, please don't be mad at me. To tell you the truth, other
than this..." He briefly raised the hand that was currently petting
Eming, "I also, *ahem*, fought with you."

"..." Hua Cheng eyed him doubtfully. "We...had a fight?"

Xie Lian met his gaze earnestly, face carefully neutral. "We did.
Look, our fight made quite a mess of the hall."

"..."

There was a pause, then Hua Cheng puffed a sigh of relief and rested his head on his hand.

Now that Hua Cheng was no longer hounding him for answers, Xie Lian finally released the breath he'd been holding and let himself relax.

"It opened," Hua Cheng muttered.

"What did?" Xie Lian asked.

Hua Cheng lifted his head and clarified with a somber voice. "Mount Tonglu reopened."

Both were entirely aware of what that meant. Xie Lian's eyes widened.

"A new ghost king...is about to be born?"

When Xie Lian returned to the Heavenly Capital to report in, thunder was rumbling loud enough to match the news of Mount Tonglu. As he stepped into the Palace of Divine Might, Xie Lian subconsciously looked to a particular spot to inquire about this.

"What's the matter with Lord Thunder Master?"

He only realized after he voiced his question that the spot where the Wind Master once stood was now empty. The Water Master in the front-most row and the Earth Master in the farthest corner—they, too, were gone. He blinked, before sighing softly to himself.

When he cocked his head to the side, he saw Lang Qianqiu enter the hall. Xie Lian had not seen him for some time, and his entire person was one size thinner and much, much gloomier. His eyes met Xie Lian's, then he turned away without a word.

As he scanned the room, Xie Lian realized he couldn't find anyone he could casually converse with.

"It's nothing. A Ghost King is about to be born; ghosts cry and gods sound, and the thunder won't stop," a voice answered his question.

Surprisingly, the one who responded was Feng Xin. For some reason, Xie Lian found the sight of him instantly comforting. However, one of Feng Xin's eyes was blackened. Xie Lian couldn't help but turn to glance at Mu Qing, who was standing on the far side of the hall. One side of Mu Qing's face was swollen. After years of nursing their grudge, their recent brawl must've been quite brutal.

Jun Wu called everyone to attention. "I am certain you are all aware of the reason I summoned you here."

The heavenly officials all responded in the affirmative.

Jun Wu continued, his speech unhurried. "The universe is a crucible, and living creatures are the copper. Infinite adversities abide within the abyss of suffering.

"Mount Tonglu is a naturally ominous realm with a landscape most perilous; it is a live volcano that can erupt at any time.

"Every few centuries, the City of Gu within the mountain opens its gates, and its call shakes the Ghost Realm; its tremors especially affect its previous champions, the ghost kings. Every nefarious creature that desires to reach the level of supreme will make their way to Mount Tonglu. Once they have assembled, Mount Tonglu will seal itself once more, and the slaughter will officially begin.

"When only one remains, a new ghost king is born.

"Crimson Rain Sought Flower and Ship-Sinking Black Water are both Supreme Ghost Kings born by this method. The two became supremes when they emerged from the mountain. It took Black Water twelve years. It took Hua Cheng ten."

"It's already difficult enough to deal with one Black Water and one Hua Cheng; just look at what they've done," Mu Qing commented coldly. "If another one comes along, we won't sleep a wink."

"General Xuan Zhen, I won't comment on Black Water. But I don't think Hua Cheng has done anything truly out of line," Xie Lian responded temperately.

Mu Qing, his cheek puffy and swollen, shot him a look.

"They *are* quite difficult to deal with," Pei Ming noted. "So we must stop the millions of ghosts from gathering, am I right?"

"Correct," Jun Wu said. "The process will take a few months. We need to put a stop to it while we are still able."

"What if we don't stop them in time?" Xie Lian asked. "Is there any way to rally after that?"

"There is," Jun Wu assured, "but hopefully we will not reach that point. The primary focus at this juncture is that the agitation of the ghosts has created a wave of chaos. Many nefarious creatures that were once sealed away have escaped, and among them are some that are extremely dangerous—such as that female ghost Xuan Ji, the fetus spirit, and the Brocade Immortal. They are likely hurrying to Mount Tonglu as we speak. They must be immediately apprehended once more."

"They've all escaped?" Xie Lian remarked. "This is quite the disturbance indeed."

"Which is why I'm afraid every martial god must expend some effort and thoroughly investigate the domains over which they preside," Jun Wu stated.

"Then...what about me?" Xie Lian asked.

While Xie Lian was a Scrap God at the moment, he had ascended as a martial god the first two times. He was basically being used as a martial god right now too; the only difference was that he didn't have a domain.

After deliberating for a moment, Jun Wu said, "Xianle, why don't you go with Qi Ying?"

68

The Besotted Boy, Brocade Immortal Forged of Blood

AFTER A BRIEF PAUSE, Jun Wu asked, "...Where is Qi Ying?"

Xie Lian looked around, and indeed, there wasn't a shadow of that young martial god to be seen. The heavens had been plagued with nonstop incidents recently, and perhaps that was why the Palace of Ling Wen was so busy, its wheels spinning so furiously that it was about to take flight. Ling Wen had a few more dark circles under her eyes as she explained Quan Yizhen's absence.

"It's been a long time since Qi Ying has been to one of these meetings. We've never been able to connect with him."

Some heavenly officials clicked their tongues.

"Where did that brat run off to?"

"Not here again? I'm rather envious that he's managed to avoid all these meetings."

"Since we do not know Qi Ying's whereabouts, we will inform you once he is located and allow the two of you to coordinate," Jun Wu said.

Xie Lian inclined his head in acknowledgment. "Yes, My Lord."

It was now autumn in the Mortal Realm, and the weather was chilly—as it was inside Puqi Shrine. Although Xie Lian wore just one layer of clothing, he didn't feel the cold. However, on the way home, he used the money he made from collecting scraps to buy two new sets of robes for Lang Ying.

Hua Cheng had returned to Ghost City, and Qi Rong had run off with Guzi in tow, so only Lang Ying was left in Puqi Shrine at present. It had felt so cramped for a while, but now it was suddenly deserted. As he approached the shrine, Xie Lian could see Lang Ying silently sweeping the fallen golden leaves away from the entrance and raking them into a pile.

Lang Ying used to slouch, perpetually coiled in on himself in fear and anxiety. Maybe it was all in Xie Lian's mind, but he seemed to stand taller and straighter now, and he finally looked the part of a cheerful boy. Xie Lian couldn't help but feel heartened. He went over and took the broom from him, and he was just about to bring him inside when the villagers—who had been hiding in wait for some time—ambushed him. Aunties and uncles and sisters both young and old, they all clamored around him.

"Daozhang, you're back!"

"Did you collect scraps in town again? Working hard, working hard... So, um, how come we haven't seen Xiao-Hua lately?"

"Yeah, yeah, we haven't seen him for days! We rather miss the lad."

"..." Xie Lian smiled awkwardly. "Xiao...Hua went back home."

"Huh?" The village chief was puzzled. "Which home? I thought *this* was Xiao-Hua's home? Hasn't he settled in with you?!"

"No, no," Xie Lian replied. "He only came here to play. Now that we're both busy, we parted ways."

Hua Cheng had hounded him for answers that night, but Xie Lian was stubbornly adamant that they'd only had a fight. And now that Mount Tonglu had reopened, Hua Cheng had more on his plate. If a new Supreme Ghost King really emerged, it would mean an assault on all three realms.

Hua Cheng and Black Water... Though one was flashy and the other low profile, they both had considerable moral character. They more or less knew their place and had a sense of propriety. But there was no telling what kind of creature would emerge this time. It would be troublesome if Mount Tonglu birthed a madman like Qi Rong who would fight them for portions of their domains. Thus, Xie Lian used "troubled times" as his excuse and said that they had better not see each other for the time being to focus on their respective duties. And with that, they very amiably bid each other farewell.

It seemed sudden and cold, like he'd turned his back on a friend. But Xie Lian really didn't know what else to do.

He had no confidence that he could hide his feelings right now.

Behind him, Lang Ying suddenly said, "Fire."

"...?"

Only then did Xie Lian realize that the pot and spatula had somehow found their way into his hand while he was lost in thought, and he'd ruined all the meat and vegetables he'd just brought back to Puqi Shrine. The fire under the pot was almost two meters high, nearly scorching the ceiling, and Xie Lian hastily put out the flames with a slap of his palm. However, he slapped too hard and the entire stove collapsed.

After the rumbling ceased, Xie Lian stood there dumbfounded with the pot in hand, at a loss for what to do. It was just about mealtime, and the villagers were outside their homes, happily eating from massive bowls. Surprised by the ruckus, they all came around again.

"What happened, what happened?! Daozhang, did your shrine blow up again?!"

Xie Lian quickly opened the window, coughing as he did. "It's nothing, it's nothing! *Cough cough cough cough...*"

The village chief came over to take a look. "Fer heaven's sake, this is an absolute tragedy! Daozhang, I think you'd better call Xiao-Hua back."

Wordless for a moment, Xie Lian said, "It's all right. After all... he's not from my household."

By the time he snapped out of it, Lang Ying had already cleaned up the mess on the ground. A plate of something vibrantly red and purple had also made it to the table; it was a dish Xie Lian had randomly prepared while he was zoning out. If his last creation was called Love for All Seasons Stew, then this should be called Riot of Colors Stir-Fry. But other than Hua Cheng, there was probably no one on earth who could swallow the stuff. Not even Xie Lian himself could bear the sight of it, and he turned around to wash the pot, rubbing his forehead.

"Forget it, don't eat it. Throw it away."

Yet after he finished washing the pot and turned around, he saw that Lang Ying had taken the plate and silently eaten the food. Stunned, Xie Lian hurried over to stop him.

"...Heavens, are you all right?" he asked, holding him by the shoulders. "Do you feel bad anywhere?"

Lang Ying shook his head. Since his face was thoroughly covered in bandages, his expression was hidden. Even Qi Rong and Black Water had lost their minds when they ate his cooking, but Lang Ying could actually handle it... Had he really been that starving, or had he received an unexpected increase in strength and power? Xie Lian managed a chuckle at his own joke. After cleaning up, he went to bed.

There were two mats in Puqi Shrine, one for each person. When Xie Lian remembered that he and Hua Cheng had lain together upon the mat beneath him, he couldn't sleep a wink. His eyes were wide open, but he didn't dare to toss and turn lest he rouse Lang Ying.

After much internal struggle, just when he thought he might as well get up and go outside for some air, he heard the window creak. Someone softly pushed open the wooden frame and hopped inside.

Xie Lian had his back to the window. He lay there on his side, shocked.

Who was senseless enough to try to steal from Puqi Shrine? It was pointless work with no payoff!

The intruder was very light on his feet and extremely skilled; no one would've noticed him unless they had Xie Lian's extraordinarily sharp senses. After he'd hopped in, he ran straight for the donation box. Xie Lian immediately remembered that the donation box had been full of gold bars earlier; was this person here for the gold? But Xie Lian had long since brought those gold bars to the Upper Court and given them to Ling Wen, who he asked to find their real owner. Listening attentively, Xie Lian realized the person wasn't trying to break the lock—he was stuffing things into the donation box, one after the other!

After that individual finished his work, he headed over to the window to leave. Xie Lian mentally plotted his next course of action—he had a mind to follow after this person once he left to see who he was and where he was going. But in an unexpected turn of events, the person spotted the plates of food on the altar table when he passed by. Apparently he was hungry, so he didn't think twice before stuffing several bites of Riot of Colors Stir-Fry into his mouth.

THUD! A moment later, he was passed out on the ground.

Xie Lian immediately turned over and sat up. *That's saved me some trouble!*

He lit a lamp to inspect his catch. A purple-faced figure lay flat on the ground. Xie Lian rushed to the rescue and poured a copious amount of water down the person's throat, and soon he began to slowly come around.

The first thing he uttered when he woke was, "What the hell was that?!"

Xie Lian pretended not to hear that comment. "Your Highness Qi Ying, you are far too reckless," he chided earnestly. "Stuffing whatever you find in your mouth without knowing what it is."

The young man had a straight nose, a defined brow, and a head full of curly black hair. Who could it be besides the Martial God of the West, Quan Yizhen?

He glared at Xie Lian. "How could I expect someone to poison their own food, offered in their own shrine?"

"..." Xie Lian rubbed his forehead. He opened the donation box and discovered that it was filled to the brim with gold bars once more. "Was it you who filled the box last time too?"

Quan Yizhen nodded.

"Why are you giving me this?" Xie Lian asked.

"Because I have a lot of it," Quan Yizhen replied.

"..."

Truth be told, even if Quan Yizhen wouldn't admit it, Xie Lian could guess that this generosity had most likely been prompted by the incident at the Mid-Autumn Banquet when he flung a chopstick to cut down the stage curtains.

"Take these back with you. I won't accept a reward for not doing anything," Xie Lian said.

Quan Yizhen didn't reply and was very obviously not listening. Xie Lian didn't know whether to laugh or cry.

"He's telling you to take those away," Lang Ying coldly interjected.

When had he gotten up? Xie Lian gazed back at him, feeling strange. Lang Ying usually made himself invisible, desperately trying to shrink into the ground. Why was he saying so much unprompted today, and in such a shockingly unfriendly tone? But he didn't dwell on it.

Failing all else, Xie Lian figured he could give the box to Ling Wen and have her shove it back on Quan Yizhen, so he straightened his expression.

"Your Highness, you've come just in time. You didn't attend the meeting at the Palace of Divine Might today, but the Heavenly Emperor has given us a mission. Have you seen the scroll? Never mind, it's all right, I know you haven't looked through it. I've reviewed it, anyhow. We'll be working as a team, and the creature we're responsible for is called the Brocade Immortal."

The Venerable of Empty Words was called "venerable" because people didn't dare to call it a rogue, a hellion, or an annoying devil so directly; it was forced praise. So then, why was the Brocade Immortal called an "immortal"? That was because, according to tales, the creature once had the potential to become a god.

As the story goes, there was once a young man in some ancient kingdom many centuries ago. Although he was born half-witted, his intelligence no better than that of a six-year-old child, his performance on the battlefield was a different story. His martial skills were extraordinary, and he was also brave and kind. His homeland was hanging on by a thread, surviving solely because he slaved away on the front lines to charge and shatter the enemy formation whenever they collided with another kingdom in battle. But because he was mentally ill and had no family, the military achievements that he put his life on the line for were claimed by others, and he was left penniless. No one was willing to marry their daughters to such a man, and very few girls were willing to come close. The young man was also stupid in this field, since he had never once interacted with girls. He didn't even have the guts to speak to them.

However, this man possessed the potential to ascend. It should have only taken a few more years of battle for him to ascend to the heavens, so it didn't matter if no girls liked him. But the sad thing was, he fell in love with a girl, and he fell deeply.

On his birthday, the girl gifted him a brocade robe she had personally sewn.

One could call it a brocade robe, but it was extremely bizarre and looked more like a horrific pocket of cloth. This was the first time in the young man's life that he had received a gift from a girl he loved, so he was filled with utter joy. Coupled with his natural stupidity, he didn't notice anything strange as he eagerly pulled the brocade "robe" over his body.

There weren't any sleeves for his arms to go through, so he asked his beloved girl, "How come my arms can't stretch out?"

The girl smiled cheerfully. "This is my first time sewing, so I'm not very skilled. But it won't be a problem if you don't have arms."

So the young man chopped off the arms he used to wield weapons. Now, the robe fit.

However, it wasn't enough. He asked the girl again, "How come my legs can't stretch out?"

The girl replied, "That won't be a problem if you don't have legs."

So the young man asked someone to chop off his legs as well.

Finally, he asked the girl, "How come my head can't peek out?"

It was easy to imagine the conclusion.

Xie Lian had originally assumed the Brocade Immortal was a nefarious creature wearing a brocade robe; who would've thought it was actually the robe itself? When Mount Tonglu reopened and agitated millions of ghosts, someone had stolen the robe. It had become an exceedingly vicious and formidable spiritual weapon after it was soaked in that young man's infatuated blood. It had changed hands among nefarious beings over the centuries, and all of them had used it to cause harm.

Thus, let this tale serve as a warning to never accept any old, used clothing from unknown origins. If a stranger wants to gift you a brocade robe as you walk the streets at night, do not accept it—for if you wear that robe, your mind will be befuddled; trapped in a trance, you will become a pig for the slaughter, and your blood will be sucked dry.

Of course, this was only a myth, and a rather outlandish one at that. The story could have easily been invented by someone who extrapolated from the brocade robe's unique nature. Nevertheless, the Brocade Immortal had to be stopped, and they could not allow it to reach Mount Tonglu.

"Your Highness Qi Ying? Your Highness? Are you listening?"

Xie Lian reached out and waved his hand in front of Quan Yizhen. Quan Yizhen seemed to have spaced out, and only then did his spirit return to this body.

"Oh."

It would appear he wasn't listening, but it wasn't Xie Lian's place to say much about that kind of behavior. Instead, he said, "So our current main priority is to find the brocade robe, I suppose? Its original form is..."

"A sleeveless, headless, sack-like robe stained with blood," Quan Yizhen finished the statement.

Xie Lian chuckled. "So you *do* know. And I thought you didn't read the scroll. But this robe is an evil object. It's also an extremely magical one with thousands of forms. There are millions of articles of clothing in the world, and searching for this one item is like looking for a needle in a haystack."

"Oh," Quan Yizhen said. "Then what do we do?"

"Nefarious creatures who get their hands on the robe will usually disguise themselves as merchants and beseech people on busy streets to buy or exchange old clothes for new," Xie Lian explained. "But that hasn't been a normal custom for centuries; it'd be rather strange if anyone tried it nowadays. The habits of nefarious creatures don't change easily or quickly, so let's go into town and see if we can catch wind of anything like that happening."

Ghosts paid more attention to these sorts of things than mortals, and the Ghost Realm's grapevine would be better informed. In other words, asking Hua Cheng directly would surely save a lot of trouble. But Xie Lian had only just told him that they shouldn't meet for a while, and it wouldn't look good to go back on his word the moment he needed something. Besides, the Brocade Immortal had only just been stolen, so the thief wouldn't be so quick to bring it out and cause harm.

Quan Yizhen nodded, rose to his feet, and followed him for a couple of steps. Xie Lian noticed that Lang Ying followed suit.

"You stay here," he told him.

Lang Ying shook his head. Before Xie Lian could say any more, there was a sudden *thud!* behind him. Quan Yizhen had collapsed again.

Xie Lian whirled around. "What happened?"

Shades of purple colored Quan Yizhen's face. He tried holding it in, but in the end, he couldn't. He flipped over, clambered to all fours, and puked all over the floor.

"..."

After vomiting, Quan Yizhen rolled over to face the ceiling, his soul leaving his body through his mouth.

"Qi Ying...can you still come along?" Xie Lian asked carefully.

Quan Yizhen's limbs were stretched out like a starfish. "Not... anymore."

"..."

Xie Lian had to woefully drag Quan Yizhen—who had lost all will to fight—over to a corner and cover him with a blanket to let him recover for a while.

It took until the next day for Quan Yizhen to look slightly better, but Xie Lian didn't dare let him eat anything from the shrine. He asked for some congee from the village chief's home and brought it back to fill the others' stomachs. Quan Yizhen sat in the spot Hua Cheng usually occupied, and for some reason, Lang Ying kept staring at him in a very unfriendly manner.

Xie Lian placed the congee in front of both of them and unconsciously murmured, "San Lang..."

Before the words fully left his lips, the two turned to look at him. Xie Lian froze, and only then did he realize what he had blurted. He softly cleared his throat.

"Please continue."

While the two were sitting at the altar table eating their congee, Xie Lian took an axe and headed out the door. As he chopped wood, he thought back on the clues the scroll had provided.

The Brocade Immortal was imprisoned behind an extremely powerful seal in a Temple of Divine Might. The temple always has maximum security and is guarded by innumerable martial experts. A simple agitation of ghosts shouldn't have allowed it to escape on its own. Someone must have spotted an opportunity and stole it amidst the chaos...

In the past, Hua Cheng was the one who always chopped the wood. Now that Xie Lian was doing it himself, for some reason it didn't feel like his wood was chopped as nicely as Hua Cheng's.

Quan Yizhen miserably drank a few mouthfuls of watery congee, then tumbled over to sleep once more inside Puqi Shrine. Lang Ying, on the other hand, came outside looking to help.

"There's no need. San...Lang Ying, why don't you heat up some water and take a bath?"

Now that he thought about it, he didn't think Lang Ying had bathed in a while. Ghosts certainly wouldn't have to worry about skin oils and sweat, but surely there would be dirt to wash away after hanging around outside all day. Still, he couldn't say it straightforwardly to save the boy's self-esteem.

Lang Ying seemed startled into speechlessness, but Xie Lian had already carried a bundle of logs inside to heat the water.

"I sold some scraps in town yesterday and bought you two sets of autumn clothes. Once you're done bathing, why don't you see if they fit you?"

Lang Ying was just putting on the new robes, but when he heard that suggestion, he turned to leave without a word. Xie Lian grabbed him to stop his escape.

"Don't go! Bathing is a must," he chided earnestly. "Don't worry, I won't unwrap the bandages on your head."

But Lang Ying still protested, and he plodded outside to chop wood, refusing to come back in. Exasperated, Xie Lian could only grab some logs for himself. While the water heated, he peeled off his clothes. Ruoye unwrapped itself loop by loop from around Xie Lian's chest.

It was at that moment that Lang Ying came back inside carrying a large bundle of logs. When he saw Xie Lian with his upper body bare, his eyes went wide.

Xie Lian was testing the temperature of the water with his hand. Determining that it was just right, he began to climb into the bath while still wearing his trousers.

"Oh, perfect timing," he called out as he saw Lang Ying come in. "Can you please pass me the scroll hung under the bamboo hat on the wall?

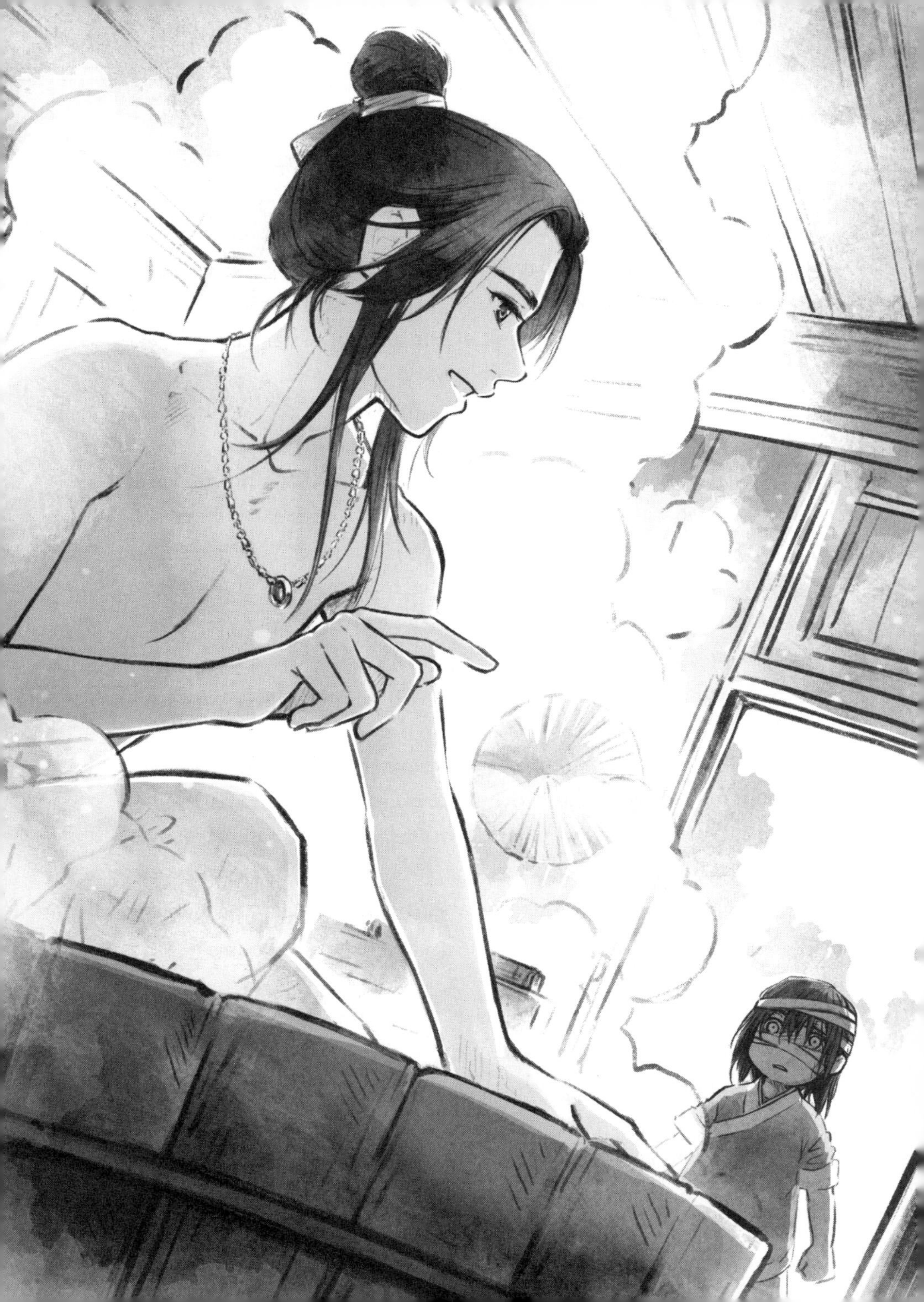

Not only did Lang Ying not come over, he backed all the way outside and slammed the door shut. Xie Lian was puzzled. Not a moment later, Lang Ying seemed to remember something and forcefully kicked the door open once more.

"Don't kick the door! The door is..." Xie Lian hastily cried.

Lang Ying kept his eyes off of him and walked straight in. Quan Yizhen lay sprawled on the floor like a corpse, and he gave no resistance when Lang Ying picked him up and dragged him outside. He appeared deeply asleep; only an event on the level of quaking earth and shaking mountains could rouse him, so he felt nothing as he was dragged along.

Xie Lian didn't know whether to laugh or cry. "What are you doing? It's all right, it's not like I'm a girl. Come in."

True, he hadn't bathed inside Puqi Shrine when Hua Cheng was around. Puqi Shrine was too small, and the conditions there were tough; having a bathtub to himself was about all he could ask for.

There wasn't a sprawling, thirty-meter-long bathing pool lined with privacy screens in which he could row a boat and bathe at his leisure, after all. But whether intentional or not, Xie Lian had never bathed in front of Hua Cheng.

But the one before him now wasn't Hua Cheng, so he didn't see the problem.

"..."

Lang Ying flipped Quan Yizhen over, then he piled a bunch of random clothes over his head. He took the scroll Xie Lian had asked for and passed it over with his head down, and then sat motionless in a corner.

Xie Lian loosened his hair and rolled the scroll open; he read through it carefully, his brows furrowed in concentration. Steam warmed his face, giving it a rosy glow. His long hair and lashes were shimmering black and dripping wet.

He suddenly noticed the thin silver necklace draped against his bare chest, and the diamond ring twinkling at the end of the chain.

Xie Lian picked up the ring, curling his fingers around it to hold it securely. At the periphery of his vision, he noticed a tiny flower sitting on the corner of the altar. Without thinking, he picked up the flower and brought it before his eyes. He felt his mind cloud like the hot air lingering around him, and he needed someone to spare a hand and help him wave away the haze.

Just then, there was a knock at the door. The sound pulled him out of his reverie, and Xie Lian set the flower back down. Before he could call out to ask who it was, he realized the knocking wasn't on Puqi Shrine's door but rather on the village chief's house next door.

A woman's delicate voice sounded between the knocks. "Is anyone home? Exchange old for new, exchange old for new. I have a brand-new robe that I have no use for, and I thought that I might exchange it for a set of old clothes that captures my fancy. Is the master of the house open to this trade? Is anyone home?"

He hadn't even needed to go searching; the creature actually came knocking all on its own!

She knocked and called out at every house, yet not a single household opened their door to her. This was hardly unexpected. When Xie Lian wasn't out collecting scraps, he hosted lectures at Puqi Shrine, educating the village aunties and grannies on hundreds of little tricks for how to identify evil. None of the villagers would fall for such an obviously strange uninvited guest who arrived in the middle of the night—the people of the modern age weren't as easy to deceive as in the olden days.

The creature knocked and knocked, but still no one responded. Finally, it came to Puqi Shrine's door. Xie Lian held his breath tensely, but it seemed that creature could feel that this wasn't a place she should call upon. With an exclamation of *"Aiyoh,"* he could hear her footsteps as she turned to leave.

"Wait! I want to trade!" Xie Lian quickly called out. Then he whispered to Lang Ying, "Open the door. Don't be scared—nothing will happen!"

Lang Ying wasn't scared in the least, and he headed over to open the door. Outside there stood a girl with a slender and sensual figure. Just by glimpsing the bottom half of her face, one could tell she was lovely. However, she was wearing a headscarf covering the top half of her face. It was as if she didn't have eyes, and the effect was rather unnerving.

She glanced inside and covered her mouth as she giggled. "Daozhang, what kind of old clothes do you want to exchange for my new ones?"

Xie Lian stayed soaking in the water tub to make it lower its guard. He smiled.

"That depends on what yours look like."

The girl extended her arm and gave it a gentle shake. A shining brocade robe unfurled from her cloth bag. It was beautiful, glamorous even, but the style seemed a bit outdated, and it reeked with an evil air.

"Beautiful. Beautiful," Xie Lian praised. "Lang Ying, give this miss the set of clothes I brought back from town."

Lang Ying brusquely handed the robe over with just one hand.[8] The girl gave him the new robe in exchange and giggled as she

---

8   *Offering someone an object with one hand is considered casual and familiar, and it is seen as disrespectful to a stranger or superior.*

received the old clothes. She was about to turn around when her face suddenly dropped—it seemed something had pinched her hand, and she screamed and threw the old robes to the ground. Ruoye had crept and coiled within the heap of hemp fabric, and it peeped out of the collar like a white viper flicking its tongue.

And this "girl" wasn't an ordinary girl. After the scream and the jump, her headscarf was knocked off by Ruoye's ambush and fell to the ground. Although the bottom half of her face was bewitching, the top half was wrinkled and aged, forming a horrifying contrast— what "girl"? She was clearly an eighty-year-old hag!

69
Separating Colors, Dyehouse Wide Open

It was a Half-MaQuillage Woman!

The Half-Maquillage Woman was a low-level ghost formed by the jealousy of older women toward young girls. Unable to accept the inevitability of aging, they were convinced that consuming the blood and flesh of young girls could restore their youth. They liked to squeak in high-pitched tones to fake maidenly voices, but as the saying goes, eyes are the windows to the soul. They couldn't hide their old age, no matter how hard they tried. The bottom half of their face would appear younger the more blood and flesh they consumed, but the upper half that held the eyes would age faster. The stark contrast was far more horrifying than normal aging, but they would still stubbornly refuse to see the error of their ways.

Xie Lian emerged dripping from the bath and set a foot on the edge of the water tub, poised to take her down with a leaping attack. But at that very moment Quan Yizhen seemed to return from the brink of death—he shot to his feet and let loose a mighty slap. The Half-Maquillage Woman was just too weak, and she was knocked to the ground with a wailing cry.

"Have mercy!"

Xie Lian unhurriedly grabbed his cultivation robes and casually draped them over himself. "So you're the one who stole the Brocade Immortal?"

"It wasn't me, it wasn't me!" the Half-Maquillage Woman quickly pleaded. "I wouldn't dare break into the Temple of Divine Might!"

That was almost certainly true, if Xie Lian thought about it. A low-level ghost like this really wouldn't have the guts to break into a Temple of Divine Might so rashly, lest she be blown to smithereens. Besides, this Half-Maquillage Woman probably had no connection to the Brocade Immortal—by a rough estimate, her ghost age was eighty-something, while the Brocade Immortal was centuries old.

"Then where did you get your hands on this brocade robe?" Xie Lian questioned.

The Half-Maquillage Woman picked up her headscarf and covered the top half of her face anew. "To...to answer Daozhang!" her voice shrieked high again. "I...I found it while browsing the shops in Ghost City..."

"..."

You could do that? Find something like that while browsing the shops in Ghost City?!

Xie Lian was speechless for a moment. Then he asked, "Who sold it to you?"

"Daozhang! I beg you, please let me off the hook!" the Half-Maquillage Woman anxiously begged. "I don't know! It's not like businesses in Ghost City need to have eighteen generations of ancestry checked!"

That was true too. If starting a business there required such a thorough background check, Ghost City wouldn't be nearly as bustling. Commerce could only come alive if there was room for loopholes.

Xie Lian interrogated her for a while, but it was fruitless. After determining that this Half-Maquillage Woman was no more than a clueless little minion, he called to Quan Yizhen.

"Qi Ying, have one of your heavenly officials come to collect this female ghost."

But Quan Yizhen replied, "No. I don't have any heavenly officials in my palace."

"Not a single one?" Xie Lian asked. "You've never appointed any deputy generals?"

"Nope," Quan Yizhen answered unapologetically.

"..."

As it turned out, the Martial God of the West always operated alone. He'd never appointed anyone to any position, not even a helper to manage the day-to-day essentials. At least for Xie Lian, it was because he couldn't afford it. Quan Yizhen's situation could probably only be explained by his eccentric character. With no other choice, Xie Lian fumbled for a clay jar and used it to seal the Half-Maquillage Woman away. Then he took the brocade robe from Lang Ying's hands and shook it open to inspect it. His brows knitted slightly.

It certainly was wicked, but...what was the best way to describe it? In Xie Lian's opinion, its evil qi was oddly superficial—like it was nothing more than a heavy layer of powder and rouge rather than emitted from deep within. Xie Lian's gut told him that this thing wasn't as dangerous as the rumors said, but he was still on guard.

Quan Yizhen glanced at the robe. "It's fake."

Xie Lian was taken aback. "How do you know?"

"It's fake," Quan Yizhen repeated. "I've seen the real Brocade Immortal before. It's way more powerful than that thing."

"When did you see it?" Xie Lian asked, curious. "There are actually quite a few people who've seen the Brocade Immortal before, but they still couldn't identify it. So how are you so certain?"

Quan Yizhen fell silent. At that very moment, Ling Wen reached out to him via the spiritual communication array.

"Your Highness, we've just received information that there is a little ghost with the Brocade Immortal in hand, spotted about ten kilometers from your Puqi Shrine," her voice rang in his ear. "We'll need to trouble you to go take a look."

"Another one? All right," Xie Lian replied. Then he glanced at Quan Yizhen, and without making a sound, he asked within the array, "Oh, by the way, one more thing. Ling Wen, has Qi Ying seen the Brocade Immortal before?"

"Qi Ying?" Ling Wen said. "He didn't just *see* it. It was much more than that."

"What do you mean?" Xie Lian asked.

"It's complicated," Ling Wen replied. "Is Your Highness aware that His Highness Qi Ying wasn't always the martial god who ruled the west? That role was once held by His Highness Yin Yu."

Xie Lian recalled the Wind Master telling him this while he stripped during their adventure at Paradise Manor, and he couldn't help but feel his heart squeeze.

"I've heard that before. Weren't the two Highnesses shixiong and shidi—a pair of martial brothers-in-arms?"

Back before Yin Yu ascended, he was their sect's head disciple. One day, he saw a brash little street urchin, and in a moment of softheartedness, he asked his shifu to take the boy in. That child was Quan Yizhen.

They were peers for many years, and Yin Yu always took very good care of Quan Yizhen. He ascended first and even appointed Quan Yizhen as a deputy general.

"You've met Qi Ying a few times, so you should know," Ling Wen said. "He's a little bit..."

"Socially unaware? That's a good thing," Xie Lian said.

Ling Wen chuckled. "Good or not depends on the person and

the situation. Some people think he's a selfish loose cannon, ignorant of manners, who doesn't give people the respect they deserve. If it wasn't for His Highness Yin Yu taking the heat on his behalf and smoothing things over when he first set foot in the Heavenly Court, who knows how many people would've tried to pulverize him."

"Those two Highnesses must share a very good relationship then," Xie Lian mused.

"It *was* good at first," Ling Wen said. "But unfortunately, later on, Qi Ying also ascended."

Both ascended from western lands, so how should it be handled? Thus, the two agreed to rule the West together.

Shixiong and shidi, presiding over their domain together— it sounded like a beautiful tale. But at the end of the day, one mountain could not support two tigers.

If Yin Yu's abilities could be called one in a million, worthy of a Heavenly Tribulation sent forth from the heavens, then Quan Yizhen's abilities could carry him through three Heavenly Tribulations. In fact, maybe not even one in a million possessed such potential. It was fine at the beginning, as the gap between them wasn't so obvious. But the more time passed, the larger the rift grew.

Quan Yizhen was clearly antisocial; not only did he not attempt to build relationships with his fellow heavenly colleagues, he also never tried to ingratiate himself with his devotees. He actually did the opposite. He didn't bother to remember the names of any heavenly officials aside from Yin Yu, and he was audacious enough to regularly tell off and even beat up his followers. He was as out of line as they came, but his domain grew bigger and bigger, and the number of his followers only increased. In comparison, the Palace of Yin Yu began to lose its shine. Finally, the Palace of Yin Yu grew restless.

This shixiong and shidi always gave each other presents on their birthdays, and one year, Yin Yu gifted Quan Yizhen a mighty suit of armor.

"...The Brocade Immortal?" Xie Lian asked.

"That's right," Ling Wen said.

Not only could the Brocade Immortal drain blood from and kill its wearer, but it also had an even more unusual ability. If a person was given the robe as a gift, they would be forced to obey every command of the one who gave it to them.

Since both shixiong and shidi had always been friendly with each other, Quan Yizhen put the armor on without a second thought. Soon after, Yin Yu played a seemingly unintentional joke while Quan Yizhen was under the control of the Brocade Immortal. And Quan Yizhen, with his mind possessed, did exactly as he was told. If not for Jun Wu, who noticed something amiss and stopped him in time, Quan Yizhen would've cut off his own head and dribbled it like a ball.

"That incident was a huge deal at the time—it caused quite the uproar," Ling Wen said. "Naturally, Yin Yu was banished from his esteemed heavenly position then and there after harming one of his heavenly colleagues."

Logically, the two of them should've fallen out afterward...but Xie Lian recalled that silly play the worshippers of the Palace of Qi Ying put on during the Mid-Autumn Festival Banquet. The clown jumping up and down behind Quan Yizhen's back was most likely Yin Yu, and yet Quan Yizhen's reaction was outrage, followed by his leaping down to the Mortal Realm to knock some heads.

"I believe Qi Ying still thinks very highly of His Highness Yin Yu. Might there have been a misunderstanding?"

"Who knows," Ling Wen said. "Whether or not there was a

misunderstanding, the person in question has been banished for so many years now. So who cares?"

Xie Lian nodded and was about to bid her farewell when Ling Wen added, "Wait. Your Highness, there's more. I wasn't done earlier. Thirty kilometers out from your Puqi Shrine, there is another unknown creature with the Brocade Immortal in hand."

"Isn't that a little too far? And why are there two?" Xie Lian asked.

"I'm not done," Ling Wen said. "Listen well: twenty-two kilometers to the northwest, seven-and-a-half kilometers southeast, eleven kilometers north..."

After reporting twenty-seven or twenty-eight locations in one breath, Ling Wen finally finished. "Yeah. That's about it for now."

By the time she was done reporting, Xie Lian had forgotten everything and felt rather woeful. "Your palace is quite efficient this time, isn't it? But 'for now'? Are you saying there might be more...? Could Ghost City be distributing Brocade Immortals?"

"Pretty much," Ling Wen replied. "In Ghost City, there are many peddlers of unknown origins who sell counterfeits while wearing fake skins. They change skins once they're done, so those in the know usually don't randomly buy things off the street. Still, there are ghosts who think of it like hunting for antiques and like the thrill of hoping they hit the jackpot. Many small-time vendors in the Ghost Realm heard through the grapevine that the Brocade Immortal has been stolen and are using this chance to scam buyers, saying any random robe they dug up is the real deal. Unbelievably enough, there are still quite a few ghosts who fall for it and try the robes out on people. It's really giving us intel gatherers a headache."

This would thoroughly interfere with their search for the real Brocade Immortal; with so many "Brocade Immortals" popping up everywhere, it would be impossible to find the real one. However, since they were assigned the mission, they had to come up with a way to complete it.

"I guess we should start with the closest one and search from there," Xie Lian said.

Xie Lian didn't have any spiritual powers, Quan Yizhen didn't know how to draw the teleportation array, and neither of them had any deputy officials. But of the locations Ling Wen had given, thankfully the closest to them was an abandoned dyehouse only two-and-a half kilometers out. Without further ado, even though it was the middle of the night, they hastily departed.

At first, Xie Lian was going to make Lang Ying stay behind at Puqi Shrine, but he tagged along and refused to be ushered back. Xie Lian figured this trip shouldn't be too dangerous and could help give Lang Ying some experience—he was planning to train the boy in cultivation anyway. So he was allowed to stick around.

The three hurried on their way under the cover of night. As they ran along, they heard creepy voices chanting a work song on the road ahead.

"Hey-hey-ho!

"Hey-hey-ho!"

Hearing that familiar work song, Xie Lian stopped his steps. A giant shadow gradually emerged from the mist ahead, along with four ghost fires floating around it. Quan Yizhen was poised to make a move, ready to beat it down without asking a single question, but Xie Lian pulled him back.

"Don't worry. I know them."

Sure enough, four golden skeletons carrying a step-litter appeared before them. Quan Yizhen had never seen anything so magical before, and his eyes went wide and shimmering.

"Is this Your Highness the Crown Prince of Xianle?" the head skeleton sang.

"It is. May I help you?" Xie Lian answered.

"No troubles here, no troubles here," the golden skeleton sang. "We brothers have time on our hands and wanted to inquire if His Highness the Crown Prince is in a hurry. Perhaps we can give you a ride?"

The journey wasn't long, so Xie Lian wanted to decline, but Quan Yizhen cut in and exclaimed *"Yes!"* He was already eagerly climbing aboard and looked like he really wanted to give this strange-but-majestic step-litter a try. Xie Lian didn't know whether to laugh or cry. He'd just climbed up to grab Quan Yizhen when the step-litter tipped and chucked the intruder out. Xie Lian swayed as well, but someone steadied him.

"San..." he blurted, but when he looked back, it was Lang Ying. He'd climbed on without anyone noticing and was holding tightly onto Xie Lian's arm. A pair of inky black eyes watched him silently.

The skeletons hastily picked up the step-litter, and their eight legs spun like four fiery wheels. They dashed steadily away while shouting into the night.

"Move, move! Don't block the way, don't block the way!"

Quan Yizhen was heartlessly thrown onto the ground, but he jumped to his feet, clearly not giving up. He was determined to leap on, but the skeletons were too fast and he was always a step behind. He remained in hot pursuit, looking like he really, really wanted to ride in the step-litter, just to feel the thrill, just once. Xie Lian watched Quan Yizhen give chase so vigorously as he rode along, and he couldn't help but feel that this was a little mean. Wasn't this like they were bullying a child?

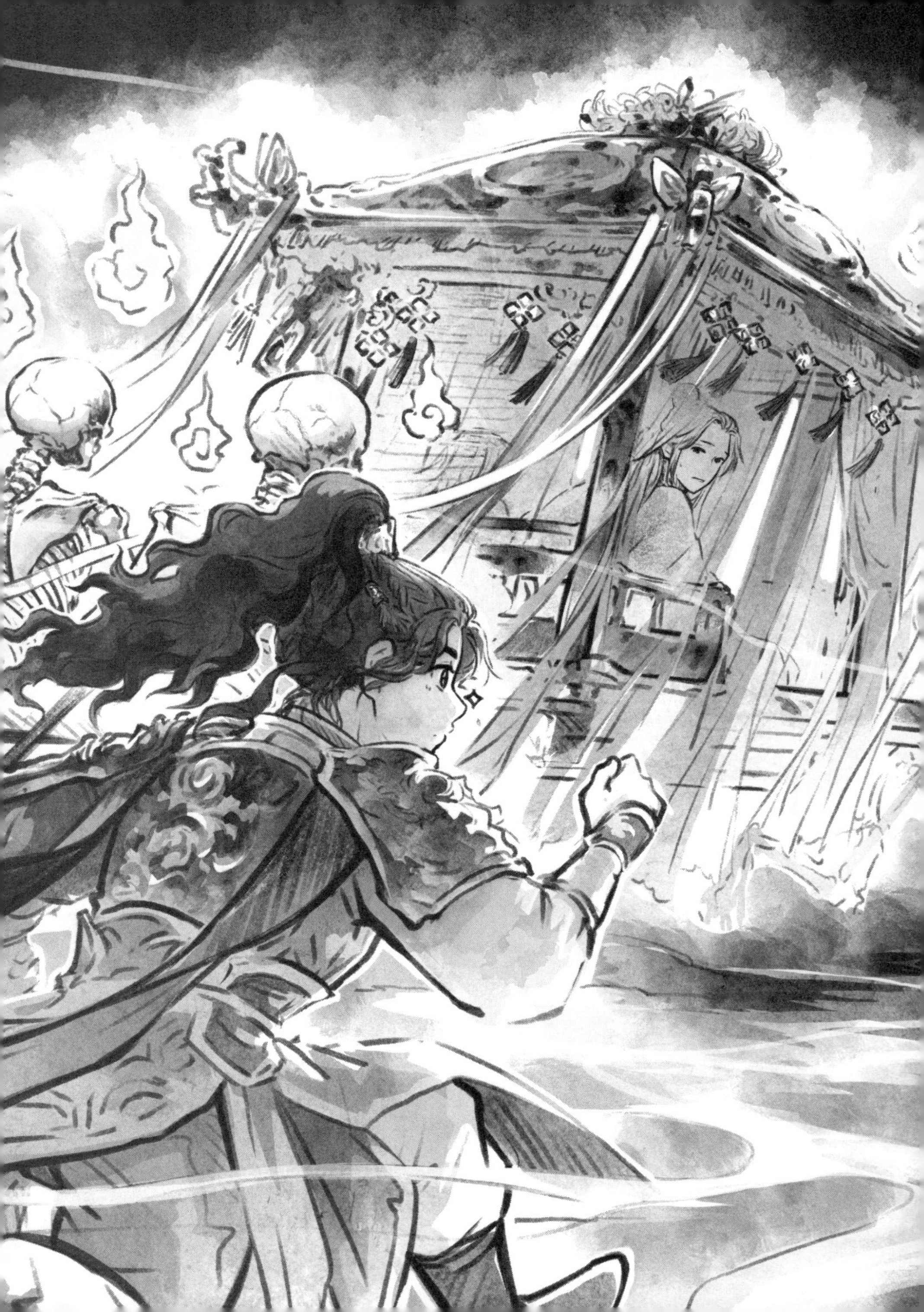

Even though he knew this step-litter belonged to Hua Cheng and he might not welcome other heavenly officials riding it, he couldn't help but ask, "Um...can't this litter carry three people?"

"It can't, it can't! It can only seat two!" the skeletons sang.

They ran at top speed the entire way, and Quan Yizhen chased them the whole time. Once they arrived at their destination, the golden skeletons allowed Xie Lian and Lang Ying to disembark, then picked up the step-litter and ran off, speedily disappearing from sight. In the end, Quan Yizhen never managed to board it, and he watched the step-litter disappear with extreme disappointment and visible longing.

Xie Lian stepped off the litter holding Lang Ying's hand. Ahead of them, he could hear loud cries and wails coming from that abandoned dyehouse. Xie Lian was puzzled. Didn't Ling Wen say this dyehouse was abandoned?

As they walked closer, the wailing voices grew clearer.

"This lowly one won't ever dare to sell counterfeits in ol' lord Hua-chengzhu's territory again!"

"We'll really never do it again! But please tell the good ol' Chengzhu that I got those fake Brocade Immortals from other ghosts! I'm a victim too!"

The three arrived at the dyehouse and bumped into a black-clad, ghost-masked man who had only just emerged from within. It seemed he'd been waiting for a long time, and he bent slightly to greet them.

"Your Highness."

The voice belonged to the officer who had once helped Xie Lian by catching Lang Ying on the streets of Ghost City. At the time, Xie Lian had seen a cursed shackle on his wrist.

The Wind Master had once told him that this person might be

Yin Yu, as there were only so many heavenly officials who had been banished in recent years.

Xie Lian asked, "How do I address you, sir?"

"Please, Your Highness. I am but a nobody," the masked man replied.

As they entered the abandoned dyehouse, Xie Lian was blown away. There were all kinds of clothes hung on countless wooden racks: wedding robes, government attire, ladies' satin, uniforms, children's clothes... There were also crude hemp shirts stained with copious amounts of blood, so much it was like they were afraid people couldn't tell that there was something off about them. Piles upon piles, layers upon layers, and they were all sinister and heavy with evil qi, like each and every one was a living corpse standing before them. Even if they weren't the Brocade Immortal, they certainly couldn't be anything good.

Long strips of fabric dyed in many colors were hung high from the wooden stacks, some ghastly white, some filthy. It had been a long time since anyone last touched them. Quan Yizhen crouched next to a large black vat of dye and became singularly fixated on the contents—the fluid had a funny color and emitted a strange smell. Xie Lian was afraid that he was going to dip his finger in and lick it at any second, so he hastily dragged him away.

Outside in the yard, a band of ghosts were bound by a single iron chain, and they crouched low, hugging their heads.

"This is...?" Xie Lian wondered.

"All the nefarious creatures guilty of selling the Brocade Immortal in Ghost City are here, as are those who attempted to use it anywhere nearby," the ghost-masked man answered. "A total of ninety-eight pieces of clothing have been collected."

Ninety-eight pieces, and they must have all been caught extremely quickly. Xie Lian was slightly touched.

"If there is any new movement, we will proceed with the utmost haste on Your Highness's behalf," the ghost-masked man continued.

Hearing this, Xie Lian couldn't help but say, "There's no need. Please tell San...Hua-chengzhu that he really doesn't need to trouble himself like this. I can take care of it myself too."

The results would've been the same, it just would've taken a little more time and energy. He was a titled heavenly official working for the heavens, after all; even if he didn't have many worshippers, this was still his job.

"Naturally, Chengzhu understands that Your Highness is capable of doing this effortlessly," the masked man replied. "But this is also precisely why he hopes My Lord won't waste energy on small errands that anyone could accomplish. Your Highness's time and effort should be spent on more important matters."

"..." Xie Lian deliberated for a moment, but in the end, he still asked, "May I ask how your Chengzhu is doing right now...?"

Lang Ying nonchalantly swayed back and forth next to Xie Lian.

"Chengzhu is very busy at the moment," the ghost-masked man replied.

"Oh. That's good," Xie Lian said quickly. "Hopefully everything goes well for him. I wish him success."

They questioned every single ghost that had been arrested, and each and every one was adamant that their product had been distributed to them by a mysterious masked individual. They didn't seem to be lying. But in a place like Ghost City, how many hundreds of masked individuals roamed the streets every day?

The interrogation was fruitless. And so, the ghost-masked man yanked on the chain and bid them farewell as he led those yowling ghosts away. The ninety-eight pieces of ghost clothing were left behind. Xie Lian felt that in all the years he had spent collecting old clothes, he had never seen so many in one place. As he rummaged through them, he suspected that not a single one was the real thing.

"Qi Ying, why don't you come and take a look?" he said to Quan Yizhen.

However, Quan Yizhen only scratched beneath his loose, curly hair and shook his head. "Too many."

Too many ghost robes. Every single piece of cloth emitted evil qi, now all intermingled. It made it impossible to tell what each one was. If someone possessed a sharp sense of taste, they would be able to differentiate between the flavors of candied pear and apple stuffing, but they could hardly do the same if ninety-eight different kinds of fruit stuffing were mixed together and presented to them to try. Xie Lian tried to think of another method, but when he turned his head to look, he saw that Quan Yizhen had picked up a robe and was about to try it on then and there. Xie Lian hastily stopped him and hung the robe back onto the rack.

"Stop, stop, stop. Qi Ying, let's agree on two things: first, don't put random things in your mouth, and second, don't put on random clothes. Those are both very dangerous things to do."

Quan Yizhen pointed behind Xie Lian. "Then what about him?"

Xie Lian suddenly smelled something burning, and he followed the direction of Quan Yizhen's pointing finger. Lang Ying had lit a match he had found in some corner and was calmly setting the bottom hem of a ghost robe ablaze with practiced ease.

"...Don't...play with fire either?!" Xie Lian exclaimed.

The ghost robe seemed to feel pain from being burned; its hem rolled upward, and it was twisting like mad, trying to get away. It looked more like a live eel than a piece of clothing. The image, surprisingly, looked rather cruel. And although Xie Lian could smell burning, there was no evidence of it on the fabric. It appeared these ghost robes had soaked in enough yin energy that they resisted destruction by fire.

Upon hearing Xie Lian telling him not to play with fire, Lang Ying casually tossed the match and stepped on it to put out the flames, looking entirely obedient once more. Xie Lian didn't know whether to laugh or cry, and he walked over.

"What's with you today...?"

He trailed off, and his face stiffened. This was because he saw, not too far away, a long white piece of fabric hanging high up on a rack and gently fluttering in the night breeze. The silhouette of a human was slowly creeping across the cloth's surface.

This shadow had no head.

Xie Lian pulled Lang Ying behind him. With one swift movement, he drew his sword and slashed. "Everyone, watch out!"

His swing cut the fabric and the shadow in half. However, when the cloth landed on the ground, there was nothing behind it; the headless silhouette had disappeared. Xie Lian had no chance to rush over to check before he felt a chill on his neck. He snapped his head back, and his pupils shrank. A beautifully dressed woman had appeared silently behind him.

No! It wasn't a woman but a robe!

What he had just slashed in half was also a robe, and once it fell to the ground, it was covered by other textiles. From all around, countless humanoid figures emerged, swaying and rocking slowly, gathering around the three of them. They had hung those ninety-eight ghost robes in the yard, on the verandas, and inside the dyehouse—and somehow, without them realizing it, all the robes had struggled free of the racks!

Xie Lian was dumbfounded. "They were all fine before! What's going on?"

Beside him came a quiet voice, "The agitation of ghosts."

Xie Lian turned his head to look, and the one who spoke was Lang Ying. Although his expression showed no unease, veins were bulging on the back of his pale hands. He was very obviously being affected by something as well.

Another wave of ghost agitation! As the day when Mount Tonglu would open its gates approached, its tremors grew more and more deafening in the ears of ghosts to remind them.

The first thing Xie Lian thought was: *How is San Lang doing?*

However, the current situation didn't give him much time to think. While his mind was rapidly spinning, over twenty ghost robes had already flung themselves over. Quan Yizhen swung his fist without a second thought. If that punch landed on the wall or the ground, it would surely rock the earth—but this thousand-pound fist collided with nothing but clothes. Even children know that in "Rock, Scissors, Cloth," cloth traps rock, and that light, malleable cloth was perfect for subduing fists! No matter how hard he launched his punches, the fabric could simply wrapped around them and incurred no damage. Only Xie Lian's sword was effective. But those ghost robes were extremely light and agile as they evaded; a simple spring backward could put over a dozen meters between them. Since they barely weighed anything, there was practically no sound or breath of air that gave away their movement. Avoiding their ambushes was much more difficult than avoiding a human opponent.

Usually, it was people who picked clothes, but now it was clothes picking people. The ninety-eight ghost robes each eagerly searched for a body that fit them, a person they fancied. Among humans, it was women who loved picking out clothes; among ghost robes, it was the female styles that loved picking out humans. Dozens of long ladies' skirts, all in different colors and styles, urgently pressed themselves against Xie Lian—even the threat of his sword couldn't force them away. It was a battle more heated than a group of women fighting over a pretty robe they fancied. Xie Lian was surrounded by blooming flowers and silk, squeezed between those female robes and pulled from all directions.

Quan Yizhen yanked off several pieces of children's clothing that were stubbornly trying to lower themselves over his head and tossed them aside. He was puzzled as he looked at Xie Lian.

"How come all the women's clothes like you so much?" he wondered.

"Maybe because they think I look friendlier?" Xie Lian answered.

However, not a single ghost robe went to harass Lang Ying. Perhaps they knew he was also a ghost and that there would be no point in siphoning from him, so they didn't approach. Xie Lian swung his sword and sliced a number of ladies' dresses, but the robes that were cut in half still moved as they wished, their dodges even more agile. From the corner of his eye, Xie Lian saw several ghost robes sneaking toward the window.

"Close the door, cast an array! Don't let them out!" he shouted.

With two gods and one ghost on hand, they could deal with this situation, but it would be a bit more difficult if the ghost robes snuck outside to seek trouble. His shout came too late, though—the dyehouse's yard was open air, and a long robe was already outside fluttering its expansive sleeves. It soared into the air like a giant bat and shot away into the night sky.

Xie Lian groaned mentally, then shouted, "Qi Ying! I'll leave the dyehouse to you!"

Then he pushed off with the soles of his feet and flew outside the walls, catching the bottom hem of that long ghost robe.

The long robe tried in vain to flutter its sleeves as hard as it could, but with the added weight of an entire person, it couldn't help but plummet to the ground. Xie Lian still held its hem in a death grip. However, it was exceedingly cunning, and with a loud *rrrrrrip!* it tore off its own corner like a warrior chopping off his own arm. It hastily slipped away from Xie Lian's hands.

A random passerby happened to be on his way home after a night of drinking, and he screamed in fright at the sight of a headless creature flying at him.

"*Aaaaaaaaaaah!* A headless ghost! It's headless!"

Xie Lian charged over and seized the robe again, then showed it to that passerby to comfort him. "Don't be scared, don't be scared! See? It's not headless! There's no body in there at all!"

The passerby looked, and sure enough, it was completely empty inside the folds of that robe! This was definitely more horrifying than a headless ghost, and his eyes rolled back as he fainted on the spot. Xie Lian quickly caught him and gently laid him on the ground.

"So sorry! I'll take care of this right away."

After that chaos was over, Xie Lian could finally get to work seizing all the ghost robes that had flown out of the dyehouse. He counted them, making sure not a single piece was missing, before letting out a sigh of relief.

With things settled, Xie Lian said, "I suppose our only option is to use Qi Ying's simple, crude method. Let's try each of these robes on and see."

He wouldn't have minded putting them on himself, but that could go badly for his two partners. If he did actually put on the

Brocade Immortal, who knew if they would be able to deal with any accidents that might happen? In the end, they decided that he would stand watch while the other two dressed.

Both Lang Ying and Quan Yizhen peeled off their outer robes and started trying on one robe after the other. With every new robe, Xie Lian would give simple commands to see if they would obey, like "jump" or "spin around."

They tried on every single one of the ninety-eight robes, both testing forty to fifty apiece, but they didn't seem to have any strange reactions. Not a single piece in this pile of ghost robes was the Brocade Immortal, and they had worked all night for nothing.

Both still dressed in only a single layer, Lang Ying and Quan Yizhen squatted on the ground while Xie Lian sat atop a mountain of clothes of all sorts.

Supporting his forehead with his hand, Xie Lian mumbled, "There really is no value in buying fakes..."

He sat there like that for a while before seeking out Ling Wen in the communication array.

"Ling Wen, I've collected some ghost robes. Even though the real Brocade Immortal is probably not in the pile, they're still rather wicked and troublesome to deal with. Can you send someone down to take them away?"

"Acknowledged. I'll coordinate it promptly. How many pieces have you gathered?" Ling Wen answered.

"Ninety-eight," Xie Lian replied.

"...Your Highness truly is a capable man, collecting more than what I reported to you," Ling Wen remarked.

Xie Lian softly cleared his throat. "It actually wasn't me..."

But before he finished his sentence, a familiar chill ran down his spine. Xie Lian paused, then looked up.

Upon the rows of light, flowy white fabrics in front of him, there was the dark, shadowed silhouette of a human.

This time, it wasn't headless, nor was it fluttering. The one standing behind those long curtained fabrics was very much a man, and the edges of his features could be easily distinguished—such as his remarkably tall height and the disheveled state of his hair.

70
The Ninety-Ninth Ghost Robe Hidden in Danger

XIE LIAN SHOT TO HIS FEET. "The Brocade Immortal?!"

Naturally, the silhouette didn't respond. It also did not move, standing there motionless.

Xie Lian set a hand on the other two's shoulders to pin them where they were. "Don't move," he whispered.

A night breeze blew by moments later, and that man's silhouette seemed to sigh, then dispersed with the wind. Xie Lian abruptly stood. Then, a knock sounded from the door of the dyehouse. All three of them looked toward it.

"Who is it?" Xie Lian raised his voice to ask.

A man's voice answered from outside. "Your Highness, it's me."

Xie Lian walked over to open the door, and on the other side was a man with bright, proper features and an upstanding divine form. He entered with his hands clasped behind him.

Xie Lian was a little stunned. "Ling Wen, why did you come in person?"

Ling Wen fixed his sleeves. "Since I heard Your Highness say things were difficult, I figured typical heavenly officials wouldn't be able to assist, so I've come to see what's going on for myself. Greetings, Your Highness Qi Ying. Why are you sitting on the ground? What's wrong? What's with that look?"

It was Ling Wen in male form. Xie Lian walked to the cloth

curtain and flipped it open. Sure enough, there was nothing behind it. He turned to address Ling Wen once more.

"The Brocade Immortal showed itself."

"What?" Ling Wen replied in amazement.

"It must have been it. I'm quite sure," Xie Lian said. "It was a young man, very tall—maybe seven centimeters taller than me. Judging by his physical structure, he must be skilled in martial arts."

Ling Wen was somewhat doubtful. "Your Highness, are you sure? We've never had word that the Brocade Immortal showed itself to anyone in the past few centuries. Besides, didn't you say that none of these ninety-eight ghost robes were the real thing? Could someone be playing a trick?"

"I'm afraid that's not possible," Xie Lian replied. "After that wave of agitation was over, we shut the door and windows and set an array to prevent ghost robes from sneaking out and harassing mortals. Things inside couldn't get out, and things outside couldn't come in. There are only the three of us here; who among us would play tricks?"

After mulling it over for a moment, Ling Wen said, "Then perhaps the real thing encountered some special circumstance...or maybe what you saw was a vengeful spirit possessing one of the ghost robes?"

Lang Ying and Quan Yizhen were both crouched on the ground, staring blankly and daydreaming, while Xie Lian and Ling Wen stood with their arms crossed, assuming the stance of adults as they engaged in serious discussion.

In the end, Ling Wen suggested, "Why don't I take these ghost robes to the Palace of Ling Wen and have my people examine them? If they don't find anything, we can make inquiries at the next meeting. I'm sure someone in the Upper Court is an expert."

Giving the idea some thought, Xie Lian nodded. "That's probably a good idea. But this mission was assigned to us, so I want to be a little more thorough. Since the real Brocade Immortal is mixed into the pile, let me think up some methods and give identifying it another shot. If I haven't managed any progress by tomorrow, I'll hand the ninety-eight ghost robes over to you."

After all, this case wasn't under the jurisdiction of the Palace of Ling Wen.

"There's no need for Your Highness to be so polite," Ling Wen said. "Oh, and if you'll be sending them over tomorrow, it will be one hundred and one pieces, correct?"

Xie Lian was puzzled. "Why are there suddenly three more?" Then it dawned on him. "You're suspicious of the robes we're wearing right now?"

"It's not impossible," Ling Wen noted.

Xie Lian's cultivation robes were so worn that they were fraying at the edges, and he lifted the corner of one sleeve to demonstrate. "I've worn this robe for several years now; it definitely doesn't have issues. I recently purchased the one Lang Ying is wearing right now, but he didn't obey my commands, so it also shouldn't be a problem."

He had told Lang Ying not to do housework, but Lang Ying still chopped wood. He had told him to stay home like a good boy, but Lang Ying still came along.

However, Ling Wen shook his head. "That's not what I mean. Your Highness, you might not be aware of this, but the evil qi on the Brocade Immortal is strong. It will pass on to other normal articles of clothing nearby. So don't wear the clothes you have on anymore, just to be safe. Get rid of them."

Hearing this, Xie Lian quickly went over and started to peel both Lang Ying and Quan Yizhen out of their outer robes. "Don't wear this anymore, don't wear this. Take it off, take it all off. I'll pack up the clothes and bring them to the Palace of Ling Wen tomorrow."

"I'll send people to come pick them up," Ling Wen offered.

"No need, no need," Xie Lian said. "It's already embarrassing enough to trouble you like this every time without you personally making a trip on top of that. Your palace is busy—I can handle this myself."

The next day, Xie Lian painstakingly packed the huge piles of clothes and carried the large bundles up to the Heavenly Capital by himself.

When he arrived, it seemed that Ling Wen had been waiting for him in her palace for a long time. Her palace wasn't as hustling and bustling as usual today, packed with gods flowing in and out. Xie Lian untied the large bundles, and the brightly colored ghost robes burst out of their wrappings, spilling onto the floor and covering the ground. He casually wiped away the sweat on his forehead as Ling Wen strolled over.

"Was your investigation fruitful?"

"Much ashamed, it's been fruitless," Xie Lian sighed, sounding resigned. "I apologize in advance. I don't have any helping hands, so unfortunately things are a bit scattered. After all the chaos yesterday, I don't know if I brought all of the robes. I keep feeling like I'm missing one or two pieces, but I'm not sure."

"That's not an issue," Ling Wen said. Then she looked down and made a rough count. "There are indeed a few pieces missing. Your Highness, I don't think I see the robe that the little ghost next to you was wearing."

Xie Lian tapped his palm with his fist. "Ah, you're right! I remember now. Lang Ying has already gotten used to wearing it, and I forgot to collect it. I'll go grab it right now."

Ling Wen chuckled. "No rush. Take care, Your Highness."

However, Xie Lian didn't move to leave—he instead remained planted in place, his expression growing solemn. Ling Wen was about to summon her subordinate heavenly officials to collect the ghost robes, but she was puzzled when she turned and saw that he was still there. It was just the two of them in the hall.

"Your Highness, is there something else?"

Xie Lian watched her with a complicated expression. "No, nothing. It's just that I wonder...if I did bring you the real Brocade Immortal, would you hide it away if I took my eyes off you?"

"..." Ling Wen's smile receded, but she still was extremely polite as she asked, "Your Highness?"

Xie Lian watched her mildly. "I've had an inkling from the very beginning."

Ling Wen remained at ease. "What of?"

"Most people—or ordinary nefarious creatures—wouldn't dare break into a Temple of Divine Might. Not many individuals aside from Jun Wu himself are familiar enough with the layout of them to steal objects under such heavy lockdown, let alone escape capture. I'm afraid that Ling Wen-zhenjun is the only other one who would know her way around so well."

After all, the Palace of Ling Wen roamed every other god's palaces each and every day. It was more than familiar with everyone's domains.

Ling Wen grinned. "Your Highness, your reasoning is a little too simplistic. 'The person with the easiest access is the most suspicious.' Based on that line of thinking, isn't it more likely that the Heavenly Emperor robbed himself?"

Xie Lian nodded. "I must admit, you're not wrong. But what made me start to suspect you was the Half-Maquillage Woman."

"What about the Half-Maquillage Woman?" Ling Wen asked.

"She had the fake Brocade Immortal in her possession and just happened to come to my door," Xie Lian replied. "How could such a huge coincidence happen? Besides, she'd practically written 'suspicious' on her face; like she was scared I wouldn't immediately find her dubious. Her intent was too obvious."

"Oh? What intent?"

"Didn't she already say it herself?" Xie Lian said. "'Exchange old for new.' What she wanted was the old clothes in my Puqi Shrine!"

When the Brocade Immortal was stolen, the Palace of Divine Might found out extremely quickly and reacted equally fast. An investigation started the moment it was stolen. Therefore, the thief might not dare keep it in their own possession and would instead hide it away. But where would be the best hiding place?

Hide a leaf in a forest.

If Xie Lian wanted to hide the Brocade Immortal, he would turn it into an extremely inconspicuous and normal-looking hemp robe and toss it into the markets of the Mortal Realm, then keep an eye on it from afar. Normally, no one would want to buy such a coarsely made robe. But the life Xie Lian led couldn't be called normal. He had been wearing the same frayed cultivation robe for the past several years; he could only afford such clothing with the money he had. As long as clothing was clean and kept him warm, that was all he asked for, and he wasn't picky. In addition, he was the kind of person who possessed the incredible ability to pick out the most dangerous article of clothing out of countless other pieces in the big discount bin. And it was in this fashion, in self-congratulatory cheer at finding such a major discount, that he bought and brought home the legendary Brocade Immortal.

"Your Highness, your accusation is quite undue," Ling Wen said. "You are from a martial god background, after all. You would subdue a Half-Maquillage Woman in no time if she approached your door. She wouldn't be able to take any robes away, old or new."

"She certainly wouldn't, but who says she had to? How would she have been dealt with if this unexpected turn of events hadn't happened?" Xie Lian said.

If Xie Lian had assumed the Half-Maquillage Woman had the real Brocade Immortal, then he would have surely reported it to Ling Wen, and Ling Wen would've most likely descended personally. And, like she had the day before, she would've probably told Xie Lian that all the clothes needed to be brought back to her palace to be assessed just to be safe.

It was too bad that Quan Yizhen was there at the time. Ling Wen couldn't have expected that he'd be so knowledgeable after having only worn the Brocade Immortal once, and that he could correctly identify the Brocade Immortal in the Half-Maquillage Woman's hands as a fake. This meant it was no longer easy nor logical for Ling Wen to whisk away all the clothes at Puqi Shrine.

All of Xie Lian's information was provided by Ling Wen. She could also openly make inquiries and keep constant track of Xie Lian's progress. When the Half-Maquillage Woman was exposed, Ling Wen immediately sent Xie Lian new communication through the array that Ghost City was distributing counterfeits that had to be managed. She had wasted no time in throwing new missions at him, giving him little time to think too deeply about anything questionable with her requests.

"I don't know if you were the one who distributed the counterfeits, but it was indeed you who provided me with intel. You probably wanted to draw me away from Puqi Shrine before coming for Lang Ying," Xie Lian said.

But Lang Ying had tagged along with him.

"I don't know if you anticipated that the Brocade Immortal would show himself so suddenly, but you have no trouble improvising."

There were so many ghost robes with authenticity unknown. A chance would surely arise to slip the real Brocade Immortal away amidst the chaos. And when the Brocade Immortal showed himself, Ling Wen could also use that as an excuse to personally and openly confiscate all clothing on-site. As for how things would be assessed, how the real thing would be identified, and the explanation for that silhouette—that would all be on Ling Wen's word.

Having listened to that point, Ling Wen gestured for him to pause. "Your Highness, please stop right there. So you believe that—Lang Ying, that's his name, right? You think that the robe he was wearing is the Brocade Immortal? Don't forget, he didn't obey your orders when he put it on. Am I wrong? You said so yourself. You have to know that the Brocade Immortal is extremely powerful. Even a Ghost King would not be able to resist a direct order if he wore it."

"You also said that it 'must've encountered some special circumstance,'" Xie Lian replied. "As for what that could be, I'm sure you know better than I do. I hope you can answer the question."

Ling Wen frowned slightly and folded her hands behind her. "Your Highness, does this mean you have deemed *me* the thief?" she asked softly. "Pardon my bluntness, but this makes me somewhat... displeased."

Xie Lian inclined his head. "I apologize."

"Apology accepted," Ling Wen said. "However, Your Highness, as long as you have the evidence, you may make your adamant accusations. But this is nothing but speculation."

"I didn't have any evidence before today," Xie Lian replied slowly. "In fact, I didn't have anything to go on at all before I stepped into the Palace of Ling Wen. But I've gotten it during this conversation."

Ling Wen gestured an invitation for him to proceed. "Please."

"The evidence is this: You never bothered to count the exact number of ghost robes," Xie Lian stated.

Ling Wen's expression barely changed aside from the slight stiffening of her brows.

"The number of ghost robes I brought was indeed lacking, but there wasn't just a single robe missing," Xie Lian continued. "In fact, I only brought eighty-eight pieces—a deficit of ten!

"I kept every piece of clothing I considered suspicious away from you. You never mentioned that the count was off, but with one look you noticed that the one Lang Ying was wearing wasn't here. So, pray tell, how did you know that particular one was missing?"

Ling Wen raised her hand. "Please wait."

She unhurriedly recounted the ghost robes and discovered that there were indeed eighty-eight pieces of clothing. Maintaining her impassive tone, she replied, "I suppose you can say that no one is perfect and something will always be overlooked."

"Very well," Xie Lian said. "Since you've counted seriously this time and have looked over every single piece, then let me ask whether you noticed this: the robe Lang Ying wore yesterday is among these eighty-eight ghost robes!"

"Your Highness, what are you implying?" Ling Wen asked.

Xie Lian crouched and pulled a robe from the pile of random clothing, shaking it open. It was a plain white hemp robe.

"The one Lang Ying wore yesterday is obviously here. Why didn't you notice it when you were counting?"

"Your Highness should also know that there's nothing special about that hemp robe. You can't blame me for not recognizing it at a glance," Ling Wen replied.

"It really is nothing to write home about," Xie Lian agreed.

"So then, as Ling Wen-zhenjun is so competent and reliable, so hard-working and cautious, why would you so rashly declare that such an inconspicuous robe was missing when you hadn't fully counted?"

Ling Wen's smile did not falter. "There are too many robes; my eyes glazed over. The scrolls on my desk are piled high as mountains, and my mind blanks at the sight of them."

"Your eyes didn't glaze over, it's the opposite," Xie Lian said. "Your eyes are too sharp. Let me tell you something else—I *didn't* actually bring the robe Lang Ying wore yesterday. The one in my hands right now is a replica of the original. I was careful with the details. How were you able to tell with just one look that the real one Lang Ying wore isn't here?"

Ling Wen was baffled. "Fake or not, either way, I didn't see it. Your Highness, have you worked on so many cases that you're constantly overthinking things? Why would you spend so much effort creating a replica?"

Xie Lian could tell that she was dodging the question. "I'm not done yet. I'll tell you one last thing." He lifted the white hemp robe and said softly, "...This hemp robe was just a random one I pulled from the pile. That 'replica based on the original,' 'careful with the details' was just nonsense I made up. As you said, why would I waste my time making a replica? You've been tricked; this one isn't even the same color as the robe Lang Ying wore yesterday. Did you not think anything was off when I questioned you with it as evidence?"

"..."

Xie Lian stared at Ling Wen with intent. "Ling Wen, right now, I only need you to answer a very simple question: what color was the robe Lang Ying wore yesterday?"

Ling Wen didn't answer immediately. She slowly raised her eyelashes.

The white hemp robe fell to the ground.

"You are the esteemed top civil god, and countless scrolls detailing the matters of the Upper Court pass through your hands," Xie Lian said. "Your memory shouldn't be this bad. Why can't you even recall the color of the robe Lang Ying wore yesterday?

"You can't answer because you're guarding against my potential trickery. You *daren't* answer because you never knew what color it was in the first place—because yesterday, what you saw him wearing was simply a headless, sleeveless, ragged cloth sack!"

He made sure she could hear every word in his accusation clearly. "The Brocade Immortal takes on thousands of forms, but that's nothing more than an illusion. But no matter how powerful the illusion is, it will always be ineffective on one individual—the one who created it!

"No matter what shape it takes, it will always show its true form to its creator. You glanced through these eighty-eight ghost robes and didn't see a strange, headless, sleeveless cloth sack. Of course you knew at once that the Brocade Immortal wasn't in the pile!"

71
Seen Through the Ghost King, Delights in Teasing the Ghost King

XIE LIAN HAD INITIALLY ONLY PLANNED on keeping the suspicious ghost robes to thoroughly reexamine them himself, but he hadn't realized that he would catch this huge hole in Ling Wen's lies with her one offhand comment. The moment Xie Lian wrapped his head around what it implied, he went with the flow and managed to blow apart Ling Wen's armor with his crafty words.

Ling Wen stood there, frozen.

"Of course, you can deny all of this," Xie Lian granted. "But it would be easy to prove the robe's authenticity. All I would need to do is bring the robe to the Palace of Divine Might. Then I can have it change its form before the Heavenly Emperor and ask you to describe what it looks like. And the truth would come to light."

The Brocade Immortal sucked the blood of over five hundred people when it roamed freely in the Mortal Realm. It was a sinister object of great evil. Even if Ling Wen had simply broken into the Temple of Divine Might to steal the robe and hadn't yet had the chance to use it to cause harm, it wouldn't have been such an unforgivable crime. But Ling Wen was an appointed deputy general before she ascended, and the earliest stories of the Brocade Immortal surfaced long after Ling Wen's tenure in that position.

Which meant that Ling Wen created the Brocade Immortal *after* she had taken up her duties in the Heavenly Realm and become a heavenly official!

A heavenly official, who was duty-bound to protect humanity, had seduced and murdered a human; that alone called for a severe criminal sentence. Furthermore, the human who had been lured to his demise was a future heavenly official. Alas, the court would not handle this case with a light hand.

"Your Highness, you are honestly..." Ling Wen sighed. After a pause, she continued, "Maybe it's just my bad luck that this mission was given to you. There are only the two of us here at the Palace of Ling Wen today, and we've got centuries of friendship between us... but I doubt you'd agree to it if I pleaded for you to turn a blind eye because of that. So now you're going to encourage me to turn myself in to the Palace of Divine Might. Am I right?"

Xie Lian sighed too. Although he and Ling Wen had known each other for centuries, it had always been pure business; they had never developed a closer bond. Nonetheless, their relationship was fairly good. When he ascended for the third time, Ling Wen never looked down on him even when all the others taunted him as the Scrap Immortal. On the contrary, she had assisted him and taken care of him. But this Brocade Immortal mission just had to land on his head. Now that the truth was revealed, it was hard to report it and harder to stay silent.

"My luck is bad too," Xie Lian replied earnestly.

Ling Wen crossed her arms and shook her head. "Your Highness, you... Sometimes you're smart, but sometimes you aren't smart at all. Sometimes you're softhearted, but sometimes your heart is as hard as iron. You are rigid as always." After a pause, she asked, "So where is the robe now?"

"It's in my custody," Xie Lian replied. "After we're done here, I will personally deliver it to the Palace of Divine Might."

Ling Wen nodded, seemingly having nothing more to say.

"Can you tell me something?" Xie Lian asked. "Why didn't the Brocade Immortal work when Lang Ying wore it?"

"I can probably guess," Ling Wen said. "But if Your Highness wants the answer, will you first agree to a request?"

"What is it?" Xie Lian asked.

"Will you let me see it? The Brocade Immortal."

Xie Lian was taken aback.

"I only need one day," Ling Wen said. "If I am to turn myself in to the Palace of Divine Might, there may not be any opportunities to see it after. Don't misunderstand me, I'm not going to tamper with it. I was just shocked when you said he'd shown himself."

She shook her head, then her eyes stared off in reverie. "...It's been so many years, and I've never seen Bai Jing appear once."

"That young warrior's name was Bai Jing?" Xie Lian asked.

Ling Wen seemed to snap out of it. "Oh. Yes. But people usually called him Xiao-Bai."[9]

"Xiao-Bai?" Xie Lian wondered. "That sounds like..."

Like they were calling him a dog, or an idiot.

Ling Wen chuckled. "It means what you're thinking of. I'm the one who gave him the name Bai Jing. No one ever called him that, so not many knew the name. But he'll be very happy if you do."

In the legend of the Brocade Immortal, the way the young man's beloved treated him made her seem cruel and terrifying. If she didn't have a bone-deep hatred for him, then she was born cold-blooded.

---

9   [白錦] "Bai Jing" can be translated as "White Brocade," thus making the term "Brocade Immortal" a play on his name. 白 means "white," as well as "blank," and is not a polite word when used to describe someone's mental faculties. Xiao-Bai ("Little White") is a common name for pets, but it can also be read as "Little Blank."

Yet Ling Wen's tone was amiable when she spoke of that young man—there was neither affection nor hatred.

"So will you? If Your Highness is worried I'll run away, you can have Ruoye bind me. I won't be able to escape—I'm not a martial god."

For some reason, Xie Lian felt he should trust Ling Wen. After considering it for a moment, he nodded cautiously.

"Very well."

They left the Palace of Ling Wen like nothing was wrong; they greeted other passing heavenly officials as usual while they strolled down the Avenue of Divine Might. Ling Wen looked the same as always, and nothing gave away the fact that her hands were firmly bound by Ruoye under her sleeves. They didn't get very far before they ran into Pei Ming, who had just returned from his street patrol. The two greeted each other, then stood on the side of the road for a bit to chat and make perfunctory pleasantries. Pei Ming stared at Xie Lian the entire time, and Xie Lian grew slightly apprehensive.

"Why is General Pei looking at me like that?"

Pei Ming stroked his chin. "Not gonna lie, Your Highness. I get the jitters whenever I see you now. It feels like anyone standing next to you is going to have something go wrong," he replied earnestly. "So my poor heart started pounding when I saw you walking with Ling Wen. Ling Wen, you'd best watch your step for the next little while."

Ling Wen laughed. "How could that be? General Pei, please stop joking."

Xie Lian, didn't know whether to laugh or cry. On some level, Pei Ming's instincts were right on target.

Once back in the Mortal Realm, they could see Lang Ying leaning against the old tree out front as they drew close to Puqi Shrine.

He was spinning the broom in his hand without a care, and next to his feet was a tidy pile of fallen golden leaves. Xie Lian watched him for a while before he purposely put more weight into his steps to make his approach heard. Lang Ying didn't look back, but he must've noticed their presence and quite naturally changed his posture. He returned to sweeping, then turned around and acted like he'd only just noticed Xie Lian and Ling Wen.

Xie Lian lightly cleared his throat. "Sweeping again?"

Lang Ying nodded. Seeing him like this, Xie Lian couldn't resist patting his head like an elder would.

"What a good child," he praised.

Lang Ying accepted the gesture without reservation. Ling Wen watched them without comment.

Xie Lian led her to the shrine's entrance and opened the door. "It's in here…"

The moment he opened the door, he saw a figure crouched in front of the donation box, sneakily stuffing in gold bars. Xie Lian hurried over to drag him away.

"Qi Ying, stop stuffing it full! That's really enough. I haven't even taken out the ones you put in there last time. You've jammed up the opening with them now."

Ling Wen nodded. "Greetings, Your Highness Qi Ying."

Qi Ying acknowledged her too. "Hi."

There was a wooden rack set up in the center of Puqi Shrine, and a plain hemp robe hung there. Of course, that was only what Xie Lian saw. Ling Wen approached and gazed at it solemnly, but the robe did not react, even as the minutes stretched on.

She cocked her head. "My Lords, I want to look at it alone. Is that all right?"

"That's fine," Xie Lian said.

Xie Lian wasn't that worried; Ruoye had her hands bound and she wasn't a martial god, so there wasn't much she could try. He laid a hand on Quan Yizhen's shoulder.

"Let's go outside."

This case was more or less closed, and Xie Lian could feel himself relax. The neighbors had recently given him a bunch of fruits and vegetables, so Xie Lian took them to the kitchen, ready to cook. His undefeated spirit should be admired as an example to all.

Now that he'd stayed there for a few days, Quan Yizhen seemed to have taken Puqi Shrine as some sort of happy farm. He kept leaping around, climbing trees, stealing squash, snagging fish, and catching frogs. In a moment of Xie Lian's carelessness, Quan Yizhen snuck into the kitchen and swiped a yam. Feeling the empty spot on the counter, Xie Lian turned to see Quan Yizhen slipping out of the kitchen with the yam dangling from his mouth, hurrying away like a fish who had escaped the net.

"It's not cooked yet, don't eat it!" Xie Lian cried.

It was precisely because it hadn't been cooked yet that it had to be eaten quickly. Once Xie Lian cooked it, it wouldn't be edible anymore. Xie Lian shook his head, then he saw Lang Ying walking over and his eyes turned crescent as he smiled.

"Lang Ying, are you free? Come help me chop some vegetables."

Lang Ying seemed to have been planning to snatch the yam back from Quan Yizhen, but when he heard Xie Lian's request, he came over to help without a second thought. Taking his task very seriously, he picked up the knife from the cutting board and sliced into the cabbage, cutting with the utmost concentration. Xie Lian watched him for a moment, then turned to rinse the rice as he chatted.

"Lang Ying, you've seen quite a number of gods and ghosts coming and going from our little Puqi Shrine by now, right?"

Each of them more bizarre than the next. From behind him, Lang Ying answered, "Mm."

"Then let me ask you something," Xie Lian continued. "If you had to pick, who among them do you think is the handsomest?"

Lang Ying was engrossed in chopping the vegetables and seemed to be thinking hard. Xie Lian lightly arched his brows.

"Go on, tell me. Just say whatever you think is the truth."

Lang Ying answered, "You."

Xie Lian laughed. "Besides me."

"The one in red," Lang Ying said.

Xie Lian was going to bust a gut trying to contain his laughter. "Mmm. I think so too," he responded seriously. After a pause, he asked again, "Then who do you think is the coolest?"

Lang Ying still answered, "The one in red."

Xie Lian swiftly continued his questions without skipping a beat. "Who's the richest?"

"The one in red."

"Who do you admire the most?"

"The one in red."

"Who's the silliest?"

"The one in green."

The questions came one after the other without pause, but he was surprisingly able to change his answer in time. It spoke for his quick wit and reactions.

"It seems you quite like the gege dressed in red," Xie Lian commented. "His name is Hua Cheng—remember it well. So does this mean you think he's nice?"

The chopping of the knife in Lang Ying's hand had gotten many times faster, seemingly without the wielder noticing. "Very nice."

"So then, once we're free, do you think we should invite him here again?" Xie Lian asked.

"Mmm. Of course. It's a must," Lang Ying replied.

"I think so too," Xie Lian said. "But his subordinate said he's been very busy lately, so he must be occupied by very serious business. I think it's best if we don't disturb him."

After that comment, the crunching sound of vegetables being chopped grew more heavy-handed. Xie Lian gripped the edge of the stove to support himself, his stomach straining from trying to hold back his laughter. Quan Yizhen poked his head in the window, sweeping a look over the kitchen as he took a bite of the yam.

"You chopped it to shreds. It won't taste good anymore," he said to Lang Ying.

"Hmm? What did you say?" Lang Ying threatened.

Xie Lian turned to look; the cabbage wasn't just shredded, it was pulverized into tiny scraps. He cleared his throat softly.

"My gosh, your knife work is really bad."

"..."

After throwing all sorts of seasonings into the pot, Xie Lian dusted off his hands and decided to let it simmer for two hours, then left the kitchen. He glanced at Ling Wen; she was still behaving herself in the shrine, so he continued to do his chores. He picked out a larger plank from the pile of firewood and borrowed a brush and ink from the village chief's house, then sat in front of the door lost in thought. One hand held the plank and the other held the brush. Lang Ying walked over, and Xie Lian looked up.

"Lang Ying, can you read? Do you know how to write?" he asked warmly.

"Yes," Lang Ying replied.

"How's your writing?"

"Mediocre."

"That's all right. As long as it's legible. Come give me a hand again." Xie Lian passed the plank and brush over to Lang Ying and smiled. "Our shrine doesn't have an establishment plaque. Why don't you draft one for me?"

"..."

Lang Ying picked up the brush at Xie Lian's insistence. The little brush in his hand seemed to weigh a thousand pounds and wouldn't be moved no matter what. A moment later, he seemed to concede defeat and put down both the brush and plank. A helpless voice came from underneath the bandages.

"Gege...I was wrong."

That voice didn't belong to Lang Ying at all—though it was crisper and more boyish than it normally was, it was clearly the voice of Hua Cheng. Xie Lian had been leaning against the wall with his arms crossed, and after watching him struggle for so long and finally surrender, he could no longer hold back and sank to the ground in a fit of laughter.

"San Lang really is extremely busy!"

Since they hadn't seen each other for a long time, Xie Lian had missed him dearly—even though that "long time" was no more than a few days. Yet who would've thought Hua Cheng had been hiding right by his side all this time? Xie Lian's mood brightened immediately, and all his previous concerns were completely forgotten. He was laughing so hard he was having trouble getting up.

"Gege, you played me," Hua Cheng accused.

Xie Lian picked up the brush and plank. "Don't turn this on me; San Lang played me first. Let me guess...you've been around ever since I broke the stove, right?"

"Ah, that's true. Gege, how did you know? You're amazing!" Hua Cheng complimented him.

Xie Lian waved dismissively. "Amazing? San Lang, if you want to wear a disguise, don't be so lazy about it. It would be more amazing if I hadn't seen through it. And here I thought there really *was* a second person who could eat...ahem. Honestly...'Who's the handsomest? Who's the coolest? Who's the richest? Who do you admire the most?' Ha ha ha ha..."

"...Gege, please forget that ever happened," Hua Cheng pleaded softly.

Xie Lian was resolute in his refusal. "No. I will remember this forever."

"Gege, although I'm happy you're so happy, is it really that funny?" Hua Cheng asked in a woeful tone.

Xie Lian hugged his belly as he laughed. "Of course! Only since meeting you have I rediscovered how simple it is to be happy, ha ha ha ha ha..."

Hearing this, Hua Cheng blinked. Xie Lian's laughter quieted as he realized that his words were a little too frank. Even *he* thought they were a little corny now that he'd calmed down. Clearing his throat quietly, Xie Lian rubbed at the corners of his eyes and forced himself to school his expression.

"All right, enough playing around. Where's the real Lang Ying? Why are you disguised as him? Bring that child back now."

"I sent him to Ghost City as a guest," Hua Cheng replied languidly.

Since Hua Cheng was the one who took him away, Xie Lian wasn't worried. He nodded and was about to continue their conversation when the wooden door creaked open. Ling Wen walked outside Puqi Shrine with her hands clasped behind her back.

"Your Highness."

Hua Cheng had no intention of revealing his identity, so Xie Lian didn't mention it and pretended he was still Lang Ying in front of others. Seeing Ling Wen's solemn expression, Xie Lian's smile faded unconsciously.

"What is it? The Brocade Im—is something wrong with Bai Jing?"

"No. There's nothing wrong with him," Ling Wen said. "There's a weird smell coming from the kitchen. Is Your Highness cooking something?"

"Oh, I am. It's simmering on the stove," Xie Lian replied quickly.

After some thought, Ling Wen used a courteous tone to say very discourteously, "Please clear it away, Your Highness. Whatever you're cooking, it's probably ruined by now."

"..."

Two hours later, evening had come.

Inside Puqi Shrine, Hua Cheng, Ling Wen, and Quan Yizhen sat around the little wooden altar table. Xie Lian brought a pot from the kitchen and set it on the table. He opened the cover to reveal dozens of cute, round, smooth, snow-white little meatballs sagely curled inside.

"Weren't you stewing something? How did it turn into meatballs?" Quan Yizhen demanded.

Xie Lian introduced his creation. "This dish is called 'Incorruptible Chastity Meatballs.'"[10]

"Weren't you stewing something? How did it turn into meatballs?" Quan Yizhen demanded.

"Kneading meatballs requires delicate strength, not too hard, not too light," Xie Lian continued his presentation. "That's why so much time went into these."

---

10 [玉潔冰清] "Clean as Jade, Clear like Ice" is an idiom that means "pure, noble, and uncorrupted," and is usually used to describe girls. Xie Lian is using the idiom's imagery to describe his cute little meatballs.

"Weren't you stewing something? How did it turn into meatballs?" Quan Yizhen demanded.

"..." Since Quan Yizhen was so relentless, Xie Lian explained warmly, "It was originally more of a stew, you're right. But because there was a small mishap with time and controlling the fire, all the water boiled off, so I mixed in new ingredients and made meatballs instead."

Hearing this, Ling Wen praised him wholeheartedly. "Your Highness truly thinks outside the box. There is no one like you in all of history. I am steeped in deep respect."

"Please, that's too much praise," Xie Lian said.

"It's not," Ling Wen said. "At least, I certainly do believe there will never be another person in history able to create a dish called 'Incorruptible Chastity Meatballs.'"

Xie Lian passed chopsticks around. "Thank you, thank you. Everyone, please."

Ling Wen and Quan Yizhen took chopsticks with one hand and at the same time reached for the cold buns sitting at the edge of the table with the other. Only Hua Cheng reached for an Incorruptible Chastity Meatball and popped it into his mouth.

After a moment, he remarked, "Pretty good."

Quan Yizhen's eyes widened at the sight.

"A bit bland," Hua Cheng added.

"Okay. Duly noted," Xie Lian said.

Quan Yizhen watched with wide eyes as the bandaged boy next to him ate several of the abnormally glistening meatballs and gave such sincere feedback. After some thought, he seemed to be persuaded and reached for his own meatball.

Xie Lian maintained his smile. He smiled and watched Quan Yizhen swallow. He smiled as Quan Yizhen's face turned pale. He smiled as Quan Yizhen crumpled to the floor.

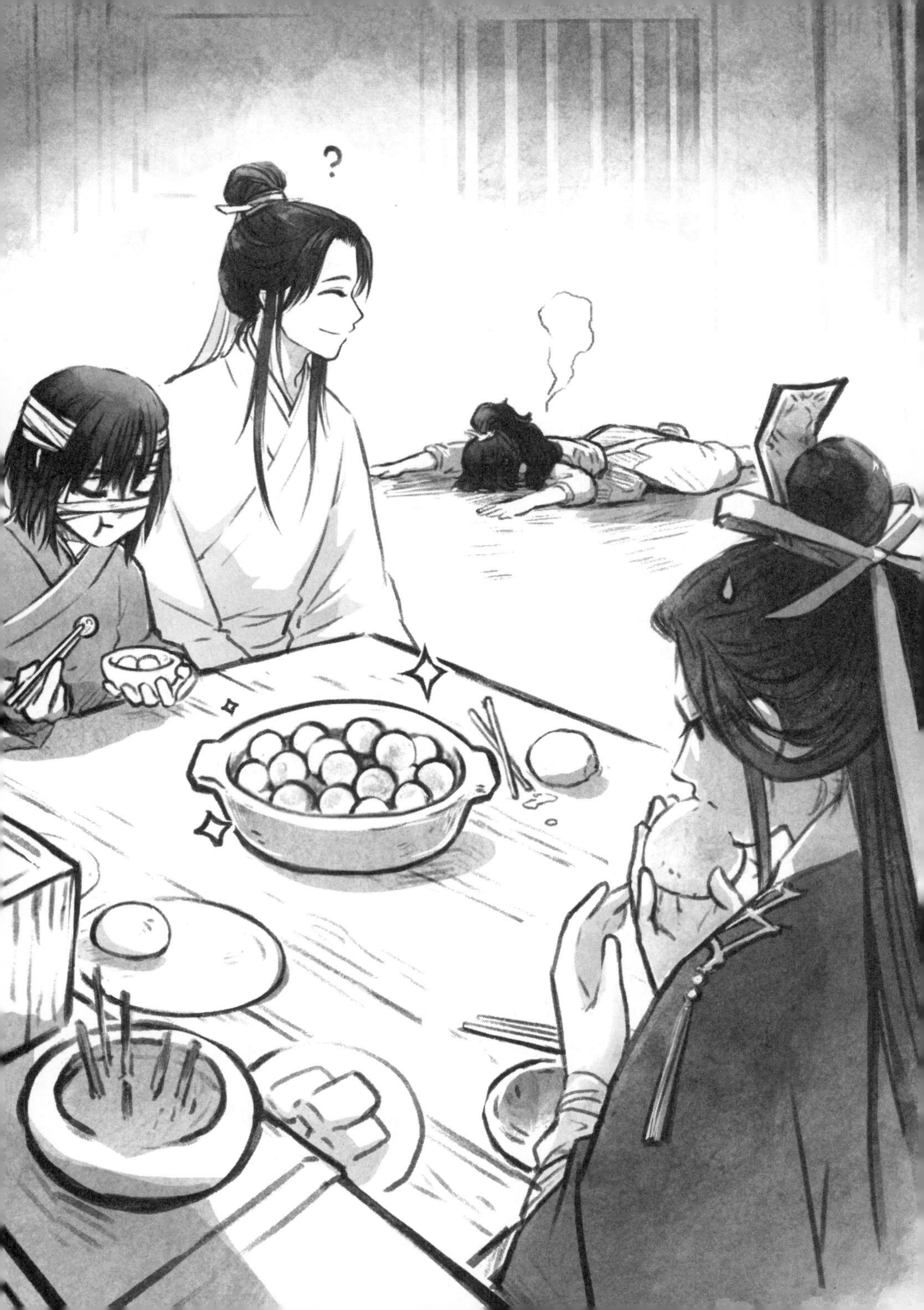

Xie Lian continued smiling as he asked, "Is something the matter?"

"Probably ate too fast and choked," Hua Cheng advised.

Ling Wen grinned.

All of a sudden, Xie Lian heard a familiar voice in his ear. "Gege."

It wasn't Lang Ying's mumbling voice, nor was it the crisp and languid voice of Hua Cheng in his boyish form. It was the voice of the usual Hua Cheng, and he was speaking to Xie Lian through their private communication array.

Xie Lian raised his lashes slightly. "What is it?"

"Ling Wen is cruel and cunning, heartless and merciless. Things might not end so easily now that you've brought her here."

This was the first time Xie Lian had ever heard anyone make such comments about Ling Wen. He thought for a moment and then replied, "It seems to me she harbors some goodwill toward the Brocade Immortal. That much at least I believe is true."

"Harboring goodwill and being merciless don't conflict. She's the number one civil god in the heavens—her eyes and ears are everywhere, and her arms are far-reaching. Gege needs to guard against her seeking out helping hands."

"General Pei?" Xie Lian asked.

"Unlikely," Hua Cheng replied. "She certainly would have asked the Water Tyrant for his assistance in suppressing the matter if he were still around, as Shi Wudu always acted on acquaintance and not reason. But Pei Ming might not be willing to aid corruption as long as you inform him of the truth. Gege, be careful."

"All right, I will be careful," Xie Lian said. "Good thing a day goes by fast."

However, Hua Cheng's voice was dark in his ear. "No. Gege, you've misunderstood. I'm telling you to be careful of something else. We have visitors."

The clinking, crisp sounds of bells reached Xie Lian's ears. Hua Cheng frowned slightly. Xie Lian looked through the window and saw a middle-aged cultivator approaching the entrance to Puqi Village and ringing a bell as he strutted forth.

The cultivator wore a rather magnificent cultivation robe and carried a treasure chest on his back that was covered in yellow talismans. As he walked along, his bell rang with each step. Xie Lian recognized it as a good tool; he had an eye for these things. The sound of that bell would give a piercing headache to any low-level evil beings that were near enough to hear it, and they would steer clear.

Before the cultivator got any closer to the shrine, he was joined by a few other large, white-browed, yellow-robed monks carrying staves in their hands, their gaits steady as they approached.

Soon, a crowd of fifty or sixty had gathered, and Puqi Shrine was heavily surrounded. It was as if they had planned this meeting and were unsurprised to see one another present.

These people weren't just putting on a show. Their bodies were hung with spiritual weapons, and their forms were composed and obviously very skilled. Heavenly officials took spiritual power from their worshippers' offerings, and likewise, certain Daoist and Buddhist cultivators could request spiritual power from the heavenly officials they worshipped. And so the monks and cultivators gathering at the shrine might possess greater spiritual power than Xie Lian, a heavenly official.

So many of them swarming outside all at once couldn't herald anything good. Xie Lian sensed that the newcomers didn't come in peace and knitted his brows in concern.

Hua Cheng put down his bowl and chopsticks and rose to his feet. Xie Lian heard his *humph* in the private communication array.

"Those foul old monks and cultivators dared chase me all the way here. I'm sorry that I brought trouble to your door, gege. I'll leave and lead them away."

Xie Lian grabbed him. "Don't move."

Ling Wen was bewildered. "What's going on?"

Xie Lian spoke to Hua Cheng through their private communication array. "Don't go. Tell me honestly, is the reopening of Mount Tonglu affecting you greatly?"

"No," Hua Cheng replied.

Xie Lian stared intently at the eyes behind the bandages. "Stop lying. You're a Supreme Ghost King. You don't need to be afraid of mortals like them. Why would you lead them away and not *beat* them away? You weren't just playing a prank when you changed into this form, were you?"

The stronger the nefarious creature, the more they felt Mount Tonglu's effects. Xie Lian had witnessed with his own eyes just how much misery Hua Cheng had suffered the first time the ghosts were agitated, and the tremors would only intensify as the gate's opening approached. If Xie Lian had been the one suffering such a thing, he would have chosen to temporarily seal his true form. To avoid going berserk and conserve his spiritual powers, he would transform into a small creature and wait it out until after the mountain had finally formally opened.

That would be a way to avoid the torment of Mount Tonglu's aggravation, but because his powers were sealed, it gave others the opportunity to ambush him.

Xie Lian cursed. "Qi Rong, you..."

That night, Qi Rong had threatened to bring forth all the Daoists and Buddhist monks who had grievances with Hua Cheng, but

Xie Lian was shocked to see that he hadn't been bluffing. Hua Cheng shook his head.

"Gege, they're only targeting me. It'll be fine once I'm gone. Although I can't kill them with a single move in my current form, I can at least make them get lost."

But Xie Lian threatened, "If you leave now, don't ever come back to see me again."

"...Your Highness!" Hua Cheng cried, shocked.

Hua Cheng was usually so flawlessly composed. He had helped Xie Lian so many times in the past, so now that Xie Lian finally had the chance to help him, how could he possibly allow Hua Cheng to leave all alone?

"Sit down. I'll go meet with them," Xie Lian said darkly.

Quan Yizhen opened his eyes with great difficulty. "Is...someone here?" he asked in a daze. His voice was hoarse. "Do you...need me to beat them up?"

"..." Xie Lian helped him close his eyes. "Qi Ying, just keep lying there. Also, you can't just beat up mortals—it'll cost you merits."

Xie Lian pressed himself against the wooden door to listen for any movement outside. Some villagers who had just finished their work for the day were still out and about and hadn't yet gone home for dinner, and they were amazed to see so many Daoists and monks.

"What're the masters doing here?" they asked. "Are you here for Xie-daozhang?"

A murderous-looking monk put his hands together in prayer. "Amitabha Buddha. Benevolent donor, are you aware that this place has been invaded by wicked creatures?"

"What?!" the villagers were shocked. "Wicked creatures?! What kind of wicked creatures?"

"A hell-raising ghost king, singular in his evil throughout the ages!" another monk replied enigmatically.

"W-what should we do?!" the villagers exclaimed.

The splendidly dressed cultivator had been the first to arrive, so he took it upon himself to announce their intent. "Leave it to us! Today, we who walk the same path are gathered here for one reason. We have been blessed with the chance of a lifetime to capture that vile ghost!"

However, before he could rush the shrine, the village chief pulled him back. The cultivator glared at him.

"Who are you? What are you doing?"

"Um, masters," the village chief laughed nervously. "I'm the leader of this village. We're very thankful you're here, but to tell the truth, y'all look very expensive..."

"...We've come to defeat evil. Do you think we're here for a reward?!" the splendidly dressed cultivator said, offended.

They tried to charge again, but the villagers stopped them once more. Although the monks and cultivators were growing irritated, they couldn't just shove themselves through.

"What now?!" they demanded with forced patience.

The village head wrung his hands nervously. "If it's free, then that's great; our thanks to the masters for coming here to defeat evil with benevolent hearts. But...it's just that all such work here in this village is taken care of by Xie-daozhang. It's hard on me as the village chief if the masters have come to steal Xie-daozhang's work."

The band of monks and cultivators looked at each other in dismay.

"Xie-daozhang?"

They huddled around.

"Is there a well-known, mighty Daoist school in the trade with the name of Xie?"

"Don't think so."

"Either way, *I've* never heard of him. Probably some nobody."

"If we haven't heard of him, then he's not well known, so who cares?"

After their discussion, the splendidly dressed cultivator turned back around. "The Xie-daozhang you speak of, is he the one living in this place?"

"Yeah." The villagers then shouted in the direction of Puqi Shrine. "Xie-daozhang! Xie-daozhang! Your peers are here! There're so many of them! Are you home?"

A yellow-robed old monk pressed his hands together in prayer. "Amitabha Buddha. It doesn't matter if Xie-daozhang is here. That wicked creature is hiding in this house right now!"

The villagers were stunned. "Huh?!"

At that point, Xie Lian pushed the door open and leisurely strolled out. "I'm here. What's going on, everyone?"

"Daozhang, these eminent monks and cultivators are saying that in your house, there's a...a...ghost..." the villagers stammered.

Xie Lian smiled. "Eh? You can tell?"

The crowd outside the shrine was shocked.

"It's true?"

"What a quick confession of guilt!"

Xie Lian tossed a jar to them. "That's right, there really is a ghost!"

The splendidly dressed cultivator caught the jar and was delighted at first, but his smile collapsed when he opened it.

"A Half-Maquillage Woman?" He tossed the jar back, looking very obviously displeased. "Don't pretend, my friend. A vulgar ghost like this isn't even at the level of a fierce! You know exactly what we're referring to."

Xie Lian caught the jar and could tell that the man's throw wasn't weak. It was obvious that he had cultivated for many arduous years and had considerable strength.

"Dao-xiong, I can sense that this cultivator's body is full to bursting with evil qi," a number of monks said to the splendidly dressed cultivator. "Could he be..."

"I, Heaven's Eye, can determine such things with just one glance!" the splendidly dressed cultivator stated.

With a loud shout, he bit his finger and drew a line of blood down his forehead, and a moment later, a third eye looked like it sprouted on his face. Xie Lian silently praised this demonstration of skill, and he leaned against the door to enjoy the show. The splendidly dressed cultivator glared at him for a moment with great concentration.

"I knew it... There it is, ghost qi! Such sinister ghost qi! You did change your face after all, *Ghost King!*"

Xie Lian was struck dumb.

How could he, an esteemed and titled heavenly official, have ghost qi on him? He was just starting to think that this man might have some skill, so why was he spewing nonsense not a moment after?

At this accusation, the fifty or sixty masters in the gathering looked like they were steeling themselves to face a great enemy. Each of them went into a fighting stance.

"These people are so annoying," Hua Cheng said to Xie Lian in their private communication array.

"It's fine. It's not that bad. Just sit tight," Xie Lian replied.

The splendidly dressed cultivator spoke up again a moment later, but he sounded doubtful. "...That's not right?"

"What's not right?" the monks next to him asked.

The splendidly dressed cultivator rubbed the blood mark on his forehead. "This is weird. When I look at this man, he's sometimes covered in ghost qi, sometimes glowing with spiritual light, and sometimes dull and colorless... This is really strange."

"Huh? How can that be? Dao-xiong, can you handle this? If you can't, let us take over."

"Yeah, how could it be so bizarre?"

The splendidly dressed cultivator was miffed. "What? You think I can't do this? If I can't, do you think *you* can? I, Heaven's Eye, have been in the trade for years and years, and I've rarely gotten anything wrong!"

Xie Lian rubbed his forehead and shook his head. "Then why don't you take another look and tell me which part of me has the strongest ghost qi?" he asked temperately.

Heaven's Eye rubbed his forehead hard and studied him again for a moment. "Your lips!" he firmly declared.

"..."

72
My Puqi Shrine Will Collapse Supremely (Part One)

"THAT'S RIGHT, it's your lips!"

Heaven's Eye proclaimed this with complete certainty, but the monks and cultivators were perplexed.

"Why his lips?"

"How can ghost qi be only on the lips? Is it a Lip Balm Spirit?"

Xie Lian's hands unconsciously flew to cover his mouth. Hua Cheng had stained him with his scent when they embraced and kissed the night away at Thousand Lights Temple—Xie Lian never could've imagined that it hadn't yet faded!

Heaven's Eye pointed at him. "Well, well, well! Do you all see? He knows his guilt!"

Xie Lian hastily dropped his hands. He forced down the urge to turn and see what expression Hua Cheng wore after hearing that accusation—even though his face was currently covered in bandages and Xie Lian wouldn't have been able to tell.

"Um, my fellow Dao friend, you've mistaken," he explained amiably. "I live a humble life, so each household item is used for many purposes. Take this jar, for example." He raised the clay jar in his hand and continued with earnest conviction. "Although I sometimes use this to catch ghosts, I normally use it to pickle vegetables. The pickles from this jar have a unique flavor, and once you eat one you'll naturally... If you don't believe me, you can try it yourself."

...Technically, this explanation could make some sense. The monks and cultivators were still dubious, but all the villagers covered their mouths as well.

"Huh?! Xie-daozhang, have all those pickles you've given us been pickled like that?"

"Won't our mouths be full of ghost qi too?!"

When the villagers offered him fresh fruits and vegetables, Xie Lian would usually return the favor by giving them some of his pickled vegetables. He quickly waved his hand.

"Don't worry, I use different jars to make the pickles for everyone else!"

"Are you mental?!" Heaven's Eye said angrily. "Aren't you afraid eating stuff like that will take years off your life? Enough talk! There's still someone hidden in your shrine—and not just one! Move aside!"

Afraid that the village chief would stop him again, he charged forward before he even finished speaking. Seeing the situation change so quickly, Xie Lian hurriedly retreated into the house. He pulled the unconscious Quan Yizhen upright, madly shook his collar, and shouted into his ear.

"Qi Ying! Listen! I am going to feed you more Incorruptible Chastity Meatballs!"

Quan Yizhen's eyes shot open the moment he heard this. Heaven's Eye had only just barged into the shrine when he immediately leapt back outside shrieking and covering his forehead.

"Don't anyone go in! There's an ambush!"

The crowd of monks and cultivators didn't dare to move rashly, and they gathered around to shield him.

"Heaven's Eye-xiong, what did you see?"

"I didn't see anything! There was an immense, blinding white light!" Heaven's Eye said.

"Oh my gosh, Dao-xiong, this is bad! Your heaven's eye is smoking!"

Heaven's Eye felt his forehead, and sure enough, that red mark on his forehead had turned black. It was emitting a soft line of white smoke like a blown-out candle.

"What...what?!" he exclaimed as the color drained from his face.

Ling Wen lazily put down her half-eaten steamed bun. "It's so noisy outside. What's going on?"

"Heaven's Eye-xiong, look," a monk said. "There are two children and a woman inside that shrine, as well as that cultivator. Of those four, which one is *him*?"

Heaven's Eye vigorously rubbed his forehead, but he couldn't reopen his eye no matter how hard he tried. The ball of white light had been Quan Yizhen's spiritual aura. When a heavenly official sensed they were about to face grave danger, or that their life would be threatened, the spiritual aura that shielded their body would expand explosively. It was this flash of protective light that Xie Lian had used to blind the cultivator Heaven's Eye. It wasn't like Xie Lian had ruined ten years of his cultivation, though; he just wouldn't be able to use his third eye for a few days.

Xie Lian picked up the pot holding the meatballs. Quan Yizhen was fully conscious now, and he gripped Xie Lian's hand.

"I won't eat it," he croaked.

Xie Lian reversed the hold and held his hand reassuringly. "Don't worry, these aren't for you!"

The band of masters surrounding Puqi Shrine shared looks with each other, then shouted and rushed forward in near unison. However, they were bounced away by an invisible barrier before Xie Lian could meet them.

A deep voice sounded from the skies above. "You foul old monks and cultivators are pesky as flies. And now you've become addicted to harassment? You dare pursue me all the way here? You're asking for death!"

"Hua...Hua...Hua..." Heaven's Eye stuttered "Hua" several times, but in the end, he still succumbed to Hua Cheng's might and didn't dare call him by his full name. Instead, he stammered, "...H-H-Hua-chengzhu! S-stop bluffing. We know you've sealed away your powers to avoid the effects of Mount Tonglu's imminent opening. Th-there's no way you're your usual insolent self. S-s-surrender yourself..."

The more he spoke, the less strength there was in his words. Xie Lian could tell that Hua Cheng was *really* angry now, and he rushed back inside to gather him into his arms.

"Don't say anymore!" he whispered. "Stop wasting your powers, conserve your strength. Leave everything to me!"

Hua Cheng's body was tense at first, but he seemed to slowly calm down after being picked up. "All right," he replied in a low voice.

As he held him, Xie Lian could sense that Hua Cheng's age had regressed again; he was now probably no more than twelve or thirteen. Xie Lian couldn't help but be worried. With one arm holding Hua Cheng and the other hand clutching Fangxin, he walked out.

"Did none of you consider that you were deceived by the Green Ghost Qi Rong?"

Unexpectedly, the monks and cultivators looked confused at this.

"Green Ghost Qi Rong? What did he lie about? Why would he deceive us?" Heaven's Eye asked.

Xie Lian frowned slightly. "Wasn't he the one who told you to come here?"

Heaven's Eye clicked his tongue. "Who do you think we are? You think we'd need a wrath to tip us off? Why would we float on the same boat as him?!"

It wasn't Qi Rong? Then how did the information leak?

Before Xie Lian could consider it further, the monks and cultivators launched their attacks. Xie Lian blocked strikes from multiple swords and several staves with a single swing of Fangxin.

"Amitabha Buddha, why must our Dao friend protect this creature of evil?" a monk questioned.

Xie Lian wouldn't back down an inch. "Master, it's not nice to ambush people when they're down, no matter who they are."

"He's a ghost, not a person! Don't cling to outdated morals, you immature young'un!" Heaven's Eye shouted.

Countless spiritual staves and treasured swords came attacking at once. If Xie Lian unsheathed Fangxin, he might hurt one of the humans present. Morally speaking, mortals could hit heavenly officials, but heavenly officials could not hit mortals. Heavenly officials must be tolerant, generous, compassionate, and caring toward mortals, and never squabble with them. Merits would be deducted if one dared to hit them. Xie Lian wasn't as unrestrained as Quan Yizhen, nor was he as wealthy. He didn't have many merits in the first place, so he'd end up in the negatives if he incurred a fine.

Thus, he put away his sword and shouted, "Ruoye, come! Qi Ying, watch Ling Wen!"

Ruoye was always aggrieved when it had to bind men, but it'd change face when asked to bind a woman. Xie Lian had to call for it a couple times before it reluctantly peeled itself from Ling Wen's wrists. In the blink of an eye, a white flash whipped the hands of every monk and cultivator in the mob, loosening their grips on their spiritual weapons.

Bewildered, they all wondered, "What kind of spiritual weapon is that?"

"Was it a spiritual weapon? ...It looked like a white silk band that someone would use to hang themself. It reeks of evil..."

"Whaddaya know, this brat actually has a couple moves!"

Taking advantage of Xie Lian fending off the mob of masters, Ling Wen shook her head, dusted off her sleeves, and rose to her feet.

"Thank you for your warm hospitality, Your Highness. I will take my leave now."

Xie Lian was slightly taken aback. "Ling Wen, the day's not over yet! Where are you going? Are you going to break your vow?"

"That's correct. I am indeed going to break my vow," Ling Wen said.

Her voice was unapologetic, like she was stating that she was about to slay evil by heaven's will. Xie Lian was struck speechless by it. Moments later, he said, "It wasn't Qi Rong who leaked the information. It was you."

Ling Wen smiled. "I may not be a martial god, and I was bound by Rouye, but one can accomplish much with just the communication array."

He knew it! But how did Ling Wen know that the bandaged boy was Hua Cheng? She barely spoke to him and barely even saw him—Xie Lian hadn't figured it out as fast as she did!

Xie Lian still couldn't get away from the fight, and he saw that she was about to take her stately leave. "Qi Ying! Don't let her escape!" he shouted.

Although he had eaten an Incorruptible Chastity Meatball not long ago, Quan Yizhen's strength was returning, and he could now pull himself upright. And Ling Wen was a weak, powerless civil god; Quan Yizhen could stop her without even lifting a finger. Hearing Quan Yizhen acknowledge *"Okay!"* from afar, Xie Lian relaxed and went back to fighting the crowd. A moment later, there was a sudden rumble, and a figure was blown high into the air, straight through the roof of Puqi Shrine.

Aghast, Xie Lian shouted toward the shrine, "Qi Ying! Don't fight like that!"

It was nothing for martial gods to get tossed around; all martial gods grew up getting beaten. But Ling Wen was a female heavenly official, and a civil god at that—she'd be pulverized if Quan Yizhen fought so ruthlessly!

A person strolled out of the shrine's front door. "Bai Jing, don't fight like that," she chided leisurely.

The cool voice obviously belonged to Ling Wen. But the moment she walked out, Xie Lian thought he saw a fleeting illusion—like the one who came out wasn't Ling Wen but an extremely tall young man with an aura of vengeance that roared to the heavens. When Xie Lian squinted, it was still the lone figure of Ling Wen.

Ling Wen was a civil god, that was certain. Even if she had tried to hide her strength in the past, she wouldn't have been able to deceive Xie Lian. How did she manage to blow Quan Yizhen into the sky?!

"Gege, be careful. She put on the robe," Hua Cheng darkly warned.

So that was it! To the untrained eye, it looked like Ling Wen was still clad in black. But in reality, a simmering dark aura covered her. It was this aura that made it seem like she had changed into a completely different person. Killing intent ran wild in the air, forming a peculiar contrast with the calm expression on her fair face. Xie Lian tried testing the waters by lunging at her with his sword, but Ling Wen deflected the blow with a wave of her sleeve.

Quan Yizhen came plunging down just in time to witness this scene. As he crashed hard into the ground, his eyes lit up in an instant.

"Beautiful!"

Xie Lian's eyes lit up too, and he also exclaimed, "Beautiful!"

Ling Wen's move just now was truly a beautiful one. Or rather, it should be said that the Brocade Immortal's move was beautiful—it had used its powers to help Ling Wen block the attack!

When others wore the Brocade Immortal, they either lost their minds or were sucked dry of blood. But when Ling Wen wore it, there was no weapon that could pierce its defense, and she could attack with such strength that even the Martial God of the West was blown away. Who would've thought that it would still allow her to use its power after she had chopped off its head and limbs?

Now, not only were the villagers of Puqi shocked, even the band of monks and cultivators were stupefied.

"What do you mean, 'beautiful'?!" Heaven's Eye exclaimed. "Is it so good to be hit? Is there anyone normal inside that shrine? I think not a single soul in there is human!"

Quan Yizhen was itching to spar, and he leapt to his feet to attack once more.

"I *said*, don't linger here!" Ling Wen hissed.

Those words were directed at the Brocade Immortal, but her body wouldn't listen to her. Her elbow blocked Quan Yizhen's punch, which led into an all-out brawl. Fighting and parrying, parrying and fighting, the blows of fists and palms rattled the old walls of Puqi Shrine, and it shook like it was ready to collapse. As expected of the Brocade Immortal, one with the potential to ascend, even Quan Yizhen was falling behind.

Xie Lian couldn't help but cry out to them. "Um...excuse me, can you both fight further away? Further away, please!"

But just as he spoke, the monks and cultivators surrounded him again. Forty or fifty blades, swords, hammers, and staves came crashing forward, and Xie Lian's face dropped as he raised his hands.

"Wait, don't! *Nooo!*"

Puqi Shrine had remained standing even as it suffered ceaseless abuse over the past few months. But now, punctuated by that tragic wail, it finally completely collapsed.

Xie Lian was dumbfounded, and bleak desolation filled his heart. "I just knew none of my houses would ever last six months. Now I *really* need to beg for donations for repairs..."

"Gege, don't be sad. It's just a house, there are plenty of others around," Hua Cheng consoled him.

Xie Lian tried to stay strong, but then Heaven's Eye came stumbling over, one hand covering his forehead and the other pointing at him.

"You! Young'un! You've got nothing but petty tricks! You dare ruin my cultivation?! Who's your shifu? What generation do you belong to? Which temple are you registered under? What god do you worship?!"

Xie Lian whirled around, and a biting chill flashed over his face. He straightened and replied with intense and furious dignity.

"You ask who *I* am?! Listen well! *I* am His Eminent Highness the Crown Prince! Bow down before me, you riotous, unruly horde!"

His voice boomed like a bolt from the blue. There were actually a few who dropped to their knees and didn't snap out of it until their companions pulled them up.

"What are you doing? Are you actually kneeling?"

"Th-that's weird, I did it before I realized..."

Xie Lian continued in a sharp tone.

"*I* am over eight hundred years old. Older than all of you combined! I have crossed more bridges than all the roads you have walked!

"*I* possess shrines and temples across this land! My worship has spread to the four seas! If you do not know my name, it is because you are uneducated and ignorant of the world!

"*I* do not worship gods—

"I *am* god!"

This speech was incredibly shameless, yet it was spoken with an incomparably impressive presence. The mob was astonished and stood there silent and slack-jawed.

"...Huh?"

Xie Lian had made up all that nonsense because he was waiting for this very opportunity. He flung forth the pot in his hand, and the little white meatballs shot through the air and scattered in all directions like iron pellets. Without a single miss, each and every one landed in the open mouth of one of the shocked monks and cultivators.

Xie Lian wiped away his sweat. "Will everyone please forget everything I just said? I'm actually only a scrap collector!"

The face of everyone who ate a meatball drained of all color.

"Huh?! We...we've been had!"

A few who were quicker on their feet had stopped the incoming meatballs with their swords, but when they peeked around to inspect, those meatballs were still spinning rapidly on their blades and creating sparks from friction. The mob was terrified.

"What...what is this hidden weapon?! Incomparably solid with a peculiar shine—could this be? The legendary..."

"That's right!" Xie Lian declared. "They're the legendary Incorruptible Chastity Pellets! They are extremely poisonous, and they will explode in your stomach if you don't drink eighty-one cups of plain water within a day to flush away the toxin!"

Although none of them had ever heard of such a thing before, the mob grew even more panicked.

"Hey! Is it really that poisonous?!"

"Either way, we gotta go drink water! The antidote is just water! Let's get outta here! Go find water!"

In an instant, a large portion of the crowd had fallen for the trick and fled.

On the other side of the temple grounds, Ling Wen was fighting with increasing aggression. She picked up Quan Yizhen in a stranglehold. But despite having the obvious upper hand, Ling Wen didn't look pleased at all.

"Bai Jing! Are you trying to kill him?" she barked with a low voice. "There's no need to fight anymore! Let's just go!"

Fortunately, Xie Lian had one meatball remaining. Just as Ling Wen said the word "go," he lobbed a meatball into her mouth with his swift hands. The light in Ling Wen's eyes was extinguished in an instant, like it had been snuffed out by the thing she had swallowed. The black aura surrounding her body also lightened a shade. With an expression like she was forcing back the urge to vomit, she glared at Xie Lian, her lips quivering soundlessly. After enduring for as long as she could, she threw Quan Yizhen to the ground and left the scene with her hand supporting her temple.

Quan Yizhen leapt to his feet to chase after her. Xie Lian wanted to follow, but the mob of monks and cultivators blocked his way.

"Everyone, hang on! More reinforcements are on the way!" they shouted.

More?! He couldn't stay in Puqi Village any longer. It would be best if he left first and thought later. Quan Yizhen was nowhere to be found; his pursuit of Ling Wen had already carried him far away.

Xie Lian cradled Hua Cheng in his arms. "Hold on tight to me!"

He bounced off from his toes into a sprint, easily outpacing the mob in an instant. Hua Cheng followed his instructions and embraced him tightly. For some reason, this felt familiar to Xie Lian, but he had no time to reminisce about the past; this affair needed to be reported to the Heavenly Court as soon as possible. Without thinking, he sent a message to the private communication array as he always did.

"Ling Wen, something's happened! I..."

"...I know," Ling Wen said.

"...So sorry to bother you," Xie Lian replied.

An instant later, Ling Wen cut their communication first.

Xie Lian was also speechless. He had always communicated directly with Ling Wen in the past, but now Ling Wen herself was the problem. His brain hadn't caught up, and he'd actually reported the incident to her. He didn't know whether to laugh or cry.

As he dashed away with Hua Cheng in his arms, Xie Lian entered the public communication array to frantically inform the others of the situation at hand.

"Everyone! Please alert the whole court! Ling Wen ran off wearing the Brocade Immortal!"

THE STORY CONTINUES IN
Heaven Official's Blessing
VOLUME 5

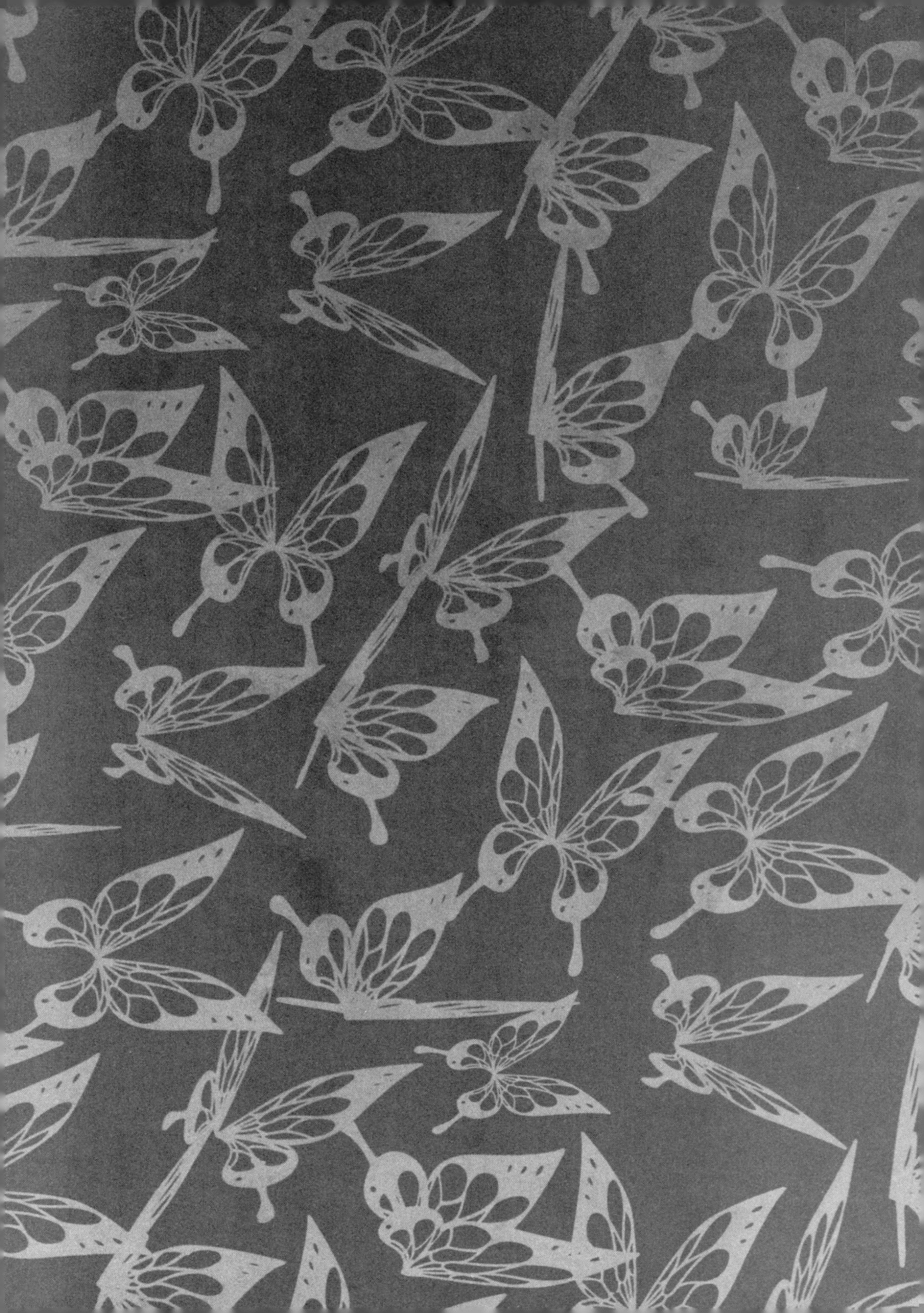

Heaven Official's Blessing

TIAN GUAN CI FU

Character & Name Guide

Characters

The identity of certain characters may be a spoiler; use this guide with caution on your first read of the novel.

Note on the given name translations: Chinese characters may have many different readings. Each reading here is just one out of several possible readings presented for your reference and should not be considered a definitive translation.

MAIN CHARACTERS

Xie Lian
谢怜   "THANK/WILT," "SYMPATHY/LOVE"

HEAVENLY TITLE: Xianle, "Heaven's Delight" (仙乐)

FOUR FAMOUS TALES TITLE: The Prince Who Pleased God

Once the crown prince of the Kingdom of Xianle and the darling of the Heavens, now a very unlucky twice-fallen god who ekes out a meager living collecting scraps. As his bad luck tends to affect those around him for the worse, Xie Lian has spent his last eight hundred years wandering in solitude. Still, he's accepted his lonely lot in life, or at least seems to have a sense of humor about it. Even for the perpetually unlucky, there's always potential for a chance encounter that can turn eight hundred years of unhappiness around.

Xie Lian has seen and done many things over his very long life and originally ascended as a martial god. While it was his scrap-collecting that saw him ascend for the third time, Xie Lian's feats of physicality are hardly anything to scoff at...though he'd sooner use them as part of a busking performance than to win a fight.

His title Xianle is a multi-layered nickname. "Xianle" is Xie Lian's official heavenly title and also the name of his kingdom. "Xianle" itself can translate to "Heaven's Delight," which ties into Xie Lian's "Four Famous Tales" moniker, "The Prince Who Pleased God." Jun Wu referring to Xie Lian as "Xianle" sounds professional and businesslike on the surface (as Jun Wu generally refers to gods by their heavenly titles only), but it deliberately and not-so-subtly comes across as an affectionate term of endearment.

Hua Cheng
花城   "FLOWER," "CITY"

NICKNAME: San Lang, "third," "youth" (三郎)
FOUR CALAMITIES TITLE: Crimson Rain Sought Flower

The fearsome king of ghosts and terror of the heavens. Dressed in his signature red, he controls vicious swarms of silver butterflies and wields the cursed scimitar known as Eming. His power and wealth are unmatched in the Three Realms, and for this he has as many worshippers as he does enemies (with considerable crossover between categories). He rules over the dazzling and otherworldly Ghost City in the Ghost Realm and is known to drop in to spectate at its infamous Gambler's Den when he's in a good mood.

In spite of all this, when it comes to Xie Lian, the Ghost King shows a much kinder and more respectful side of himself. He does not hesitate for a moment to sleep on a single straw mat in Xie Lian's humble home, nor to get his hands dirty doing household chores at Puqi Shrine. That being said, it's impossible to deny that as he and Xie Lian grow closer, Hua Cheng seems to be growing more and more mischievous... From the very start, his secret identity as

San Lang seemed to be no secret at all to Xie Lian, but Xie Lian still calls him by this name at Hua Cheng's request.

Honghong-er
红红儿 "RED," "RED," FRIENDLY DIMINUTIVE

A young street urchin who Xie Lian saved from certain death long ago, when Xie Lian was a prince in Xianle. Honghong-er is tiny, emaciated, and hardly looks like the ten-year-old child that he is, nor does he act like it. He is constantly on guard and quick to attack, though he strangely seems to become tame—and quite bashful—when Xie Lian is around. He bears immense shame regarding his supposedly ugly appearance and refuses to remove the bandages he wears to cover half his face.

Honghong-er's life has clearly been one of immense suffering and hardship, and he clings to every one of Xie Lian's fleeting acts of kindness toward him as if he has never experienced anything like it before.

The name "Honghong-er" is clearly a nickname—it can be roughly translated to "Little Red."

Young Soldier

A nameless young soldier in the Xianle army. He keeps half of his face hidden beneath bandages at all times and seems determined to stick by Xie Lian's side in battle to protect him, even if it takes him to the most dangerous parts of the battlefield. His remarkable skill with the sword caught Xie Lian's attention and made the god-prince remember him fondly even during the difficult times leading up to Xianle's fall.

HEAVENLY OFFICIALS & HEAVENLY ASSOCIATES

Feng Xin
风信   "WIND," "TRUST/FAITH"

HEAVENLY TITLE: Nan Yang, "Southern Sun" (南陽)

The Martial God of the Southeast. He has a short fuse and foul mouth (especially when it comes to his longstanding nemesis, Mu Qing) but is known to be a dutiful, hardworking god. He has a complicated history with Xie Lian: long ago, in their days in the kingdom of Xianle, he used to serve as Xie Lian's bodyguard and was a close friend until circumstances drove them apart.

Jun Wu
君吾   "LORD," "I"

HEAVENLY TITLE: Shenwu, "Divine Might" (神武)

The Emperor of Heaven and strongest of the gods. He is composed and serene, and it is through his power and wisdom that the Heavens remain aloft—quite literally. Although the Heavens are full of schemers and gossipmongers, Jun Wu stands apart from such petty squabbles and is willing to listen to even the lowliest creatures to hear their pleas for justice. Despite this reputation for fairness, he does have his biases. In further contrast to the rest of the rabble in Heaven, he shows great patience and affection towards Xie Lian to the point that many grumble about favoritism.

Ling Wen
灵文   "INGENIOUS LITERATUS"

HEAVENLY TITLE: Ling Wen

The top civil god and also the most overworked. Unlike the majority of gods, she is addressed by her colleagues and most others by her heavenly title. She is one of the rare female civil gods and worked tirelessly (and thanklessly) for many years to earn her position. Ling Wen is exceedingly competent at all things bureaucratic, and her work keeps Heaven's business running (mostly) smoothly. She is the creator and head admin of Heaven's communication array.

These days, her name Nangong Jie [南宫杰, "South" 南 / "Palace" 宫 / "Hero" 杰] is only used by her close friend Pei Ming—though he usually calls her the friendly nickname "Noble Jie." She is also close to Shi Wudu, who is known in the heavens for his self-serving personality. Their friend group is dubbed the "Three Tumors."

Ming Yi
明仪   "ILLUMINATE/UNDERSTAND," "INSTRUMENT/CEREMONY"

HEAVENLY TITLE: Earth Master

The elemental master of earth. Taciturn, sullen, and always looking for a reason to go home—even so, he is often seen out and about with Shi Qingxuan. Shi Qingxuan calls Ming Yi their closest friend and exclusively uses the nickname "Ming-xiong." Ming Yi claims to not enjoy the Wind Master's company.

Mu Qing
慕情   "YEARNING," "AFFECTION"

HEAVENLY TITLE: Xuan Zhen, "Enigmatic Truth" (玄真)

The Martial God of the Southwest. He has a short fuse and sharp tongue (especially when it comes to his longstanding nemesis, Feng Xin) and is known for being cold, spiteful, and petty. He has a complicated history with Xie Lian: long ago, in their days in the kingdom of Xianle, he used to serve as Xie Lian's personal servant and was a close friend until circumstances drove them apart.

Pei Ming

裴茗   SURNAME PEI, "TENDER TEA LEAVES"

HEAVENLY TITLE: Ming Guang, "Bright Illumination" (明光)

FOUR FAMOUS TALES TITLE: The General Who Snapped His Sword

The Martial God of the North. General Pei is a powerful and popular god, and over the years he has gained a reputation as a womanizer. This reputation is deserved: Pei Ming's ex-lovers are innumerable and hail from all the Three Realms. He is close friends with Ling Wen and Shi Wudu, who are also known in the heavens for their self-serving personalities. This friend group is dubbed the "Three Tumors."

Pei Xiu is Pei Ming's indirect descendant, and Pei Ming took him under his wing to help advance his career in the Heavens. He was very displeased when Pei Xiu ruined that career for Banyue's sake, but he seems to have accepted the situation and does not hold a grudge against Xie Lian for his involvement in uncovering the scandal.

Quan Yizhen

权一真   "POWER/AUTHORITY," "ONE," "TRUTH/GENUINE"

HEAVENLY TITLE: Qi Ying, "Stupendous Hero" (奇英)

The (current) Martial God of the West. He previously shared this title with his shixiong, Yin Yu. Since Yin Yu was banished from heaven, Quan Yizhen holds the title alone.

Quan Yizhen has a single-minded focus on martial arts and is considered a prodigy even among heaven's elite. He also has a reputation for beating up his own followers, though this somehow does not damage his popularity in the Mortal Realm. While his skill cannot be disparaged, he is widely disliked in the heavens for his lack of social etiquette. He cares not for the friendship or opinions of his fellow gods, though he seems to have warmed up to Xie Lian.

Rain Master

HEAVENLY TITLE: Rain Master

The elemental master of rain who ascended to the heavens shortly before Xie Lian's first ascension. Rain Master is a reclusive heavenly official who is known to reside on a secluded mountain farm with many subordinates working in the fields. One of those subordinates is an intelligent talking ox who is capable of transforming into human form, one that's equally as beefy as his bovine build.

Shi Qingxuan
师青玄 "MASTER," "VERDANT GREEN/BLUE," "MYSTERIOUS/BLACK"

HEAVENLY TITLE: Wind Master

FOUR FAMOUS TALES TITLE: The Young Lord Who Poured Wine

The elemental master of wind and younger sibling of the Water Master, Shi Wudu. Shi Qingxuan ascended as a male god, but over the years, he began to be worshipped as a female version of himself. Shi Qingxuan eagerly embraced this, and she leaps at any opportunity to go out on the town in her female form...and will try to drag anyone she's traveling with into the fun.

Shi Qingxuan is as flighty and pushy as the element they command, and as wealthy as they are generous with their money. They possess a strong sense of justice and will not be dissuaded by notions of propriety. They appear to be close friends with the Earth Master Ming Yi, despite the latter's insistence to the contrary.

Shi Wudu
师无渡 "MASTER," "WITHOUT," "CROSS," "PASS THROUGH"

HEAVENLY TITLE: Water Master

The elemental master of water and elder brother of the Wind Master, Shi Qingxuan. He is also known as the Water Tyrant because of his domineering and relentless personality. Despite his callous reputation, he is devotedly loyal to his younger sibling and to those he considers part of his inner circle. He is close friends with Ling Wen and Pei Ming, and even entrusts them with his darkest secrets. Because Ling Wen and Pei Ming are also known in the heavens for their self-serving personalities, this friend group had been dubbed the "Three Tumors."

GHOST REALM & GHOST REALM ASSOCIATES

Lang Ying
郎萤   "YOUTH," "FIREFLY"

A mysterious ghost child afflicted with Human Face Disease. He has known nothing but abuse for hundreds of years due to his horrifying appearance, save for the fleeting kindness and warmth of the human girl Xiao-Ying. The combination of this trauma and his almost total lack of human interaction has left him mostly mute and constantly on high alert. Xie Lian was the one to give him this name: Lang being the national surname of Yong'an, and Ying to commemorate the girl who once took care of him.

Bai Jing
白锦   "WHITE BROCADE"

The human spirit fused with the Brocade Immortal. He was once a young man with immense talent in martial arts who was destined for godhood. However, his life was gruesomely cut short when the girl he was in love with manipulated him into dismembering himself.

Qi Rong
戚容   "FACE OF SORROW" OR "RELATIVE," "TOLERATE/FACE"

FOUR CALAMITIES TITLE: Night-Touring Green Lantern

One of the Four Calamities, also called the "Green Ghost." Unlike the other three Calamities, he's actually only a wrath ghost, not a supreme. Gods and ghosts alike agree that he was only included in the group to bump up the number to an even four. (Also, he's just that big a pest.) He is infamous for his crude behavior and ostentatious attempts to copy the style of the more successful Calamities, as well as for his ravenous appetite for human flesh.

More recently, his crimes have expanded to include kidnapping and body-snatching. In an attempt to hide from heaven's detection, he possessed the body of a human man and in doing so acquired a young son named Guzi.

Qi Rong is Xie Lian's younger cousin on his mother's side, much to Xie Lian's everlasting dismay. Surprising no one, Qi Rong has been a source of stress and trouble ever since their mortal childhoods in Xianle. His royal title in Xianle was Prince Xiao Jing.

Ship-Sinking Black Water
黑水沉舟

FOUR CALAMITIES TITLE: Ship-Sinking Black Water

One of the Four Calamities. Ship-Sinking Black Water is a mysterious and reclusive water ghost who rules the South Sea. Like Hua Cheng, he won the bloody gauntlet at Mount Tonglu and wields the power of a supreme ghost. In life, he was known as He Xuan (贺玄 "Congratulate" / "Mysterious," "Black").

Waning Moon Officer
下弦月使

Hua Cheng's right-hand man, subordinate, and all-around errand runner. He bears a cursed shackle on his wrist, which marks him as a banished heavenly official. He is feared and respected in Ghost City, but what kind of face lurks behind that daunting, mysterious mask?

White No-Face
白无相 "WHITE NO-FACE"

FOUR CALAMITIES TITLE: White-Clothed Calamity

One of the Four Calamities, White No-Face is mysterious, cruel, and powerful enough to battle with the Heavenly Emperor himself—truly, a supreme among supremes. He destroyed the Kingdom of Xianle with the Human Face Disease pandemic. His peculiar fixation on Xie Lian is unnerving, as are his equally peculiar displays of affection.

MORTAL REALM & MORTAL REALM ASSOCIATES

Guzi
谷子 "MILLET"

A young human child that Qi Rong kidnapped as a byproduct of stealing the body of the boy's father. Because Qi Rong is possessing Guzi's father, the poor little boy seems blissfully unaware that he's in any danger at all, though that hardly prevents him from enduring plenty of suffering at Qi Rong's hands.

Lang Ying
郎英　　"YOUTH," "HERO"

A Yong'an man that Xie Lian made the acquaintance of in the Xianle era. He is a troubled man who has lost much—some might say everything—to the drought and famine that has struck his home region.

Heaven's Eye
天眼开　"HEAVEN'S EYE"

A wealthy, pompous human cultivator who leads a team of cultivators with a similar member profile. Despite his personality flaws, his powers are the real deal. His third eye can see the unseen, and in the process inadvertently reveal exactly how you've been "borrowing spiritual energy" recently.

State Preceptors of Xianle

A quartet of cultivators who serve as Xianle's state preceptors. They are also the religious leaders and head instructors at the Royal Holy Temple, Xianle's premiere cultivation school and largest place of worship for several gods. They are highly skilled cultivators and specialize in the art of divination, though they are very easily distracted by the allure of a game of cards.

The Chief State Preceptor, Mei Nianqing (梅念卿 "plum blossom," "to lecture/to long for," archaic word for minister/high official) is the most talkative of the bunch and has a close relationship with his most cherished student (and biggest headache), Xie Lian. While the names of the three deputy state preceptors are unknown, Xie Lian clearly respects their skill and wisdom.

The plum blossom in Mei Nianqing's name is a symbol of endurance in Chinese flower language, as it blooms in the depths of winter. The plum blossom is also one of the four flowers of the *junzi* (the ideal Confucian gentleman).

Xianle Royal Family

The king and queen of the Kingdom of Xianle, and Xie Lian's parents. Xie Lian's father is of the ruling Xie (谢 "to thank/to wilt") clan, and his mother is of the Min (悯 "to feel pity for/commiserate with") clan. Xie Lian is very close with his mother, who is a doting—if rather naive and sheltered—parent. Xie Lian has a more contentious relationship with his father and frequently squabbles with him.

When Xie Lian's given name (怜 / lian) and his mother's clan name (悯 / min) are written together, they form the word "compassion" (怜悯 / lianmin).

SENTIENT WEAPONS AND SPIRITUAL OBJECTS

Brocade Immortal
锦衣仙 "BROCADE," "IMMORTAL"

A semi-sentient brocade robe possessed by the ghost of a human man, Bai Jing. The name of this object is meant to be a play on the name of the spirit of the man that inhabits it. The Brocade Immortal is an immensely powerful and dangerous artifact—those who wear it can be controlled like puppets if they were given the robe by a person with nefarious intent, and even gods are not immune to its effect.

Eming
厄命   "TERRIBLE/WRETCHED," "FATE"

Hua Cheng's sentient scimitar. With a single blood-red eye that peers out from its silver hilt, it is a cursed blade that drinks the blood of its victims and is the bane of the Heavens. It enjoys nothing more than receiving praise and hugs from Xie Lian, and its childish, forward personality is a great embarrassment to its ghostly master.

Fangxin
芳心   "AFFECTIONS OF A YOUNG WOMAN"

An ancient black sword with ties to Xie Lian. An antique, it easily tires when dealing with high-flying heavenly adventures. Xie Lian used the sword's name as an alias while serving as the state preceptor of Yong'an.

Ruoye
若邪   "LIKE/AS IF," "EVIL" OR "SWORD"

Xie Lian's sentient strip of white silk. It is an earnest and energetic sort, if a bit nervous sometimes, and will go to great lengths to protect Xie Lian—quite literally, as it can stretch out to almost limitless dimensions.

Locations

HEAVENLY REALM

The Heavenly Capital is a divine city built upon the clouds. Amidst flowing streams and auspicious clouds, luxurious palaces dot the landscape, serving as the personal residences and offices of the gods. The Grand Avenue of Divine Might serves as the realm's main thoroughfare, and this road leads directly to the Palace of Divine Might—the Heavenly Emperor's residence where court is held.

The Heavenly Court consists of two sub-courts: the Upper Court and the Middle Court. The Upper Court consists entirely of ascended gods, while the Middle Court consists of officials who—while remarkable and skilled in their own right—have not yet ascended to godhood.

MORTAL REALM

The realm of living humans. Often receives visitors from the other two realms.

Kingdom of Xianle
仙乐   "HEAVEN'S DELIGHT" OR "HEAVENLY MUSIC"

A fallen kingdom, once glamorous and famed for its riches and its people's love for the finer things in life—such as art, music, gold, and the finest thing of all, their beloved crown prince, Xie Lian. Xianle's gilded exterior masked a declining kingdom plagued by corruption, and Xie Lian's meddling hastened its inevitable collapse in a most disastrous fashion.

Xianle's largest cultivation center, the Royal Holy Temple, sprawled across the peaks of the auspicious Mount Taicang. Its qi-rich landscape nurtures the blanketing forests of fruit trees and flame-red maples. The mountain hosted the kingdom's largest Palace of Xianle for worship of Xie Lian after his ascension, and the Xianle Imperial Mausoleum is located far underground.

Kingdom of Yong'an
永安   "ETERNAL PEACE"

A fallen but once-prosperous kingdom. Yong'an began its existence as an impoverished and poor city located within the Kingdom of Xianle. It later became a powder keg of social unrest which kicked off a lengthy and bloody civil war that eventually resulted in Xianle's end.

The Kingdom of Yong'an rose out of the ashes of the Kingdom of Xianle after the latter's collapse, but it very soon fell to the very same corruption and excess that doomed Xianle.

Puqi Village
菩荠村   "WATER CHESTNUT"

A tiny village in the countryside, named for the water chestnuts (*puqi*) that grow in abundance nearby. While small and unsophisticated, its villagers are friendly and welcoming to weary travelers who wish to stay a while. The humble Puqi Shrine—under reconstruction and welcoming donations—can be found here, as well as its resident god, Xie Lian.

GHOST REALM

The Ghost Realm is the home of almost all dead humans, and far less organized and bureaucratic than the Heavenly Realm. Ghosts may leave or be trapped away from the Ghost Realm under some circumstances, which causes major problems for ordinary humans and gods alike.

Black Water Demon Lair

The domain of the reclusive Supreme Ghost King that rules the South Sea, Ship-Sinking Black Water. If one is unfortunate enough to wander into his territory, it will quickly become their final resting place. Should they avoid being eaten alive by the colossal skeletal fish that serve as threshold guardians, the sea itself will devour them instead. Nothing can float upon the waters of the Black Water Demon Lair—all intruders are forfeit to the abyss.

It is said that Ship-Sinking Black Water dwells on Black Water Island, located at the heart of his realm. His residence on the island is called the Nether Water Manor. In stark contrast to Hua Cheng's lively Ghost City, Black Water Island is a silent, gloomy place with few residents other than the master himself.

Ghost City
鬼市   "GHOST CITY"

The largest city in the Ghost Realm, founded and ruled by Hua Cheng. It is a dazzling den of vice, sin, and all things wicked, which makes it the number one spot for visitors from all three realms to shop for nefarious goods and cavort under the glow of the blood-red lanterns.

Hua Cheng is rarely present in the city and does not often make public appearances. On the occasion he is in the mood to do so, he is met with considerable adoration; clearly, Ghost City's citizens love their Chengzhu and respect him immensely. His residence within the city is the secluded Paradise Manor, which has never seen guests—at least until Xie Lian came to call, of course.

The city is also home to the beautiful, secluded Thousand Lights Temple, which Hua Cheng dedicated to Xie Lian for reasons the man seems reluctant to elaborate on. It serves double-duty as a place of worship and private school of calligraphy, though Xie Lian doesn't seem to be making much progress on teaching Hua Cheng to write legibly.

OTHER/UNKNOWN

Mount Tonglu
铜炉山 **"COPPER KILN MOUNTAIN"**

Mount Tonglu is a volcano and the location of the City of Gu. Every few hundred years, tens of thousands of ghosts descend upon the city for a massive battle royale. Only two ghosts have ever survived the slaughter and made it out—one of those two was Hua Cheng.

Name Guide

NAMES, HONORIFICS, & TITLES

Diminutives, Nicknames, and Name Tags

-ER: A word for "son" or "child." Added to a name, it expresses affection. Similar to calling someone "Little" or "Sonny."

A-: Friendly diminutive. Always a prefix. Usually for monosyllabic names, or one syllable out of a two-syllable name.

XIAO-: A diminutive meaning "little." Always a prefix.

Doubling a syllable of a person's name can be a nickname, and has childish or cutesy connotations.

FAMILY

DIDI: Younger brother or a younger male friend. Casual.

GE: Familiar way to refer to an older brother or older male friend, used by someone substantially younger or of lower status. Can be used alone or with the person's name.

GEGE: Familiar way to refer to an older brother or an older male friend, used by someone substantially younger or of lower status. Has a cutesier feel than "ge."

JIEJIE: Familiar way to refer to an older sister or an older female friend, used by someone substantially younger or of lower status. Has a cutesier feel than "jie," and rarely used by older males.

MEIMEI: Younger sister or an unrelated younger female friend. Casual.

XIONG: Older brother. Generally used as an honorific. Formal, but also used informally between male friends of equal status.

YIFU: Maternal uncle, respectful address.

YIMU: Maternal aunt, respectful address.

Cultivation, Martial Arts, and Immortals

-JUN: A suffix meaning "lord."

-ZUN: A suffix meaning "esteemed, venerable." More respectful than "-jun."

DAOZHANG: A polite address for Daoist cultivators, equivalent to "Mr. Cultivator." Can be used alone as a title or attached to someone's family name—for example, one could refer to Xie Lian as "Daozhang" or "Xie Daozhang."

SHIDI: Younger martial brother. For junior male members of one's own sect.

SHIFU: Teacher/master. For one's master in one's own sect. Gender neutral. Mostly interchangeable with Shizun.

SHIXIONG: Older martial brother. For senior male members of one's own sect.

YUANJUN: Title for high class female Daoist deity. Can be used alone as a title or as a suffix.

ZHENJUN: Title for average male Daoist deity. Can be used alone as a title or as a suffix.

Other

CHENGZHU: A title for the master/ruler of an independent city-state.

GONGZI: Young master of an affluent household.

Pronunciation Guide

Mandarin Chinese is the official state language of China. It is a tonal language, so correct pronunciation is vital to being understood! As many readers may not be familiar with the use and sound of tonal marks, below is a very simplified guide on the pronunciation of select character names and terms from MXTX's series to help get you started.

More resources are available at **sevenseasdanmei.com**

Series Names

SCUM VILLAIN'S SELF-SAVING SYSTEM (RÉN ZHĀ FǍN PÀI ZÌ JIÙ XÌ TǑNG):
ren jaa faan pie zzh zioh she tone

GRANDMASTER OF DEMONIC CULTIVATION (MÓ DÀO ZǓ SHĪ):
mwuh dow zoo shrr

HEAVEN OFFICIAL'S BLESSING (TIĀN GUĀN CÌ FÚ):
tee-yan gwen tsz fuu

Character Names

SHĚN QĪNGQIŪ: Shhen Ching-cheeoh
LUÒ BĪNGHÉ: Loo-uh Bing-huhh
WÈI WÚXIÀN: Way Woo-shee-ahn
LÁN WÀNGJĪ: Lahn Wong-gee
XIÈ LIÁN: Shee-yay Lee-yan
HUĀ CHÉNG: Hoo-wah Cch-yung

XIǍO-: shee-ow

-ER: ahrr

A-: ah

GŌNGZǏ: gong-zzh

DÀOZHǍNG: dow-jon

-JŪN: june

DÌDÌ: dee-dee

GĒGĒ: guh-guh

JIĚJIĚ: gee-ay-gee-ay

MÈIMEI: may-may

-XIÓNG: shong

Terms

DĀNMĚI: dann-may

WǓXIÁ: woo-sheeah

XIĀNXIÁ: sheeyan-sheeah

QÌ: chee

General Consonants & Vowels

X: similar to English sh (**sh**eep)

Q: similar to English ch (**ch**arm)

C: similar to English ts (pan**ts**)

IU: yoh

UO: wuh

ZHI: jrr

CHI: chrr

SHI: shrr

RI: rrr

ZI: zzz

CI: tsz

SI: ssz

U: When u follows a y, j, q, or x, the sound is actually ü, pronounced like eee with your lips rounded like ooo. This applies for yu, yuan, jun, etc.

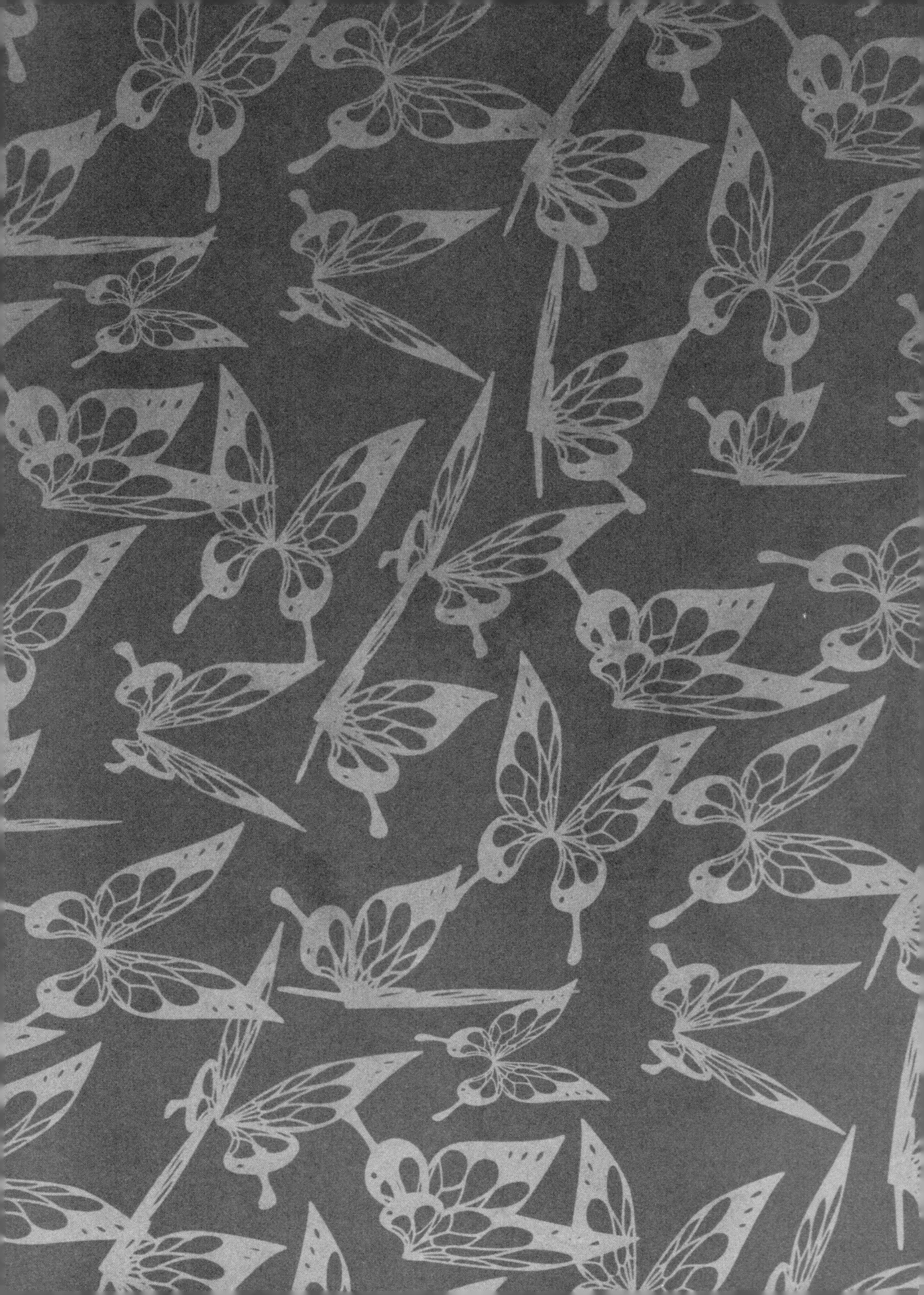

Heaven Official's Blessing

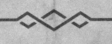

TIAN GUAN CI FU

Glossary

Glossary

While not required reading, this glossary is intended to offer further context to the many concepts and terms utilized throughout this novel and provide a starting point for learning more about the rich Chinese culture from which these stories were written.

China is home to dozens of cultures, and its history spans thousands of years. The provided definitions are not strictly universal across all these cultural groups, and this simplified overview is meant for new readers unfamiliar with the concepts. This glossary should not be considered a definitive source, especially for more complex ideas.

GENRES

Danmei

Danmei (耽美 / "indulgence in beauty") is a Chinese fiction genre focused on romanticized tales of love and attraction between men. It is analogous to the BL (boys' love) genre in Japanese media. The majority of well-known danmei writers are women writing for women, although all genders produce and enjoy the genre.

Wuxia

Wuxia (武侠 / "martial heroes") is one of the oldest Chinese literary genres and consists of tales of noble heroes fighting evil and injustice. It often follows martial artists, monks, or rogues, who live apart from the ruling government, which is often seen as useless or corrupt. These societal outcasts—both voluntary and not—settle disputes among themselves, adhering to their own moral codes over the governing law.

Characters in wuxia focus primarily on human concerns, such as political strife between factions and advancing their own personal sense of justice. True wuxia is low on magical or supernatural elements. To Western moviegoers, a well-known example is *Crouching Tiger, Hidden Dragon*.

Xianxia

Xianxia (仙侠 / "immortal heroes") is a genre related to wuxia that places more emphasis on the supernatural. Its characters often strive to become stronger, with the end goal of extending their life span or achieving immortality.

Xianxia heavily features Daoist themes, while cultivation and the pursuit of immortality are both genre requirements. If these are not the story's central focus, it is not xianxia. *The Scum Villain's Self-Saving System*, *Grandmaster of Demonic Cultivation*, and *Heaven Official's Blessing* are all considered part of both the danmei and xianxia genres.

Webnovels

Webnovels are novels serialized by chapter online, and the websites that host them are considered spaces for indie and amateur writers. Many novels, dramas, comics, and animated shows produced in China are based on popular webnovels.

Heaven Official's Blessing was first serialized on the website *JJWXC*.

TERMINOLOGY

ARRAY: Area-of-effect magic circles. Anyone within the array falls under the effect of the array's associated spell(s).

ASCENSION: In typical xianxia tales, gods are conceived naturally and born divine. Immortals cannot attain godhood but can achieve great longevity. In *Heaven Official's Blessing*, however, both gods and immortals were born mortal and either cultivated deeply or committed great deeds and attained godhood after transcending the Heavenly Tribulation. Their bodies shed the troubles of a mortal form and are removed from the corporeal world.

AUSPICIOUS CLOUDS: A sign of good fortune and the divine, auspicious clouds are also often seen as methods of transport for gods and immortals in myth. The idea springs from the obvious association with clouds and the sky/heavens, and also because yun (云 / "cloud") and yun (运 / "luck") sound similar.

BOWING: Bowing is a social custom in many Asian nations. There are several varieties of bow in Chinese culture, which are distinguished by how low the bow goes as well as any associated hand gestures. A deeper bow indicates more respect, and those with high social status will always expect a deeper bow from those with low status. The kowtow (see associated glossary entry) is the most respectful level of bow. "Standing down in a bow" means holding a bowing position while leaving someone's presence.

BUDAOWENG: A budaoweng (不倒翁, "wobbly old man") is an oblong doll, weighted so that it rolls back into an upright position whenever it is knocked down.

CHINESE CALENDAR: The Chinese calendar uses the *Tian Gan Di Zhi* (Heavenly Stems, Earthly Branches) system, rather than numbers, to mark the years. There are ten heavenly stems (original meanings lost) and twelve earthly branches (associated with the zodiac), each represented by a written character. Each stem and branch is associated with either yin or yang, and one of the elemental properties: wood, earth, fire, metal, and water. The stems and branches are combined in cyclical patterns to create a calendar where every unit of time is associated with certain attributes.

This is what a character is asking for when inquiring for the date/time of birth (生辰八字 / "eight characters of birth date/time"). Analyzing the stem/branch characters and their elemental associations was considered essential information in divination, fortune-telling, matchmaking, and even business deals.

Colors:

WHITE: Death, mourning, purity. Used in funerals for both the deceased and mourners.

BLACK: Represents the Heavens and the Dao.

RED: Happiness, good luck. Used for weddings.

YELLOW/GOLD: Wealth and prosperity, and often reserved for the emperor.

BLUE/GREEN (CYAN): Health, prosperity, and harmony.

PURPLE: Divinity and immortality, often associated with nobility.

CONFUCIANISM: Confucianism is a philosophy based on the teachings of Confucius. Its influence on all aspects of Chinese culture is incalculable. Confucius placed heavy importance on respect for one's elders and family, a concept broadly known as *xiao* (孝 / "filial piety"). The family structure is used in other contexts to urge similar behaviors, such as respect of a student towards a teacher, or people of a country towards their ruler.

COUGHING/SPITTING BLOOD: A way to show a character is ill, injured, or upset. Despite the very physical nature of the response, it does not necessarily mean that a character has been wounded; their body could simply be reacting to a very strong emotion. (See also Seven Apertures/Qiqiao.)

CULTIVATORS/CULTIVATION: Cultivators are practitioners of spirituality and martial arts who seek to gain understanding of the will of the universe while attaining personal strength and extending their life span. Cultivation is a long process marked by "stages." There are traditionally nine stages, but this is often simplified in fiction. Some common stages are noted below, though exact definitions of each stage may depend on the setting.

- ◇ Qi Condensation/Qi Refining (凝气/练气)
- ◇ Foundation Establishment (筑基)
- ◇ Core Formation/Golden Core (结丹/金丹)
- ◇ Nascent Soul (元婴)
- ◇ Deity Transformation (化神)
- ◇ Great Ascension (大乘)
- ◇ Heavenly Tribulation (渡劫)

CULTIVATION MANUAL: Cultivation manuals and sutras are common plot devices in xianxia/wuxia novels. They provide detailed instructions on a secret or advanced training technique and are sought out by those who wish to advance their cultivation levels.

CURRENCY: The currency system during most dynasties was based on the exchange of silver and gold coinage. Weight was also used to measure denominations of money. An example is something being marked with a price of "one liang of silver."

DAOISM: Daoism is the philosophy of the *dao* (道), known as "the way." Following the dao involves coming into harmony with the natural order of the universe, which makes someone a "true human," safe from external harm and who can affect the world without intentional action. Cultivation is a concept based on Daoist beliefs.

DEMONS: A race of immensely powerful and innately supernatural beings. They are almost always aligned with evil.

DISCIPLES: Cultivation sect members are known as disciples. Disciples live on sect grounds and have a strict hierarchy based on skill and seniority. They are divided into Core, Inner, and Outer rankings, with Core being the highest. Higher-ranked disciples get better lodging and other resources.

When formally joining a sect as a disciple or a student, the sect becomes like the disciple's new family: teachers are parents and peers are siblings. Because of this, a betrayal or abandonment of one's sect is considered a deep transgression of Confucian values of filial piety. This is also the origin of many of the honorifics and titles used for martial arts.

DRAGON: Great chimeric beasts who wield power over the weather. Chinese dragons differ from their Western counterparts as they are often benevolent, bestowing blessings and granting luck. They are associated with the Heavens, the Emperor, and yang energy.

EIGHT TRIGRAMS MAP: Also known as the bagua or pakua, an eight trigrams map is a Daoist diagram containing eight symbols that represent the fundamentals of reality, including the five elements. They often feature a symbol for yin and yang in the center as a representation of perfect balance between opposing forces.

ENTRANCE COUPLETS: Written poetry verses that are posted outside the door of a building. The two lines of poetry on the sides of the door express the meaning/theme of the establishment, or are a wish for good luck. The horizontal verse on the top summarizes or is the subject of the couplets.

FACE: *Mianzi* (面子), generally translated as "face," is an important concept in Chinese society. It is a metaphor for a person's reputation and can be extended to further descriptive metaphors. For example, "having face" refers to having a good reputation, and "losing face" refers to having one's reputation hurt. Meanwhile, "giving face" means deferring to someone else to help improve their reputation, while "not wanting face" implies that a person is acting so poorly/ shamelessly that they clearly don't care about their reputation at all. "Thin face" refers to someone easily embarrassed or prone to offense at perceived slights. Conversely, "thick face" refers to someone not easily embarrassed and immune to insults.

FENG SHUI: Literally translates to wind-water. Refers to the natural laws believed to govern the flow of qi in the arrangement of the natural environment and man-made structures. Favorable feng shui and good qi flow have various beneficial effects to everyday life and the practice of cultivation, while the opposite is true for unfavorable feng shui and bad qi flow.

THE FIVE ELEMENTS: Also known as the *wuxing* (五行 / "Five Phases"). Rather than Western concepts of elemental magic, Chinese phases are more commonly used to describe the interactions and relationships between things. The phases can both beget and overcome each other.

◇ Wood (木 / mu)
◇ Fire (火 / huo)
◇ Earth (土 / tu)
◇ Metal (金 / jin)
◇ Water (水 / shui)

Flowers:

LOTUS: Associated with Buddhism. It rises untainted from the muddy waters it grows in, and thus symbolizes ultimate purity of the heart and mind.

PINE (TREE): A symbol of evergreen sentiment / everlasting affection.

PLUM (BLOSSOMING TREE): A symbol of endurance, as it blooms in the depths of winter. The plum blossom is also one of the four flowers of the ideal Confucian gentleman.

WILLOW (TREE): A symbol of lasting affection and friendship. Also is a symbol of farewell and can mean "urging someone to stay." "Meeting under the willows" can connote a rendezvous.

FUNERALS: Daoist or Buddhist funerals generally last for forty-nine days. It is a common belief that souls of the dead return home on the night of the sixth day after their death. There are different rituals depending on the region regarding what is done when the spirit returns, but generally they are all intended to guide the spirit safely back to the family home without getting lost; these rituals are generally referred to by the umbrella term "Calling the Spirit on the Seventh Day."

During the funeral ceremony, mourners can present the deceased with offerings of food, incense, and joss paper. If deceased ancestors have no patrilineal descendants to give them offerings, they may starve in the afterlife and become hungry ghosts. Wiping out a whole family is punishment for more than just the living.

After the funeral, the coffin is nailed shut and sealed with paper talismans to protect the body from evil spirits. The deceased is transported in a procession to their final resting place, often accompanied by loud music to scare off evil spirits. Cemeteries are usually on hillsides; the higher a grave is located, the better the feng shui. The traditional mourning color is white.

GHOST: Ghosts (鬼) are the restless spirits of deceased sentient creatures. Ghosts produce yin energy and crave yang energy. They come in a variety of types: they can be malevolent or helpful, can retain their former personalities or be fully mindless, and can actively try to interact with the living world to achieve a goal or be little more than a remnant shadow of their former lives.

Water ghosts are a notable subset of ghosts. They are drowned humans that haunt the place of their death and seek to drag unsuspecting victims underwater to possess their bodies, steal their identities, and take their places in the world of the living. The victim then becomes a water ghost themselves and repeats the process by hunting new victims. This process is known as 替身 / *tishen* (lit. "substitution"). In *Heaven Official's Blessing*, there is a clear story parallel between the behavior of water ghosts and the birth and actions of Ship-Sinking Black Water.

GUQIN: A seven-stringed zither, played by plucking with the fingers. Sometimes called a qin. It is fairly large and is meant to be laid flat on a surface or on one's lap while playing.

GU SORCERY: The concept of gu (蛊 / "poison") is common in wuxia and xianxia stories. In more realistic settings, it may refer to crafting poisons that are extracted from venomous insects and creatures. Things like snakes, toads, and bugs are generally associated with the idea of gu, but it can also apply to monsters, demons, and ghosts. The effects of gu poison are bewitchment and manipulation. "Swayed by gu" has become a common phrase meaning "lost your mind/been led astray" in modern Chinese vocabulary.

HAND GESTURES: The baoquan (抱拳 / "hold fist") is a martial arts salute where one places their closed right fist against their open left palm. The gongshou (拱手 / "arch hand") is a more generic salute not specific to martial artists, where one drapes their open left palm over their closed right fist. The orientation of both of these salutes is reversed for women. During funerals, the closed hand in both salutes switches, where men will use their left fist and women their right.

HAND SEALS: Refers to various hand and finger gestures used by cultivators to cast spells, or used while meditating. A cultivator may be able to control their sword remotely with a hand seal.

HEAVENLY REALM: An imperial court of enlightened beings. Some hold administrative roles, while others watch over and protect a specific aspect of the celestial and mortal realm, such as love, marriage, a piece of land, etc. There are also carefree immortals who simply wander the world and help mortals as they go, or become hermits deep in the mountains.

HEAVENLY TRIBULATION: Before a Daoist cultivator can ascend to the heavens, they must go through a trial known as a Heavenly Tribulation. In stories where the Heavens are depicted with a more traditional nine-level structure, even gods themselves must endure and overcome tribulations if they want to level up. The nature of these trials vary, but the most common version involves navigating a powerful lightning storm. To fail means losing one's attained divine stage and cultivation.

HUALIAN: Shortened name for the relationship between Hua Cheng and Xie Lian.

IMMORTALS AND IMMORTALITY: Immortals have transcended mortality through cultivation. They possess long lives, are immune to illness and aging, and have various magical powers. An immortal can progress to godhood if they pass a Heavenly Tribulation. The exact life span of immortals differs from story to story, and in some they only live for three or four hundred years.

IMMORTAL-BINDING ROPES: Ropes, nets, and other restraints enchanted to withstand the power of an immortal or god. They can only be cut by high-powered spiritual items or weapons and usually limit the abilities of those trapped by them.

INCENSE TIME: A common way to tell time in ancient China, referring to how long it takes for a single incense stick to burn. Standardized incense sticks were manufactured and calibrated for specific time measurements: a half hour, an hour, a day, etc. These were available to people of all social classes.

In *Heaven Official's Blessing*, the incense sticks being referenced are the small sticks one offers when praying at a shrine, so "one incense time" is roughly thirty minutes.

INEDIA: A common ability that allows an immortal to survive without mortal food or sleep by sustaining themselves on purer forms of energy based on Daoist fasting. Depending on the setting, immortals who have achieved inedia may be unable to tolerate mortal food, or they may be able to choose to eat when desired.

JADE: Jade is a culturally and spiritually important mineral in China. Its durability, beauty, and the ease with which it can be utilized for crafting both decorative and functional pieces alike has made it widely beloved since ancient times. The word might cause Westerners to think of green jade (the mineral jadeite), but Chinese texts are often referring to white jade (the mineral nephrite). This is the color referenced when a person's skin is described as "the color of jade." Other colors of jade will usually be specified in the text.

JADE EMPEROR: In Daoist cosmology, the Jade Emperor (玉皇大帝) is the emperor of heaven, the chief of the heavenly court, and one of the highest ranked gods in the heavenly realm, lower only to the three primordial emanations. When one says "Oh god/lord" or "My heavens", it is usually referring to the Jade Emperor. In *Heaven Official's Blessing*, Jun Wu's role replaces that of the Jade Emperor.

JOSS PAPER: Also referred to as ghost paper, joss paper is a form of paper crafting used to make offerings to the deceased. The paper can be folded into various shapes and is burned as an offering, allowing the deceased person to utilize the gift the paper represents in the realm of the dead. Common gifts include paper money, houses, clothing, toiletries, and dolls to act as the deceased's servants.

KOWTOW: The *kowtow* (叩头 / "knock head") is an act of prostration where one kneels and bows low enough that their forehead touches the ground. A show of deep respect and reverence that can also be used to beg, plead, or show sincerity.

MERIDIANS: The means by which qi travels through the body, like a magical bloodstream. Medical and combat techniques that focus on redirecting, manipulating, or halting qi circulation focus on targeting the meridians at specific points on the body, known as acupoints. Techniques that can manipulate or block qi prevent a cultivator from using magical techniques until the qi block is lifted.

MID-AUTUMN FESTIVAL: Zhongqiu Jie (中秋節), or the Mid-Autumn Festival, falls on the fifteenth day of the eighth month of the Lunar Calendar. It typically falls around September-October on the Western Calendar. This festival is heavily associated with reunions, both family and otherwise. Mooncakes—also known as reunion cakes, as they are meant to be shared—are a popular food item associated with this festival. Much like the Shangyuan Festival, the Mid-Autumn Festival involves the lighting of lanterns to worship the heavens. It is also commonly associated with courtship and matchmaking.

Numbers

TWO: Two (二 / "er") is considered a good number and is referenced in the common idiom "good things come in pairs." It is common practice to repeat characters in pairs for added effect.

THREE: Three (三 / "san") sounds like *sheng* (生 / "living") and also like *san* (散 / "separation").

FOUR: Four (四 / "si") sounds like *si* (死 / "death"). A very unlucky number.

SEVEN: Seven (七 / "qi") sounds like *qi* (齊 / "together"), making it a good number for love-related things. However, it also sounds like *qi* (欺 / "deception").

EIGHT: Eight (八 / "ba") sounds like *fa* (發 / "prosperity"), causing it to be considered a very lucky number.

NINE: Nine (九 / "jiu") is associated with matters surrounding the Emperor and Heaven, and is as such considered an auspicious number.

MXTX's work has subtle numerical theming around its love interests. In *Grandmaster of Demonic Cultivation*, her second book, Lan Wangji is frequently called Lan-er-gege ("second brother Lan") as a nickname by Wei Wuxian. In her third book, *Heaven Official's Blessing*, Hua Cheng is the third son of his family and gives the name San Lang ("third youth") when Xie Lian asks what to call him.

PHOENIX: *Fenghuang* (凤凰 / "phoenix"), a legendary chimeric bird said to only appear in times of peace and to flee when a ruler is corrupt. They are heavily associated with femininity, the Empress, and happy marriages.

PILLS AND ELIXIRS: Magic medicines that can heal wounds, improve cultivation, extend life, etc. In Chinese culture, these things are usually delivered in pill form. These pills are created in special kilns.

PLAGUES AND DISEASE: In ancient China, plagues and pandemics were considered to be the work of demons or other evil creatures, and were thought to be karmic punishment from the heavens for humanity's evil deeds. It was thought that the gods would protect the righteous and innocent from catching the disease, and mass repentance was the only way to "cure" or banish a plague for good. When the gods determined the punishment served to be sufficient, they would descend and drive out the plague-causing demons.

This outlook is why Human Face Disease is considered in-universe to be a mark against the Kingdom of Xianle's morality and a mark against Xie Lian as both a leader and a god—the plague only affecting Xianle is "proof" that they angered the heavens, and Xie Lian being unable to cure it by his own power is "proof" that he does not have heaven's blessing and is not a true god.

PRIMORDIAL SPIRIT: The essence of one's existence beyond the physical. The body perishes, the soul enters the karmic wheel, but the spirit that makes one unique is eternal.

STEP-LITTER: [步辇] a "litter" is a type of wheelless vehicle. Palanquins and sedan chairs are in the same category of human-powered transport, but they often have boxed cabins. A step-litter is an open-air platform with a seat/throne atop it, often with a canopy of hanging silk curtains for privacy. Step-litters are usually reserved for those with high status.

QI: *Qi* (气) is the energy in all living things. There is both righteous qi and evil or poisonous qi.

Cultivators strive to cultivate qi by absorbing it from the natural world and refining it within themselves to improve their cultivation base. A cultivation base refers to the amount of qi a cultivator possesses or is able to possess. In xianxia, natural locations such as caves, mountains, or other secluded places with lush wildlife are often rich in qi, and practicing there can allow a cultivator to make rapid progress in their cultivation.

Cultivators and other qi manipulators can utilize their life force in a variety of ways, including imbuing objects with it to transform them into lethal weapons or sending out blasts of energy to do powerful damage. Cultivators also refine their senses beyond normal human levels. For instance, they may cast out their spiritual sense to gain total awareness of everything in a region around them or to feel for potential danger.

QI CIRCULATION: The metabolic cycle of qi in the body, where it flows from the dantian to the meridians and back. This cycle purifies and refines qi, and good circulation is essential to cultivation. In xianxia, qi can be transferred from one person to another through physical contact and can heal someone who is wounded if the donor is trained in the art.

QIANKUN: *Qiankun* can be translated to "universe." Qiankun pouches (乾坤袋) or Qiankun sleeves (乾坤袖) are containers that are bigger on the inside, used to easily carry cargo a person normally couldn't manage. Qiankun items are common in fantasy settings.

RED STRING OF FATE: Refers to the myth in many East Asian cultures that an invisible red string connects two individuals who are fated to be lovers. The string is tied at each lover's finger (usually the middle finger or pinky finger).

SECT: A cultivation sect is an organization of individuals united by their dedication to the practice of a particular method of cultivation or martial arts. A sect may have a signature style. Sects are led by a single leader, who is supported by senior sect members. They are not necessarily related by blood.

SEVEN APERTURES/QIQIAO: (七窍) The seven facial apertures: the two eyes, nose, mouth, tongue, and two ears. The essential qi of vital organs are said to connect to the seven apertures, and illness in the vital organs may cause symptoms there. People who are ill or seriously injured may be "bleeding from the seven apertures."

SHANGYUAN: Shangyuan Jie (上元節), or the Lantern Festival, marks the fifteenth and last day of the Lunar New Year (usually around February on the Solar Calendar). It is a day for worshipping and celebrating the celestial heavens by hanging lanterns, solving riddles, and performing Dragon Dances. Glutinous rice ball treats known as yuanxiao and tangyuan are highlights of this festival, so much so that the festival's alternate name is Yuanxiao Jie (元宵節).

SHRINES: Shrines are sites at which an individual can pray or make offerings to a god, spirit, or ancestor. They contain an object of worship to focus on such as a statue, a painting or mural, a relic, or a memorial tablet in the case of an ancestral shrine. The term also refers to small roadside shrines or personal shrines to deceased family members or loved ones kept on a mantle. Offerings like incense, food, and money can be left at a shrine as a show of respect.

SPIRIT BANNER: A banner or flag intended to guide spirits. Can be hung from a building or tree to mark a location or carried around on a staff.

STATE PRECEPTOR: State preceptors, or guoshi, are high-ranking government officials who also have significant religious duties. They serve as religious heads of state under the emperor and act as the tutors, chaplains, and confidants of the emperor and his direct heirs.

SWORDS: A cultivator's sword is an important part of their cultivation practice. In many instances, swords are spiritually bound to their owner and may have been bestowed to them by their master, a family member, or obtained through a ritual. Cultivators in fiction are able to use their swords as transportation by standing atop the flat of the blade and riding it as it flies through the air. Skilled cultivators can summon their swords to fly into their hand, command the sword to fight on its own, or release energy attacks from the edge of the blade.

SWORD GLARE: Jianguang (剑光 / "sword light"), an energy attack released from a sword's edge.

SWORN BROTHERS/SISTERS/FAMILIES: In China, sworn brotherhood describes a binding social pact made by two or more unrelated individuals. Such a pact can be entered into for social, political, and/or personal reasons. It was most common among men but was not unheard of among women or between people of different genders.

The participants treat members of each other's families as their own and assist them in the ways an extended family would: providing mutual support and aid, support in political alliances, etc. Sworn siblings will refer to themselves as brother or sister, but this is not to be confused with familial relations like blood siblings or adoption. It is sometimes used in Chinese media, particularly danmei, to imply romantic relationships that could otherwise be prone to censorship.

TALISMANS: Strips of paper with spells written on them, often with cinnabar ink or blood. They can serve as seals or be used as one-time spells.

THE THREE REALMS: Traditionally, the universe is divided into Three Realms: the **Heavenly Realm**, the **Mortal Realm**, and the **Ghost Realm**. The Heavenly Realm refers to the Heavens and Celestial Court, where gods reside and rule, the Mortal Realm refers to the human world, and the Ghost Realm refers to the realm of the dead.

VINEGAR: To say someone is drinking vinegar or tasting vinegar means they're having jealous or bitter feelings. Generally used for a love interest growing jealous while watching the main character receive the attention of a rival suitor.

WEDDING TRADITIONS: Red is an important part of traditional Chinese weddings, as the color of prosperity, happiness, and good luck. It remains the standard color for bridal and bridegroom robes and wedding decorations even today. During the ceremony, the couple each cut off a lock of their own hair, then intertwine and tie the two locks together to symbolize their commitment.

WHISK: A whisk held by a cultivator is not a baking tool but a Daoist symbol and martial arts weapon. Usually made of horsehair bound to a wooden stick, the whisk is based off a tool used to brush away flies without killing them and is symbolically meant for wandering Daoist monks to brush away thoughts that would lure them back to secular life. Wudang Daoist Monks created a fighting style based on wielding it as a weapon.

YAO: Animals, plants, or objects that have gained spiritual consciousness due to prolonged absorption of qi. Especially high-level or long-lived yao are able to take on a human form. This concept is comparable to Japanese yokai, which is a loanword from the Chinese yao. Yao are not evil by nature but often come into conflict with humans for various reasons, one being that the cores they develop can be harvested by human cultivators to increase their own abilities.

YIN ENERGY AND YANG ENERGY: Yin and yang is a concept in Chinese philosophy that describes the complementary interdependence of opposite/contrary forces. It can be applied to all forms of change and differences. Yang represents the sun, masculinity, and the living, while yin represents the shadows, femininity, and the dead, including spirits and ghosts. In fiction, imbalances between yin and yang energy can do serious harm to the body or act as the driving force for malevolent spirits seeking to replenish themselves of whichever they lack.

ZHONGYUAN: Zhongyuan Jie (中元節), or the Ghost Festival / Hungry Ghost Festival, falls on the fifteenth day of the seventh month of the Lunar Calendar (this usually falls around August/

September on the Solar Calendar). The festival celebrates the underworld, and offerings are made to the dead to appease their spirits and help them move on.

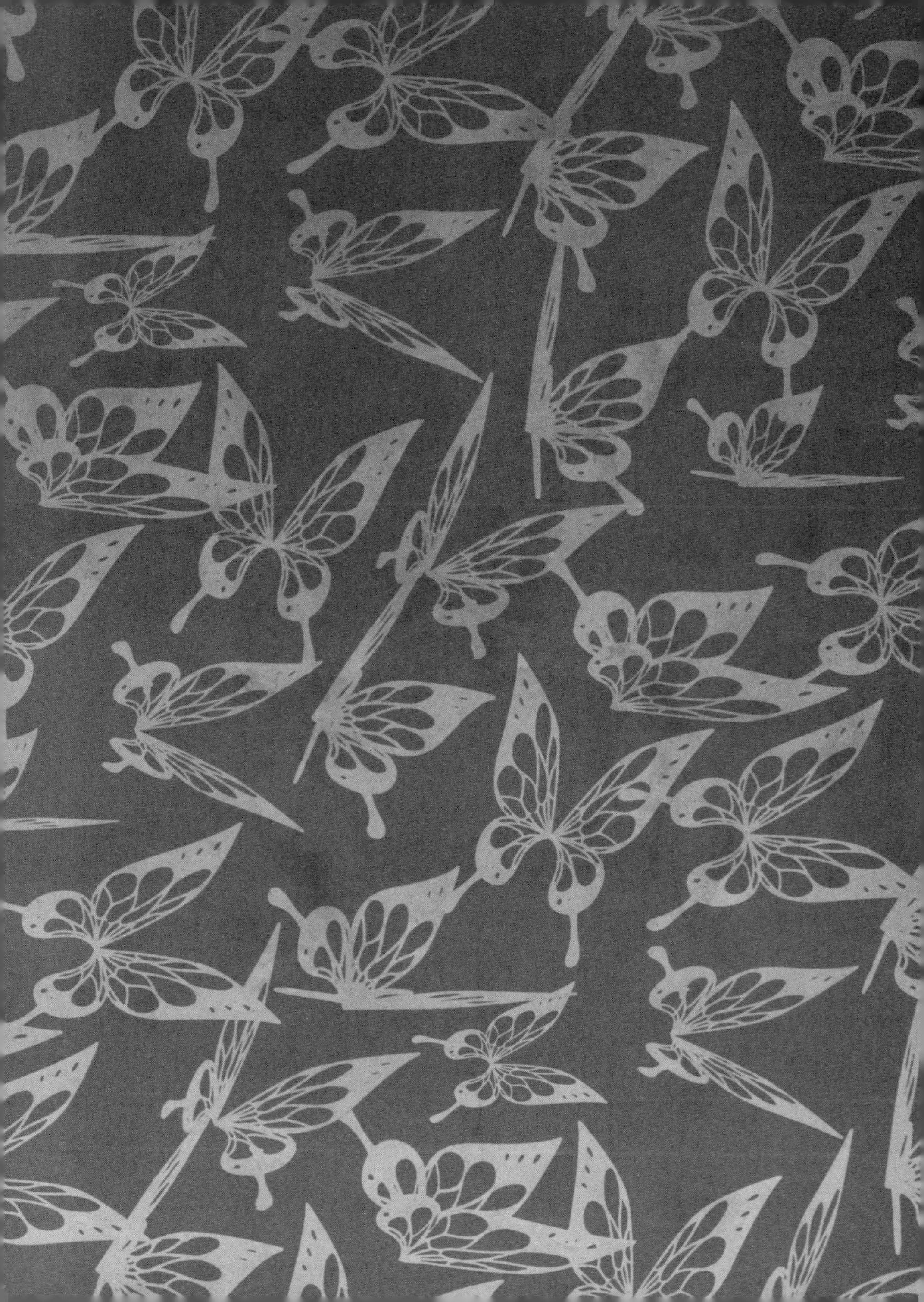

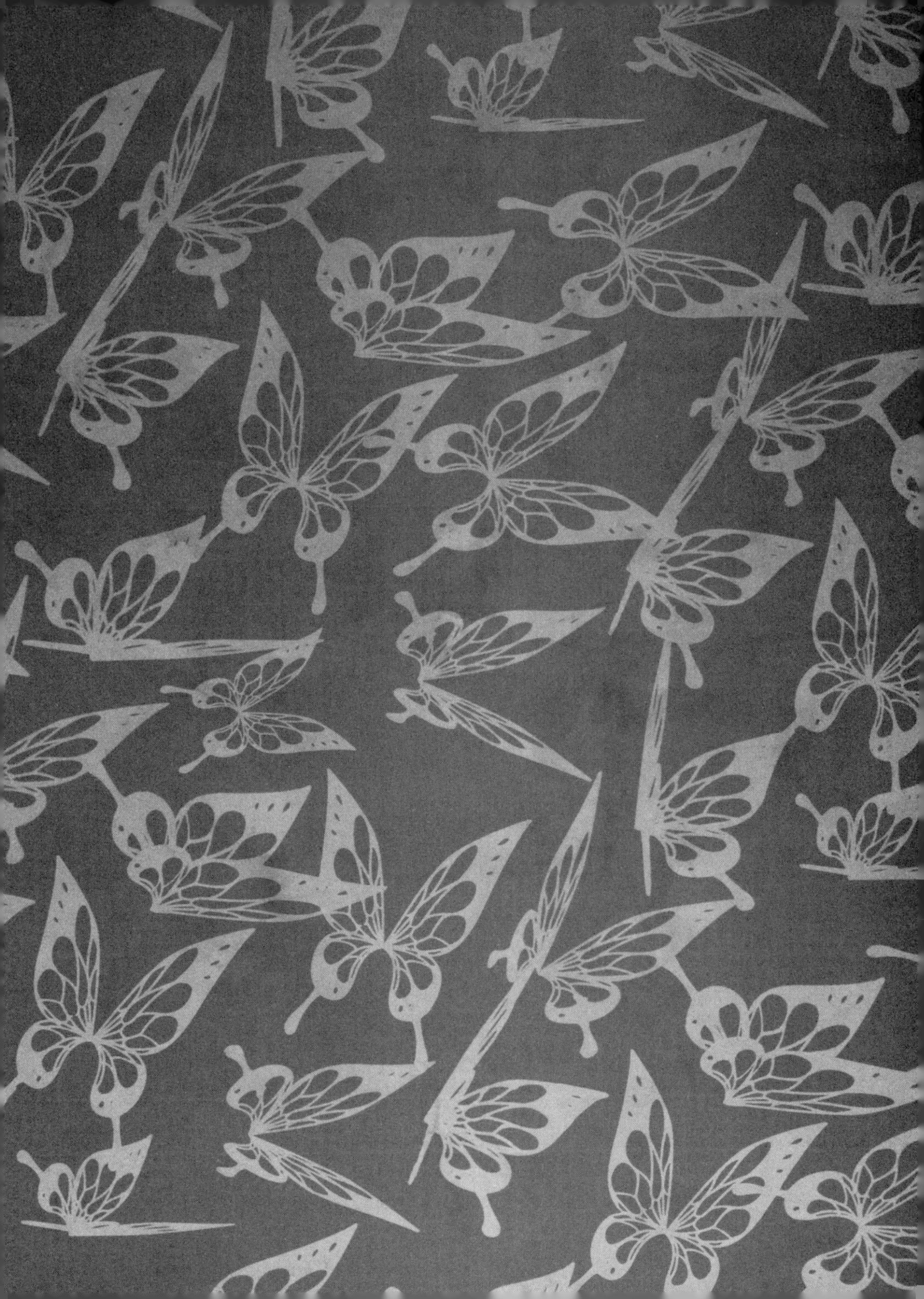

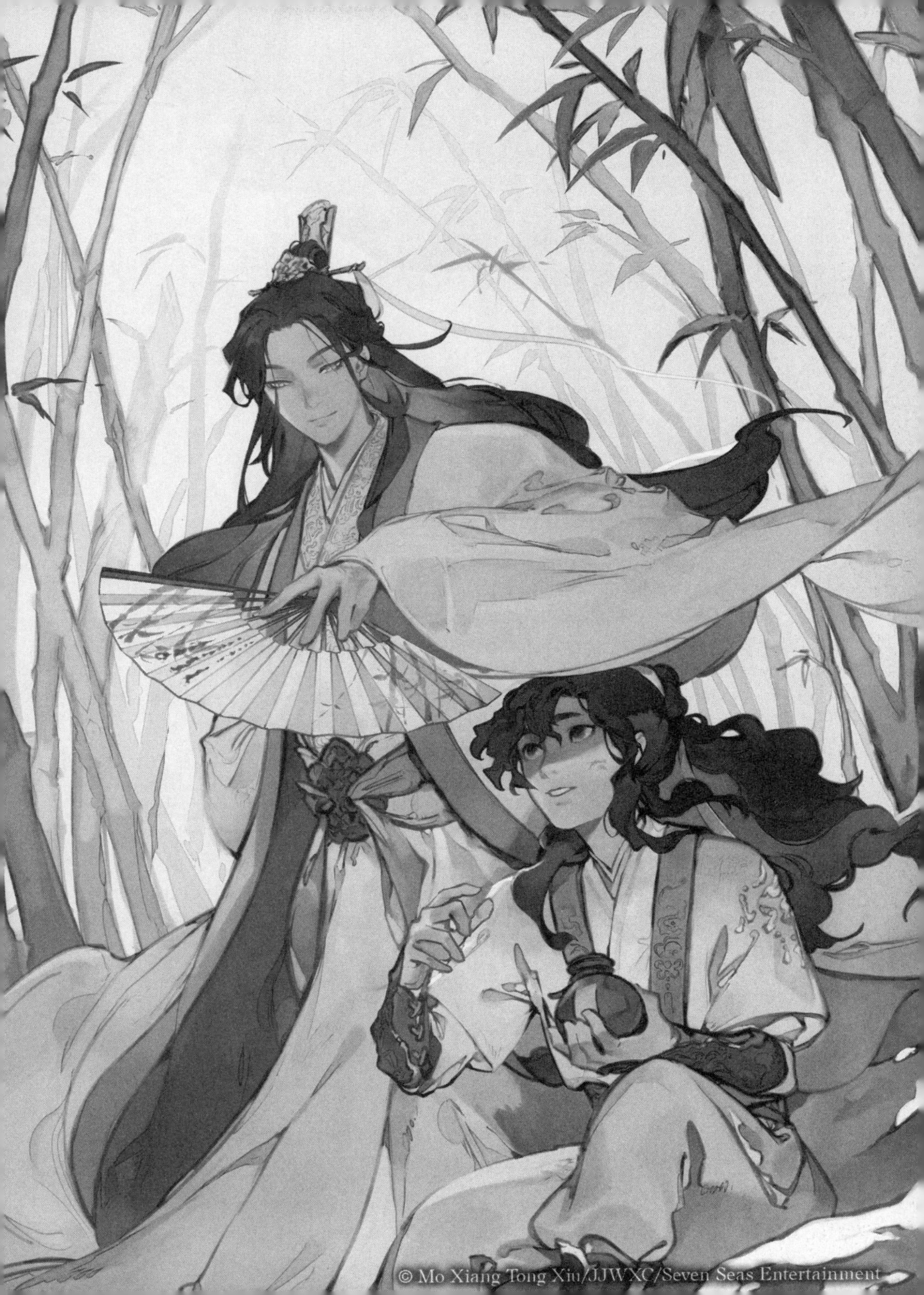

FROM BESTSELLING AUTHOR

MO XIANG TONG XIU

Grandmaster of Demonic Cultivation

MO DAO ZU SHI

Wei Wuxian was once one of the most outstanding men of his generation, a talented and clever young cultivator who harnessed martial arts, knowledge, and spirituality into powerful abilities. But when the horrors of war led him to seek a new power through demonic cultivation, the world's respect for his skills turned to fear, and his eventual death was celebrated throughout the land.

Years later, he awakens in the body of an aggrieved young man who sacrifices his soul so that Wei Wuxian can exact revenge on his behalf. Though granted a second life, Wei Wuxian is not free from his first, nor the mysteries that appear before him now. Yet this time, he'll face it all with the righteous and esteemed Lan Wangji at his side, another powerful cultivator whose unwavering dedication and shared memories of their past will help shine a light on the dark truths that surround them.

Available in print and digital from Seven Seas Entertainment

Seven Seas

耽美Danmei

Seven Seas Entertainment

sevenseasdanmei.com

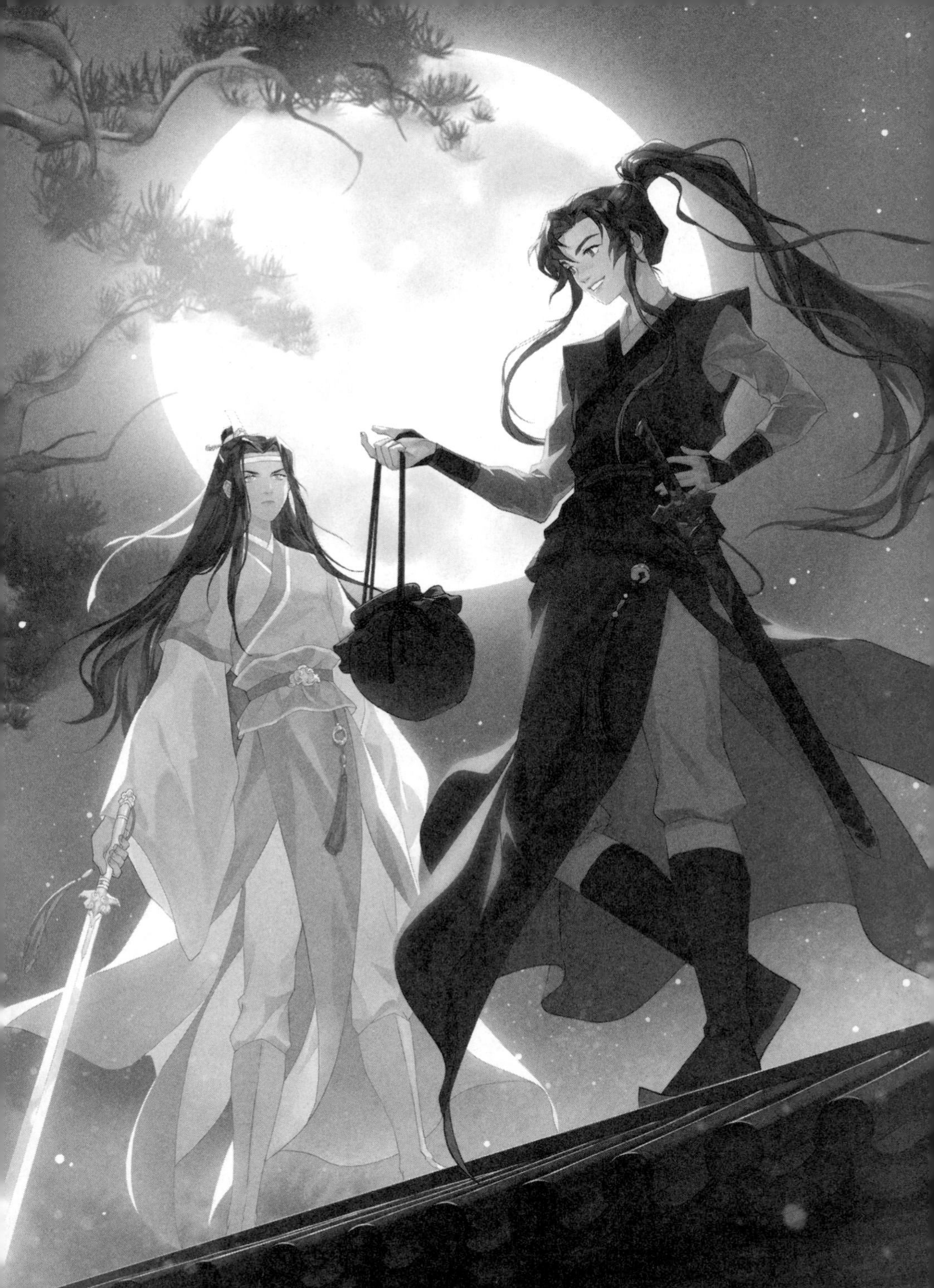

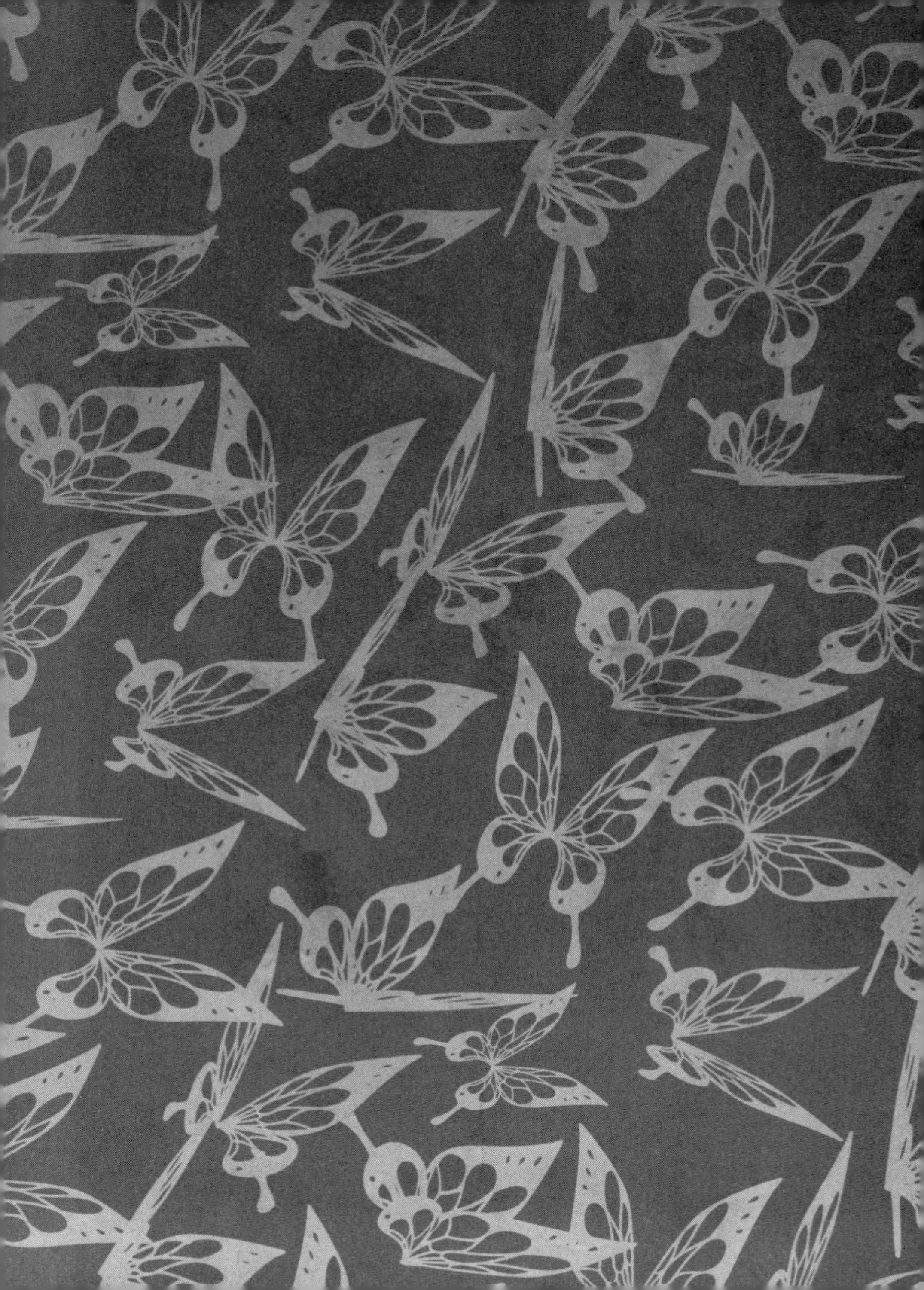